EXIT WOUNDS

ALSO BY THE AUTHOR

High Crimes

E·X·I·T
WOUNDS

·JOHN WESTERMANN·

SOHO

Copyright © 1990 by John Westermann
All rights reserved under International, Berne and Pan-American Copyright Conventions. Published in the United States by
Soho Press, Inc.
1 Union Square
New York, NY 10003

Library of Congress Cataloging-in-Publication Data
Westermann, John, 1952–
Exit wounds / by John Westermann.
p.   cm.
ISBN 0-939149-27-3:
I. Title.
PS3573.E856E95   1989
813'.54—dc2089-38351 CIP

Manufactured in the United States
10 9 8 7 6 5 4 3 2 1
Book design and composition by The Sarabande Press

FOR JAKE

"If all you've got to live for
is what you've left behind,
get yourself a powder charge
and seal that silver mine."

"Mississippi Half-Step Uptown Toodeloo"

The Grateful Dead
Words by Robert Hunter
Music by Jerry Garcia

EXIT WOUNDS

1

"So what landed you here?" asked the Reaper, as he drove the county morgue wagon away from a two-car accident that hadn't produced any customers.

"General naughtiness."

The Reaper nodded. "Yeah, most of my associates over the years have been bad boys."

Orin barely glanced at him as he pulled down the top half of his gray jumpsuit, with POLICE in large yellow letters on the back. The Reaper wore an identical outfit, although his was several shades darker; Orin doubted if it had been ever washed.

Emil "Reaper" Dell was pushing forty, pocked with acne scars and boasting less than a full set of teeth. Some minor infraction had gotten him assigned to the morgue wagon three years ago and the system had forgotten about him. He'd been mislaid. Of such oversights, thought Orin Boyd, dedicated employees are born.

Orin had dealt with remains before, in other places and other times. But he had never shared such chores with someone who enjoyed them.

What was normally the least desirable post in the job, often given out as punishment, was Officer Dell's permanent assignment. The Reaper liked driving the white unmarked van and being the meat wagon man. Orin hated it, had from the first instant, and he'd been assigned now for two weeks.

"Come on," Officer Dell said. "The gig ain't bad. Ain't no one looking over your shoulder and the clients never bitch."

Orin forced a toothy grin. "Right, Reaper."

The radio interrupted. In a wooded area on the western perimeter of the 13th Precinct, near some railroad tracks, was Swilly Pond. Somebody had bobbed to the surface.

Dell acknowledged the call, then turned to Orin. "A floater," he said, almost gleefully. "Some just blow up like the Michelin Man and explode."

"Please," Orin said. "Shut the fuck up."

"You'll get used to it."

"I don't want to get used to it."

A uniformed cop was at the fence gate at Swilly Pond, logging arrivals at the scene. Outside the fenced area were parked cars and trucks of the investigators. Some of them were leaning on fenders, taking their after-noon coffee break away from the smell. All were smoking. By the pond, further on, a team of four divers suited up, preparing to search the murky bottom with powerful flashlights. A lady homicide dick balanced on one foot and wiped mud from her other high-heel. The first two divers went in.

Dell stopped the van at the gate. "Reap-man" said the cop with the clipboard. "How you been?"

"Can't complain," said Dell. "Business is picking up."

They parked against the chain-link fence and rolled the collapsible stretcher from the back of the van. The uniform said, "Down there, by the big evergreen. Foley is catching."

Officers Dell and Boyd found the detective-in-charge at the edge of the pond, ankle deep in muck, directing two detectives as they searched the area. The floater was in the tall grass a few feet away, face up, eye sockets open. His hands looked like boxing gloves, his T-shirt and blue jeans were nearly bursting.

"Hi, Reap," said Foley. "How ya doin'?"

"Better than this guy."

Detective Foley said, "You sure it's a guy?"

"From the size of the sneakers—yeah."

"Looks like Oprah when she was fat," Foley said, then sighed. "Shit, if he'd 've drifted to the other side he'd be in Queens instead."

"Them guys," Dell said, "they probably sailed him over here to duck the paperwork."

Foley agreed and said, "Try to keep the remains intact, willya."

"Will do," said Reaper. "Continuity of evidence is paramount." He pulled his rubber gloves out of his back pocket and slid them on, his hands held aloft like a surgeon's. The detectives, who had gathered, stepped back. Foley said he had to run, his long day was getting longer. Reaper looked sorry to lose any part of his audience. "Okay, Orin. We tip him one way and work the bag underneath. Then we do the other side. A piece of cake, a walk in the park. Come on, Officer Boyd. This boy can't hurt you now."

Orin grunted and the two men bent to their work. The unzipped bag at their feet, they slid their gloved hands underneath a soggy shoulder and hip, and slowly rolled the body onto its side. Gas escaped. Orin turned his face to one side and winced. The smell was enough to gag a maggot.

Reaper tittered. "Was that a dying declaration?"

"Long-winded son of a bitch," said Orin.

It took them nearly a quarter of an hour to wrestle the bloated corpse into the rubber bag, and another ten minutes to cart it up to the van. When they got there a squad car was parked next to it. The cop at the wheel had come to fetch Officer Boyd.

I'm the wrong guy for the job, Orin Boyd told them right there in the commissioner's office. Sergeant Daniels just adjusted the cuff of his immaculate white shirt, tugging it down over his scented brown skin. The sergeant liked his cologne. "Bull shit," he said. "Make yourself the right guy."

"Fuck." Orin tried to look away, out the wall of windows, but the glare was too heavy. "I've got problems of my own."

"You don't do this, you'll have more."

"Is that a threat?" Orin said, staring down the sergeant.

The commissioner shook his head. "Not at all, Boyd. It's an honest assessment of your future."

"You wanna break it to me gently?"

Commissioner Trimble rocked in his high-backed swivel chair. "Your illustrious partner is out of the picture. From here on you sink or swim on your own. No more winking at your screw-ups, no more breaks, no favors, no slack. Like the morgue wagon—you fuck up, you pay. You and Kenny Demarco gave us great numbers, great cases. But—no offense—Kenny was the brains and you, Orin. . . ."

"Muscle's cheap, my man," said the sergeant.

Orin Boyd glanced around the spacious office, stalling. His gaze settled on the precise crease in the sergeant's pin-striped trouser leg. He wondered if it was sewn in place.

"Talk to us, Boyd," the commissioner said.

"Why me?"

Sergeant Daniels crossed his arms. "You're perfect. You're not a detective, you're a street cop. But you've done some undercover and worked bunco. Your lousy record is real. In a precinct full of . . . rugged individualists, your arrival would hardly be noticed."

"Thanks so much for saying so."

"Hey," Daniels said, "we're not the fellas who had all the fun. You did. And everybody covered for you two. Up until now. Kenny Demarco is on the beach, and you are looking at more unpromising reassignments."

"Persuaded?" the commissioner said, raising an eyebrow.

Orin noticed the collection of glass paper weights on the credenza behind the vast desk. The glinting light stabbed at the last of his hangover.

"What's in it for me?" Orin said.

Commissioner Trimble and Sergeant Daniels looked at each other. Daniels said, "What do you want?"

"I want to be gone."

"Meaning?"

"My last five years you guys mail me my paychecks. At twenty I pick up my pension."

"Done," Commissioner Trimble said, so quickly that Orin wished he had thought to ask for more.

"Would you wear a wire?" Daniels asked.

"No way. I'm a cop, not a snitch." He looked straight at Commissioner Trimble. "And no little guys. Don't expect to hear about cooping or whoring. My brothers on the bottom of the municipal barrel don't need more abuse."

"That's fine," Trimble said, sounding faintly bored. "We're after crooks, not goof-offs."

"Don't look so glum," Daniels said. "You get a nice vacation beforehand, anyway."

"Yeah. I can hardly wait."

Detective Sergeant Daniels was driving the unmarked car, Officer Boyd rode alongside, dozing. They crossed the Throgs Neck Bridge, then stopped and started in traffic until turning north onto the New York State Thruway.

As they drove, the detective spoke freely of the pressures of the job, the stress cops live with, subjects generally considered admissions of weakness. The sergeant was not afraid to admit his mistakes. Daniels had turned out to be a decent guy. It was hard for Orin to believe this wily cop had ever been a juice-head.

"When did you say you stopped?" Orin asked.

"For good?"

"Yeah."

"Well . . . there were several false starts. Basically, eleven years ago." Daniels popped a sunflower seed.

"Damn," Orin said. "I'll bet you could sure use a taste."

"Not funny, Boyd."

"Sorry." Orin did not want Daniels to think his efforts were not appreciated. "Should I look forward to this?"

"It doesn't suck, if that's what you're asking me."

"Early to bed and early to rise, that kind of healthy?"

"Just like everything else, Orin, Camp Cope is what you make it. Monsignor O'Rourke is one of those guys who likes cops so much, he makes you feel good about being one. The Monsignor can show you the way, but if you don't really want to change, you ain't gonna. In which case, you'll do a little fishing, hear a little bullshit, watch a few propaganda movies, and then go on home, back to the job, where you will eventually fall through your asshole and hang yourself."

"I think I got the picture." Orin said, and stared out at the dairy farms and apple orchards, at the flat, chalky Catskill Mountains, and noted how much bigger the sky looked when you got away from the urban sprawl. He sighed. "I didn't know mandatory rehab was part of our deal."

"It isn't," Daniels said. "But you're gonna be at the camp anyway, and your problem is crystal clear. There's no mistaking what's ailing you."

"God, I hate to hear that."

"There ain't no Easter Bunny either."

"Leave me something, hey?"

"How about your wife and kid?"

Orin chortled. "Now it's you with the comforting delusions, Sergeant. Me and Judy wouldn't take each other back with guns to our heads."

"Never say never."

Orin shook his head. "Where was she when I needed her?"

"Where were you?"

Orin frowned. Daniels glanced over and looked back to the road. He said, "I'll don't know why we try living life with our heads befuddled by booze and chemicals."

"Because anyone can do it sober."

Daniels eased the car onto the exit approach. It was a long way to the toll booth. He slowed and stopped to pay it. Orin opened his window a crack. The air was crisp and clear, free of the humidity and heat back in the city and out on the Island.

Daniels said, "You'll be happy to hear your old partner, Kenny Demarco, is up at the camp, too. Not that he's having much fun."

Tell me life don't run in circles, Orin thought. "The last time we talked," he said, "Kenny was staying with his daughter in North Carolina, waiting to cash in his chips."

"He called the chaplain last month and told him that he was going out of his skull with boredom down there. The Department offered to let him finish up his sick leave at the camp."

"Kenny Demarco deserves to be taken care of. He's the most decorated officer in the job—by a mile. Everybody but the bad guys loved his ass."

"Which is why he always got away with his shit," Daniels said. "And a fat lot of good it did both of you."

Orin fell silent and thought for a while about running with Kenny: the bar fights, the big collars, the all-night drunks. He leaned his back against the headrest and drifted in the sounds of the engine and tires and the air rushing by. Daniels woke him when they had reached the treelined driveway of Camp Cope. He pulled over, reached across Orin's lap and shoved the door open.

"From here on in you're on your own. I promised myself eleven years ago I'd never go back in there."

Orin shook the cobwebs from his head and the sleep from his eyes, then thanked Daniels and climbed out of the car. He pulled his suitcase out of the back seat and set it on the side of the country road. His joints cracked and his back ached as he leaned down to the open passenger's window to say good-bye.

Daniel's said, "The Monsignor isn't in on this thing in the 13th. He likes helping cops in trouble. Let 'im. Do yourself a favor."

Orin gave a non-committal nod and Daniels dropped the gearshift, made a U-turn and disappeared around the bend. Orin picked up his bag and walked down the long wooded driveway into the camp. The first building he came to had someone on the porch. The Monsignor was waiting for him by the small white cabin that served as his office and residence. He was drinking carrot juice, and wearing a New York Yankees baseball cap and a Holy Name Society sweatshirt. O'Rourke showed Orin in and sat down behind his desk. "How ya doing, guy?"

"Can't complain, Father. I'm Officer Boyd. Sergeant Daniels just dumped me at the curb."

"I got your papers right here, kid. You're all set. Old Man Trimble sent a teletype Tuesday night and Daniels called me this morning from his house. He's quite a man, Alonzo Daniels. You couldn't have found yourself a better sponsor."

"I know."

"You like to fish?"

"I love to fish."

"You got it. You like to play golf?"

"Sometimes more than I like to fish."

"What's your handicap, and remember that it's a mortal sin to lie to a man of the cloth."

"Twelve," Orin said with a straight face.

"You're a nine for the purposes of your recovery here. The aggravation will do you good."

"Yes, sir."

Orin wondered what had happened to the how-are-you-my-son conde-
scension he had grown accustomed to getting from clerics.

O'Rourke licked his lips. "You know Gary Jerezuk, the highway
sergeant?"

"Sure," Orin said.

"He's the temporary golf pro—one of my boys. Once you're one of my
boys, you're always one of my boys. He'll set you up with clubs and shoes
and whatever else you need."

Orin wondered who else was here whom he might know. The guest list
was kept confidential by both the Department and the recoverees, but
there were always rumors.

"You know Johnny Macon, too?"

"Sure." Orin nodded. "Wild Johnny" Macon was a captain from the
11th and the rare boss Orin liked. He could make this an outright pisser.

"Son, this program works as long as you really want to dry out. Guys
worse than you have come back from the dead here. We work hard and
play hard and pray hard, and that way we don't need to medicate ourselves.
Simple as that. We're not perfect but we're getting there. And we have the
time."

"I'm a believer, Monsignor. Honest. I ain't here five minutes and you've
already adjusted my handicap."

The monsignor sat back in his chair and smiled at Orin. "Why do I have
this feeling that you're gonna break my balls every step of the way?"

"Probably because I like getting wasted better than anything else I do."

"At least you're honest. Not many admit that. Most guys'll bitch about
stress, or their parents or their wives or their kids, or the next-door
neighbor's kid. It's never their fault. It's never that getting drunk or stoned
or coked is marvelous fun for certain people, even if it's killing them.
That's a good start," said the monsignor. "Come on, I'll show you around
the grounds."

Monsignor O'Rourke walked Orin around the sixty-acre farm he had
donated to the police department for the purposes of drug, stress, and
alcohol rehabilitation. He proudly showed Orin the eight wooden cabins
tucked among the evergreens, and the large red barn that served as a
lecture hall and dining room. The softball field was lined with chalk.
There were nets on both baskets. Orin was impressed.

They followed a wide dirt path down to the boathouse on the lake, and then continued through the woods in silence. Soon they reached the chain-link fence that marked the southernmost boundary of Camp Cope. Halfway up the hill, the monsignor showed Orin a section of the fence that had been clipped out and then refastened with speaker wire. The tributary path through the patched hole in the fence was embarrassingly well worn.

"The escape hatch," said the monsignor. "In case you have a setback."

"Excuse me?"

"I'd hate to think of my boys sneaking past my cabin in the dark."

"I can see how that might make you feel queasy."

"I'm not Father Flanagan and this ain't Boy's Town. Nobody is gonna hold your hand. Everybody gets a couple of chances, usually as many as they need. Most make it, some don't. It comes down to whether you still want to be a cop or not. If you don't get better sooner rather than later, you're gonna get the old heave-ho."

As they followed the path back to the center of the camp, it dawned on Orin that they had not seen another living soul, that the camp resembled a ghost town. When their rounds brought them back to the monsignor's office, Orin picked up his cabin assignment, and then asked where everyone was.

Monsignor O'Rourke checked his watch. "They're in town, bowling for milkshakes, I believe. They ought to be back pretty soon."

Orin scoffed. "Kenny Demarco's not bowling, I know that. He always thought bowling was beneath him."

O'Rourke's wizened face took on a peeved expression. "Cancer has a way of making certain long-cherished opinions appear absurd."

"I guess it does, Father. I'm sorry."

"Go settle in, Orin. Make yourself at home. Then get your tail over to the dining hall by six. I think we're having salisbury steak."

Orin left the office and found his assigned bunk in the corner of cabin number six, a two-room, one-bath firetrap that was home to three other patients, all of whom were away, probably bowling in town, like the good father said. Orin stowed his gear in a locker and sprawled across the musty mattress. Talk about laid-back, he thought. This place was softer than a politicians' prison. No wonder rehabilitated guys spoke of their time at the camp with great fondness. No wonder so many suffered relapses. He rolled onto his back and stared at the rough-hewn ceiling, then at the sign on the wall by the swinging bathroom door:

DON'T KID YOURSELF. YOU WOULD NOT BE HERE IF YOU WEREN'T ONE.

Kenny Demarco was not at dinner that night, but his seat at the head of the table remained vacant, his place set, a reminder of his full-time status at the colony. The monsignor told Orin that Kenny was sick from his medicine. Tomorrow, God willing, would be another day.

So there were nine of them in the dining hall his first night, seated around two picnic tables, smoking cigarettes, swilling coffee, laconically planning the next day's leisure activities. Two foursomes were arranged for a morning golf match, with only Police Officer Francis X. Berillo—a hopeless klutz—excluded. Then lunch and a film, *The Addictive Personality*. A tennis tournament was a possibility for the afternoon, depending on the weather. A barbecue. A little poker. Curfew. Prayers.

Before the monsignor left the dining hall, he told Gary Jerezuk to put Orin on his team for the following morning, declaring the new arrival a fourteen handicap, and a rusty one at that.

Orin crushed his cigarette in the aluminum ashtray and looked across the table at Wild Johnny Macon. "So?" he said. "That takes care of tomorrow. What are we gonna do tonight?"

"Not drink," said Detective Duncan Miles.

"Or fuck," said Berillo.

"That's for damn sure," said Wild Johnny Macon. "The nearest whorehouse is a hundred miles." He was a tall athletic man with thick black hair and a reputation for slapping his ladies. "We couldn't get there and back before the old man's up for morning vespers."

"I'm gonna read," said Berillo.

"Whew," said Wild Johnny, wiping his forehead with the back of his hand. "I'm glad that's settled, aren't you, Orin. Francis is gonna read a couple of smut mags and then he's gonna whack his beef. Something new and different."

"M-Y-O-B, please."

Wild Johnny laughed in his face.

Francis X. Berillo was chubby and short, with thinning brown hair and wire-rimmed glasses. All his life people had been laughing in his face.

Berillo's problems, Wild Johnny explained, had absolutely nothing to do with substance abuse. Berillo was addicted to strange pussy, a situation he insisted to the departmental psychiatrist was job-related. He had never cheated on his wife when he was a civilian. But from the police academy on, women flagged him down and offered to stiffen his nightstick. Things got completely out of hand. It was the uniform, he insisted. It was forcing him to be something he was not.

Then Berillo and a couple of bachelor rookies paid twenty bucks apiece for a dose of the clap from a Hempstead hooker on the night of a big retirement party. The cure: antibiotics and abstinence for a fortnight. And, of course, the next six nights his wife made her move on him without a satisfactory result. Francis X. Berillo ran out of excuses for her. If his damn back hurt so much, she was going to make an appointment for him with the chiropractor.

Berillo drove to the 7-Eleven store on Merrick Road and bought a quart of Budweiser beer. He drank half and spilled the rest over his chest and crotch. Then he walked in the front door of his station house and fell to the floor, faking delirium tremens in front of four cops and three civilians. His PBA delegate was apprised of the situation and had him on the next bus north. His wife was dumbstruck to hear of his drinking problem. She was reassured that sometimes loved ones were the last ones to know.

"Hey, Francis," said Wild Johnny. "I bet you cry when you're done flogging that thang. I bet you run straight to the monsignor and confess your act of emission before the soap is dry on that hairy palm of yours. And the shame of it," he said, turning to Orin, "is that he'll probably be thinking of his wife when he makes his moment."

"I've done that," said Orin.

"What did you say?" cried Berillo.

"Not with *your* wife, asshole," Macon snapped.

"Oh." Berillo removed his glasses and wiped the lenses with his napkin. While his vision was impaired, and he mumbled to himself, Johnny lobbed a kernel of corn through the air that bounced off his forehead. He leapt to his feet in surprise.

"While you're up," said Wild Johnny, "how about letting 'em know in the kitchen we need another pot of mud."

Berillo made a face. Rank was not supposed to mean anything at Camp

Cope. But that was a double-edged sword: if he told Wild Johnny to fuck off, there was a chance Wild Johnny might slap him silly. He walked disgustedly into the kitchen to find a coolie.

Wild Johnny leaned against Orin and smiled, showing his chipped front teeth. "The movie tonight is *Lost Weekend*."

"How apt."

"What say we duck through the wall?"

"On my first night? Do you really think we should?"

"I'm sure of it."

Wild Johnny and Orin Boyd slipped out the door of cabin six with flashlights and slipped across the softball field to the edge of the woods. From there they followed the dirt path down to the lake. The air was cold, the stars bright, leaves crackled underfoot. Wild Johnny switched off his flashlight and they turned south along the lakefront until they found the chain-link fence. They made their way along the path to the escape hatch in trembling darkness.

"Just a sec," Johnny said huskily. "Ya gotta untie it."

A twig cracked in the distance, a branch moved without the aid of wind. Johnny suddenly dropped to his haunches.

Orin hit the earth flat, half a second ahead of him. They held their breath and hugged the ground. The woods were deathly still.

"What do you think?" Orin whispered after a moment.

"I think someone's out there."

"Who?"

"Goddamn, Orin, I don't know. I've made this trip a hundred times and no one's ever fucked with me."

"And us without our guns."

Johnny held his finger to his lips. "Get comfortable. We'll wait them out."

"Them?"

"Sssshh."

Orin rolled onto his back and relaxed his muscles, molding himself to the contours of the cold earth. He slowed his pulse and respiration the way he had learned from a prostitute in Bangkok. Soon the gears of time slipped to a different speed as he stared through bare trees at the stars, detached, yet vigilant, aware of his surroundings. Then Johnny tapped Orin on the shoulder and retrieved him. Thirteen minutes had passed.

"Whoever it was must be gone," said Johnny.

"Or better at playing dead than us."

Johnny stood up and dusted himself off. "Jesus H. I was flashing on Korea."

"I hear ya," said Orin.

"And, Lord, I'm thirsty."

"I hear that too."

Johnny pulled Orin to his feet. "Let's go get us a drink."

"O Captain, my captain. . . ."

Wild Johnny held back the gate in the fence for Orin and then followed him through. He turned the flashlight on again and started through chest-high rocks to a path that exited some eighty feet below, on the main road into town. Orin stayed close to Johnny's back as they squeezed between two boulders.

"Watch your step here," Johnny told Orin. "We had a guy break his leg one night and then we had to sell the monsignor a midnight hockey game on the lake. Not that he really believed us. He just wanted something reasonable to write on the aided card."

"Is that so?" a voice cried out from above.

Wild Johnny spun in his tracks, a yelp escaping from his throat. Orin flushed red, felt the helplessness of an ambush victim, the shame and chagrin of a cheater caught.

Above them, sitting on a large flat rock with a flashlight in his hand, was Monsignor O'Rourke. "Out for a little stroll, boys?"

"Yes, sir," said Orin. "I suppose it was inevitable."

"Inevitable?" O'Rourke shined his light in Orin's face. "On your first night in camp?"

"I'm sorry."

"You should have known better, Johnny," said O'Rourke. "It's one thing to have fun, and quite another to facilitate a suicide. This guy right here," he said, dropping down to their level and then poking his finger in Orin's chest, "he needs all the help he can get."

"Sorry, Father. I wasn't thinking."

"Then I guess it's a good thing I was."

Orin and Johnny mumbled more apologies until the monsignor told them to knock it off. "Get on back where you belong, before I change my Irish mind." He pointed with his flashlight in the direction from which they had come. "Johnny will know the way."

The monsignor made the sign of the cross over their heads and they watched him descend to the side of the road and climb quickly into his Blazer. The headlights snapped on and O'Rourke drove away.

"Jesus," said Orin. "That was fucking weird."

"He's never done that before, I swear it. Not in all the time he's had the camp. I mean the doctors are strict and the piss tests are real, but I really didn't think the old man gave a shit one way or the other, as long as he got to talk shop with us."

"I guess we were wrong," said Orin. "I guess he thinks this shit is real."

2

Wild Johnny was gone in the morning. His cabinmates told Orin at breakfast that the monsignor woke Johnny at dawn and said to get packed, a cab was waiting. No explanation was given, and from the look on Johnny's face, none was needed.

Kenny Demarco was also absent from the morning meal. No one had seen him. His cabin door was closed, the shades drawn.

While Orin was eating a corn muffin and drinking a second cup of coffee, Francis X. Berillo entered the dining hall in a heavy sweater and his tennis whites and told him that Monsignor O'Rourke wanted to see him right away.

"Should I bring my playbook?"

"Huh?"

"Never mind."

It was a cool and sunny morning, and as Orin crossed the compound he could see white clouds sitting on the distant mountaintops. The sweet smell of wet leaves and pine needles drifted up from the woods, and birds were screeching overhead. O'Rourke was waiting for him on the porch, sitting in his rocking chair, wearing a First Squad windbreaker and Sex Crimes sweatpants, reading yesterday's *New York Times*. He saw Orin coming and laid his paper aside, then motioned for Orin to sit on the steps at his feet. "Thanks for coming right away," he said. "We have a disaster on our hands, you and I."

"I know," said Orin. "But don't you feel bad about this. There really are people you cannot help."

"But you're not one of them, Orin."

"I don't understand."

"Come on inside, I want you to hear something." Monsignor O'Rourke stood up and led the way to his cabin and his office. After he had closed the door behind them, he turned on an answering machine and played for Orin a recording of an incoming telephone call, one that he said was received at the camp switchboard on the day before Orin arrived. The machine had unintentionally recorded the conversation, he said.

The caller never identified himself, simply asked to speak to Captain Macon. Orin heard several clicks, then Wild Johnny's whiskey voice: "Yeah?"

"Hey, Johnny."

"What's so wrong that you're calling me here. Don't tell me somebody's pregnant."

"Relax. I need a favor."

"Name it."

"A guy named Boyd is coming to the camp."

"I know Orin. He used to work for me, back when the job was still a job."

"He's a scumbag, Johnny. We don't want him down here. I want you to jam him up."

"He's not a scumbag at all. I used to—"

"You owe me, Johnny. You owe me a big one."

A moment's silence, the flick of a Bic, then a long exhalation of smoke.

"I'm not asking for all that much. Just take him over the wall and get him twisted, then let Mother Nature take its course. Leave him in town. He's sure to do something to fuck himself."

"And then we're even," said Johnny.

"A clean slate."

"You got it, gumba. I'll see you when I'm well."

Click.

"Orin!"

A door had opened behind them. Then Kenny Demarco was hugging him.

One look at Kenny's face sent him reeling. His partner had aged years. He was completely bald and there was room in his collar for another neck. Orin had all he could do not to cry. Kenny Demarco was forty-eight years old. He looked seventy-eight.

Orin's chest heaved once involuntarily, and Kenny squeezed him tighter. "I know," he said. "I look like—" They hugged again, until they became self-conscious. Then Kenny broke free and held Orin at arm's length. "What the fuck. We're acting like a couple of skirts."

Orin grinned sadly.

Kenny said, "So what do you think of the Monsignor's wiretap? Did you recognize that bastard's voice?"

"You knew about this?"

"What the fuck did you think? The monsignor told me as soon as it happened. I stayed out of sight to make it easy for Captain Johnny, the bootlicking turd, to make his move."

Orin turned to O'Rourke. "Why'd you let it go so far? Why didn't you just put me wise?"

"I honestly wanted to see what Johnny would do. I wanted to see what you would do. I considered calling the commissioner, but I would rather know what's going on first."

"You don't have to worry about a thing, Father," Orin said. "I'm gonna take care of this."

"Tell me what's going on," O'Rourke said.

"I have a lot of work to do."

Monsignor O'Rourke shook his head vehemently. "No," he said. "You have nothing to do that is more important than drying out from booze."

"With all due respect, sir, I'd rather be a drunk cop than a sober victim. If I don't make some moves right now, I'm history—an asshole precinct cop with a sheet full of shit. Kenny knows."

"Can we help you?" O'Rourke asked. "You know I have access to Commissioner Trimble."

"His sheet really *is* full," Kenny said. "You might not want to risk the farm on this."

Orin said, "Monsignor, you gotta graduate me early."

"But surely—"

Kenny said, "Orin's right. The high command, hey, they like you, and the camp is good publicity. But you're not a cop, and that's the first thing they'll say."

O'Rourke sat down in his chair, wounded. He was not a cop, he would never be a cop. He was a buff, which was well on the way to buffoon. Years of hale and hearty slaps on the back would be negated in an instant. He was humored, a gadfly, a boy with a need for men.

"Hey, Monsignor," Orin said. "You may not be a cop, but you just saved my bacon. And I thank you for it."

O'Rourke raised himself up in his chair and sighed. Kenny sat down on the couch and put his feet up on the arm. He coughed into his hand.

"Orin's not your run-of-the-mill drunk," Kenny said. "We didn't used to live on booze when we worked together. We didn't need to. We were having so much fun most of the time that it never came up."

O'Rourke looked Orin in the eye. "Tell me the truth, Orin Boyd. Are you a drunk or a nut?"

"I'm a nut."

"I'm glad to hear it—I think."

Orin and Kenny went to Kenny's private cabin and locked the plywood door behind them. Kenny pulled his tackle box from under his cot and produced from it a loosely rolled joint. "The doctor gave me a prescription, to level out the chemo."

"Do it up."

Kenny took a hit and held it in his lungs for a moment, then hacked violently and spat. He took another hit and then another and then he smiled dumbly at Orin as the wave of relief flooded his brain. He half-heartedly offered the joint to Orin.

"No thanks."

"How's Judy doing? She making a million bucks yet?"

"She threw me out."

"Hey, you *are* on a roll," Kenny said. Then, less sharply: "It was only a matter of time."

"I was getting in the way, on her climb to the top."

"I'm sure you were . . . among other things."

Orin nodded. "Among other things."

"Any chance of getting back together?"

"She's already out of mourning."

"That's too bad. I mean, she wasn't a bad broad, all in all."

"Everything she liked about me turned into everything she didn't like. I always found myself working against her."

Kenny smiled and pointed at Orin. "That's *your* trick," he said.

"That ain't it," Orin said. "This new job she's got made her change."

"Come on, man. Judy Boyd ain't no big deal. The problem is she don't know that yet. She'll change back," Kenny said. "Ride it out."

"But she's such an asshole these days."

"Remember when you were a rookie?"

"No," Orin said. "Well, maybe bits and pieces."

"Write her a love letter, whether she deserves it or not."

"Hey, Kenny . . ."

"Okay. I'll stop. At least you've got Dawn out of the deal." He stubbed the roach out on his antique bedside table with his hand, all bone and tendon. His clothes sagged around his withered frame as he stretched out on his cot. He said, "Linda knows I'm dying. After eighteen years of marriage she wouldn't take the time to drop me a note. And yet my daughter told me that when her mom first heard the news, she burst into tears."

"Goddamn," said Orin. "We didn't do so good with the chicks, did we, partner."

Kenny shook his head. "Not really." He reached under his pillow for a pack of Camel cigarettes and lit one up. "You gonna tell me who that was on the phone?"

"I don't know."

"Why does he want to hurt you?"

Orin shrugged.

"You don't have any idea why he's out to get you?"

"No."

Kenny Demarco sat up painfully. "Look in your cases," he said. "I once had a boss up my ass because I'd burned his brother-in-law, not that the little shithead ever said anything when I had him pulled over. All of a sudden I was doing traffic in the cold and wind and rain." He paused. "Maybe he thinks you've got something on him."

"Maybe."

Kenny made the face he made when he was thinking hard. "I need to know more," he said. "You gotta tell me everything you can about this."

"I don't gotta do nothing. I'm going home and I'm going back to work."

"Do it quick, then, eh? I want to be around to see it."

Orin didn't know what to say to that. He walked aimlessly around the dreary cabin, looking at but not really seeing Kenny's toiletries on his bureau, his alarm clock, all the pills he wouldn't need much longer.

"Did you hear me?"

Orin nodded.

3

Orin Boyd walked backward along the shoulder of the Southern State Parkway with a knapsack on his back and his thumb in the air. He wore the same clothes he had worn for the past three days: faded jeans, white Reeboks, and a black Harley-Davidson T-shirt. There was little hope of getting a ride.

He was westbound, squinting into the sunrise. It was seven A.M., the first of September, and the temperature was already rising through the eighties. The only relief was the breeze billowing through his sun-lightened hair and desperado mustache. Rush-hour traffic on the parkway moved past him at a crawl. Through a chorus of open windows blared a montage of drive-time morning shows. The drivers were preoccupied with a variety of tasks: last-minute touch-ups to face and hair, telephone calls on their cellular phones, dashboard fast-food breakfasts. An alarming number were reading the morning paper.

The Marine Corps knapsack grew heavier, the shoulder straps rubbing raw skin once toughened to this particular abuse. Orin continued to walk backward, his thumb out. A half mile back, near the Wantagh Avenue exit, his pickup truck was dead in the center lane. The old once-red Ford had coughed and sputtered, then rolled, engine silent, like a glider, its motion progressively slower as the other vehicles barreled past on either side, allowing no room to pull over. Orin had ridden out the momentum, then abandoned the truck where it stopped, right in the middle of the centermost lane. He imagined the beloved wreck was an object of considerable discussion by the traffic helicopters hovering over the Long Island rush hour, giving out the bad news to the drive-time radio listeners.

The Island was more like the city every day: an ordeal to traverse, impossible to afford. Clean water was running out and the garbage piling up. I gotta get away, Orin told himself, as he walked backward into the branches of a sapling. Only five more years to retirement, one thousand one hundred and eighty rotating shifts to go. And maybe zero. They wanted him out and they were going to use him to flush out some others. Flotsam and jetsom, fuckups and felons. The whirlybirds circled like vultures overhead.

The truck's checking out wasn't a good omen; he was going to be late to work. Nobody in his right mind would pick up a thirty-eight-year-old burnout wearing biker tweeds and both arms embroidered with tattoos celebrating the golden age of the Grateful Dead and the siege of Khe Sanh.

Nobody except a couple of well-groomed, well-armed, and very young New York State troopers eager to enforce the prohibition against solicitation of a ride. Orin smiled warmly as the blue-and-yellow cruiser rolled to a stop just in front of him, inches from his toes.

"What's the story, Ace?" said the trooper riding shotgun.

Orin was used to people taking him for a jerk. He smoothed his mustache and spread his feet a little wider. "Bad gas."

Both officers glanced around, frowning. "What the hell you talkin' about?" said the driver.

"The gas in the truck—about half a mile back? The one that's got traffic backed up to Montauk." Orin bent down and glanced at their faces.

"What are you doing with a truck on the parkway?" the trooper driving wanted to know. "Didn't you see the signs?"

"No," said Orin. "I didn't see the signs. I was late."

"You were late," the second trooper mimicked. "I love it."

The officers grinned at each other. The driver turned to Orin. "Why don't you be a good fellow and hop in the back seat. We'll take care of everything from here."

"Whatever you say, officer."

Orin opened the back door and slid into the caged rear seat. He couldn't believe what greenhorns they were, not even frisking him. They smiled and he smiled, sharing their pleasure—however transient—in the certainty of multiple summonses, maybe enough to coast on for a couple of days.

To help embellish their fantasies, Orin said, "She's unregistered."

"Unregistered?"

"Yep. Uninspected, too."

"Uninspected?"

"And uninsured."

"You don't say."

"Yeah," Orin said. "I hope you guys don't mind."

"Mind?" said driver. He put the car in gear. "We don't mind, but it might honk off the judge."

The two thought this was hilariously funny. The troopers kept giggling. Orin tapped the cage with his shield.

"Judge?" he said. "What judge?"

The troopers were crestfallen. They tried to hide it as they mumbled fraternal greetings, but Orin could tell they were disappointed over the lost tickets, and the hard evidence that someone who looked as bad as he did could actually be a cop, too.

"Where do you work?" the driver said. "Motor pool?"

"I wish," Orin snorted.

"So where?"

"Unfortunately, gentlemen, I've just been reassigned to the banana republic of Nassau County, the gulag *policia*. I'm supposed to be in Belmont in"—he glanced at his watch—"thirty short minutes."

"The Lucky Thirteenth, eh?" the second one said, as if that explained Orin Boyd's low-life appearance. "What didya do?"

Orin studied the blond hair on the back of his hands. Rookies, he thought, fucking new guys. They were invariably dangerous douchebags, at least until their hearts were broken and they got suitably uncivilized.

"I was framed," Orin said. "Internal Affairs called it blatantly miscreant behavior, but you know how those uptight pricks can blow things out of proportion."

A look of revulsion passed over the driver's pale Irish face as he glanced back at Orin through the grille. "Yeah, sure. Whatever you say."

"Square business. I shit you not."

The truth was a lifetime of sloth had caught up to him on a very bad day when his partner of fifteen years announced over morning coffee that he was going to die of bone cancer within the year.

He and Kenny had started drinking shots of vodka around noon at Kenny's house, to warm up for the topless bars in Lindenhurst. Around 3:30 his partner had driven home, and Orin reeled into the precinct house to report for work.

The desk officer that night knew enough not to let him drive. He assigned Orin to a uniformed foot post and told him to stay out of sight. Which Orin took to mean that he should wear a windbreaker over his uniform and hole up in one of the local pubs with his radio transceiver off. Orin only left his barstool to call in his hourly reports. "Boyd on a ring," he said at 1700 hours. "Boyd with a dring," he said at 1800. "Bird on a string," at 1900. At 2000 hours he had mumbled, "Wha' the fu'k you want?" Orin later heard himself on a tape saying, "Kiss my wahzoo!"

Orin missed his next ring. Brother officers were dispatched to find their missing man. As luck would have it, the headquarters shooflies caught him in the Sunoco station next to the bar. He had the no-lead nozzle in his ear and was pouring gas onto his head and person, screaming, "Answer the phone, you fucking morons!"

The fine was three days pay—the eighth such punishment in fifteen years. He was slated for counseling at a time convenient to the department, and assigned to the morgue wagon. The hearing officer, a deputy chief in Legal, called him a juvenile delinquent and a disgrace. His estranged wife just called him a fool.

So he preferred vague lies to reliving the gory details. What did he care what the troopers thought of him? He probably had more time suspended than these two had on duty.

The officer riding shotgun used the dashboard radio to arrange a tow for Orin's truck as they took to the grassy shoulder of the road and drove around the traffic jam. The tires popped and the car bounced, trailing dust in its wake. Orin sat back and slid his head against the seatback.

At the Belmont exit, where the streets got rapidly meaner and more littered, Orin opened his eyes and saw that they had arrived in the realm of the Lucky 13th, the clapboard slum on the south shore of Nassau County. Once idyllic and clean, even sparsely populated; now overrun, teeming. The cruiser lurched into a cobblestone driveway and stopped. The second officer opened Orin's door. Before even a handshake, the trooper was back in his passenger's seat and speeding away. The back tires threw stones against Orin's jeans.

Disheartened but on time, Orin Boyd turned his gaze upon his new business address, the 13th Precinct house, standing alone in the middle of nowhere. He could see how it had come to be called "The Little Out House on the Prairie." He shielded his eyes with his hand and looked over at Needle Park across the street where homeless junkies felt safe enough to sleep on summer nights, then looked again at the two-story municipal building that was the precinct house. It had green globes over the double front doors, and a copper plaque that said Nassau County Police Department, Erected 1950. Orin wondered if calls for help went out over the radio antennae on the roof, or if they just used smoke signals.

I've seen worse, he thought, in Harlem and Bed-Stuy, and East New York, station houses like bases under siege, war zones where big-time police work got done. The 13th was dark and dangerous but strictly minor league.

He squared his shoulders and walked in, then had to wait to introduce himself while the desk officer took bail from a black girl in a very revealing red dress. When the released prisoner had finally wiggled out the door and the six arresting officers had nothing more to leer at, Orin held up his shield.

"Police Officer Orin Boyd," he said. "I'm a transfer from the One-One."

Lieutenant Vincent Fazio squinted at the badge, as if making sure it was genuine.

"It's real," said Orin.

"No doubt. Welcome aboard." Fazio leaned over the chest-high desk and shook hands.

"Glad to be here," Orin said.

"No you're not," Fazio replied. "But what the fuck? You might as well enjoy it. Right now, go down the hall and sign in with Sergeant Ril. And if the sleazy bastard asks you to kiss his ring, think long and hard about doing it. He's a rotten little piss ant and the pipeline to the boss, who happens to be a big rotten piss ant. You with me? When that's done, if you still have possession of your soul, look under the stairs in the basement for Captain Archibald Blogg, also known as the Geek. He'll see you get a map of this dump and a list of the local ordinances. He'll give you applications for the Holy Name Society, the Emerald Society, Cops for Christ, Guns for God. Do with them what you will. After that, grab a locker and saddle up. I'll find you someone to partner with."

"Okay if I just go out on the stoop and eat my gun?"

Lieutenant Fazio ran his hand through his slicked-back hair. He smiled sadly. "You wouldn't be the first, sorry to say."

Orin found Sergeant Dominick Ril in his office, sitting in a beautiful wingback chair behind a large mahogany desk. He was reading *Hustler* and smoking a cigar.

Ril was small and dark and handsome, going smartly gray at the temples. His uniform was immaculate, the pleats in his shirt razor-sharp. The walls of his office were covered with pristine duty charts and calendars. As an obvious joke, fellow officers had put a kneeler in front of the desk so they could be more comfortable when begging for whatever.

"I'm Orin Boyd, Sarge. The D.O. said you were the dude to deal with."

Sergeant Ril marked his place in the magazine and slipped it under his blotter. "Orin Boyd, eh? Is that fucking typical or what? Nobody told me you were coming."

"Internal Affairs sent a teletype Friday."

"*Those* idiots." Sergeant Ril cursed the inefficiency of the system, the bureaucratic incompetence, the downright criminal negligence, and then handed Orin two silver 13s from one of his many desk drawers.

Orin looked at the collar studs in his hand. "That's it?"

"That's it."

"Don't you wanna wish me good luck?"

Ril cocked his head to one side. "Why would I want to do that?"

"No reason."

"What exactly did you do to land your dumb ass here, Boyd?"

Before Orin could frame a reasonable-sounding answer, the telephone on the desk rang. Off the hook, thought Orin. Except Ril made no move to answer it. It rang again and again. The sergeant laced his fingers behind his head. Orin cupped his ear.

"It's been good talking to you, Officer Boyd. You get the rest of your stuff from Archie the Geek, in the basement. Did they"—the phone rang again—"tell you that?"

"The phone," Orin said. "It's ringing, sir."

"Don't pay it any mind." Sergeant Ril rose from his wingback chair to see Orin out. The telephone was still ringing when Ril abruptly slammed the door.

"Hey!" a voice boomed. "You!"

Orin turned, pointing a finger at his own chest. "Me?"

A tall man with thick white hair and stevedore shoulders, wearing the star-spangled blues of a police inspector, marched from the office at the end of the hall toward Orin.

"Prisoners are not allowed back here." The name tag said Donnelly; the aroma said whiskey and cigars.

Orin snapped to attention and gave the inspector a military salute. "Police Officer Boyd, sir. I just rode into town."

Inspector Donnelly frowned, then bared his teeth, then burped in Orin's face.

"God bless you, sir."

"Get bent." Donnelly stepped around him and entered Ril's office unannounced. The door slammed.

Orin exhaled and headed for the basement.

Captain Archibald Blogg. His was a small metal desk in the corner of a small darkened room under the stairs in the basement. From the doorway Orin couldn't tell if he was dead or sleeping. He cleared his throat and raised his hand to knock.

"Yes . . . Officer Boyd." The desk lamp blinked on. "Come in. Good of you to pay us a visit."

Archibald Blogg stood up as far as the ceiling would allow and offered his thin hand. He was taller than Orin and very much skinnier. His uniform pants were baggy and drawn closed around his waist like a sack. Dark circles ringed his eyes and his hands felt clammy as he used both of them to shake Orin's, pumping slowly for a long time as he spoke.

"We've been waiting for you. With great anticipation."

Orin recoiled and raised his hands as if to surrender. "Look, Captain. I don't know what you've heard, but it wasn't really a sexual advance, okay? That was bullshit. Just boys being boys."

Captain Blogg raised a hand to his lips. "I understand . . . completely. We'll speak of this no further."

Orin shook his head in dismay. He was beginning to see why the psycho rate in this precinct was so much higher than the norm, why no women officers ever worked the 13th, or even requested the opportunity.

"Uh, Lieutenant Fazio said you would—"

"Great challenges await you here." The captain was beaming. "Tests of the mind and the heart."

"Sir?"

"We need men like you down here: men willing to stand up and be counted, willing to draw the line."

Orin laughed.

"Never laugh in the face of destiny, Orin. The Lord works in mysterious ways."

"Captain Blogg, why are you fucking with my head?"

"I'm not."

"Come on."

"I wouldn't. I think you can be saved. You're the first transfer in four years without a criminal conviction on his record, or out-patient status at one of our local rehabs. Your file has only minor transgressions. On the plus side: medals for bravery, commendations for actions above and beyond. I assure you, I'm not—ah—diddling with your head. Heaven forbid. I'm on your side." Blogg leaned closer. "The only man here you can trust."

"You trust anyone around here but me and you're out of your freakin' mind," George Clarke told him in the locker room ten seconds after they had first met. "The walls have ears and the clouds got eyes. If Kenny Demarco hadn't called ahead, I would have searched you for a wire before I took you for a partner."

Orin laughed out loud. Never before in his life had so many people assumed he was on the side of the angels. As he changed from his street clothes into his navy blue uniform, he felt himself in the awkward position of wanting to explain himself.

"Look," he said, "I—"

"The last guy they tried to slip in here had a blanket party you wouldn't believe. Three broken bones and a pension I heard he got for his troubles."

"Is that so?"

"Fucking A."

George Clarke was still wearing his Bermuda shorts, a blue, flowered Jimmy Buffet shirt, and black, zippered Beatle boots. He stood in front of the open locker deciding which of his uniforms would least offend the duty sergeant. George was forty-five years old, with silver hair combed forward like a little boy's, eyes surrounded by crow's-feet, and somebody else's perfect nose surgeoned onto his mug, paid for with a uniform allowance check. He was coasting to retirement like Kenny Demarco, before the white cells went berserk and the bones changed to twigs.

Orin said, "What happened to your old partner? How come you're working alone?"

"The dopey fuck." George snorted. "We fell out over pussy. I couldn't believe it." He wriggled out of his wedding band and pinned it to the back of his shield, over his heart.

Orin considered wearing his bulletproof vest but decided against it. Nobody got shot on their very first day, and besides, he was already sweating and the locker room was air-conditioned. "Must be over ninety out there," he said to nobody in particular.

"I'd die if I got transferred," George said. "Having to find a new string of bimbos, new places to coop, finding out the hard way who's righteous and who's a fucking scumbag." He shook his head and made the sign of the cross.

"I'm an extraordinarily lucky man," Orin said. "I married my bimbo, I don't trust a soul, and I haven't had a good night's sleep since 1968."

"You don't got bimbos?" George said. "What the hell's the matter with you, boy? Eight hours in the freakin' street, my dick gets hard and my balls start smoking. I need some pussy, and I ain't joking. Something my new bride don't quite understand yet."

"Yeah? How many before her?"

"Two," George admitted.

"So then maybe it *is* you."

"Funny guy," said George. "I do hope you drink at least."

"Dewar's scotch. Maybe you saw me on the back ad of that magazine. The last book I read was *Yertle the Turtle*."

"Yeah?" said George. "I don't get to read much."

They finished strapping on their gear. The locker-room phone rang once.

"It's time," George said. "They want us upstairs."

Orin looked at the clock on the wall, frowning. "And no word from the governor?"

"He doesn't even know we exist."

Twenty male uniformed cops dragged their butts up the staircase to roll call. Most of them took the trouble to draw their nightsticks and beat on Captain Archibald Blogg's office door. The rest, except for Orin, yelled "Geek!" as they passed. It was like a ceremony.

Blogg opened the door and stuck out his head, blinking.

"Geek! Geek!" The cops surged forward, up the stairs, trampling those in front, giggling as they went. "Geek!" they called out. "Geek!"

Sergeant Reginald "No Relation" Reagan stood on the landing, blowing his whistle. Cajoling and shoving at them, he eventually formed two uneven ranks of the tittering cops whose job it would be to protect the unincorporated Village of Belmont for the next eight hours. Sergeant Reagan put on his bifocals and read to them from the roll-call book, enumerating which merchant thought his place might get robbed next, which shopkeeper was complaining of the kids drag racing, and which corners were not currently open-air drug markets (that being quicker than naming territory lost). At the end of the melancholy recital, a crackling fart erupted in the ranks and everyone moved away from somebody.

Lieutenant Vincent Fazio stood up behind the duty desk to read out the post assignments: "Hoskinson and Garrett, thirteen-oh-eight. Carson and Healy, thirteen-ten . . ." At the end, he said, "George, you and the new man are walking the Strip. This here's Orin Boyd, who comes to us by way of a disciplinary hearing that didn't exactly go his way. He's no Gestapo plant, so you don't have to chill his ass for the next six months. That's about it, kids. You're on your honor."

4

Officers Clarke and Boyd were dropped off by Sergeant Reagan at the corner of Tompkins Avenue and DuBois Boulevard, the northern boundary of the foot post referred to interchangeably as the Strip or the Vil, a commercial area that catered to walk-in customers with cash. The visible street people wore the legal minimum on their hard-muscled black bodies. From doorways the disembodied heads of young men glared at them, like trophies. His kind of neighborhood, Orin thought, full of men on the side of the road, hiding in plain sight.

He pushed back his visored hat and pulled his map out to get his bearings. George told him to put it away, that there wasn't anything useful to see there anyway. He spread his hands as if he were holding a serving platter.

"This is it," he said. "The end of the freaking line."

"Where's this road go?" Orin asked.

"Nowhere."

"You're a depressing guy, George. Have you ever considered professional help?"

"I'm serious, man. It ends at a concrete abutment under the Mead-owbrook Parkway."

"Just like that," Orin said, snapping his fingers. "Four-lane main drag runs right into a wall, huh?"

George smiled lewdly. "You wouldn't believe the number of juiced-up spooks been surprised by that freakin' wall."

"What about putting up signs?" he said. "Like, 'Dead End,' 'No Way Out'?"

"The fucking kids would just swipe them," George said, and motioned him to follow, so that they might continue the "nature walk," as George called it. "First the Bohack closed, then the Dodge dealer, then Carvel. Now we got nigger social clubs and pig-knuckle delis run by nasty little A-rabs. Driving schools. *Abogados* scamming green cards for the illegals and chargin' C-notes to even talk to Immigration. Right there's Clay-borne's Funeraleria, offering the finest in previously loved coffins. And that big brick baby over there—with the satellite dish?—that's the Church of the Midnight Light, one of them e-lec-tronic ministries."

"This looks like Africa, George. It's making me very thirsty."

George thought this over for a moment. "What exactly are you saying?"

Orin patted George on the back. "Do you really think there's anything we can do for these people? You and me . . . by ourselves, given our limited resources? I mean, think about it."

"Are you trying to tell me you're ready for a cold one?"

Orin threw his arm over George's shoulder and gave him a cheerful squeeze. "Jeez, George, I thought you'd understand."

"Thanks be," George said. "A man after my own heart. I think we're damn lucky to hook up here. There ain't many of us left, you know."

"The word, I believe, is extinct."

They crossed the street to Maria's Corner Counter and pressed the buzzer by the door. A fat Puerto Rican woman pulled aside the shade. "It's me, babe," George announced.

She forced a smile and let them in. The two cops followed her to a kitchen in the back and sat down on small wooden chairs at a table under a skylight reinforced with a chickenwire mesh. Maria handed George an ice-cold six-pack. "You need more," she said, "you let me know."

"Thanks, babe." George popped one open.

Orin chuckled. "It's true," he said. "Everything I heard is true."

George looked quizzical. "You heard about Maria's?"

"The Lucky Thirteenth."

"Oh, yeah," George said. "We're out of control. For at least a couple of years now. It's a pisser. I love to come to work."

"What about Sergeant Reagan? What if he was to catch us dumping beers?"

George burped. "Forget 'No Relation.' He's afraid to get out of his car."

Orin took a long swig, loving every icy swallow. George swallowed his beer whole and crushed the can. "You want a straw for that?"

Orin smiled and knocked back the rest. "Inspector Donnelly burped a little Jackie Daniel's in my face this morning. He's an earlybird, I take it."

"He's a crude old fart. But he listens to reason. When you get jammed up, at least you can talk to the guy."

"And then he owns you," Orin said.

"More like rents. With an option to buy. But hey, it's a cold cruel world. A man needs all the friends he can get."

Before George could opine on the practice of sucking up to the boss, the portable radio on his belt ordered them to a disturbance in front of the Stallion Bar, corner of North Main and Broadway, at the southernmost boundary of the post.

They each left a dollar on the table and tugged their gunbelts into place. Outside, in the bright sunlight, they walked quickly past the empty lots and boarded buildings, past surly pockets of unemployed black youths and overdosed skeletons, on over to the sidewalk in front of the Stallion, where they found one Abraham "Batman" Wilson slumped over, drunk, in the gutter. He was curled up into a ball and unconscious.

Three old-timers standing watch over the body moved reverently aside to allow the cops room. The prostrate man was bleeding from the nose and mouth. His yellow T-shirt was tattered, rows of old shrapnel scars visible on his back.

George said to the oldsters, "We have the technology. We can rebuild him." He nudged Abraham Wilson's head with the tip of his boot. "Batman!" he yelled. "Hey! Get the fuck out of my street."

The man didn't have it in him to respond. A bubble of blood grew from one nostril and popped. His encrusted eyelids flickered. Orin asked a man in the growing crowd if Batman Wilson was an epileptic.

"No, sir. He a Baptist."

"Does he get seizures?"

"What do you mean—them athletic fits?"

"Yeah."

The man shoved his porkpie hat back on his head and spit. "Naw, man. He got his butt kicked." He looked at his friends. They looked away. He looked back down at Batman, as if he were peering into a hole.

Orin said, "I'm all ears. Are you your brother's keeper?"

"Forget it, homeboy," the man said, and then spun on his heels and went back into the bar.

George mopped his brow. "Who cares what happened to him. Let's just get him the hell out of here before No Relation to Reality drives by and makes a big deal of it. I don't know about you, but I don't plan on spending my whole day with this freaking mope."

Orin nodded. "So we'll call for a car and take him home."

"We can't."

"Why not."

"He hasn't got one. There ain't no place to take him, unless your wife don't mind the extra company."

Orin knew the paperwork for a veteran's hospital would flip George out. "Whatever," he said. "Your post, your call."

"Fucking A, partner." George nursed a pair of ammonia capsules from his gunbelt and stooped to roll Batman onto his back. "Lieutenant Fazio has a ten-minute rule. Meaning, if you can't stroke the complainant and shitcan the call in ten minutes, you gotta take a case report. Which any fool can see isn't necessary here."

George inserted a capsule in each of the large, bloodied nostrils. Gauze patches and a swatch of adhesive tape secured them. "Lock and load!" he called out.

While George Clarke was bent over the victim, Orin noticed that the grips of his revolver were notched in three places. One for each wife? It occurred to him that George might have some kind of difficulty getting along with persons of color. Or maybe everybody.

"Watch yourself," George said. "This guy's one strong mother," and he pinched Abraham Wilson's nose hard and gave it a clockwise twist. Then he jumped back like a kid who had lit a firecracker. Batman sat up howling, pawing at his face with scarred hands, his eyes filled with wild surprise.

"Beat it down the road, Batman!" George shouted. "Before I lock your dumb ass up."

Abraham Wilson went cross-eyed for a moment, then ripped the dressing from his nose. He lurched to his feet with the aid of a parked car, grunted something unintelligible, and stumbled away, veering along the sidewalk.

Most of the onlookers laughed. Some didn't. George clapped Orin on the back. "You gotta love it. That guy starts up better than my LawnBoy."

"No wonder they hate our guts."

George frowned. "Fuck 'em."

The man in the porkpie hat was watching them from the doorway of the Stallion Bar.

"Hey," Orin said to George, "go get us a couple of beers and tell the bartender how glad we are that we don't have to report him to the State Liquor Authority for serving Batman here into a comatose state."

"Hey!" George brightened. "Good idea."

George lumbered past the black man in the doorway. Orin nodded greetings. The man sipped from a brown paper bag. "Let me hold a cigarette," he said.

Orin gave him a cigarette.

The black held the white stick daintily. "Man, why you let your partner do him like that?"

"He's hard to handle when he's been drinking."

"That ain't no excuse."

Orin said he would try to get George to lighten up.

"Man, I wish I was white."

"I wish you were, too."

"Serious. They'd do something if I was to complain about him?"

"He's out of here in less than a year," Orin said. "Tell your friends and neighbors there's a light at the end of the tunnel."

The old man's dark face wrinkled in disbelief. "I ain't sure if you jackin' me up or what, but you slicker than that Nazi son of a bitch. Nice to meet you, Officer. My name's Wallace Higgins. I used to drive a cab in New York City."

"Orin Boyd. I used to be a cop."

A patrol car pulled up in front of the bar. Sergeant Reagan. Orin said good-bye and walked toward the cruiser. George Clarke passed him before he reached it and quickly explained to the sergeant that nothing at all had happened. "Probably just another of them hoax calls we've been getting. I told you, Sarge, making 911 calls free was a terrible mistake."

"Whatever you say, George. As long as it doesn't reflect disfavorably on my command."

"The sarge went to college at night," George said to Orin. "That's why he talks so funny. So presidential."

Reagan ignored the jibe. "Hop in the car, Boyd. They want you inside forthwith."

"Really. What for?"

"How the fuck should I know? They told me to pick up *you* and a couple of light and sweets."

Orin looked at George and shrugged. "Been nice working with you, George. A real experience."

Sergeant Reagan drove Orin to the station house and told him to report to Sergeant Ril's office. Dominick Ril, in turn, informed Inspector James Donnelly, via intercom, that Officer Boyd was waiting to see him. Inspector Donnelly duly instructed Sergeant Ril to "send the fucking shithead in."

Ril escorted him. He opened the door to the inspector's office and they walked inside together. Ril left Orin standing in front of the inspector's desk and went to stand next to Donnelly. The office, Orin noted, was like Inspector Donnelly—pompous.

Donnelly was smirking. Orin gave a wise-ass salute to the American flag on the wall next to the softball plaques, obscene cartoons, the picture of Police Commissioner Trimble, a picture of Donnelly in a rented tuxedo shaking hands with Cardinal O'Connor, and a cross-stitched sampler in a wooden frame that read, *Fuck 'em if they can't take a joke.* On the desk was an appointment calendar courtesy of the stewards of Belmont Park and a commemorative lucite block with a crack pipe embedded in it, a trophy of a skirmish won.

"It says here you're a fuckup," Donnelly said. He looked up from the confidential file conspicuously opened on his desk.

"Does it?"

"In a nutshell."

"There must be some mistake," said Orin. "I got a pisspot full of medals home that say I'm a fucking hero."

Donnelly's eyes lit up and he laughed in Orin's face. "You got some set . . . bluffing when you ain't got no cards."

"I don't understand what you're talking about, sir. But then it's been that kind of day for me."

Sergeant Ril said, "We got word that you're a plant. An Internal Affairs snitch." He pointed past his boss's shoulder. "This file, it's a fucking fantasy, Boyd. A fairy tale. Nobody pulls the stunts you're alleged to've pulled and then gets off with just a transfer."

"Your source," Orin said, "is full of shit."

Ril grinned like Frank Sinatra and pulled at his cuffs. "I'll tell him you said so."

"I'm sure you will."

"Then you really did all this shit?" Donnelly said. He eyed an item. "You actually beat a prisoner with his dead cat."

"No."

"No?"

"The cat wasn't dead."

"Jesus," Ril said.

Orin shrugged. "The perp was a rapist. He had just done a ten-year-old."

Donnelly said, "What about this off-post violation back in January? It says you were filmed at a Mafia wedding at a time when you were supposed to be on a stakeout?"

"We went to high school together."

"A car accident. A barroom brawl. One, two . . . three brutality complaints. Two insubordinations. Seven fines." Donnelly tossed the file aside. "It sounds to me like I could call Internal Affairs right now and tell 'em I caught you jerking off in front of Sunday school kids and they'd buy it."

Orin didn't say anything. Sergeant Ril said, "I can see it already. Little girls in school uniforms using anatomically correct dolls to recreate the incident, mommies wailing, daddies pounding nails into the gallows." He tittered.

Donnelly smiled. "I guess what I'm trying to tell you, Boyd, is that we work together here, or I cut your fucking throat."

Orin glanced out the window, doing his best to ignore the provocation. They had called him in for a humbling session. He took a deep breath and spoke.

"I'll come to work every day, put in my eight, and keep my mouth shut." He looked back at Donnelly. "You won't even know I'm here."

"I can't stand heroes," Donnelly said, "and I can't stand rats. You got a problem? Tell it to the fucking wall. 'Cause I'm a prick. The biggest one you ever met. I thought it fair to both of us that you know that."

George dropped Orin off at the Goodyear service center on Sunrise Highway. A hundred bucks it cost him for the emergency tow and repairs.

The mechanic said, "I did the best I could for you. Used parts and whatnot. She's only worth a couple of times the bill, not counting the police discount. You sure you don't want to just unload her?"

Orin shook his head no. "Sentimental value," he said. "Made in the U.S.A."

"Then you ought to get it registered and inspected. And washed."

Orin nodded, checking under the seat. Crushed cigarette packs, coffee containers, empty bottles and cans, fishing gear, rock and roll tapes, and a beanbag ashtray that he banged empty and threw up on the dashboard. "Soon," he said, and climbed into the cab. "You're absolutely right."

The engine turned right over and all was well with the world. He smiled. He was not a man in love with his vast possessions, he thought, but he did require reliable transportation. He put it in gear and pulled out. Orin believed the truck helped him appear useful, a contributing member of society, doing for him what a clipboard does for an army private, a microphone for a politician. Also the pickup provided substantial protection from rain and solid objects and did not tip over as easily as the Volkswagen Beetle he used to drive.

Five years ago, drunk as a lord, he had rolled the Scum Bug. And he did it in front of a traffic cop at Franklin Avenue and Old Country Road, a block from headquarters, at high noon on a sunny day, with Kenny sitting wide-eyed next to him. Whistles blew and women screamed as bits of windshield glass kept cascading down on them every time they moved. Orin climbed out the side window like an astronaut after splashdown, the startled traffic cop just staring at him. Orin saluted, then pretended not to understand English as he pulled Kenny out, righted the car with his bare hands, pushed Kenny back in, and drove away. The image of the patrolman running after them, waving frantically and getting smaller and smaller in the rearview mirror, made him laugh even now.

It took twelve minutes and he was there: the head shop, as ordered. Orin parked behind the redwood medical building on Hempstead Turnpike. He climbed the back spiral staircase to the empty third-floor lobby, checked the menu board, and found that Juliet Cammer, M.D., saw her patients in Room 303.

But there was no receptionist there when he arrived. And where were the others, he wondered, glancing around the empty waiting room. Where were the bearded ladies, the eunuchs, the droolers. And where was the departmental shrink, whom he had to assume was working for the county because she couldn't cut it on her own. Was she napping in the back? Was she observing him through a peephole?

He sat down on one of the pea-green vinyl couches and thumbed through a pack of his bills that he had been carrying. He opened the MasterCard statement and saw the interest piling up, muttered "Shit," and shoved it and the rest into his back pocket. He opened an old copy of *Golf Digest* and was skimming Jack Nicklaus on intuition and putting when the door to the waiting room flew open. A woman burst in: late twenties, auburn hair, five feet seven, a great set of wheels, and arms loaded with paperwork.

"Officer Boyd?" she said.

"That's me."

"I'm Dr. Cammer. Sorry I'm late."

"That's okay."

"One of your brother officers—I had to make an emergency admission to South Oaks."

"No problem."

She opened the door to her office. "Please."

Orin entered. She slid in behind her desk, piled with correspondence and files, and rifled through the messages, tossing them one by one into the wastebasket propped atop an adjoining chair. A schedule was tacked unceremoniously to the wall behind her where most physicians usually displayed degrees or photographs of vacations with their brilliant kids.

Orin sat down across from her in a leather scoop chair. The room was comfortably air-conditioned. On the small table alongside him was a huge clamshell ashtray and an economy-size box of tissues.

"Do I have to smoke and cry to get my money's worth?" he said.

Juliet Cammer looked up from the drawer she was stuffing with more paper. "No. You have to stop drinking."

She held a finger up to indicate she needed a moment more to get organized. Orin took the opportunity to check her left hand for a wedding ring and found none, then wondered what possible use the information could be. This chick was not merely out of his league, they didn't even play the same game. He was, however, pleased that the department's seventy dollars per would not wind up in some hunchback's wallet.

"So," she said, sitting up straight in her chair and folding her hands atop the desk. "Most of my patients call me Julie."

"Most of my doctors call me Orin."

She smiled thinly. "Have you spent much time in therapy previously?"

"At the V.A."

"After Vietnam?"

"During . . . after. Most of my unit wound up there sooner or later."

"Did you see a great deal of fighting?"

"How old are you?" Orin said.

"Twenty-seven. Why?"

"No reason." He sat back in the chair and lit a cigarette. Juliet Cammer stared at him as if she expected something more. Did she want him to replay for her the war movies in his head? Fuck that, he thought. She had been what—nine? He had been twenty. He gave her the blankest stare he could muster.

"Talk about why you're here," she said.

"To keep my job."

She frowned. "Aren't you at all interested in your mental well-being?"

"What are you talking about?"

"I'm talking about a marriage in jeopardy. I'm talking about an incipient ulcer . . . a thirty-eight-year-old male with the drive of an octogenarian who is at risk of losing his job because he's an addict."

Hardball, he thought. The detailed history of his degeneration was there somewhere in her pile of papers. He sighed. What had happened to cops taking care of their own? The extended family of brother officers? Omertà?

"You do admit you're an alcoholic?"

"Yeah. Sure."

She made a note of this. "Drugs?"

"When I was younger."

"What did you take?"

"I don't think I should answer that."

She put the pen aside. "Nothing leaves this office, Orin. I work for you, not the county or the police department, even though they ordered you here."

"Fine," he said. "Put down everything but heroin and crack."

She raised her eyebrows. "Everything? Like LSD, PCP? Seconal? Coke."

"Like it was alphabet soup."

"What made you stop?"

"Watergate."

"Are you serious?"

"Actually, I was tripping in a topless bar in Bangkok and the girl on stage turned into a monkey. It really blew the mood, as you might imagine."

"What *about* women?" she said. "In general, how do you get along with the opposite sex?"

"Famously."

"Any problems with impotence?"

"I beg your pardon."

"You'd be surprised," she said. "Lots of alcoholics can't, or won't, relate sexually to their mates."

"I can do it just fine by myself," he said. "That way I get to skip the lies."

"Being out of love doesn't have to be so bleak," she said.

"Bleak? Who said anything about bleak?" He put his cigarette out half-smoked and instantly wanted another.

"You have a child," she said.

"Yes. A daughter. She's five and a half."

"Do you see her regularly?"

"Not often enough."

Dr. Cammer nodded. "Are there what you might call considerable differences between you and your wife?"

"I'd say so. She'd say so. What's this got to do with drinking?"

"What about your parents?"

"My mother is deceased. The old man is missing in action."

"Do you miss them?"

Orin lit another cigarette and wondered if she was counting. He wondered if asking to go to the bathroom in the middle of the session would tip her off to how close she was coming to his unreasonable fear of the known but not admitted.

"That's a tough question," he said. "My mother is dead eighteen years now, right after I got home. And the Old Man left when I was ten, so he's a dead issue, too. We were not what you'd call a close family." He paused to take a drag and saw the ash from the tip of his cigarette. "Do I miss them? I don't know. I miss being eight years old, when we were together and the world made a little more sense. I suppose my daughter will miss being four."

"Not if you stay in her life."

"That's true," he said, with little conviction. Orin was sweating through his shirt and sticking to the leather of the chair. He could smell his armpits and hoped that she couldn't.

"Your partner. Tell me about that."

"Don't you want to know about the first time I cut school?"

"I'm bouncing around," she admitted. "I'm going for a quick read, a general impression from which I can structure an overall plan for your recovery."

"Well, that really sounds impressive, Doctor, but it feels like you're playing Ping-Pong with my brain."

"Sorry," she said. "But that's no more than what you've been doing to it, and without a license. Tell me"—she looked away—"do you feel guilty about it being him instead of you?"

"Right, lady. Survivor's guilt. Gimme a break. Forgive me, Dr. Cammer, but you've been reading too many textbooks. I've seen a lot of guys go instead of me."

"Because it's interesting that you used the expression 'cutting school' and—"

"No it's not. None of this shit is interesting."

Dr. Cammer looked at her watch. "One more question, Orin—the big one where clinically depressed cops are concerned."

He thought briefly about telling her the truth, then remembered that he needed his gun and badge. Maybe she caught it in his face, probably she hadn't.

"No, Doctor," he said. "Rest assured. I do not now, nor have I ever contemplated oral sex with my gun."

She just gazed at him for a moment. "I'll see you next week," she said. "Same time."

"I'll be here."

"You're sure?"

"No surer than you."

He stopped at the beer dock on Merrick Avenue for a case of Bud Light in bottles, then drove down the Meadowbrook Parkway to the Jones Beach Pier. It was a beautiful evening and he needed some beach time, a chance to think and drink and ruminate on twists of fate. Specifically, his new boss, and his new partner. Two more of life's sudden derailments. Like wives and children and taxes. Obstacles and opportunities. Orin knew all about shoulda, woulda, coulda, and failure. Sometimes, usually when he was melancholy drunk, he wondered if, but for a shot of booze here and there, he might be sitting in a corner office somewhere, or running back punts in the NFL.

Fishing was good for his soul, he thought, even better than golf, and it could be adjusted to take more time or less time than eighteen holes of self-abuse. At a favorite spot near the end of the pier, he abandoned the truck and expertly dropped a line over the side, then cracked a beer. Next to him was an old black lady whose plastic bags were nearly filled with the day's catch.

"Nice night," he said.

"Been good to me."

"You want a beer?"

"Heavens, no."

"Good. More for me."

The old lady chuckled. Orin drank. The alcohol eased into his bloodstream and he relaxed. Soon string lights flashed on the coastal bridges and above them a half moon hung over the water like a hammock.

5

George Clarke was George Clarke: not bad as partners go, but not great, like Kenny Demarco. A week went by walking alongside George. The day shifts turned to evening tours, four-to-midnights. Four-to-forevers, Judy had called them when she felt like breaking his stones.

The new job was tedious but tolerable. Orin worked every day, did his eight and kept his mouth shut, just like he had said. But the thirst a man could build increased in direct proportion to the workload, which on warm nights in the 13th was considerable. So he began casual friendships with a few of his co-workers over happy-hour cocktails, but it was nothing like it had been with Kenny and the beer-for-lunch bunch from the 11th. Guys mostly went their own way in the One-Three. They whispered, hunched over the phones in the squad room, and gave vague descriptions of their personal lives instead of sharing the gooey details.

On the night that he had exactly four years and thirty-eight weeks to go to retirement, he and George were assigned to handle traffic outside the Church of the Midnight Light during a memorial service for some matriarch who had left behind sixty-one grandchildren in Belmont. The Reverend Sims, voice and guiding spirit of the church's radio crusade and its founding pastor, appeared alongside their patrol car in his full magenta robes. He thanked them personally for their cooperation with the black community and withdrew, robes billowing, into the church. A black-suited deacon slipped an envelope onto the dashboard in front of George and proceeded after the reverend.

George's "Thanks" went unheard. "What a stud," he said. "You gotta appreciate Bubba Sims. I hear he's banging half the congregation. You gotta give the devil his due."

"No, you don't," Orin said. "Not right out in the open. Considering that I'm on probation, and maybe the unwitting star of Internal Affairs's latest feature film, it wasn't the brightest thing you could have done taking money like that."

"Shit," George said, glancing around. He slid lower in his seat. Holding the envelope below the dash, he ripped it open and fished out two tens. "What do you think we should do?" he said, looking mildly worried.

"I think we should drink the evidence as quick as possible."

"M' man!" George hooted. "What the hell are you scaring me for?"

After the shift George brought Orin with him to Red's, there to drink the Reverend Bubba's money and to celebrate the capture of a Lebanese burglar they had nabbed on a fire escape with someone else's VCR. Red's was a large, dark cheater's bar with little to recommend it except its hard-rock jukebox, discreet off-road parking, and its female patrons, a collection of loose and willing women who could sometimes be talked into parking-lot quickies or adventures under the stars at the pistol range. What they saw in the mostly married cops—beyond the probability that they wouldn't be axe-murdered—was anybody's guess. But tonight the place was empty, except for the two of them and a couple of other One-Three misfits.

George told Orin about his last assignation at Red's—"Linda, the Liplock"—who had subsequently flipped out and pulled a "Tokyo Rose" on him.

"Her little shitsack brother got popped for selling crack and the next day Linda storms into Donnelly's office and claims sexual relations with half the precinct. How dare we lock up her bro, she says, she's fuckin' family. My God, that was embarrassing. Freakin' Donnelly made us all line up and Linda cruised the ranks like a visiting dignitary. 'He fucked me, he fucked me. Him, him . . . This guy a blow job, him, him too. Him, him . . .'"

"What did she say about you?"

"The skank told everybody I ate her, which of course I categorically denied. Fuck. She took the pipe in California and named the Thirteenth in her swan note. It made the papers out there."

"Swan note?" somebody said.

"Yeah," said George. "Sucked off a Chevy, the dumb bitch. But that was terrible: casting perversions on us like that. I laughed when I heard she was dead."

Newt, the ancient operator and proprietor of Red's, was a tiny bald man with thick glasses that sat on the end of his nose. He brought them both another round of drinks.

"Here you go, Speedrack," he said to George. "Bad whiskey and watered-down beer will ease your grief."

George raised a glass. "The best things in life are cheap."

Orin leaned across the bar toward Newt. "Where are all these hot mamas I've been hearing about? This isn't much of a reception."

Newt ventured a guess: "Maybe they have real dates tonight."

"No fuckin' way," George said, "not unless they suckered some other schmucks with them bogus ads in the personals."

"Go home to your wife, you big asshole," suggested Newt. "Have a piece of something strange."

"Later," George said. "I'm still breaking her in."

Orin hadn't even thought of going home. Instead, he drank beer and played eight ball with the boys, listened to George tell Donnelly stories and tales of the Geek and the Reverend Bubba, who sounded like he was running half the town. It went on till four A.M., until Orin was finally bored and the bar was closing.

He stood up from his stool and announced that he was going fishing. Anyone who wanted to could come.

George grimaced. "I gotta go home and turn the old lady over. She gets bedsores sleeping on the couch."

The others begged off too, claiming errands and family obligations. Just as well, Orin thought, the tide was running out. He drove home alone instead.

Orin unlocked the door to his basement apartment, a tiny studio George had christened the Hole. It was.

The sickly smell of fuel oil from the boiler flavored the air. He turned on the overhead fluorescent, set his pistol on the aluminum snack tray near the tiny stove, and threw his windbreaker on the floor in the corner. Above it, the view through the one window was of hub caps and tires and the base of the dumpster. There was a mattress on the tile floor and dumbbells scattered all around, so that you had to step carefully not to crack your ankles. Orin put on an Allman Brothers album, took off his clothes, and stretched out on the mattress. The record was worn, the speakers giving out the sound of eggs frying behind the music. He closed his eyes and listened to the clunk and whir of the elevator. From the garbage chute down the hall came the clinking of cans and breaking glass, and Willie the janitor screaming at the lazy, ignorant, useless shitheads pitching metal and glass into the incinerator, and at five in the morning, too. Orin chuckled and slipped into sleep.

He woke up fifteen hours later, feeling lousy. He was hungry and his head hurt, so he opened his knee-high refrigerator and gargled down a pair of aspirins with a Diet Dr. Pepper. Then he called Sal's House of Pizza and arranged for breakfast to be delivered while he showered.

Orin was sitting on the second-hand couch in his boxer shorts, watching a *Magnum* rerun and eating from the white cardboard box in his lap, when somebody knocked on his door. Food in hand, he opened it.

Judy appeared startled. Her estranged husband, unshaven and undressed, stood mutely in the doorway of what appeared to be a furnished storage room with a slice of pepperoni pizza in his hand. He could see sorrow well up in her face at the sight.

"Hey!" he said. "Come on in. This is . . . ah. Forgive the mess, okay? We separate our trash here at Alimony Acres and I'm afraid I've fallen a week or two behind."

"You're in arrears, alright. You owe me a check."

Orin pulled on a black police raincoat that was hanging on the back of the door and modestly zipped the front. Judy had on a kelly-green dress, silk, and perfectly applied makeup.

He said, "You don't look like you need money."

"What I look like is none of your business. You and me, we have a child to raise. That's our mutual responsibility. You could make it easier on both of us if you'd do this like an adult."

Orin stepped back from the door and Judy Boyd stepped in past him. "I thought I sent you the check," he said, taking a paper bag from the floor and rifling through the rubble of his financial records. "You want a drink?" he said.

"No." She shook her head. "Jesus."

"How's Dawn?" he said, still rummaging.

"If you cared that much, you'd come to see her."

He exhaled audibly, leaving the accusation unanswered. In truth, he did not understand himself why he hadn't gone to see his child since the breakup. Finally he said, "If I saw her, I'd have to see you."

"Orin, I'm late for an appointment."

"Oh," he said, "is that like a date?"

"You're a fool!" she said.

"At least we agree on something."

His checkbook materialized from under a stack of unopened mail lying in the silver cup he had won wrestling in high school. Using the top of the pizza box like a writing board, he wrote her a check for one month's child support and another a month ahead.

When he handed them to her, she said, "These had better not bounce."

"Don't think much of me, do you?"

"Take a good look at yourself," she said. "What am I supposed to think?"

"You know, you're not pretty enough to be such a bitch."

"I was pretty enough when you married me."

"You were pregnant."

Judy pursed her lips. "I'm sorry. Did I forget your one good deed?"

Orin tossed the checkbook back into the silver cup.

"Listen," she said. "Dawn needs a father."

"Great. Maybe you can advertise for one in the *Wall Street Journal*."

"She needs you to teach her about something other than alcoholism and abandonment."

"Get off it. You sound like a goddamn soap opera." He turned away. "I'm not gonna change just so you don't have to."

"You haven't got any choice. She needs you to. Look, this isn't about some one-night stand cheat with some bar pickup. Or about coming home dead drunk to your nagging wife. Okay?" She gestured helplessly. "Okay. We're over. This isn't about us. This is about her, and you. You love her. You've got to do something about yourself, for her, for you."

He rolled his eyes.

"Think about it," she said, her voice wavering. "Do you want her growing up feeling about things the way you do?"

Orin paced to the door and threw it open. "You've got appointments, remember?"

"Giving me the gate, eh?" She made to follow. "I see you're still wearing your wedding ring, which tells me you're not accepting this."

"I'm gonna have it removed, with an ax."

Her eyes filled. It softened him a little, which made him more resentful. "What are you looking at?"

She said, "Are we in any way going through this together?"

"Yeah. Sure," he said. "It's . . . It's late. You'd better get going."

She nodded. "I'm going to miss you," she said, and left.

Orin threw on gray slacks and a corduroy sports jacket, and jumped into his shoes. Then he ran outside. Judy was obviously dressed for an evening out. He was going to follow.

He got to the parking lot in time to see her taillights flash at the stop sign near the end of the block. "Shit."

He raced to the truck and peeled out in pursuit. He was three cars back by the time the light turned green on Sunrise Highway. He wasn't worried about her spotting him. The sun was down, the shoppers out in force. She wouldn't notice him behind her, lurking.

In the glove compartment he found the dregs of a vodka bottle and drained it. Judy turned north onto Meadowbrook Parkway, then west on Stewart. She pulled into the municipal parking lot between Seventh Avenue and the railroad tracks and entered the Tap Room through the rear door.

Orin gave her ten minutes, then followed. Inside, the restaurant was crowded with the well dressed and well heeled. The laughs were loud and the smoke as thick as the steaks the joint served. Orin confiscated a stool at the bar, behind several standing drunks, lawyers he knew by sight. When he asked about the food, the bartender gave him a menu to peruse. Orin sipped his beer and slipped along the bar to a better vantage point, using the crowd and the menu to shield himself.

Judy was halfway across the room, smoking and talking animatedly. He recognized the guy as her boss. Mister red suspenders himself: married, no children, a southerner. Orin was pleased to see that the man was balding prematurely and drinking a margarita. He was also staring deep into Judy's baby blues.

"See anything you like?" the bartender asked.

Orin forced a small smile and shook his head no. He left the bartender a three-dollar tip and returned to his truck to wait them out. A half a pack later, Judy and her boss came out, arm in arm and obviously tipsy. The guy walked her to her car, opened the door for her, brushed off her seat, and helped her get in. Then he squatted next to the window for a long five minutes.

"The dopey fuck should keel over from the exhaust," Orin muttered, but the guy stood up and rubbed his back, Judy reaching under his coat to help. "Shit." They both laughed and he bent down once again to kiss her. Orin exhaled, cheeks puffed. Judy waved, rolled up her window, and drove away.

The date checked his watch and sauntered to a red BMW the same color as his braces. He looked pleased with himself. Orin had trouble catching his breath as the BMW pulled out.

Alone in the dark parking lot, Orin thought about following, stopping alongside and giving him the old smile-at-the-traffic-light, and then putting a bullet in his brain. But it was too risky, he decided. Homicide would reconstruct the victim's last hours and know immediately who had done it.

Orin groped in the glove compartment some more, but without success. The BMW sped away. He drove around for a while, then decided to go to the house, make an honorable offer to settle their differences. He would toss her a bone: agree to daily head sessions with Cammer and a family counselor. He would try to mend his ways and his heart. There would be something between them again, circuits would reconnect. For the good of their child, he would say. Take it or leave it. And if that didn't work, he could always kill her suitors at his leisure.

Confidence filled his empty heart. It was all simple, terribly simple, and he wondered why he hadn't made this move before. Half a block from the house, he found some gum sliding around on the dashboard and popped a stick in his mouth. He felt like a teenager picking up his first date; he vowed to say nothing dumb.

The yellow light of the living-room window played on the dogwood tree in front of the house. It glinted off the chrome of the BMW in the driveway behind Judy's Mazda. Orin shut off his lights and coasted. He rolled past the house and stopped the truck at the end of the dead-end street. The light in the cab unscrewed easily. Orin opened the door and slid out. He walked casually down the street, smelling the fetid summer grass, remembering births and barbecues, pushing Dawn in her carriage. At the corner of his property line, he slipped into the side yard and followed the concrete walk to the back of the house, watching the windows for signs of life. Upstairs, in the darkened dormer window his baby girl slept. Above the rooftop the sky was clear, the stars bright. Light from the double glass doors of the den fell on Dawn's two-wheeler on the patio. The training wheels were gone, a kickstand in their place.

He climbed onto the roof of the tool shed, the apex of which he straddled. From there he could see Judy sitting at the kitchen table, sipping coffee, the date pacing back and forth, gesticulating, driving home his points. The red suspenders were in full view: the guy's coat was off and his tie pulled down.

Orin thought to leave, to climb down from his perch and walk away. He could stop back at the Hole, pick up his stuff, and still make Richmond, Virginia, by daybreak. The pain would go away, he supposed, if he was anything like his father. Then the guy took her hands in his and Orin slid off the low roof like a snake and slithered to the edge of the patio to eavesdrop.

"Thank God," the guy exclaimed, "that you're not like this in your work. I've always admired the way you decide right off what you want and go for it."

"Thank you, Jonathan. I mean that."

They turned away, back into the house, and he couldn't hear them very well anymore. They had settled in the living room on the other side of the house.

Orin hunched over and circled around. When he reached the window the lights inside had been dimmed. Judy was on the couch and so was he, on top of her, his hand groping, head twisting as he wetted her down.

They looked like they were in heat. Judy's legs went over the guy's shoulders.

Orin tugged the five-shot Smith & Wesson Chief out of his ankle holster. He pressed his face against the bricks, the gun alongside his cheek. All he had to do was align the sights with his bald spot and gently squeeze the fuck into forever. It was like sex or riding a bicycle: you never forgot.

His breathing grew rapid, the night air scorching the inside of his head. He wondered if the bullet would blow the guy's brain across the new wallpaper, or ricochet down his spine and dribble out his asshole.

He thought about flying glass shredding Judy's cheek, slicing her arteries. He closed his eyes and thought about putting the cold barrel inside his own right ear, imagined pulling the trigger, the impact—going out with the kind of rush found only at ground zero.

6

The rookies pushed aside the front door and approached the platformed duty desk. The taller one, a freckle-faced redhead, held up his shiny new shield to the lieutenant looming above him.

"I'm Jack Gaines and this is Paul Kellog, sir. We were ordered to report here for the eight-to-four shift."

The lieutenant leaned forward onto his hands. "What did you guys do, fuck up in school?"

"Excuse me?" Jack was unsure he had heard correctly over the background jabber of police calls.

The lieutenant said, "Just breaking your balls. They don't usually send us rookies, is all. What ya got here are zookeepers, every one of them a fuckup. Great guys, but—Anyhow, welcome to Jungle Habitat. I'm Vince Fazio."

"Yes, sir," Paul Kellog said.

"You got your shit?" the lieutenant asked. "Bullets and like that?"

"Yes, sir," said Paul Kellog, stepping forward to show the duty officer his new shield, too, while holding up his kit bag as well. His academy crew cut had yet to grow out.

Fazio laughed. "Great, kid. Good-lookin' badge. Okay, you two go down that stairs there and hang a left. Ask for Clarke or Boyd. They've been assigned to break you in." He motioned to a sergeant coming down the stairs. "Hey, Dom. Give these guys a quick tour of the premises and show 'em the locker room."

Sergeant Ril made a face and sighed wearily. "Right. Follow me, fellas." The rookies fell in behind Ril, admiring his starched uniform and polished shoes as he marched up the stairs, all the while reciting the spiel he obviously could have given them in his sleep: "What you got here is a total manpower of 220 cops: 150 patrolmen, 50 sergeants and officers, 20 detectives. There are five dicks per tour to handle the misdemeanors and felonies. Anything heavier than that, homicides or kidnappings, brings in the specialized squads from headquarters. This way," he said.

They had reached the upper floor. The sergeant led them through double doors into a large bright room with six regulation metal desks and plainclothes cops sporting all varieties of clothes and weapons. The squad room was busy. Along the walls, prisoners slumped on wooden slat benches, one wrist cuffed to a steel bar that circled the room, while cops in sweat suits and blue jeans sat thumping typewriters, preparing case reports, property invoices, physical descriptions, and crime reports on each of the half-crucified unfortunates.

Sergeant Ril pointed and spoke. "Evidence lockers, two weapons lockers, fingerprints over there by the interrogation room, some of the five detectives on duty, a couple of patrolmen working vice undercover. Come on."

He walked back the way they had come. On the stairs, he resumed the rapid recitation: "We've got fifteen posts to cover, a twenty-two-squad system. We cover the posts with eight guys in cars, two walking beats . . . roughly. It's a four and ninety-six schedule: Five eight-to-fours and seventy-two hours off, meaning you'd be due back at four o'clock of the third day off. You with me? Then it's five four-to-midnights, another seventy-two off. You're back at midnight of the third day. You'd work the next four midnight-to-eights and go off for ninety-six, then come back in the same time as you got off, except of course four days later. Got it?"

Officer Gaines rolled his eyes at Officer Kellog behind the sergeant's back. Six months in the academy and Ril was acting like they didn't know anything. The sergeant led them back across the main floor, talking all the way.

"On the ground floor you have your duty officer, the signal monitor next to him, the desk sergeant over there, back there report rooms where you'll spend many happy hours doing your paperwork, the ad-min office, officers' offices, clerks, et cetera. Watch your step."

The trio descended the stairs to the basement.

"Okay. More weapons lockers—"

"What've you got in them, Sarge?" Jack said.

"Tear gas, riot helmets along the top there, plastic shields to protect your looks, gas masks, automatic shotguns, Uzis, Thompsons."

Jack Gaines whistled.

"The muster room," said Sergeant Ril, and he led them into an area forty feet long and just as wide. There was a set of barbells in one corner, a Universal Gym rig, a color television, couches, pictures on the walls of various social and sporting functions from years past, and a long conference table surrounded by metal folding chairs. Each had a small plaque on the back, Kellog noticed. The plaques read: Courtesy of Huntington and Clifford Funeral Home.

Ril pointed to the long table. "We do roll call down here with the street supervisor. If there's no street boss on duty, then roll call's upstairs, in front of the desk. Got that? This way."

Gaines shook his head at Kellog and followed the sergeant out of the room, past the holding cell area. They stopped in front of an open door.

"This is the locker room," said Sergeant Ril. "Your other teachers are inside." He pointed over his shoulder with his thumb as he walked away, leaving them on their own.

"Whew," Paul said. "What an asshole."

"Keep your voice down, stupid. This place gives me the creeps."

Together they walked in. The locker room was as big as the muster room. It was grungy: yellow walls, four rows of battered metal lockers, bulletin boards with softball schedules, announcements for the next sergeants test, and *Playboy* centerfolds, tastefully altered.

Jack and Paul picked adjacent stalls and quickly changed into their uniforms. In the facing stall a handsome blond cop was pulling on his trousers.

Jack nonchalantly said, "We were told to ask for George Clarke." He was not yet comfortable talking to cops.

"He owe you money?" said the blond.

"No. He and his partner are supposed to break us in."

"George? That's great." The guy snickered. "You know what he did when he broke me in? Drove me into the woods in the middle of the afternoon and told me to listen to the radio calls, that he was gonna take a nap. We sat there for a couple of hours doing shit. At sundown we went hunting rabbits with our pistols."

"Not much help, huh?" Jack said.

"Actually he got his message across. Taught me to do as little as possible. They can't sue you if you don't bother nobody. The idea is to act like a number and every two weeks there'll be a paycheck waiting."

"Sounds dismal," Jack said.

"It is. My name's Tony Kole," he said, offering his hand to Jack, then Paul. "The mean-looking guy over there is Clarke." He nodded down the aisle. "You better go meet him. We only got about twelve minutes left." He pointed to a twenty-four-hour clock overhead. It was ringed by what looked like pubic hair. "Time," Kole said, philosophically, "the ultimate cunt."

Clarke was wearing the dirtiest, most tattered uniform that Jack had ever seen. On a thin leather strap above his shield were six commendation bars awarded by the county for heroism. The guy was six feet, better than two hundred pounds, most of it firm. A dangerous dude, Jack concluded. He and Paul approached warily, both noting the notches on the grips of George Clarke's sidearm.

"Uh, Officer Clarke?" Paul said. "Lieutenant Fazio told us you'd show us the ropes—you and your partner."

"Fucking beautiful," said a guy in the far corner of the locker room. He was lying on a long table in his undershorts, holding an ice pack on his forehead, and staring at the steam pipes on the ceiling. "Come on, George. Show the kids your rope."

George Clarke yanked down his fly and reached in like he was drawing a sword. The two rookies stepped back, startled.

Clarke chortled. The guy racked out on the table said, "Aw, don't tease them. George here's hung like a gas pump."

Jack quietly said to Paul, "It's nice to feel welcome."

"Yeah," Paul agreed.

"Fuck 'em. We'll be okay."

Sergeant Reagan sauntered in: stocky, gray-haired, uneasy. "Let's get upstairs, gentlemen, shall we." His voice was whiney, like a siren. "The sooner we start, the sooner we finish." He folded his arms across his chest and rocked on his heels. Jack noticed Reagan wore gold-buckled black loafers with his uniform.

A black cop danced in, humming "I've Got Rhythm."

George said, "How's your hammer hangin', Moses?"

"Neglected," the black replied.

"Meet Paul Kellog . . . Jack Gaines. This is Michael Malcolm Moses."

"Hi, hi, hi," Moses said.

"And that pile of shit there," continued George, "is Officer Boyd."

Orin propped himself up on an elbow and took a deep swig of coffee from his mug, trying to nurse his murderous gin hangover. He said, "Run now, while you still can. I'm serious. Oh, Jesus." He covered his eyes with the ice pack.

"Hey, man," Moses called out to Orin as he buttoned his shirt. "What was Donnelly shouting about you for just now?"

"When?"

"Upstairs, two minutes ago." Moses strapped on his gunbelt, pulling closed its Velcro tabs.

"Fuck," Orin said. "I knew it. They had me working radio last week, filling in for somebody, and *Newsday* called the desk. Like they always do, you know—looking to see if anything is going on, or if we're fucking up . . . their favorite pastime. I told the bitch we found a dinosaur egg. I said it was big and blue and that we found it in a vacant lot. So she asks why we think it's a dinosaur egg, and I tell her 'cause when we cracked it open, it spit fire."

Moses and a couple of others howled with glee. "Then what?" he shouted.

"Fuck if the bitch don't file a story about how the cops in the One-Three don't have nothing to do but jerk off the working press. It ran this morning, I guess. Donnelly just took his morning shit."

"Sensational," Moses said, then looking around: "When's Jerry coming back to work? They done fryin' his balls yet?"

George said, "Couple a' more days. They're not quite browned."

"Who's Jerry?" Jack asked, sounding casual. Paul was still concentrating on Boyd, again dozing on the table.

"Jerry Santos," Moses said. "Good guy. He broke up a robbery a while ago and killed the bad guy."

Paul said, "I thought you got medals for that kind of stuff." And notches on your gun, he thought.

George smirked. "One of his rounds got away and seminicked a civilian. It's our own little 'excessive force' incident. Jerry will come out on top, though."

"There ain't a mean bone in his body," Moses said.

Five minutes to roll call, Orin Boyd was finally dressing. George glanced over at a tall, skinny cop sitting silently in front of his locker, waiting. "Hey, Benny," George half shouted. "How did you make out on the dick list?"

The skinny cop colored. "Some clerk nerd got my slot, the fuck."

George said, "Ah, the merit system. It ain't who you know, it's who you blow."

Sergeant Reagan reappeared in the doorway. "If you and Boyd are gonna be teaching these new men police work, why don't you start by showing them a proper attitude."

"Oh, excuse me," said Orin, imitating the sergeant's irritating tone of voice. "George, how could we have forgotten?"

"Don't know. Must be the pressure of workin' in the ghetto."

"Boyd," Reagan whined. "If you ever want to get out of the doghouse, you better clean up your act. I'm not hearing good things about you. Mount up, gentlemen."

"Oh, yes, sir," Orin muttered. "I'm working on it, sir."

"Upstairs in three minutes," Reagan announced.

Jack Gaines and Paul Kellog nervously checked their equipment.

"Take your time," George said. "We got two minutes left to be white men."

The rookies went into the bathroom and stood before the full-length mirror, inspecting themselves. Jack looked pleased. Paul looked anxious, noticing that the collar of his white T-shirt was visible above the black clip-on tie because his uniform was too big.

"Come along, children," George called to them. "The boogies ain't gonna give a shit what you look like. They either eat you or they don't."

" 'Ten-tion!" Reagan called out.

The morning shift ambled into formation in front of the desk. Ranks formed, after a fashion. Sergeant Reagan listlessly read off the eight-to-four assignments. A fart sounded in the ranks. Men edged away from George Clarke.

"Clever," said Sergeant Reagan. "Real goddamn clever. You're a real animal, George. You know that?"

Mazzarappolli stepped to George's side and threw an arm over his shoulder. "Send for a breathalyzer technician at once," he said. "My client is innocent!"

"Fall in!" yelled Reagan, then resumed the recitation of assignments. Once finished, he turned and faced Lieutenant Fazio behind the desk and saluted. "All present and accounted for. Second Platoon fit for duty."

Before Fazio could dismiss them, Inspector Donnelly appeared on the platform behind the duty desk. The room fell silent. Donnelly looked up and down the ranks, back and forth, hunting. He found his man.

"Boyd," Donnelly said, "any more shit with the press and I'm gonna ship your insolent ass to Internal Affairs. Just one more silly-ass prank and you're gonna be crossing goikers at the Wilhelm Clinic for the rest of your stay with us."

" 'Goikers,' sir?" Benny Sarina said, his voice trembling. He was in the line behind Orin's. "What do you mean 'goikers'?"

"Retards then, okay, Sarina?"

"No, it's not okay, Inspector."

"Drop it, Benny," Lieutenant Fazio said very evenly.

"Sir—" Sarina began to say something.

Orin interrupted: "Back off, Benny. The inspector didn't mean anything by it. It's the biggest word he knows, is all."

Donnelly walked around the desk and stepped off the platform. With a languid gait, he came up to Orin and got right in his face. Donnelly's shoulders were squared. He was taller than Orin, and wider. Orin snapped to attention, his eyes on Donnelly's Adam's apple, his face deadpan.

"I've had it with you, Boyd. You're a punk and a loudmouth. Hear me?"

"Sir, yes, sir."

"I've a good mind to suspend you right this minute. Look at you. You're a bum in blue. You belong with them goikers."

"Yes, sir."

"Inspector?" It was Sarina's voice.

"Stay out of this, Sarina," Donnelly said, without taking his face out of Orin's.

"Inspector, my son is one of those 'goikers.' You know that?"

"No, Sarina," Donnelly replied, eyes still locked on Orin's. "I didn't," and he walked away, down the hall to his office, and closed the door.

The ranks stood silent. "Okay, men," said Lieutenant Fazio. "Take your posts."

The twelve-to-eight shift sauntered in as the eight-to-four sauntered out, cops slapping high-fives as they passed friends in the other group.

"Yeah," George said, stretching. "Time to stalk the Wild Negro."

"Look at this place," said George to the rookies. "Outrageous, ain't it? Plywood City, all boarded up. The Bohack went first, then the Oldsmobile dealer, the ice-cream parlor, Arnie's Pizza. The Domino Theory."

"Jeez," said Paul Kellog. "I thought Belmont was supposed to be making a comeback."

"Don't believe that Chamber of Commerce bullshit. All the scumbag boogie kids chased away every decent person who ever lived around here."

Orin said, "That's why the Vil is such a good post. It's just like guarding a cemetery."

"There are *some* businesses left," said Jack, pointing with his chin.

George mopped his brow. "Yeah," he said. "A few diehards who own their own buildings and are afraid of fire. But they hide in their stores, doors locked, barely hanging on. There's Rocky, that old guy in the paper store. He's been robbed twice in the past year but don't know enough to lay down. Clayborne's Funeraleria, two storefront churches, a check casher, two social clubs . . . Ain't much to stick in a brochure."

"Come on," Orin said. "Let's get a cold one."

George grinned. "Beats standing here like Jack Kemp and pretending we're gonna do something for these animals."

Jack looked at his watch and arched an eyebrow at Paul. But neither of them said anything about drinking on duty, much less about drinking at nine in the morning. Instead they followed Clarke and Boyd across the littered street to a corner luncheonette. A fat smiling Spanish woman followed them to the booth in back with a cold six-pack in hand. She pulled beers from the plastic rings and handed them out like Halloween candies. Clarke and Boyd disposed of theirs in single gulps.

Paul Kellog said, "Not to be a wise guy or anything, but this isn't what we're supposed to be doing, is it?"

Orin said, "You wanna go look around outside, be my guest. Me, I'm hurting."

"What about Sergeant Reagan? What if he drives by?"

"Ha," George said. "He's an old cunt. Just putting in time like the rest of us."

"God," Paul said. "You guys are crazy."

"So what are you doing here?" Orin said. "Saving society?"

Paul shrugged. "Damn. I don't know. Maybe. I dropped out of college and went to work for my uncle. Got tired of it. Took the test for this as a lark."

"Maria," George called out. "Bring another round. We're hearing life stories."

The Spanish woman stopped chopping onions on the blue Formica counter and delivered another six-pack to the cops. Someone called her to the window counter, Jack noticed, and passed her money and some slips of paper. Jack nudged Paul.

Quite a few blacks stopped at the window to hand Maria money and slips. Jack's heart surged. In his head he started reviewing the academy lecture on policy games. He turned to Boyd, who was slowly shaking his head and grimacing.

"Be serious, kid."

"Hey," said Paul. He pointed to two men across the street menacing one another.

"Ease up," George said. "It's nuthin'. Although, if you see it getting out of hand, you might want to jump in and feed those brand-new sticks a little meat. Otherwise, when you got a couple of splibs going at it, hang back and then lock up the loser."

"What if he resists?" Jack said.

"You beat his ass. What else?"

"Of course," Paul said, "what else."

George finished his second beer and rose to leave. "There ain't a one of them worth getting hurt for. Let's go, children. The safest target is a moving target."

Paul pulled out two dollar bills. "Don't we—?"

"It's on the arm," Orin said.

Out in the street an old black man in a blue sweatsuit pushed a rag-filled shopping cart along the opposite sidewalk. Four young girls, two Hispanic and two black, batted a pink rubber ball against a brick wall. Five trucks were parked side by side against a chain-link fence. One had something written on the tailgate in red paint: *Pass this way and be the leader*, on the left; on the right, *Pass this way and meet Saint Peter*.

Three hard-muscled boys, their shaven heads gleaming, swaggered toward them, knuckles dragging. Closer, they loosened their gait, adding a hitchstep. Two of them spit as they passed.

The cops walked south, George and Orin in front, Jack and Paul two steps behind. Theirs were the only white faces in sight. The morning sun was already intense.

Between the different skin colors and languages that floated along the street, and the new cooking smells wafting from the walkup apartments all around, the rookies felt like they were in a foreign country.

Jack said to George's back, "Weren't they playing numbers back there?"

"So?" George said without looking back.

"That's illegal."

"No shit," said George.

Orin said, "So's adultery. You see anybody getting bagged for that?"

"No, but—"

"Hold it right there," said George, pausing to face the two young men. "I'll say what's illegal around here. You dig?"

"Okay," Paul said. Jack said nothing.

"Besides," said George, "these people need to gamble. It's in their genes."

"It's not in their genes," Jack said.

"College boys, huh?"

Orin wiped his forearm across his chin. "White people gamble all they want."

"Yeah," George added. "Why not niggers? You remember the big spread in *Newsday* on the gambling ring at Grumman? Big caper, right? Three and a half million a year. Everybody they collared copped a plea to all kinds of bullshit charges. A truckload of action and the main guy goes down for attempted possession of gambling records. Gimme a fuckin' break. Three point five mil and the stiffest fine was five hundred bucks to the guinea ringleader. He probably spent more getting his tube cleaned Friday night."

"I don't know," Jack said.

"That's right, rook." George looked him in the eye. "You don't."

A radio call distracted George. Jack and Paul strained to hear what it was but weren't yet used to the constant static.

"What is it?" Paul said.

"Nothin' much," Orin answered. "Sarina's calling for a homicide dick. He's found a body."

"Now *that*," said George, "can fuck up your day."

Benny Sarina flipped Detective Alonzo Daniels a bored salute from the doorway. The black in plainclothes identified himself to the ladies gathered in the hallway of the senior citizens' complex. He stepped away from the crowd of old women in cotton housedresses and puffball slippers and slipped by Officer Sarina into the apartment.

"What have we got?" said Detective Daniels.

"Homicide," said Benny Sarina as he marked Detective Daniels present at the scene.

"Any ideas?"

"About what?" Sarina replied.

"The earthquake in Tashkent, Benny. What the fuck do you think?"

"I haven't got any ideas about anything."

"Gave up, huh?"

"Really."

Daniels's question was academic. He had seen the list of new detectives days ago.

Sarina said, "I wanted to make detective, sure. The opening in the Thirteenth went to a goddamn fingerprint technician, for Chrissake. His daddy's connected. Well, good, that's it for me. The guy couldn't find a Jew in Long Beach, but they make him all the same."

"What can I tell you, Benny. Just keep plugging."

Sarina shook his head. Daniels moved past him and began to roam the apartment, checking for clues, giving the lab men orders. He paused to take in the two foot high word scrawled in lipstick across the living room wall: JUSTICE

Detective Bobby Shaw and the new man, Freddie Ryan, were still in the bathroom staring at Doris Williamson's nude body, lying facedown in brackish bathwater. An extension cord ran from the wall socket to the tub.

Daniels said, "Okay, guys, enough gawking. How about a canvas, her phone book—you know all this shit. Don't make me tell you."

Bobby Shaw and Ryan left the scene to look for witnesses. The lab techies were finishing up in the living room. Daniels turned to Sarina.

"You gonna wait for the wagon and basket?"

"Who else?"

"Who found her?"

"I did. She didn't show up at the Salvation Army kitchen for lunch."

"Okay," said Daniels. "I gotta go, but write a good report for me, will ya? Don't let your shitty attitude sabotage this case. I'm on your side, eh?"

"Whatever. Only you and I know it should be me outside asking the questions, and those two muscle brains ought to be the ones havin' to fish the old girl out of the tub."

Daniels smiled and nodded. "You've still got time," he said, on his way out. "Later, babe."

Alone, Sarina sat down in the living room and turned on the black-and-white television. He didn't watch it but was grateful for the company. Unlike the hostess, the TV screen was at least animated. He smoked a cigarette and paced slowly, killing time.

When he went to flush the cigarette down the toilet, from the corner of his eye he thought he saw Doris change position. Quickly he stepped from the room.

Exhaling deeply, he wandered around the apartment, halfheartedly sifting for clues. The woman had loudly complained about the crack dealers on her block. A real activist. Ballsy. He wondered how he would have handled the case if he were Daniels. In the bedroom he found a photograph of Doris holding a windblown granddaughter on the back of a pony, her smile matching the child's in intensity. In a wood frame on her reading table was a purple heart, also eyeglasses and rosary beads. Doris had joined the medal winner, Sarina thought; he believed in life everlasting.

There was a shoe box of pills on the dresser and an aluminum walker that hadn't been used much or else had been recently refitted with rubber tips. A distasteful odor hung in the air.

The stripped bed had been the stage for one last nightmare. Sarina lifted the mattress from the boxspring and slid his hand between them, feeling for the money he was almost sure would be there. Old lonely women were predictable. Bingo. Taped to the mattress. Sarina stuffed the five hundred odd dollars into his pocket and headed back along the dark hallway to the television in the living room.

A cooking demonstration was in progress. Sarina sat down. He had stopped looking for clues. The lure of the puzzle, he decided, just wasn't that compelling now that he was an accomplice.

"Sure, I hit him!" Lucy Harris yelled through the screen door. "What the fuck do you think?"

George Clarke pointed a thumb at a thermometer nailed to the aluminum siding. "Trouble. You watch. It gets up past ninety-five degrees and things always get downright so-ci-o-logical."

Orin smiled at her. She was short and fat and naked, her nipples pointing at the ground. She smiled back, sensing that she wasn't in any real trouble. The raggedy cop was too relaxed.

Abraham "Batman" Wilson sat on the porch next to Jack Gaines, holding a blood-soaked rag to the right side of his face. A thin red stream meandered down his arm, beaded briefly, then fell, landing in tiny splats at his feet.

"Honey," Orin said. "Let me in a minute. Just to talk."

"J'st you, not that raggedy-ass nigger. *You hear that, you fucking porch monkey. You ain't never coming near my black ass again.*"

She let Orin into the house, leading the way to the living room, where she turned on the lights. The cockroaches scattered. Call in an air strike, Orin thought. Napalm the little bastards. He felt like he was walking on Rice Krispies.

"What did you hit him with?" he said.

"You see," Lucy Harris began, "we was fuckin' on the couch and ma little boy, Billy—he only three—he was cryin', so's I pushed ole smelly ass offa me and goes to help ma kid. Well, Abe, he was about to make his moment, I guess, and he got pissed off. He went soft 'n all." She giggled.

Orin pretended to write all this dutifully on his clipboard. "Then what?" He noticed Kellog standing fast by the screen door, listening intently.

"He was gonna spank my baby, so I come up 'side his head."

"With what?"

Lucy smiled shyly and tiptoed to the fireplace. She held up a sooty iron poker. "This."

Orin shook his head in amazement. "You know you can't be doing things like this, Lucy. You could have really hurt him. Maybe killed him."

"Yay. I knows it. But he ain't got no right hittin' ma kids. He ain't the father of but two of 'em."

"Okay." Orin nodded. "You're both wrong. We'll call it a draw. Go make your kids some lunch and I'll get Abe stitched up. Fair enough?"

"Thank you, Officer. You a nice man."

Orin went with Abraham Wilson in the backup squad car to the hospital on Merrick Road. He signed Batman in and sat down in the brown-tiled waiting room to have a smoke. He had just lit up and inhaled deeply when a severe-looking head nurse reprimanded him for smoking. He stubbed it out, then lit up again when she had gone.

A resident finally sewed up Batman's head. Orin scratched out his report, putting down exactly what Abraham Wilson told the doctor—that he had fallen down a flight of stairs while drinking. A felony flagged and justice served. A second-degree assault reduced to an indiscretion. Without lawyers. He deserved another medal.

Sergeant Reagan panted in and ordered Orin to go with him. Outside a full squad car waited, engine revving. They were all rushing to a crowd control call in the projects. The awards ceremony would have to wait.

Two feuding families had drawn blood: sons and daughters and cousins slashing at one another with knives and car antennas and bicycle chains. Orin arrived with the second wave of police and one ambulance. An earless teenage girl, her face flooded with blood, was taken to the ambulance, where she told Moses and Orin Boyd what other girl had cut her and where she was hiding: an apartment on the fourth floor of Building C.

They grabbed Tony Kole and two other uniformed men and made their way through the crowd of fifty shouting blacks into the building.

From the first-floor landing Orin could see that the ambulance had been surrounded in the courtyard and that the crowd was rocking it. The driver was hanging out the open side door like a sailor tacking against a gale. Kole radioed for more help.

The girl who had done the initial violence was waiting for them and gave up with no resistance. She was, in fact, glad to see them, for they would offer her safe passage from the building before the victim's family could retaliate. Moses cuffed her and they started downstairs, then stopped. On the landing below them were twenty or so women armed with knives, chair legs, baseball bats, and a vacuum-cleaner pipe.

"Goddamn," Moses said, "and they all mine!"

Kole dispersed them with a spray of Mace. The cops then formed a triangle around the prisoner and walked her downstairs, their nightsticks raised. They forged through the crowd at the door and out into the courtyard. A full milk carton smashed at their feet, splattering them all. An elderly woman in shorts and see-through plastic sandals tried to spray the prisoner with a mixture of Coca Cola and lye. She got Kole in the face instead. He groaned and fell to his knees.

Orin snapped his stick across the woman's face. The crowd roared. He pulled Kole to his feet and dragged him to a second ambulance that had pulled up. More cops had arrived, too. The mob now numbered upward of three hundred.

The cops formed a riot line and penned the mob into the courtyard. Missiles landed all around, thrown off the roof. There were bricks, garbage cans, then a dog. Radios the size of suitcases blared ghetto anthems. At the curb an old blue Chevy, with dingle bells and Dominican decals, caught fire. The crowd cheered. Somebody on the third floor was videotaping it all.

More patrol cars, more cops. Sirens, flashing lights. A pumper from the firehouse arrived but refused to fight the blaze when missiles rained down around the bonfire. Sergeant Reginald "No Relation" Reagan ordered the line of cops to hold fast, then disappeared.

More cops came in a paddy wagon. They passed out hardhats and bats and riot gear to the line. Orin, his face streaked with blood, his uniform ripped down the back, pulled aside a local black councilman who was vainly imploring the rioters, and dragged him over to the fire truck.

"Things can't get much worse. What do you say we hose 'em down? It's a hundred degrees. Hell, they'd probably like it."

"I don't know," said the fire chief. "How'll it look."

"Fuck," said Orin. "Like South Africa. So what. Do it!"

The councilman agreed. The pumper arched a plume of water onto the rioters, not enough to knock anyone down. A roar of surprise turned to delight. A rainbow stretched across the courtyard. Soon the little kids stripped down to their underwear and went splashing in the puddles. The cops backed off. No arrests had been made, none would be.

Orin sat down on the curb next to the frolicking youngsters and splashed himself. George came up and squatted next to him, followed by Gaines and Kellog. The rookies were pale and wide-eyed.

George yanked off his visored helmet, his cheeks streaked with sweat. "What a freakin' block party."

7

Officer Jerry Santos was cleared of all charges and specifications stemming from the liquor-store battle, and returned to active service for the Wednesday eight-to-four, where he was loudly welcomed back by everyone. But no one was as happy to see him as the rookie he had never met, Jack Gaines. Rumor control had it that Jack Gaines was to be paired with Santos for the remainder of his in-service training, and for Jack that meant the end of working with the unpalatable George Clarke. Paul seemed to like Clarke well enough, but Jack had grown weary of his barbarity. Jack also worried that George Clarke would get them into trouble with his meal period escapades, when he would dump Boyd and the rookies in the back room of a deli and sneak across the street to the Stallion Bar.

So Jack Gaines raised his freckled face to the dark-complexioned Jerry Santos and smiled with great sincerity.

"Welcome back," he said to his new partner.

Santos nodded as they exited the precinct to hitch a ride to their post. "Thanks."

In the squad car, Jack looked him over more closely. Santos was an outwardly serene man, with almost a religious air that made him seem out of place in the 13th. Yet everywhere in the house he had heard expressions of concern for the outcome of the liquor-store investigation and for Santos.

After they had been dropped off at their post, Jerry and Jack fell into an easy gait as they began their patrol.

"So how come you're walking a foot post now?" Jack asked.

Santos squinted against the glare. "I've had it with the car, is all. Too much abuse, too many chances to get involved. I feel for you kids just starting out. You'll hate it before you're through. That was my second shooting in the last nine months. Walking is safer. I figured, why push my luck with one year to go on my twenty."

"Retiring, huh?"

"I'm driving up to Albany to put in my papers the night before. My wife and I are going out to dinner and spending the night at the best hotel in town. Then file for my retirement in the morning." He smiled. "Eleven months and counting."

Jack stopped to check and adjust the angle of his uniform cap in the reflection of a drugstore window. "You're probably right," he said. "I'd ask to walk myself if I didn't want to make detective so bad."

"Come on," Santos said, "let's see what's happening on the street of broken dreams."

They started down Sunrise Highway, checking the boarded-up store-fronts and making sure whatever glass there was was in place. Santos hummed and twirled his nightstick from front to back and side to side without paying attention to it. Watching, Jack grinned sheepishly, as he recalled his own painful attempts at this all-but-forgotten tradition. After several bruised shins he had given up and removed the leather thong from his stick.

"You do that nice," he said.

"What? Oh, this—I walked my first seven years here. Taught myself just to kill the boredom. You young guys coming on now'll be pushing a patrol car around. Why learn something you'll never really use."

"Yeah," said Jack. "I'm looking forward to riding. I really wasn't enjoying walking with Clarke all that much."

"How come?"

"Aw, he was getting on my nerves, I guess. Is he as dangerous as they say?"

"Like a frog with hand grenades," Jerry said, and laughed. "Him and Boyd both look sort of loony, if you know what I mean. Neither of them has both oars in the water, but Orin you can trust is what the guys are saying. He's weird but he's okay. George you gotta watch. Do you know that he once reported sighting a UFO?"

"Jeez," Jack said. They ambled along for a few blocks in silence. Then Jack said, "Do you mind if I ask you how your trial board went?"

"It was okay. They decided I was justified in shooting. They went back to the scene and replayed it, and they saw how the old guy's clothes blended in with the background, so they figured I never saw him."

"That's a break."

"Yeah. Also he's okay. I went to visit him the other day." The stores were starting to open; the breakfast places were busy with customers. Jerry Santos smiled. "You know, on days like this I love this place. No walls. No one looking over your shoulder every second of the day. After a while you can feel an energy, or some kind of pulse—whatever you want to call it. Comes running down inside the sidewalk." Santos leaned against a mailbox to rest his feet. Hands cupped, he lit a smoke. He looked at Jack Gaines. "You like it?"

"Some."

Blossoms dusted Champagne Danny Bugs, speckling his brown skin with white. For over an hour he had been working the corner, shaking hands and smiling at anyone who passed. At three hundred pounds, Danny was an institution, if not a monument, at Filmore and Ocean avenues, where he happened to write numbers for a living. Crowded with sweatshops overpopulated by illegal aliens, it was a busy Third World intersection.

Danny stroked his clients with rap chatter, egging them on with his melodious voice and rhymes: "Hit the mark with Danny boy. Get yo'self a brand-new toy."

Paul Kellog shifted in his seat next to Orin Boyd. "Hey. How long are we gonna watch him rubbing salt up our butts?"

Orin, slouched alongside him in the front, didn't even open his eyes. "He does act like what he's doing is legal."

"Practically is in this precinct."

"Cool off, Friday. I don't make the rules here. The dicks don't want us making numbers collars."

"Well, I can't stand listening to any more of his jingles."

"Right. Move us."

"What?"

"You heard. Move the car. Take us away." He glanced at his watch. "It's almost time for my latest punishment tour anyway. Shit, at least it's not raining."

Left to his own devices, George Clarke resumed the pattern of patrol he had developed over his nineteen years in the street. He leaned against a brick wall and glared at anyone he caught looking at him, until, in his own mind, he became invisible. Then he whirled on his heels and stepped into the gloomy cool of the Stallion Bar and Grill.

The bar was damp and filthy and reeked of malt. The stools wobbled, there was no footrail, but the price was right and no one ever bothered you. Cops were welcome to drink house liquor for free; the only one who did so with regularity was George. "Speedrack" the barmaids called him, behind his back. A dollar tip was what he left, for one glass of bar booze or fifteen.

George did not stop today for his usual shot-and-shortie or to chat up the regulars. He walked straight through to the rear exit and climbed the stairs in back with a purpose, then knocked on the bright red door at the top.

"'Ello, honeybaby," Gloria said as she opened the door, a procedure that took some time and was accompanied by considerable clicking of locks, chains, and bolts. "I wondered where you were. I was getting worried."

"Sorry, babe. I got stuck." He handed her the mail.

Gloria Mendosa was thirty-one and Puerto Rican, a welfare mother with hair bleached the color of a trumpet, the sole supporter of her seven-year-old son. She wore a blouse and gynecologically crafted black slacks, and she stood on tiptoes for a kiss.

George granted her this favor, then walked past to the couch by the window that overlooked the street. He peeked through one of the holes in the shade, then unhitched his gunbelt and flopped onto the couch, a king in his castle with a view of his domain. George dug into his pocket for some money.

Gloria held her breath, thinking she was finally making progress with the big Anglo cop, that he was going to do what he said he would: such as help out with the rent, and take her on vacation, buy her clothes that she could actually wear in public. But he put away the folded twenties and held up a single five.

"Miller?" she said, with resignation.

"Michelob," said George. "And potato chips. And put on the freakin' *Family Feud* before you go."

Gloria flipped through the mail. "I howie to go back to Puerto Rico," she said as she read the dismal number on her check from Social Services. "I can no stay for this kind of money."

"What are you talking about?" George said. "You got it made." He repositioned himself and piled his gunbelt on the coffee table.

"Two people on a couple a' hundred dollars a month. Sometimes is heat, sometimes no. That is what you call having it made?" She dropped the rest of her mail on the table unopened.

"Well, yeah," he said. "It ain't exactly Easy Street, but what exactly do you do?"

"*You* got the nerve to ask me that, Georgie? Show me the numbers on your check, show me how much the county pays you to hide in my apartment."

"It's not that much, darling. Trust me."

Gloria laughed bitterly.

"I'm a little hungry," he said, picking up her newspaper.

"My son is gonna be late today," she said. "Let's go someplace."

"Huh?"

She knows he doesn't like her Anthony because she will not do it with him when the baby is home. But George never takes her to his place, so too bad. Let him pay for the short-stay motel with the dirty movies and the dirty sheets. What does she care? It would be a chance to go out, to ride in a car.

He said, "What about you just give me a blowjob? I got a lotta shopping to do, and it don't make sense me doing it out of uniform. There ain't no point in paying double for shit."

Raul Lobell was waiting for the 10:44 to Rockville Centre on the lonely Long Island Railroad platform, anxious to get home to his wife to discuss some more the contemplated down payment on a house occupying a sixty-by-one hundred-foot lot they had seen on Saturday. He didn't notice the two black teenagers approaching.

The tall, thin boy, called Rod, shuffled past him. His companion, a shorter youth wearing a T-shirt and golf hat, turned backward, moved slowly toward Raul Lobell. Rod leaned over the back of the bench and said softly, "Okay, Pedro. No hassle. J'st give up the bread."

"Huh?" Lobell's eyes blinked rapidly. He smiled.

The golfer, Doctor Justice, wound up and slapped Lobell across the face, screaming, "Now, motherfucker! You know you ain't got no right takin' down anything in our territory."

Rod looked nervously around the platform. They were alone for the moment. "Be cool, Doc. My man's gonna do it, right?" He leaned over and rubbed Raul Lobell's shoulders like a boxer's corner man.

"I got twelve dollars." Lobell tried to stand up to walk away, but Rod threw him back to the bench with great force.

Doctor Justice sneered. "Don't bullshit us, man. We want the whole bank. Nobody crowds our action with no *bolito* route. You hear what I'm sayin'?"

Lobell began weighing the odds of fighting off the boys when Doctor Justice's hand snaked into his pocket for a knife.

"Doc!" Rod shouted.

Lobell grabbed for the knife and tried to bend it free of Doctor Justice's grasp. Doctor Justice raked the knife across Lobell's palm, grinding tendon and bone. Lobell screamed and let go of the knife.

The spurting blood sprayed the platform. Doctor Justice cursed and grabbed Lobell by the hair, bending his head back over the bench. Lobell yelled for help but the cry was cut short, turning into a guttural roar as Doctor Justice drove the blade in.

Gagging, Lobell fell to his knees on the concrete. Doctor Justice raised the knife again, both hands on the handle, and drove it between the man's shoulder blades. Then he braced a forearm against the impaled back and yanked the weapon free, before following Rod, fleeing to the east.

Lobell felt cold more than anything else. Air bubbles escaped from somewhere. He got to his feet, staggered the twenty-five yards to the stairway, and clutching, sliding, half falling down them, he made the street.

An approaching car set him waving his arms, but the car swerved around him and sped off, its driver horrified at the crimson vision. Lobell turned to chase the car and fell. His momentum carried him down onto the curb, trapping his left arm beneath his body. Frustrated and too tired, he closed his eyes.

By the time Jerry Santos and Jack Gaines arrived on the run, a small crowd had gathered. Santos bent over the victim, then stepped away.

"Isn't there anything we can do?" Jack said.

"Hold his hand if you want to. That's all."

Kneeling down, Jack cradled Lobell's head and looked into his eyes for a spark, some sign. The breeze blew sand across the wound; it stuck to the congealing, stringy mass that hung from his throat. The caked lips parted to speak. There was a thin trickle of fresh blood, a tremor, and a final heartbeat. Then stillness.

Santos pulled Jack Gaines up, away from the body. "He's gone, Jack. Straighten up."

"Okay!" Sergeant Reagan bellowed. "Listen up."

The chattering in the basement muster room continued unabated.

"Shut up!" Reagan yelled.

George Clarke gave Reagan a mocking glance as the rest of the men took seats around the conference table, their equipment banging loudly on the aluminum chairs. For a moment Clarke stood considering a grand-stand play, then sat down to Reagan's obvious relief.

Reagan stepped behind the front desk, puffed out his chest, and began to address the shift: "Regarding the P.R. that got snuffed yesterday morning," he said, talking tough. "We don't have a weapon, we don't have a motive, we don't have a suspect. We got shit. *Nada.*"

"*Nada* fucking thing," George said. Reagan gave him a you're-speaking-out-of-turn frown, then looked up as a gray-haired black, wearing an expensively cut three-piece suit, entered the room. He walked to the desk and, instantly sizing up "No Relation" Reagan, dismissed him with a mild wave. Paul thought the guy might be a physician from the medical examiner's office come to give them gory details of the killing.

"Most of you know me. I'm Detective Sergeant Alonzo Daniels from Homicide. I've been reviewing your work on the train-station murder, and I don't mind telling you, I was favorably impressed. You guys do nice work.

But then this isn't Syosset, is it? From the homicide rate around here, I guess I could have expected a competent job. Thanks. You're good cops . . . no matter what they say at headquarters."

The younger guys chortled.

"Unfortunately," Sergeant Daniels continued, "in this case that's not enough. We're gonna get some pressure on this one. The public doesn't care for unsolved street murders and neither should you." Daniels paused to light a pipe. "Starting now we apply some heat to this burg and see what we get. This isn't gonna be one of those sneaky-cute investigations with the dicks grabbing all the credit at the wrap-up. That's not the way I work. We share the load and we share the glory, if there is any. Fair is fair." He opened his briefcase.

"We'll start with what we know, which isn't a whole lot. The detectives have been checking the victim's background to see if he was into anything shady, but so far nothing. I doubt he was dirty. Male, Hispanic, thirty-two, two jobs, two kids, one wife. His car was even properly registered."

"Then we know he wasn't Puerto Rican, sir," Tony Kole called out from the back. Daniels smiled.

"You uniforms have a leg up on the dicks because this was a street crime and you men are the street people of this department. Use your expertise. We're going to reorder our patrol priorities for a while. First, check and see if any of the local humps are laying low or missing. Lean on the other humps if you have to, but do it gently, please. Let them know the streets are going to be very uncool until we catch our bad guy. Work the stoolies, too. We got some cash to spread around on this. Lean on the gin mills. We start locking up drunks and the bartenders will be falling all over themselves to help us. Remember, liquor loosens tongues as well as panties. If there's any bragging being done, we want to know about it."

"What about the regular workload?" said Reagan.

"Handle it," said Daniels. "You're supposed to be pros. I shouldn't think you'd mind extending yourselves for a while. It *is* for a good cause." He paused. "We meet again in the afternoon. I want to know everything that you see, hear, and think today, no matter how insignificant it may seem to you. This is a puzzle and I'd rather play with all the pieces. Please . . . think about this murder. Let it piss you off, and then let's get this guy and stuff his ass into a cage. Take your posts."

They scoured the precinct: shook down junkies, hookers, and winos; questioned delivery men, commuters, lonely souls who walked their dogs through the area—anyone who might have seen anything. If enough pressure were applied in the right places, Daniels believed, something would pop.

Cops flooded the area, pushed their way through crowded barrooms, stared closely at pedestrians, leaned on sources. The shift passed quickly. The men had been given a direction to move in and they responded. Instead of merely reacting to situations, they were forcing breaks. For once they were being managed and by someone obviously good at it. The contrast to the haphazard command of Inspector Donnelly, who rarely even ventured out of his office, was startling.

When they returned to the station house at four in the afternoon, Daniels was still there, still looking fresh. When the men lined up for roll call, he spoke to them again: "Good effort, guys. The next tour will keep it up. Debriefing at Red's in fifteen minutes. If you can't make it, see me before you go. Dismissed," he said, and saluted them smartly.

Charlie, the day man at Red's, was shocked. Usually some of the guys stopped by in the afternoon but never the whole tour, and certainly never a boss. He was even more shocked when Detective Sergeant Daniels told him to run a tab.

While the cops feasted on cheeseburgers, chili, and beer—except for Orin, who drank martinis—Daniels moved among them sipping club soda, listening to their pet theories and suspicions and to the gossip they had picked up.

When he got around to Officer Boyd, Orin said, "Definitely the work of African subversives," but he smiled disarmingly at Daniels. "Just kidding."

"That's good," said the detective, "because I've seen bigotry foul up more than one investigation."

"That's not bigotry, Sarge. That's common sense. In a precinct of mostly blacks and Spanish, a homicide committed with a knife tells you many things. It wasn't Rastafarians. They only use guns. Whites, too; also maybe baseball bats. It wasn't his wife, she was home. And it wasn't other Ricans because they slash with knives, like Zorro. Blacks do the stabbings, the puncture work."

"That simple?"

"Check the stats."

"I'm aware of the racial profile of this precinct, Boyd, and of the various methods the citizens have for eliminating one another. All I'm asking is for an open mind."

"Couldn't be wider," said Orin, taking another sip of his martini. "The odd part is the wallet being untouched."

"Maybe he panicked."

"Maybe it wasn't about money. Still, I'll bet you twenty it was blacks."

"I'm not a gambler," Daniels said. "Whiskey was my only vice."

"Shit, Sarge. I got 'em all. Be glad to loan you a couple."

"Give them away, son, but not to me." Daniels leaned his backside against the adjoining barstool. "It's in the personality, you know, not in the booze or the drugs. It's a hell of a way to live, if you think about it."

"I think about it," said Orin, admiring the liquid in the triangular glass. "But it makes me sick to think about it so I go out and party instead."

"That's not the answer."

"Really?"

Daniels eased closer. "Anything yet?"

"Nothing."

Daniels gave him a scornful look. "Try harder, bro."

"Sure." He turned to the group at large. "Gentlemen, time to boogie."

Orin led the men of the Lucky 13th to the Outrigger Lounge and Supper Club. There, to their delight, the monthly meeting of Parents Without Partners was just breaking up and the dance floor was as well stocked as a crystal mountain lake. Orin could feel the martinis working through his system, tripping synapses in his neck and arms. This would be one of those nights when he was unable to get drunk—try though he might. He checked his coat pocket for his extra pack of Marlboros, then fought his way to the bar.

"Your pleasure, sir?" asked the bartender.

"A double Beefeater martini, on the rocks."

George ordered a shot of Jack Daniels and a beer and they stood at the bar, pressed together by the crowd, waiting for something with possibilities to stagger by. Orin scanned the faces of nearby women, hoping not to see Judy, until George poked him twice in the ribs. "There're two dancing together," he said. "Let's break them up."

Orin shook his head. "Please. Not until I have my fair share of drink."

"They'll be grandmothers by then."

"Good," said Orin.

"Come on, man, where's your confidence? The freaking Geek could score here."

"That's what I mean."

George said, "I just can't win. Here we got ourselves a room full of hose monsters just dying to make wet nasties, and you look like you're at a freaking funeral. What say we snatch a couple up and dance with them? What are they gonna do—say no?"

"With any kind of luck." Orin paid the bartender for their drinks and ordered another round. "Keep 'em coming," he said.

George knocked back his whiskey, grimaced, then downed the top half of his beer. "Come on," he said. "Next song."

"Get lost, Speedrack. I'm still not over my wife."

"Yeah," said George. "I can see you're all broken up."

Just then the band took a break and the dancers made a dash for the bar. The women's bright faces were flushed with exertion, their eyes twinkling with excitement; the hungry men followed them hopefully, some with courage enough to steer.

Orin watched George's smiling face. George was enraptured by the idea of so many lonely women. Orin himself saw nothing wonderful about hobnobbing with some other asshole's pack of woe and paying hard-won cash for the privilege. He suffered a vision of Judy telling some dink about the prick she'd been married to. And then hearing the wimp express shame and regret for the members of his sex who were nothing more than animals. And Judy, in heat, pawing the son of a bitch. He was sorry he had let George talk him out of driving his truck, whether it killed his chances with women or not. "This was a mistake," he said to George. "I gotta get away."

"Come on, man. Hold the fort," said George. "I'll scout the herd."

George slipped away through the crowd. Orin lit a cigarette and paid the bartender again. He sipped his new martini and watched young Jimmy Caprione from the precinct slow-dancing with a woman who was at least sixty years old, which looked even worse because the band was still on their break and the jukebox could barely be heard. Moses and Maxwell Hanke were arm wrestling on a video-game cocktail table and the bouncer was begging them to stop. Billy Wermer had a waitress in a headlock.

Across the room George had commandeered a rather large brunette, had backed her up against one of the plastic palms that ringed the dance floor. He was stuffing a roast beef sandwich into his mouth while he shot his rap, and she was listening to him like he was Tom Brokaw with news of The Second Coming. Orin smiled sadly. Mayonnaise was all over George's chin and she was listening, because George looked like one of those guys who was dumb enough to get married again, and again, which he was.

George wiped his mouth with his shirtsleeve, then waved over at Orin. "Yo," he yelled over the heads in the crowd. "I need you." Orin ignored him, so George marched promptly to his side. "Hey," he said. "I'm calling you. That chick I'm bullshitting has a friend."

"She's gonna need her," said Orin. "Her family and neighbors, too."

"She says her friend ain't had none lately."

"Get out of here, George. Girls don't talk like that."

"Square business. I shit you not."

"Then I'm sure there's a very good reason for that. Like maybe doctor's orders. What is she on the Richter Scale? A two? A two and a half?"

"Yeah, right. And what are you? Prince fucking Charming?"

"Vlad the Impaler, according to Judy."

"Funny." George downed the beer he had left behind, then started bitching about loyalty among friends when times were rough.

"Why don't you go have your little coup de twat and leave me the fuck alone," said Orin. "I'll call a cab or grab a ride home with Cappy and his mother there."

George hemmed and hawed for a moment, then admitted that Yolanda had told him that they came as a package deal: she was not the kind of girl who abandoned a friend to run off with a man.

Orin pinched the bridge of his nose and closed his eyes.

"Pretty please?" said George.

"Okay, big guy," he said. "How bad is she? The truth."

George pointed to a table by the bandstand where the two young women were sitting, their pale hands folded around their drinks. "The one on the left. The brunette. Lois. She's staring at you."

"Okay, George. I think I've got her zeroed in."

"She's not too bad." George smiled. "In fact, when we get over there, if you want to trade bimbos—"

"Keep it up and the first thing I tell 'em is we're married."

"Forget I said a word. What am I, crazy?"

Orin slipped his wedding ring off and hid it in his wallet; then they carried their drinks across the parquet dance floor and joined Yolanda and Lois at the table for four. George made the introductions and flagged down a waitress for more drinks.

"Make them doubles," said Orin. "The ice looks kind of thick."

His designated date stiffened her backbone. "You didn't look terribly happy, either, sitting at the bar all by yourself." Lois Perrine had very white teeth, a dazzling smile.

"Oh, really?" said Orin. "Were you staring at me for very long?"

"No," she said. "Not too."

"George tells me you boys work together," Yolanda said.

Orin grimaced. "There's no telling what George will say."

"Are you divorced, too?" she said.

Orin lowered his chin to his chest and gave a small shake of his head. Everyone suddenly focused on the pain in his face.

"Let's don't talk about those things tonight," Lois said. "We're here to have a good time, or at least I am."

"I'm a widower," said Orin. "My wife is dead."

As far as George was concerned, the band could not possibly have chosen a better time to resume their labors. He snatched Yolanda to her feet and dragged her out to the center of the dance floor in one fluid motion.

Orin smooched with his drink. His eyes glazed over as he watched the strobe-lit dancers, frozen for slices of time. Lois Perrine leaned forward to intercept his attention.

She was pretty, he thought, in a dated, laid-back sixties kind of way. Her brown hair was pulled back in a long French braid, her eyes quite blue beneath her granny glasses. She was very pretty, actually. A six, maybe a seven. He thought again of his wife and felt a tug of regret that she might be here tonight too, or somewhere just like it, that she also could be playing this grown-up version of Spin the Bottle. No, he thought with some relief. Judy was more the Divorced and Separated Catholics type. This seedy shit was his speed.

"What's wrong?" Lois asked him.

"About what?"

"Oh, I don't know. In general? With me?"

"Nothing, really," said Orin. "You're the nicest woman I've spoken to in years."

Lois sat back and sipped her Kir. His compliment seemed to have jarred her, given her some sense of the bizarre. He got back to his drinking while she looked around the room. Finally, as the band struck up "Feelings," she asked him if he liked to dance.

"No," he said, which was a lie, because he loved to dance to rock and roll.

"O-kay . . . I can understand your not wanting to dance. I really can. But is catatonia necessary? If you want to leave, feel free."

"I'm sorry," he said. "I still have trouble talking about it, is all."

"I'm not asking you to talk about it. I'm asking you to talk about anything else. Tell me a joke. Tell me about someone you hate. The last book you read . . . anything other than ga-ga-goo-goo, and, Mommy, I spilled my milk."

"Cooped up with kids all day, are you?"

"I figured I might as well give you the bad news right up front."

"How many?"

"Just two. A boy and a girl." She checked her wristwatch.

"That's not such horrible news."

"Their father is surfing Maui as we speak."

"You want to talk about it?"

Lois laughed and shook her head. "No more than you do."

Orin decided to give Lois an eight, largely because of her looks, but also because it sounded like she'd had her butt kicked a couple of times and it didn't seem fair. An eight put her out of his league, of course. He considered himself a five, and that was grading on a curve.

George and Yolanda returned to the table arm in arm. George sat down to another fresh beer, but Yolanda—whose dress was still trapped between her thighs—grabbed her pocketbook and said in a stage whisper to Lois, "Caucus."

Lois laughed and excused herself and followed Yolanda to the ladies room. George and Orin chugged the drinks in front of them and ordered more.

"We got a lock," said George. "These chicks are all over our shit."

"I'm hip. Let's book."

"Will you stop that! Please . . . I want to take them down to the Hole for a nightcap. Yolanda said Lois is probably not too keen on going it alone."

"I'd rather go somewhere and finish this drunk."

"You gotta come," said George. "Yolanda said that's part of the deal."

"I'm gonna get even with you for this. I mean it."

The girls returned a moment later, all fresh perfume and merriment. "So?" said Yolanda as she sat next to George. "What are we doing?"

"How about we swing by Orin's apartment for a little private party?" George suggested.

Orin groaned and said, "What was the point of leaving my truck home if we're gonna show them the Hole?"

"The Hole?" Lois said. "Sounds either very exciting or perfectly dreadful."

"It's both," said George. "And it's less than a mile away."

"He's right," Orin said. "But there's also a perfectly good rest room in the gas station on the corner where I'm sure we could have a wonderful—"

"Orin," said George. "Hush yo' mouth."

Over Orin's continued objections, they collected their coats and piled into George's car: three happy people thinking they were going to get something they wanted, one unhappy man certain he would get something he did not. The girls remained cheerful as George drove into Orin's run-down neighborhood. But their pretty faces changed from cheerful to brave as George pulled into Orin's parking lot, and from brave to concerned when they passed up the elevator and started down the stairs. At the door to the Hole only George remained cheerful. The girls wore expressions strikingly similar to Orin's.

"I want to talk to you, George," said Yolanda. "Privately." She took him by the upper arm and walked him back to the bottom of the stairs. "Go on in," she called to Lois and Orin. "We'll be right along."

Orin opened the door and walked inside. He put Lois's coat on the benchpress rack and gave her a beer from his little refrigerator. "Sorry about the mess," he said. "My cleaning woman got deported . . . during the French and Indian War." He returned to the door, holding it open, waiting. "What did Yolanda want with George?"

"I think to be alone . . . but somewhere else."

"And that's okay with you?"

"If it's okay with you."

"Wow," he said. "You got a lot of guts."

They didn't waste any time. Orin watched while Lois undressed. She had several curly wisps around each nipple, something he would have hated on his wife but found titillating with Lois, just as he enjoyed the thin line of hair that descended from her navel to the dark triangular swatch at her groin. Lois switched out the light and joined him in bed, coyly assuming a position for sleep: she, in front and fetal; he, behind and pressed close.

Turning slightly to look back over her shoulder, she reached behind her and tweaked the soft tissue. Orin moaned and pressed his sex against the small of her back. She reached back fully and griped the base of it, then slowly pumped.

"You like that, do you?" she said, and turned to face him. She slid slowly into the bunched sheets, and waited.

He admired her, tracing a line along her side: from the jut of her chin, along the side of her breast, her rib cage, across the taut belly.

She kissed his lips, then his navel. "I like the way you feel when you're in back of me," she said, rubbing with both hands. "We're gonna have to try that sometime."

He gasped, teeth white, as she stroked him with her thumbs.

"This is mine," she said. And then she was on him, moving to his motion.

The telephone ringing by the side of his head brought tears to his bloodshot eyes. He knocked the phone off the hook trying to pick it up. "What?" he said when he finally brought the phone under control. "Who the hell is this?"

"It's me, asshole," said George. "You're late for work in seven minutes."

"Goddamn," said Orin. "Is it that time already?"

"Oh, yeah."

"But . . ." Orin rolled over and saw that Lois Perrine was not part of a wonderful wet dream. She was Live From New York, pressed against the wall, with the sheet under her chin. Her face appeared mildly confused.

"I can't make it," Orin said to George. "If I looked in the mirror I'd puke."

"Little Lois still there?"

Orin turned his back on the naked woman in his bed. "That's affirmative."

"I knew it," said George. "I picked the wrong damn one again."

"Oh, yeah? How come?"

"Because I'm an asshole, that's why. Because while you were getting your end wet, I was getting my freaking face smacked."

"Cut it out and quit kidding me."

"I'm serious, my man. I had to ice my cheek down to get her fingerprints off it before I could go home."

"What happened?"

"Yolanda had her period. I should have noticed the water-weight buildup," he said. "The puffiness around the eyes."

"So what was the big deal?"

"That's what I said. No big deal. That's why God made paper towels. Only where this bimbo's sanitary needs are concerned, all of a sudden she's a paragon of virtue. So I told her it was cool, she could owe me one."

"And?"

"And I told her that I didn't see no string hanging out of her mouth."

"Jesus, George. I haven't had breakfast yet."

"You know *why* women have periods? Because they deserve 'em."

Lois rolled over and hung her chin on his shoulder, no longer hiding the fact that she was listening. Her breasts were warm against his back.

"Can you believe it?" said George. "I dumped her back at the bar, grabbed some ice from the kitchen, and then went home and woke up Ella. So it wasn't a total loss. She did her wifely duty."

"You're a prince," said Orin. "Now swing me into Reagan's office, willya. I gotta bang in sick before they list me AWOL."

"Okay, but you're a freaking bum for leaving me alone today."

Sergeant Reagan came on the line a moment later and accepted Orin's report to sick leave without any trace of emotion. He said nothing about the party the night before, nor did he question the cause of Orin's migraine. Orin assured him that he was not, at this time, considering legal action against the caterer or the hosts. Then he hung up the phone and hid his face under the covers.

Lois wrapped her arm around his waist and snuggled closer. "So?" she said. "How are we doing?"

"I personally feel like an elephant peed in my mouth."

Lois sat up and pulled the sheet from his face. "I have that effect on men," she said. "I've told my shrink, but he thinks that I'm making it up."

Orin smiled and patted her knee. "Not your fault," he said. "I don't remember you forcing me to drink those wifebeater martinis."

Lois forced a smile. "I was going to ask you about that."

He ran his hand through his hair and shrugged. He could smell himself, and if he could, she could.

Lois lit two cigarettes and handed him one. "Maybe another time, eh? Right now all I want is some food," she said.

He had nothing in his refrigerator but beer and Spanish olives. It would have been simpler to talk about his drinking than to rustle up an omelette. "Don't you have to be somewhere?" He could see by his clock it was seven forty-five. "You don't look like the type who can flush whole days."

"My ex-husband's parents have the kids, so actually I'm as free as a bird until Sunday at six."

Orin nodded judiciously, as if his concern were primarily for her children. "I see."

"What about you?"

"See that's where we got this little problem." There was no way on earth she was staying for the weekend. "I lied about my wife."

"Oh, did you?"

"She's more alive than you or me."

"And she's still your wife?"

"Yup. My ring is in my wallet."

"I see. And this is your summer place, where you come to relax after the rigors of serving the homicide bureau."

"Another lie. I'm a dirtbag uniformed cop. I live by myself in this dump all year round. We're separated, since the summer."

"Is your name really Orin?"

"You think I'd invent a name like Orin?"

Lois fell back in the bed and stared at the steam pipes that ran along his ceiling. "What the hell did I do to deserve this?" she wondered aloud.

Orin stared at her hard flat breasts. He wanted her again, but thought asking now might seem a little tacky. When he looked at her eyes he could see that she was crying.

"I don't do one-night stands," ·she said. "Or at least I didn't until last night. Of course you probably don't believe that and I can't say that I blame you. This sounds absurd, but I thought we had the start of something nice. At least that's what I told myself, I guess so I wouldn't feel like such a tramp."

"You were lied to, Lois. By me. You're a victim, not a tramp. I'm really sorry."

"You should be, Orin. I can't believe you'd just lie like that to a stranger. What is it: a woman alone is a joke?"

"No. A woman alone is not a joke. Maybe I was getting back at my wife. I don't know. I was drunk and you didn't seem real."

"You bastard," she said. "You insensitive creep." She punched him in the arm. "Does that feel real?" She hit him again, harder. "That? That? How about that?"

Orin absorbed the blows without flinching, as if he were dead, or so beyond compassion as to be shock-proof, until her tears splashed onto his chest and a girder rose in his boxer shorts. He sat up and put his arms around her, pinning her hands to her hips until she gave up her struggle. He kissed her softly on her forehead as if she were a child. "You're real," he said. "I'm the ghost."

"Don't patronize me."

"I can't win."

"Yes," she said. "Yes, you can."

His eyes glazed over with lust, and he therefore neglected to tell her she was wasting her time, that he wasn't worth the effort. While she kissed his neck and then his chest, he could hear Willie across the hall, playing on the electric organ plucked from the trash. It was a reasonably competent rendition of "America the Beautiful." Orin thought of a solitary man, a father of two, surfing amber waves at Maui.

8

Fernando Diaz watched the orange-and-blue police car from the window of his cousin's apartment over the Bodega Dominican grocery. Two women and a child in the room behind him were praying. His male cousin stood by his side.

The cousin said, "Just walk out there and tell them you got a warrant on you for a gas-station heist, Fernando. Believe me, friend, they will do the rest. You make your deal with them when you get inside."

"I don't know. I think I should call them and set it up first. Maybe get a lawyer. Or call the detectives and give myself up to them. Or call Bubba's people."

"What makes you think they will help? That stickup was solo work. You know Bubba don't allow no freelancing."

"Yeah."

"You been hiding five months now. You can't work, you can't rest. Trade what you got and start over someplace else."

"Yeah. Let's get it over with," said Diaz. He pulled on his denim jacket and tied a handkerchief around his neck.

"What else you gonna do," said the cousin, and shrugged.

Paul Kellog and Orin Boyd were eating Chinese takeout in the squad car and hiding out from Sergeant Reagan, who was out cruising, establishing his command presence on the scene as the cops sifted their snitches for leads in the Raul Lobell killing. All the activity and the presence of headquarters personnel had energized him. He was definitely scheming a way out of the 13th.

Paul noticed the two Hispanics first and nudged Orin, causing him to spill pork fried rice into the dark blue crevices of his pants.

"Hey!"

"I wonder what they want?" Paul said, while Orin dug for fried rice between his legs.

Orin said in a Spanish accent, "Pleese, meester. My baby es bery sick."

The cousin heard them laughing as he stepped up to the car, his relative standing next to him. "My cousin wants to give himself up," he said. "There is a warrant for him, I think."

Orin forced a smile. People were always turning themselves in on their meal break. "Look, man, we're eating. Hows about waiting until tomorrow? Actually, hold it. Paul, you want some overtime?"

"Nope." Paul speared a piece of pork. He had a date.

"Yeah," said Orin, "why don't you do that? Hang loose for a while, take two aspirins, then call us in the morning. We'll even send a car for you."

Diaz stepped forward. "My name is Fernando Diaz and I'm wanted for—"

"Robbery," Orin said, putting aside the takeout container. "Okay. We'll take you."

They cuffed Diaz and put him in the caged back seat. Paul grumbled.

Orin said, "You're meeting a bimbo, right?"

"She's not a bimbo."

"She's still gonna have to learn to wait." Paul didn't appear convinced. "Kid," Orin said. "You want to make detective, you gotta make good collars. Diaz here is a good grab. He shot a guy in the back before you came on the job."

Paul reached for the dashboard radio to call in the arrest. Orin pulled his hand away. "Wait. Let's have some fun with this."

"Whaddaya mean?"

"Make a caper out of it. Call in that we're chasing this guy, then play it by ear. Reagan's working the street, looking for points, and he'll try to horn in on the grab."

"Won't we get into trouble?"

"Shit, not a chance. No Relation is too stupid. George told me that Reagan once went to a house that was getting ripped off and this guy walked out the door just as Reagan arrived. The guy sashays over and thanks him for the quick response, tells him someone's in the basement. Reagan shakes the man's hand, tells him he's glad to be of service, spells his name for him. Then he runs into the house, gun drawn. Of course, he'd shaken hands with the burglar." Orin keyed the microphone. "Car thirteen-two-one to headquarters. My partner is out of the car on Grand Avenue in foot pursuit of a robbery suspect. I'll be assisting."

"Okay, thirteen-two-one. Any available units and supervisor, assist thirteen-two-one in pursuit on Grand. What is your exact location, thirteen-two-one?"

Orin smiled. "Suspect is a male Hispanic, about twenty-five, wearing blue denim jacket, dungarees, and purple shoes."

"Information received, thirteen-two-one. Give location."

Paul and Orin tittered as they peeled out. Diaz cursed in the back, dumbfounded.

"Thirteen-two-one," said the radio, *"what's the closest side street?"*

Orin pulled in behind an apartment building and shifted into park.

"What the fuck is this?" Diaz half shouted. "You tryin' to scare me, man?"

The two cops didn't even hear him, so intent were they on listening to the radio chatter, eager voices offering suggestions and advice on where the chase might be. Patrol cars saturated the area, racing up and down Grand, sirens blaring.

"Hey!" Diaz shouted. "This is bullshit! I was giving myself up. I know stuff. What are you tryin' to do?" He was squirming all over the back seat. This hadn't been what he'd had in mind at all. "I'm surrendered, damn it!" He was terrified they would press additional charges for this mock resistance or, worse, set him up to be shot while escaping.

A large black woman was handing preschoolers in through an apartment window and screaming. Sirens wailed in every direction.

"Hey, man," Diaz said, trying to sound reasonable. "I just want to go to jail, okay?"

"Relax," said Orin. "Everything's cool."

"What the fuck you mean 'cool'?"

Reagan sped past their hiding spot, lights and sirens on max.

"Listen," said Diaz, "maybe we could make a deal. I know stuff."

Paul looked back over his shoulder, Orin was busy chortling. "What?"

"Like one of the hitters who iced the *bolito* guy at the railroad station. You call this off and I'll give you the information."

"What's a *bolito*?" Paul said.

"Spanish numbers game," Orin said. Then to Diaz: "Tell us the story and we'll call the hunt off."

The radio calls came at short intervals.

"Bester," said Diaz. "His name is Rod Bester. He lives in the projects."

It was cloudless and moonlit, the stars almost country bright over the Roosevelt projects. The brick towers loomed over the highway, their hollows black.

They climbed out of their cars calmly, quietly. Daniels believed in taking perps at night, while they slept. He liked the advantage and the odds of catching them in their cribs.

Finding Rodney Bester had proven simple. High-school truancy records and juvenile offender files and several rap sheets had given them all they needed to know, including the kid's usual partner in crime. Warrant in hand, Daniels secured a pass key through the security office of the complex. With another dick named Higgins, and Officers Boyd and Kellog, Sergeant Daniels stopped in the dismal hallway outside the door to the Besters' apartment. Mercifully the family was away.

Kneeling, Daniels worked the lock. It opened. They slipped inside. As previously rehearsed, one man took each of three internal doors beyond the tiny living room: bathroom, bedroom, kitchen. At Daniels's signal, they flipped on the lights. Orin's door opened on the prize.

Rod Bester rolled over, pulling the sheet to his face. "Yo, turn off the light, man," he whined.

Orin sprang onto the bed. He grabbed a handful of Rod's face and pulled him upright, pushing a pistol against the chin.

"Don't move, motherfucker! Not an inch. He's in here!" Orin felt around beneath the covers and found a lead pipe hidden in the pillow. He tossed it to the floor and slapped Rod hard. "What's that for, scumbag? Huh?"

Rodney Bester remained rigid—petrified. Kellog burst in, nervous and panting; Higgins slipped past him, calm and collected.

"Easy," Daniels said. "Don't hurt him, Boyd. He's gonna help us." Daniels and the others stood over the bed, guns drawn. "You know your constitutional rights, don't you, Rod?"

Sitting naked in bed, Rod nodded. "I wanna get dressed."

"Sorry," Daniels said, holstering his revolver. "That's not in the Constitution. Now, why did you off that Puerto Rican at the train station?"

Rod Bester's face barely moved, a mere slackening of the jaw. Then a look of sublime boredom came over him and Daniels knew he had him. "Shit," said Rod. "I didn't cut nobody."

"How did you know it was a stabbing?" Orin said, and rose from the bed.

"It was in the papers, man. I know what stabbing you're talkin' about."

"He follows current events," Higgins said. "A smart boy. Good."

"Hope so," Daniels said. "Jerome said *you* did it."

Rod screwed his face into a look of extreme anguish.

"He said he tried to stop you. You know you got the wrong guy, don't you? Jerome said you were crazy that day. All souped up on something— crack, coke." Daniels shrugged. "He signed a statement, Rodney."

"Jerome?"

Daniels feigned an inquisitive expression. "Detective Higgins, what was Jerome Jackson's street name?"

"Doctor Justice," Higgins said.

"Doctor Justice," Daniels repeated to Rod.

"Doc didn't sign shit," Rod said. "You guys are fishin'."

Orin stepped around Daniels and sent Rod spinning with a backhand to his face. Daniels and Higgins restrained him as he hovered over the suspect.

Rod pulled the sheet off the bed to cover his crotch. "Yo, cop. Get a grip," he said.

"Rod," Daniels said, "I'm gonna let this cop here pound the dog shit out of you in a minute, you think you're so bad. I'll give you one chance to use that little brain of yours. If Jerome didn't talk, then what the hell are we doing here? Why are we talking to you at five in the morning? We know it was Doctor Justice did the cutting. He confessed. All you gotta do is back that up in a statement. Believe me, Jerome is going away on a long trip. You don't want the same ticket."

"No," said Rod, shaking his head. "He did it. It was all Jerome Jackson."

9

The squad went on four-to-midnights. An hour before going on duty, George and Orin stood on a bridge over one of the canals that passed through the town. A twenty-eight-foot cruiser approached from the east.

"George," Orin said, checking the time. "We should head for the house soon. It's almost that time."

"Got a live one," George said gleefully.

Orin shook his head in disbelief and leaned his chin on his hand, his elbow propped on the concrete balustrade.

Aboard the pleasure craft were two young women, lying facedown, sunning themselves, their bikini tops unfastened.

"Here comes," George said, priming the Polaroid camera borrowed from the evidence locker and putting his left hand on the empty beer can poised on the stonework. A fishing line was knotted around the tab of the can, its other end wound around an ornament on the railing. "Okay," George said, "camera ready."

"You should have had it with you when you saw the flying saucer."

"Fuck you, pal."

The cruiser lurched forward, as if starting through a car wash, its keel caught in the rushing current beneath the bridge. George leaned farther over the rail, giggling. "Hey!" he yelled. "Look out down there!" and pushed the empty beer can over the side. The girls on the bow screamed and turned over to scramble for cover. The camera clicked. The beer can stopped its plunge and harmlessly dangled over the spot where the boat had been.

"Got it," George said, looking very proud.

Donnelly was out of his office for the second time in recent memory and once again in Orin's face. The men standing in ranks to either side of Orin cringed.

"Foot pursuit, eh?" Donnelly bellowed. "Games. Grab ass. *Bullshit.*"

Sergeant Reagan was trying not to look self-satisfied. Orin put on an expression of utter incomprehension.

"*Funny man!*" Donnelly screamed an inch from his nose. The inspector's blue blouse and white eyes were in sharp contrast to the bright redness of his face and neck.

Orin resisted the temptation to look at George Clarke, to see if the bigmouth's face was also turning colors. George was the only one he and Paul had told about the phony chase that had sent Reagan zipping all over, trying to horn in on a collar. Officer Clarke had vowed absolute secrecy on the graves of his blessed parents.

Inspector Donnelly sputtered out, regained his composure, then whispered something to Lieutenant Fazio and returned to his office.

Fazio dismissed the troops, saying, "Do it by the numbers tonight," and told Orin to see him in the radio room. As the door closed behind them, he said, "The boss wants you buried."

Orin nodded, saying nothing.

"Every shithouse gig that comes along is yours until somebody else fucks up bigger. Which, considering the way you piss the man off, may be never. I'm sorry, Boyd, but that's the way it's gonna be. You got to pay for tellin' the bosses to kiss your ass, if you know what I mean."

"No problem," Orin said. "Eight hours is eight hours. There ain't none of this shit that's so much fun that I'd miss it."

"Okay," said Fazio. "You can start by taking the first two hours of the school crossing in front of the Wilhelm Clinic. Get one of the car guys to drive you out."

"Georgie Clarke, okay?"

"Pick your poison."

Orin caught George in the parking lot. He hopped in the passenger side of the patrol car and slammed the door against the downpour. The rainwater glistened on his slicker.

"Drive," he said, "before I change my mind and rip your fucking tongue out."

If George had been innocent, he would have blustered denials as he drove Orin out to his foot post. But George kept his mouth shut, as did Orin, who rhythmically tapped the dashboard with his nightstick as they rode.

"I thought," Orin said, "that I was a better judge of character. You were the last guy I thought would be a rat."

"Jesus Christ, Orin. I didn't say nothin' to no bosses. I only told a couple of the guys at Red's."

"Who told a couple of other guys, who told a couple of more, until some stupe told Inspector Donnelly. And now, when all I wanted to do was be a number around here, I'm on center stage with my pants around my ankles."

"I hate these fucking guys," George sputtered. "You can't trust nobody!"

Orin laughed, in spite of himself. The car slowed as they approached the crossing he would be guarding in the rain.

"I'll see you later," Orin said. "You think of me standing out here while Gloria's licking your balls."

"You're asking an awful lot," George said. "I been with her so long now, I have to think about my wife to keep it stiff."

"Nice talk." Orin pulled the hood of the slicker over his cap.

"Hang in there, buddy. I'll bring you a beer."

"Sure. Thanks," said Orin.

Orin met with Dr. Juliet Cammer in the early afternoon at their new time. He reported to her on his continuing sobriety and the apparent ease with which he was maintaining control. He didn't miss booze anywhere near as much as he had thought he would, he claimed. He didn't miss the bar talk, he didn't miss the hangovers. He could use a little sexual attention, he told her, but other than that, things were fine.

"Bullshit," she said flatly. "No one gets better that fast. Especially not someone like you."

"Someone like me?"

"A person who has managed to expose himself to the most stressful of events, who would have everyone believe it's no big deal, while his peers are running up personal crisis statistics that are breaking all the records."

"I never said it was no big deal. I just said I wasn't interested anymore."

"Exactly," she said. "You're so tough you don't even acknowledge that you handle it well."

"Handle what?"

"You see what I mean?"

"No, tell me what you mean." Orin settled into the leather chair thinking these visits were more fun than seeing a hooker, and wishing he and Juliet Cammer were of equal caste. Never before in his life had a woman of uncommon beauty shown such an interest in him. He could listen to her empathize for hours.

Dr. Cammer brushed back her hair with her hand and said, "You're a war hero."

"I stepped on a mine."

"You're a decorated police officer."

"I'm lucky I haven't been fired."

"You're a parent."

"I'm a fraud."

She leaned back. "Were your parents frauds?" she said.

Orin tapped a cigarette up from his pocket and lit it. He held his hand in front of him and wiggled it, as if to say, perhaps.

Juliet Cammer had noticed his eyes fill. "Tell me," she said.

"They got me this far."

"Yes?"

Orin remembered his merchant seaman father, those days when the Old Man was in port, the trees in autumn colors, smoke from fires hanging in the air, the smell of roast beef and corn on the cob, his dad gathering them around the dinner table and telling about the places he had been. Paris. Amsterdam. Singapore. Honolulu. When he was ten his father began making more frequent appearances at the house—back from shorter trips along the coast. Each time he packed a little more. One day his mother checked her husband's sock drawer for a little pin money they kept there. The money was gone. So were the socks.

"Orin?"

"Actually I wouldn't know my father if I fell over him."

"That must be tough."

"I don't dare say that it isn't, do I?"

"You'd only be fooling yourself."

"Well, that's it then," he said. "The answer."

"Tell me how you were wounded."

"I did," he said. "I stepped on a mine. The next thing I knew my ears were ringing and I was looking down at my buddies from the treetops. I landed on my ass, with my balls on the ground between my feet."

"Did they manage to put you back together again?"

"I managed to father a child."

"After the war you joined the police department, ready to save humanity, looking for that common thread to stand all the puppets up at once—"

He inhaled smoke. "No," he said. "A lot of guys joined the cops. I just knew I wouldn't be able to hack a nine-to-five gig. After the war, I found that I had a very low tolerance for bullshit. I mean, if it ain't life and death, don't bother me. Profits and losses, inventories, production schedules—I mean, who gives a good goddamn about shit like that."

"Your wife, for one."

"Yeah. Ain't it amazing?"

Juliet Cammer nodded. "We'll pick this up again next week."

Orin drove to the Long Island Railroad station to wait for his wife, arriving on the 1:40, coming home early to see him.

The back of the battered pickup was loaded with rods and tackle and bait for a midnight outing on the beach, after his shift. Pulling into a tow-away zone, he cut the engine and poured himself decaffeinated coffee from his thermos and smoked a low-tar cigarette, his best shot at following doctor's orders. Orin sat watching the sky grow heavy and threatening. The tree leaves flashed their shiny undersides like a football cheering section. The seasons were changing: the light was different; the wind off the water, chilling. He watched the early commuters arrive on trains from the center of the world, middle managers and executives getting a jump on the Indian summer weekend.

Seventy-five yards away a blonde in her thirties was lugging an army blanket and a cooler past the drunks outside the waiting room and the yearbook black-and-white of Doctor Justice flashed in his memory. A little girl trailed behind the woman. For a moment they looked similar to his wife and child, and he felt compelled to follow them, to make sure they were safe. When he pulled abreast, they were strangers; the mother looked away, frightened, and took her child's hand without losing a step.

Orin gave her a good-natured smile and drove back to his parking spot. Without the uniform, he thought, I must be a sinister dude. What had Judy ever seen in him, considering her love of the orderly. A reclamation project? Her earthly opposite? A Catholic boy who would go down on her?

The next train pulled in, depositing a few young fogeys and a crowd of black construction workers. Old folks and unregistered nurses were the last ones out of the train's brand-new cars. Judy appeared out of nowhere at his elbow: gray suit, red bowtie, gleaming shoes. His hand shook as he rolled the window all the way down.

"Sorry to be late," she said. "I missed the 12:12."

"Hop in," he said, and held the door open for her from the driver's seat. She went around and got in; he did not look directly at her. His stomach burned and his legs trembled; he was grateful to start up, his feet busy with the clutch and accelerator. She did not say anything about why she wanted to meet; she did not say anything at all. They drove in silence all the way to the house.

Orin stumbled on the threshold and bumped his shoulder on the hutch, rattling her collection of spoons from the capitols of Europe. She looked at him and told him to stay in the kitchen while she drove the housekeeper home.

"Don't touch anything," she said. "You don't live here anymore."

"Fine," he said. "I'll play with Dawn until you get back. Okay?"

"Dawn is at Hannah Greenberg's house—a play date."

He sat at her kitchen table, smoking, and waited. When Judy returned she quietly unpacked her attaché case, as if searching for something.

"What's up?" he said.

"Our time."

"Excuse me?"

"Get a lawyer, Orin. From now on I'd rather we have minimal contact."

"You make it sound like we're through with the preliminaries."

"Yes. I've discussed it with my attorney."

"And that's what you wanted to talk about this afternoon?"

"I owed you the warning," she said. "Face to face, like men."

After work that night Orin drove his truck to Field 4 at Jones Beach, locked the doors, turned on some heat, and fell asleep across the seat. A park ranger woke him.

"You can't stay here," he said. "The fine for trespassing is two hundred, fifty dollars."

Orin looked at himself in the rearview mirror and thought littering a more appropriate charge.

The unincorporated Village of Belmont, viewed from the roof of the abandoned factory, stretched out flat before him like an African savannah, the tar-paper roofs connecting in the distance, punctuated by water towers and treetops, all bathed in mercury vapor. The streetlights made the human activity below seem subterranean and strange. He opened a can of beer and washed the taste from his throat. Everything was wrong in this precinct, he thought. Out of whack. Real cops don't openly admire wiseguys, no matter how much pussy they score. They take it personal, like the asshole is getting over on them. They take offense. But not in the 13th.

Or maybe it was him, and the way it just wasn't the same without Kenny. When they were the overtime stars of the 11th Precinct's plain-clothes squad, racking up big-time "collars-for-dollars," he and Kenny would scout their turf off-duty, drinking and carousing, setting traps and snares, but also watching and learning, doing homework. They identified and catalogued patterns of behavior, so they would notice whenever something was different, when the smallest thing felt out of place. Nothing like that went on in Belmont.

It was obvious to Orin that no one was doing much police work in the 13th; obvious that the Reverend Sims and others were having their own way. Besides saving souls, the good reverend also ran illegal leisure activities: numbers, drugs, hookers. Orin watched the reverend's boys make their supervisory rounds in the small hours of the night, unimpeded in the slightest by the precinct's midnight shift, all of which seemed inured to the sight of the chrome-embroidered red Eldorado on patrol. The collector was brazen. Orin watched the Caddy ooze around a pothole in the street directly below him, and park next to a bank of public phones at the curb.

A skinny black dealer in a sweat suit and gold chains hung up a phone and ambled over to the car, his hands held low and behind his back, the fingers splayed. A large black hand emerged from the passenger window. The kid slapped it five, then filled it up with cash. The hand disappeared and the car pulled away.

Adrenaline surged through Orin's chest.

He watched the kid in the gold chains go back to the phone booths and again pretend to be engaged in conversation. A patrol car passed; the kid actually waved. A baby-blue Mazda, with white girls in it, rolled up to the curb. The kid hung up the phone and made his sale. He stuffed the money in his pants, then picked up the phone and resumed his charade.

It was time to shuck and jive. He climbed down from the roof of the factory and got into his ancient truck. Where, he wondered, could he find the components he needed? Ah, yes. Of course. He drove to a park across from a large apartment building whose tenants were permitted pets. He found his flashlight and an old paper bag in the truck and walked carefully into the knee-high grass, searching for specimens.

If Judy could see me now, he thought, rolling a beauty into the bag with a stick. He held the bag in his fingertips and placed it on the flatbed, next to the tailgate. Then he drove to another set of public phones and made his call.

The communications center answered. "Police department, operator twenty-one."

"Police?" said Orin. "Listen . . . there's an old man at the corner of Broadway and Trenton with his dick out, and he's masturbating all over the store windows. Some little children are watching. Please, God . . ."

"Dispatching a car immediately, sir. May I have your—"

But Orin had already hung up and run back to the truck. He arrived, huffing and puffing, at his rooftop observation tower in time to see that the response to his call was immediate and enthusiastic, enough to please even the harshest of the police department's critics. Six cops and a sergeant had converged within minutes, nightsticks at the ready, and itching for the chance to open some sicko's dome. And, as Orin had expected, Bubba's teenage dealer beat a hasty retreat down the alley, leaving the phones temporarily unattended.

"Run, my little gangster," Orin said to himself. "Just make sure that you come back."

When the policemen gave up their hunt for the phantom pervert and retired from the field, Orin climbed down from the roof and walked across the street to the phones with his paper bag. Looking first one way, then the other, he filled each earpiece with a scooping motion. The moist remainder, still wrapped in the brown paper bag, dropped to the sidewalk with a thud.

Back on the roof again, waiting in the darkness for the dealer's return, Orin felt terribly silly, trying to imagine any other thirty-eight-year-old behaving as he was this chilly evening. He imagined Judy trying to explain to her business colleagues what exactly her husband had done to get suspended this time. Not that she would anymore. He had to admit, though, he was having a wonderful time.

To Orin's delight and surprise, before the dealer felt it safe to reopen for business, the red Eldorado reappeared. The collector stepped from the passenger side and posed elegantly next to the booths. He looked around a moment with his hands on his hips, then leaned back into the car. When he stood up again, he was holding a little black book.

"My kingdom that he might have a quarter," Orin said softly.

The man stepped up to a phone and spun that quarter into the slot with a long reptilian finger, then nestled the receiver next to his ear.

"Bingo!" said Orin. "Zap!"

"Oh, my God!" the man screamed, loud enough for Orin to actually hear him. "Yo, Sherman. Get your ass out here."

The fat hand of Sherman Clayborne, the reverend's main man, extended from the car. Orin could see that he was pointing to something.

This was wonderful, thought Orin. Police work the way it ought to be. He climbed down the fire escape and casually crossed the street.

The collector didn't see Orin coming. He was too busy digging the crap out of his ear. Sherman Clayborne didn't see Orin either; he was too busy trying not to laugh.

"Yo, blood. What it is," said Orin, slapping the man on the back, hard. "You got any shit on you? I was told I could get some at this corner."

The collector got over being startled. He towered over Orin, glaring down at him, wondering where he had seen the face before. "What? You think you funny?"

"Why no, m' man. But then I'm not the one with the dog doo in my ear."

The man's jaw dropped. The driver's door of the Caddy flew open. Sherman Clayborne jumped out and started around the car. Orin pulled his off-duty revolver from the waistband of his blue jeans and stuck it in Sherman Clayborne's face. "Back in the car, Cato, before I launch one up your nose."

Sherman raised his hands above his head and backed away. "Is you crazy, motherfucker? Does you got any idea who you fucking with?"

"Absolutely, my good man. I'm on a mission from the Lord. He wants you both to clean up your act."

"You got a name, homeboy?" the bagman wanted to know.

"Jack MaHogoff," said Orin. "I'm in the book."

"Yeah? Well now you in my book," said the collector.

"Good," said Orin. "Now get out of here. You're drawing flies."

The hood never took his eyes off Orin as he got back into the car. He held his head out the window so as not to soil the upholstery. An enraged Sherman Clayborne made a seven-point U-turn that snapped the man's head back and forth. He was still howling and cursing as the limousine finally sped off.

10

Paul Kellog dropped Orin off in 1308 and drove away. George was picking him up in two hours. Orin took up his familiar position on the windy corner opposite the Wilhelm Clinic and leaned against a mailbox, his hat tipped back and his hands in his pockets. The street was quiet, the handicapped adults were in classes and workshops, and some in preventive detention. He had to stand there in case any wandered off.

He thought of his own daughter, healthy and happy, telling her kindergarten friends that her daddy was a policeman. He thought of Judy, and the night she told him that devotion to her job gave her more satisfaction than her home life, and that he really ought to try to make something of himself, to concentrate more on career advancement.

Could she have possibly meant this—the usual upwardly mobile day at the office, spent standing on a corner? Could he rouse himself to be the best damn crossing guard in America? He lit a cigarette and tried not to look at his watch. Maybe the next two hours would pass without him noticing. His body might be rooted to concrete, but his soul would be free, his mind on vacation. A little down-time, a moment's disconnection from the machinery.

Two minutes into Orin's disappearing act an old black woman tried to file a missing person's report with him, claiming all five of her sons had been kidnapped at birth and were now appearing everywhere as the Los Angeles Lakers. They never called. Never sent a card. Orin promised to get right on the case.

Then a pretty white girl in jeans and a red sweat-shirt wandered over and said hello. She was around twenty and wearing Air Jordan's that were much too big for her feet. Her mouth curled into a street-smart smile.

"What do *you* want?" Orin asked. "Someone steal your BMW?"

"I don't want nothin'. Just thought I'd say hello. My father was a security guard."

"Good," he said. "Get out of here."

Her smile was wounded, her eyes concerned.

"Honest, sweetheart. People will talk."

"You go!" she said.

"I'm not allowed to. I've gotta be here for another one hundred and eleven minutes. I'm being punished."

She stabbed herself in the chest. "Me, too." Then she pointed at the clinic and the words *emotionally disturbed* jumped into his head.

"What did you do?" Orin asked her, half hoping it would make less sense than what he had done.

"I lost my temper, they said. I threw my pen at the therapist's back."

"Hey," Orin said. "These things happen. I've seen guys waste whole villages over letters from their girlfriends."

She nodded as if she understood, then told him that she was learning to read and write. She said it seemed like it was taking forever.

"Well," he said. "Stick with it." He said good-bye again, explaining what his superiors would do to him if they caught him standing around talking to a nice-looking chick all afternoon.

"What's your name?" he asked.

"Lonnie Terrell."

"You know a kid in there named Sarina?"

"No."

"My name is Orin Boyd," he said, and extended his hand. She shook it.

"You married?" she said.

"I was . . . my wife ran off with a taffy salesman."

"I'm sorry."

"My little daughter thinks my name is Honky Pig."

Lonnie frowned for a moment, then laughed out loud. She looked at Orin's hand and asked why he was wearing a wedding ring.

"They were nice," he said, glancing at his hand. "I miss them."

Lonnie took a deep breath. "Where would you go if you weren't being punished?" she said.

Orin closed his eyes and smiled, imagining sunlight on the water, a cold beer. "Fishing probably. Why? Where would you go?"

"I don't know. Maybe the same. I'll see ya, okay?"

"Yeah. Take it easy."

Jack Gaines rested his foot on the dashboard and his arm on the steering wheel and looked out at the boats on the Great South Bay. Next to him Jerry Santos was doing the Sunday crossword puzzle.

"You know an eight-letter word for protective device?" Jerry said.

"How many letters in *rubbers*?"

Jerry raised the container of coffee to his lips without looking, intent on the puzzle. "Seven," he said. "I thought of that."

Jack's Styrofoam coffee cup, wedged between the dash and the windshield, steamed the dirty glass. He lit another smoke and read the rentals column of the real-estate section. The radio dispatcher gave their call number and an address. Jerry acknowledged as Jack revved it up and took off, siren cranking.

"*Umbrella*," Jack shouted over the siren.

"What?"

"Protective device. Eight letters."

Jerry shook his head. "*Insanity*."

"What?"

"Eight letters."

Jack broke into a smile. "Yeah."

The house was a tenement on Rose Street.

"Hey," Jerry said as they pulled up front. "Get a load of that Chiquita."

A thin young woman in a lacey dress was waving frantically from the front porch.

"Nice imported stuff," said Jack, killing the engine and piling out after his partner.

"What's the matter, miss?" Jerry asked.

"*Los ninos*," she said, "the children. They have been crying for hours. I don't know if the mother is home or not. This way."

They followed her up the stairs of peeling paint. The hallway smelled of socks and burnt toast. She stepped over small toys and loose piles of garbage. Santos kicked the debris aside, Jack Gaines behind him.

"Floor two," she said.

"Your name, Miss?" Jerry said.

"Consuela Tiburceo." She continued up the worn steps, past a portrait of the Blessed Mother framed in gold plastic. Jack flipped his cigarette butt out a broken stairwell window. Nearing the second-floor landing they could hear children howling pitifully.

At the apartment door Jerry knocked and the wails grew louder. He forced the lock easily. Twins, girls maybe two years old, huddled against one another next to the collapsed body of their mother. Liquor wafted up from her. A vial of pills had been spilled across the bare carpeting.

Jerry quickly checked for vital signs. "Alive," he said. "Call for a bus, Jack. And see if the kids might have eaten any."

Jack keyed his transceiver and relayed the instructions, then picked up the twin girls gingerly and carried them to the couch, checking the pupils of their eyes as he went.

"I'll change them," Consuela said protectively, and elbowed him out of the way.

"*Gracias*," said Jack, noting the thinness of her attire.

She blushed and adjusted the bodice of the house dress. He watched her soothe and comfort the kids, whose terror leveled off to childlike crying.

Jerry said, "We'd better call Child Protective Services."

"Oh, no!" Consuela said. "That is not needed. This lady is a good mother . . . most of the time." She glanced fearfully from Jerry to Jack. "I will watch them until she . . . feels better. Please. You can see"—she swept the room with her hand in a Latin gesture—"they are all she has."

Jack looked to Jerry, the senior man, who scratched his silver topped head. He winked at Jack. "Okay, Miss Tiburceo. You watch the kids. Jack, take her information," he said, and plopped down on the couch to play with the twins while his partner escorted the young woman into the kitchen to be interviewed.

Consuela Tiburceo was twenty-two, she lived across the hall, with her mother. She did not seem exactly scared, but she was tenuous. Aloof. They did not have a telephone.

"So how do boys call you up for dates?" he said.

She paused, then said, "They do not."

"*Porque?*"

Consuela shrugged, obviously caught off guard.

She was, he decided, unaware of how disarming he found her beauty, her innocence. Perhaps she was even a virgin.

"Would you," he said, "go out with me?"

"Ah . . ." Confusion was clear in her expression. What was required of her? What might be the consequences of declining? "I think so. If you wish."

"Tomorrow?"

"Tomorrow," she agreed, nodding. "Thank you."

Abraham Wilson needed food and drink but he was broke. His Social Security check wasn't due for three more days and his credit at the 7-Eleven was overextended. He had nothing he could sell, either, not even his blood. So he rode his three-speed bike to the Pathmark supermarket and locked it up next to the dumpster. He vaulted into the dumpster, landing in the middle of the store's expired items.

Tearing open a box of corn flakes, he inspected the contents, then snacked on them as he searched among the pungent garbage for something more substantial. A pound of sliced bacon.

Bacon in hand, he carried the package inside, showed the store manager the expiration date, accepted the man's apology and two fresh packets with PAID stickers.

On the way out Abraham pressed his luck. He slapped one of the labels on a case of beer. The manager stopped him at the door. "Hey, motherfucker! Put the goddamn beer down and get out of here before I call the cops." Abraham panicked, shoved the man aside and ran.

Car 1321 arrived as Batman was stuffing the bacon down the front of his pants and balancing the case of beer on the handlebars of his getaway bike.

"Good," George Clarke muttered to Orin. "It's only Batman. No fucking way did I want to make a collar."

The manager ran from the store to meet them. "That's him! Grab him, grab him!"

"Relax," said George, hiking up his gunbelt. "He's not going anywhere. Are you, Batman?"

Abraham put his booty on the ground and hung his head. Orin got out of the car and stood up behind his door. He looked at the culprit and shook his head.

"So," George said to the manager, "you got your stuff back. Is everything else okay?"

"What do you mean?"

"You want us to escort old Abraham from the area for you?"

"I want you to lock up his thieving ass."

"Well, now—"

"Well nothing. This guy robbed me, Officer. Why wouldn't I want him arrested?"

"Why?" George chuckled, trying to downplay it. "Oh, I don't know. Only the court appearances, the postponements, the countersuits, the bad publicity, the pickets, the trial—what we call the complainant's syndrome. If you've never done it before, you just don't know what a pain in the ass it can be. Why—"

"I've done it before," said the manager. "Maybe thirty, forty times, when I ran a branch in the Bronx. It's the only way to keep these animals from taking over. To tell ya the truth, I like doing it. Where do I sign?"

George said, "We're gonna have to bring the beer to the station house, to take a picture for evidence. We'll call you when you can come and pick it up."

"Forget the beer, boys," the manager said. "Take the picture and then drink it. I know the fucking score."

"Yeah," said George. "Sure you do."

George Clarke only kicked Batman once in the butt. That was on the way up the front steps of the 13th. Orin told George that, in view of how much George hated to type, he would handle all the paperwork if George would run out and pick up Chinese food.

"You mean it?"

"Yeah. I mean it. I can't stand watching you abuse these fuckers."

"Damn," said George, looking like he had just won the lottery. "You got it!"

Orin ordered a sparerib combo for himself and another for Abraham. George said he wanted egg foo yung, gathered up his clipboard and radio and left the prisoner processing room.

Orin opened Abraham's handcuffs and told him to make himself comfortable. "Let's keep it simple," he said. "We'll be gentlemen."

Batman opened his eyes a little wider and regarded Orin with interest.

Orin said, "Beautiful," his fingers poised on the typewriter keys. "Full name?"

"Abraham Atticus Wilson."

"Also known as?"

"Ah . . . Wilson . . . or Batman."

"Age?"

"Forty-two or forty-three. No one was ever sure."

"Forty-two or forty-three? You're kidding," said Orin. "And I thought I looked old for my age."

"Yeah?" Batman fixed his gaze on the cop. "How old *are* you?"

"Thirty-eight." Orin smiled.

"You right. You do look old for your age."

"Hey. I thought we agreed to be gentlemen."

"Sorry."

The prisoner's eyes, Orin noticed, strayed from time to time to the case of beer on the desk. "Occupation?"

"I picks up mongo—all them bottles and cans, and papers what land on the ground. You'd be surprised what a man can make if he's willing to get up early and work hard."

"And before that?"

"I used to caddy, up at the Rockville Links, till some of the members complained about my drinking." Abraham told Orin where he had been born, raised, gone to school.

"Married?"

"Nope."

"Children?"

"Not really."

"Home address."

"I lives outside. Have mostly since I got out of the army."

"Oh, yeah? When was that?"

"I guess 'bout twenty years now. Sixty-eight."

"Me, too," Orin said, typing. "I was in I Corps. Marines."

"Army," said Abraham, "in the Delta."

And now you're back in the boonies again, Orin thought.

"Yeah," said Abraham. "A lot of us are out there, poundin' the ground still."

"Amen. Where do you get your welfare check delivered?"

"At a lady's house. Charlene King. Me and her used to go together way back. She watches over some of my things. Sometimes I showers there. Sometimes she fix me a bowl of something to eat."

"You think she'll bring you twenty-five bucks for old times' sake?"

Abraham shrugged.

"That way me and George don't have to take you to Mineola for the night. You can skate, and we can go off duty on time."

Abraham said, "I suppose it's worth a shot."

Orin dialed Charlene King's number for Abraham, then handed him the phone.

"Charlene?" Abraham said. There was a pause. "Well then run 'round front and get her, girl. Tell her I needs help. Me—Abraham."

While Abraham waited, Orin lit cigarettes for both of them.

"Hey, honey. It's me, Abe. I got locked up . . . Shoplifting . . . I need a hundred dollars or they gonna put me in jail . . . Yeah . . . At the Thirteenth."

Orin started to correct him on the amount of bail he'd need, but Abraham shook his head and held his finger to his cracked lips. Orin laughed out loud.

"Why, you little sneak," he said, softly.

Abraham hung up and smiled. "That way they's seventy-five dollars for me. She a well-off woman."

"Would you like to try for the beer and bacon, too?"

"Don't play with me, Officer. I don't think my heart could stand it."

George was back and everybody stopped to eat dinner at the desks. Then Charlene King arrived with an envelope with five twenties and a promissory note, that she made Batman sign. She was forty or so, dark, pretty—a surprise to Orin. The pleasant scent of her perfume filled the dismal office, masking, however briefly, the odor of Abraham Wilson.

"Don't even think about cashing yo' check Tuesday," she said to him. "You and me gonna cash it together."

"Thank you, Charlene. You the best friend I got . . . after Jesus."

"Don't you Jesus me, Abraham Wilson. You ain't spent five minutes today thinking about your savior." Charlene handed him the money. Abraham nearly levitated.

While Orin was walking her back out of the house, he asked her what the deal was, why a woman like her would bail a wino out of jail. Charlene King smiled. "He wasn't always like that. At one time he was together. Even had a lot of money once."

"Really?"

"And there's the teachings of the Lord," she said. "If I don't do it, who will?"

"Nice meeting you," he said.

"Nice meeting ya'all."

George and Orin brought Abraham Atticus "Batman" Wilson, the bicycle, the bacon, the beer and the paperwork upstairs to Lieutenant Fazio. Abraham signed his release agreement in perfect Palmer script and thanked the officers for their courtesy. But he looked genuinely disappointed when George said he couldn't have the beer.

At four P.M. they reported back to the station house, where they were ordered to remain on duty and to assemble in the muster room. "Training lecture," said the desk officer. "Fifteen minutes' worth."

Fifteen minutes when they were least able to retain information. With the predictable amount of grumbling, they wandered down the stairs to the basement muster room.

Sergeant Reagan received them in his street clothes. "Okay, hurry the fuck up and sit down. The sooner we get started, the sooner we go sit in traffic."

Cops filed in and slumped in the metal funeral home chairs. Reagan rapped the red stone of his college ring on the table. Nobody paid any attention.

"Okay! Listen up," he said loudly. The chatter continued. Reagan

looked at the twenty-four-hour clock overhead, then at the shift patrolmen. "I said, 'Shut the fuck up!'"

"Easy, boss," said George Clarke. "You don't have to yell at us like we're
children." He gave Reagan a mocking smile as the rest of the stragglers
took their seats, handcuffs and revolvers and flashlights clanging against
the chairs. George remained on his feet.

Reagan ignored him. He stepped behind the table at the front of the
room and began to read aloud from the training bulletin on duties at the
scene of a crime.

"Get to the important shit, willya?" protested George. "Who do the
dicks like in the double tomorrow?"

"Must you speak out of turn every single day, George?"

George frowned, mulling a rejoinder, when Detective Sergeant Alonzo
Daniels entered, behind him Captain Blogg and Sergeant Ril, who took
chairs on the side. Daniels joined Reagan up front.

"Yes," said Reagan. "May I help you?"

Daniels said, "When you're finished."

"He was finished fifteen years ago," George announced. Cops ooohed.
Reagan bowed deeply and sat down.

"I'm Detective Sergeant Daniels, Homicide," he said. "You may remember me from the train-station killing, one perpetrator of which we
bagged, thanks to your good work, the other perp remaining at large." He
set his briefcase on the table and looked out at them, then at George, still
on his feet. "Big man," he said, "most cops I know with your kind of time
on the job would rather sit."

George suddenly looked out on a limb. His back went stiff.

Orin smartly rose to his feet beside George. "Officer Clarke was just
suggesting we form a jogging club," he said. "He's an inspiration to us all.
Right, fellas?"

The men applauded enthusiastically as the pair sat down.

"Okay, okay," said Daniels, waving them quiet. "You guys are beautiful. Now business," he said, and launched into a lecture reviewing the
duties of the first officer at the scene of a crime and even managed to make
it interesting by mixing in anecdotes from actual cases and state-of-the-art
lab techniques. When he had finished, he told the men he was switching
hats and asked them to bear with him. Out of his case came a colored
chart, which he tacked to the bulletin board behind him.

Hearing mumbling, he said, "Relax. I'm not here to break your balls. I'm here to point out a trend, a very disturbing one—the rapid rise of alcohol-related violence within the department." He tapped the oaktag. "Guns and booze don't mix, not for cops, not for anybody. We all know someone who messed up with his piece. All I want to do is remind you guys that the job runs a very effective rehabilitation center. You can get help without getting fired. There's no longer any good excuse to hide. None. I'm living proof that they don't hold treatment against you. I was a uniformed patrolman for my first ten years. During that time I ruined a good marriage and damn near drank myself out of a job. A bigger asshole you have never seen. One night I screwed up big-time and wrecked a county car. The department chaplain, Monsignor Martin O'Rourke, came to see me in the hospital, bearing a message from on high: Sign myself into the program or hit the bricks. No ifs, ands or buts. I signed. Six months after I returned to duty, I was given my gold shield and sent to Narcotics. Eight years later I passed the sergeant's test. Six months ago yesterday I made detective sergeant. Nassau County pays me seventy-two thousand dollars a year to do a job I love. . . ."

Nobody wanted to argue with the sergeant, everyone was watching the clock on the wall, well aware that—even as Daniels was humiliating himself for their benefit—the time permitted by PBA contract for these training sessions had expired.

"Any questions?" he said. There were none.

Sergeant Ril, resplendent in his many military creases and spit-shined shoes, rose from his chair and cleared his throat. "The captain has an announcement."

"Yes," said Blogg, bouncing to his feet. "Well. What I would like to announce, if I may, without wasting more of your valuable time, is that my staff and I have set the date for the Thirteenth's first annual Precinct Kick-off Dinner, to be held right here at the station house on the eleventh of next month between twenty and twenty-two hundred hours." He looked down at his file cards. "I know this will be a memorable evening for us. We—my staff and I—will serve you fellows food and refreshments. There will be motivational music and a guest speaker from headquarters."

"Wow," George whispered. "Gatorade, donuts and a circle jerk. They haven't tried this move in years."

"All the biggies do it," Blogg said proudly. "General Motors, Allied Chemical, not that our little get-together will be an exact replication of an IBM convention in Acapulco." He smiled, pausing to allow for their laughter. None came. The smile drew into a rictal grin. "Our Kick-off Dinner is a solid step in the right direction. Headquarters considers this pilot program of the utmost importance."

"Wives or girlfriends?" Moses called out.

"Excuse me?" said the captain, blinking.

Orin said, "He means is this shindig gonna be stag or do you want us to bring broads?"

Captain Blogg sputtered. "Stag . . . stag. That should go without saying. All right. See you on the eleventh. Dismissed."

George Clarke strode into the locker room and changed quickly. He left his wedding ring pinned to the back of his shield and tossed it in his gym bag.

"That fucking idiot, Blogg," Kole muttered, and slammed his gear into the locker. He said to Orin, "*What* if I had a second job? I'd be late now, about to catch shit from some other scrote boss because the Geek wants to throw us a fucking Happy Fizzies party."

"I'll catch you later at Red's," George said to Orin.

Orin tugged listlessly at a shoelace. "Say hello to Gloria for me. Hey, anybody want to stop for a taste?"

George threw his gym bag over his shoulder. "Love ya, baby. Let's do lunch."

Outside the station house, George scooped up a handful of gravel, then he wheeled, kicked and fired in the direction of Blogg's basement window. The pebbles rattled the glass; George's elbow burned with pain.

It took George fifteen minutes to drive back to the Strip. He parked his Thunderbird behind the Stallion Bar and climbed the back stairs to Gloria's door. When she let him in, and he saw she was wearing only a pink terrycloth robe and fluffball slippers, he grunted unhappily.

"The movie starts in fourteen minutes, Gloria. What the fuck?"

"I have some trouble, Georgie. Anthony, he—"

"Great," he said, pulling a beer from her refrigerator. "Just what I needed to hear. Gloria, one of the reasons I like you is because things usually run smooth. And now—"

"Thin's usually go your way," she said. "That's what you mean."

"Hey!" he shouted. "You're the one who wanted to go out in public. Now you're not even ready."

"My son is very sick," she said, and pointed to the child bundled up and sleeping on George's favorite couch. "What am I gonna do?"

"What's he got?"

"A fever and a sore throat. I cannot leave him alone."

"How do you know he's not faking it?"

"Because I can read a thermometer, you son of a bitch!"

"Yeah?" said George, digging a wad of bills from his pocket. "Oh, yeah? Watch how fast he feels better when he gets a look at these."

"Don't you dare," she said evenly, dark eyes flashing.

"Forget it," said George. "That was a joke. He's too young to be bribed. Even I know that."

He stood in the middle of the tiny living room, wondering whether to take off his jacket and stick around, or dream up some halfassed excuse and split. The TV was tuned to an English speaking station, he noticed, and something spicy and special was bubbling on the stove. The down side was, however, that she wouldn't cut loose with the good thing with Anthony home. Not now, not ever. He might as well go.

"I'm gonna take off," he said breezily. "Give you a call tomorrow morning, to see how the boy is doing."

"I knew it," she said softly. "That's why I din't even waste the time to get dressed."

"What are you talking about?"

"Why you can no stay?" She pushed back her gold and orange hair. "You got another woman, Georgie. Some *puta?* I'm gonna cut her fucking tits off."

"Don't be ridiculous."

"Ridiculous, eh?"

"Absolutely ridiculous."

"You want to keep coming here, Georgie, you gotta share."

"That's a lotta crap." George lumbered to the door, yanked it open so the walls shook, then turned and sneered at her. "This is the fuckin' thanks I get, eh? Try to do something nice for Gloria, plan a little evening out on the town, and when I get here, you cop this attitude like I'm a scumbag because I can't understand where you're coming from."

Gloria scratched her head. "I'm coming from Puerto Rico. Just like always: Why are you trying to confuse me?"

"Don't play dumb with me," he said. He put his beer on the hall table, his exit virtually assured. "You got something to say to me, sweetie, you better say it now."

"Go," she said. "Who needs you."

Paul Kellog leaned back on his stool, his foot hooked on the rail, and glanced up at the ball game on the tube, then at Orin, propped chin-in-hand on the bar.

"Are there any eligible women in here, do you think?"

"Not the marrying kind. Some riders maybe."

"You go with any riders?"

"Not anymore."

"Anything else in this town besides riders?" Paul said.

"Nothing."

"So I guess I keep drinking, huh?"

"Hey, Newt," Orin called out. "Bring us Don Juans a couple of beers."

Newt stepped into the kitchen doorway, his apron splotched with chili. "Get 'em yourself."

Orin chuckled and strolled behind the bar to replenish their glasses.

"Make that one more," George called from the front door.

"My man," said Orin. "Quick matinee?"

"Too quick. Where's Newt?"

Paul said, "In the back, jerking off in the chili."

"And where are the local sperm receptacles?" asked George, his head swiveling, taking in the room.

Paul and Orin shrugged. Orin said, "We're it."

Moses pushed in through the door.

"Mo," Orin said. "I thought you were coming straight here."

"I was. I got snagged. That fucking Donnelly was tanked again and on a rampage."

"What happened?" George said, pulling on his beer.

Moses parked on an adjoining barstool and blew on his cold hands. "All available hands had to help him find his car keys. He's gettin' to be a candidate for a latex lounge. Fuckin' head case. I don't know what's bugging him but he's been outrageous the last couple of weeks.

Drunk in his office two hours into a shift. Ril's going broke buying him bottles."

George snorted. "He goes back and forth like a waitress anyway, the little scumbag."

Moses shrugged. "I heard Donnelly is packing it in soon."

"Yeah," George sniffed, "but don't get too enthused. Rumor Control says they're replacing him with Blogg."

"Oh, God," Orin said. "The mutant from the cellar?"

"Yep," Moses said. "The Geek himself."

"He looks like he sticks his head in the freezer every night to harden it up. Say it ain't so, Mo."

George sniggered.

"What's so funny?" Orin said.

"Blogg. Before any of you guys came on he once buttered his roll with a knife that was used in a homicide and was being held for evidence."

"You're shittin' me," Paul said, snorting a laugh.

"Swear." George held up his hand like he was taking an oath.

"What kind of pull does this clown have?" said Orin.

"His old man was a precinct commander somewhere."

Paul asked George how the lovely Miss Gloria Mendosa was making out.

"Not bad," George said, "not bad. She's getting older every day, of course, but that's the problem with all my broads. Take my wife, for instance. I should have plugged her barrel up with cement a year ago."

Moses nodded. "George, you are all heart. All heart. You got a deep, deep compassion for your fellow man."

"Fuck 'em. Wait till you're forty-five and all the broads you're banging got tummies like tapioca pudding. We'll see how much compassion *you* got, m' man."

Paul looked closely at George. He could not imagine his Maggie's tummy as anything but taut.

"Newt!" Moses shouted. "Give the boys some shooters. Hey, did you catch Jimmy D's dust up?"

"What happened?" George said.

"He caught a family dispute call, wound up in the middle of two warring mamas, one with a baseball bat. He jumped her—bitch 'bout the size of a water buffalo. Some other broad went at his back with a kitchen knife. Danny opened her dome just as she was about to shish kebab his ass."

"Blackjack?" asked George.

"Nightstick . . . a real clean stroke."

George nodded. "Yeah, that'd be Danny. He's a great stickman. Quick, too. Like Orin."

Paul listened but couldn't take his eyes off the picture on the wall behind the bar: softball players, fat, white and grinning, sitting on their fire truck.

Moses nudged George. "So I thought you were camping out with your bimbo tonight?"

George made a face. "Gloria? That skank would go down on the *Titanic*."

Orin looked over at Paul. "What about you, hot pants? Got a date?"

"Actually I have two."

"You see? Why make one woman miserable when you can make hundreds happy."

Paul slid off his stool and dropped some bills on the bar. "Later, gentlemen."

"Good night, rook," said Moses. "Want a rubber?"

"Good night, kid," said Orin and raised his glass.

George leaned in toward Orin. "Word's out there's a songbird in the house. So watch what you do in public. I don't trust these fucking new guys."

"Thanks for the tip," said Orin, and drank up.

"Another round for my grandfather here," said George, pointing to Orin's glass.

I t had been snowing since two A.M. George Clarke and Paul Kellog sat in 1310, enveloped in the smell of wet wool and George's cigarettes. Accident reports were pouring in from other units. George hated to take reports.

He said, "We're crazy to sit here in the street, you know. Some creep is going to pork us in the buns. We should pull behind a factory and try for a couple of hours' sleep. This sucks." He stretched himself lengthwise, leaning backward over the seat. After silent consideration, he said with great seriousness, as if framing an important new concept, "Man is not a nocturnal animal."

"I guess not," Paul said, and wondered where George had gotten the big idea. Probably from nocturnal emission, he decided, and chuckled to himself. He slipped the car into drive and steered carefully through the fresh snow, noticing the flakes in the distance drift lazily, while those closest to the windshield raced past, like tracers.

Paul parked at the curb in front of an abandoned diner on Sunrise

Highway. He said, "Why don't you curl up in back. I'll let you know if we get anything."

"You talked me into it. Goddamned police department. Have them hold my calls. I'm in conference."

George got out of the car, took a yellow disposable blanket from the trunk to make a pillow, then got in the back and curled up across the seat. Paul pulled away again, sticking to the right-hand lane, making only right turns at the farthermost corners of their post, covering their assigned area in ever smaller orbits. George was snoring.

Near the Sunrise Highway a red Volkswagen Rabbit caught his eye. He pulled closer. Behind the wheel was Maggie. Stopping behind her, he got out and, acting very official, walked over to her car.

Her window rolled down. "Merry Christmas, Copper."

"May I help you, ma'am?" he said, and bowed from the waist.

She poked him in the stomach. "I thought maybe I could help you. I've been thinking about you all night. You know—you working, lonely, cold."

"You're crazy driving around down here at night, you know. You want some coffee?"

"Yes. I could use some. I'm a little bombed from the party at Kathy's. Stoned, too." She slipped a joint from her purse.

"Jesus. Hide that, willya."

"Ooops. Sorry, Officer."

"Follow me, lady," he said, and got back in the patrol car. He led the way to an all-night coffee shop, got some to go, then led her to a nearby Off-Track Betting parlor and hid both cars in back of it. Then he jogged over and got into her car on the passenger side.

"You left your motor running," she said.

"It's always running for you, babe. Also, Clarke is asleep in the back seat."

"A guy tried to pick me up at the party."

"Oh, yeah?"

"He said I had a nice-looking set of wheels and a bitchin' chassis."

"How old was this guy?"

"I said I was interested in someone else. I told him that there was a great deal of"—she slid closer—"passion . . . built up in me, and that it was only right that the man who so aroused me be the one to—"

"No way," Paul said. "You've got to go home now. Go to bed."

"You look so beautiful when you're anxious."

"Honey—"

"It's been on my mind for days."

"I know."

"You know?"

Paul jumped out of the car and trotted around to Maggie's side. She rolled down the window and he leaned in and kissed her deeply. The snowflakes swirled around them, glazing their cheeks, catching on their lashes.

She pulled back. "I'll see you for breakfast, okay?"

"Yeah?"

"Yeah."

Paul stepped back as she drove off, then walked back to 1310 and got in. George was slouched in the back.

"Who's the bimbo?"

"The lady's name is Maggie."

George came up front. Paul put the car in gear and pulled away. The radio calls ticked off as the midnight shift rolled on: business burglaries, car accidents, family disturbances, sick children, sick adults, family disputes, a suicide attempt—a city cop's wife, fifty pills, while her husband lay drunk in the living room.

"God, it's boring," George said.

Along the Strip the bars were closing, the night people were disappearing.

"It's emptying out down here," Paul said.

"Yeah," George yawned. "Back to the caskets."

Dawn stood on the ottoman in the living room while Judy buttoned her coat. The child was crying.

"Hey, hey. Daddy's got presents for you," Judy said, "and then he'll probably take you to the Pancake House. You love the Pancake House."

"I wanna stay with you!" Dawn said for the fifteenth time.

"I know, darling." Judy hugged her, feeling her daughter's hot breath and tiny tears on her neck. "I know. But Daddy's coming. He wants to spend the morning with you, just like we talked about."

"I don't want to."

"I *know* Daddy went shopping for you."

"Daddy's here," Dawn said over her mother's shoulder.

Through the window they watched Orin park in front of the house. Judy walked Dawn to the front door and bent down on one knee to hug her. "Now, have a nice time, and I'll see you this afternoon." She kissed her daughter again, then watched her walk down to where her father stood waiting by the beat-up old heap he was still driving.

"Merry Christmas, Orin," she said across the cold stretch of lawn.

Orin nodded, smiled feebly. He kissed Dawn, helped her into the passenger seat, and strapped her in. When he looked back at the house, Judy had disappeared behind the closed door. He didn't see any sign of her at the window. Hopping into the cab of the truck, he said, "Honey, you look beautiful," and drove away. "I missed you, baby."

"I missed you too, Daddy."

"You wanna go see what Santa Claus left you at my . . . apartment?"

The little girl nodded, wearing her mother's grave expression. Was she mad at him, making him pay his first installment for walking out on them?

"After you get your presents, we're gonna go to a party with Eddie Sullivan's kids. You remember Kevin and Kelly?"

"Mommy said I could have pancakes. At the Pancake House."

"We can have pancakes," he said in a singsong falsetto. "We can do anything you want."

Dawn didn't say much for the rest of the trip. Orin parked behind Alimony Acres and undid her seat belt. The dumpster was overflowing with empty boxes and wrapping paper.

"Come on, hon," he said to her, feeling sad that she was already old enough to wear white stockings. "I'll carry you on my shoulders."

Dawn sat there, sniffling. Tears welled up, then sped down her cheeks.

"What's the problem, darlin'?"

She didn't answer. The tears just kept streaming.

"What's wrong?"

She sat with her hands balled between her knees like she was trying not to pee. Her lips were trembling.

"Daddy?"

"Yes."

"Daddy, I don't want to go in there. Don't make me, Daddy. Please!"

"Dawn—"

"I don't want to! I wanna stay here."

He put his arms around her small torso and rocked her. "Okay, honey. Okay, okay." He kissed the top of her head, remembering her baby smell. "Listen to me good now. You don't have to go inside. I won't make you do anything you don't want to do."

Dawn shuddered, then sobbed some more before bravely regaining her composure. Orin wiped her face with a tissue from his glove compartment and kissed her cheek.

"There you go, baby. That's my girl."

"Thank you, Daddy."

"Don't mention it." He balled up the tissue. "But, listen. Can you just tell me why you don't want to see my apartment?"

"It's bad," she said.

"Who told you that?" he said.

"I heard Mommy tell Grandpa."

"Oh." Orin put his arm around her shoulder and gave her a loving squeeze. "Daddy wouldn't take you someplace bad. Honest Injun." His voice broke. "It's not Trump Tower, I know, but Daddy lives here." He bent closer. "Listen up. You stay here. I'm going to run inside and get your presents."

She considered this for a second, then said, "Okay."

"Great."

"Lock the doors."

He did. Then he walked backward, with his eyes on her and smiling, all the way to the basement door and quickly inside. Fumbling with his keys, he unlocked the door but it wouldn't open. "Come on, come on." He walked away, hands on hips, his chest heaving. He remembered he had forgotten to lock it, as usual, and must have locked it now. He turned the key, it opened.

Finally inside he exhaled through his mouth, emptying his lungs to calm himself. "Fuck!" He ripped down the Merry Christmas banner from the wall above his mattress and lashed a kick at the plastic tree. The tinsel and garlands shook, the tree righted itself.

He filled a cardboard box with the poorly wrapped presents, then took an envelope from his sports-coat pocket and dropped it among the packages. He walked out, banging the door shut behind him.

Reaching the parking lot, he jogged quickly to the truck. His little girl was crying again. Shaking, he helped her blow her nose and drove her home. When they pulled up in front of the house, Judy appeared instantly at the door. Orin unhitched Dawn's belt and the little girl bounded out and up the snowy walk. Judy hugged her daughter, the child's head to her hip.

"Back so soon?"

Orin walked up to the door and handed her the box of presents. "She didn't want to come in. She wanted to be with you."

"I'm terribly sorry," Judy said, setting the box down inside the door. "I was going to say something before."

"She was afraid."

Judy patted Dawn's fanny into the house and called after her: "Take your coat off and go to the bathroom. Mommy will be right there."

When Dawn was out of range, Orin said, "I thought we weren't going to play pinball with her head."

"I didn't," Judy said. "Not on purpose." She looked chagrined. "Dawn heard me talking to Dad one night after I'd been to your place. I was depressed. Upset. And I probably said more than I should have. I'm sincerely sorry, Orin. I really am."

Orin nodded. "Don't worry about it. Better go wipe her bottom."

Judy nodded and went in. Orin closed the door after she was gone and went back to his truck, then drove back to his place slowly, the ache in his throat working down to his stomach.

Jack Gaines climbed the creaky stairs on Rose Street, his arms laden with flowers. On the second floor he knocked twice on the door of the Tiburceos and waited until the mother let him into the pristine apartment.

"For me?" she teased. "Jack, you are too kind." Leading him in, she called, "Consuela. It is your gentleman come to call."

Consuela appeared from her bedroom, eyes excited. She stood on her toes to buss him and made a satisfying fuss over the flowers, setting them on the coffee table in the living room and inhaling deeply their fragrance.

She reciprocated with a present of her own, in a black velvet box she took from her pocket and handed to him. Inside he found a small silver medal of the Blessed Virgin on a silver chain.

"May she always keep you safe," Consuela said. She helped place the chain around his neck and clasp it.

"It's truly beautiful, Connie. Thank you."

"It is not for the looks," she said.

"I know." He wrapped his arms around her. "I do."

In the doorway of the kitchen, Consuela's mother crossed herself. A policeman, she thought, was a very good catch.

Jack and Consuela left soon after and drove down the Meadowbrook Parkway to a spot on the beach, in the dunes, that Orin Boyd had shown him the night they'd gone fishing. Sitting on an old blanket he kept in the trunk, they huddled against the wind and cold and watched the airport's incoming traffic circle and circle, slowly working their way downward in the stack, awaiting clearance at Kennedy.

"I want to marry you," he said. "I want to have children with you: little freckle-faced spics with leather vests and baseball mitts."

"Are you sure, Jack? Are you going to feel comfortable with a Latino wife? What will people say?"

"People will marvel at the beauty of our offspring and the grace with which they turn a double play."

She laughed.

"This is serious," he said. "Tomorrow I'm buying a new vehicle. If you say yes, it will be a family car."

"And if I say no?"

"A Harley Davidson."

"Motorcycle?"

He nodded.

"I couldn't stand to have you risk yourself on such a thing. We had better do it, then," she said, and kissed him.

The engagement was announced at the Santoses' Christmas party, an annual event for the rank-and-file members of the precinct and other brother officers Jerry had worked with during his nineteen years on the job.

Actually nineteen and a half, he thought, watching his guests mingle in the downstairs and basement recreation room of the house he and Christine had built twelve years ago, when land in Ronkonkoma was still cheap. It was a solid house, gaily decorated for the occasion. In another three months it would go on the market.

Yet Jerry was down, unable to shake the vague funk he had been in since the shooting. He had stopped taking his wife's Valiums when the dreams stopped, the stickup artist and the elderly bystander, both dancing madly in front of him, then collapsing inside their clothes as if he had let the air out of them. Deciding definitely to retire had helped, but still the odd feeling persisted.

Christine paused alongside him in the kitchen. "I hope we got enough of everything." She had wanted a small gathering for a change, but Jerry knew too many other cops too well. And it would be their last blowout, they both realized, although neither of them said it.

Jerry patted her arm. "We did forget something—air sickness bags?"

"Speaking of which, did you make sure George Clarke wasn't bringing another hooker this year? Did you say anything to him?"

"Of course not."

"Of course."

"Not to worry. He's here already and he came alone."

"Where?"

"Over by the bar. Where else. You want a drink?"

"No, I'm fine, honey."

Jerry Santos gave his wife a peck on the cheek and eased through the crowd to the makeshift bar in the den. The downstairs was packed.

Even Ril and his wife had come, with the sergeant faultlessly attired in a Scottish tweed sports jacket, plaid shirt, Christmasy red-green tie, perfectly pressed wool slacks, and glossy penny loafers.

Ril slipped a bottle of inexpensive scotch onto the bar, hiding it behind the others. The move was not lost on George Clarke, who was acting in his usual role as impromptu bartender.

"Pink Lady or Shirley Temple?" Clarke said.

"Scotch and soda, please," Ril said. "How are you, George? Merry Christmas."

"You want Chivas or this cheap shit?" He plucked out Ril's bottle.

"Chivas is fine."

"Sure is," George said, pouring Ril a glass of the cheap shit.

Ril gave a perfunctory nod of thanks and eased away. His wife went into the front room where the other women had gathered; Ril drifted into the foyer.

Hoots and howls erupted from the cellar stairwell. Up the stairs and out into the crowd came Danny Tucker in a rented Santa suit pulled along by a prancing Orin Boyd, who was naked, except for red paint on the tip of his nose, a black leather halter around his neck, and a matching studded G-string, no doubt borrowed from the Vice Squad evidence locker. Startled screams followed them through the front room where the older wives were gossiping.

Paul Kellog was agape, his date was doubled over laughing. She seemed entirely comfortable standing around the bar.

"Fire up the rock and roll!" Danny was shouting, momentarily drowning out the Christmas carol being sung somewhere in the house. George Clarke complied with a blast of hard rock from the confiscated ghetto blaster he had arrived with under his arm.

"Boogie!" George shouted. Maggie pulled Paul into the middle of the room and cut loose. Other couples were joining in. Just as Tony and Anita Kole came in the front door, Orin Boyd and Santa pranced out. Hooting and hollering, St. Nick and his reindeer circled the house through the snow.

Christine Santos gave her husband a knowing look. "This tops even the hooker."

Jerry nodded and stared out the window in disbelief as the pair took a second lap.

"It's a good thing we're moving next fall," she said.

12

A squall blew in from the Atlantic, flooding streets, clogging traffic, and downing power lines.

By the back door of the empty medical building Juliet Cammer waited for Orin, stepping outside when he pulled up in his truck.

"The lines are down. No lights. We'll have to cancel. I'm sorry. I tried to get a hold of you."

"I was fishing. No problem." He squinted against the drizzle. "As long as we're here, I passed a couple of restaurants down on the canal that had their lights on. Do you want to improvise a session down there?"

"I shouldn't. Unprofessional and all that," she said.

"What if I snap because we missed this very session? Besides, you must be cold and hungry."

"I am," she said. "Okay. But I've got to call my service and tell them where I'll be."

"The Grotto. Come on. Follow me in your car. We'll meet by chance."

It was chill and rainy along the Woodcleft Canal, and dark. The streetlights were widely spaced and feeble; the neon restaurants signs shone on the wet pavement. Above the canal loomed the shapes of masts, outriggers, antennas, and the decks of dry-docked boats cradled on stilts. Orin pulled into the parking lot of the Grotto, Juliet Cammer right behind him. Pads of melted and refrozen snow clung to the gravel like jellyfish.

They were seated in the back of the dining room in a drafty corner overlooking the canal. The wind vibrated the plate glass. Small pleasure boats, battened down for the winter, bobbed in their slips.

"Nasty out," she said.

"A winter monsoon." She shivered. "Cold?" he said.

"I'll be okay in a minute. How have you been?"

"Fine, and you?"

"I didn't mean it socially."

"Not bad," he said. "I cut down some on the booze. I think it might be helping. Still, I get those moments when it seems like the whole world is beaning out on crack and I've been assigned to take the report."

"We all get like that, Orin. Especially shrinks. Our jobs are not dissimilar."

"Only you get paid a lot of money."

The chunky waitress appeared to take their order. She smiled, revealing a gap in her teeth the shape of a convent door. They ordered drinks and two broiled bass dinners, and she left.

Juliet Cammer said, "I've noticed that a great many cops feel perse-cuted—like a minority group member might."

"I suppose many of us do. We're certainly identifiable. The wonderful management we work for has something to do with it, too. Plus the fact that we aren't permitted to work in bars, run for political office, wear our hair long, grow beards, et cetera. They get an awful lot of control over our lives."

"Does it make you feel . . . powerless?"

"Sort of. You show up a rookie, all enthusiastic, scared at first, then awed by what you see. No one tells you. You come to work in a place like the Thirteenth and it swallows you, takes you over almost completely. You are the job. Law enforcement, the judicial system. Most of it operates in an integrity vacuum. Reduces friction. They could knock down three quarters of the courtrooms in this country and replace them with one very large latrine to make deals in. Nobody would be the wiser."

"What about life outside, after work? Are you seeing anyone?"

"No. I just can't stomach one-night stands anymore."

"I didn't mean sport fucking. I meant love, affection, closeness."

"There really hasn't been anyone in that sense, except Judy. Living with a street cop is like living with a psychotic. They eat strange, they sleep strange; they're never home, they're always home. Normal women don't last with cops, and cops are crazy anyway when it comes to falling for somebody."

"What do you mean? For instance—"

Orin thought for a moment. "I was in love a long time ago with a girl. I met her at a police convention in the Catskills. God, she was gorgeous. Nineteen years old, wearing a green leotard top and sheer white slacks. She was a hooker. It killed me that she was doing it for money. She told me she liked her work when she was high. After I had been with her once, we were standing around the hospitality suite and this fat upstate-farmboy cop comes into the room, wearing a fucking baseball cap with police insignia on it, and he talks to her and she takes his hand and takes him to my room." Orin shook his head. "I let her. I don't think I've ever been so jealous. I hurt for weeks. Rented her four times in two days and all I really wanted was for her to like me, and maybe not charge me. What a fool. She got her money up front all four times. Pretty crazy."

"I don't think so. What else is bothering you? Your job told me about your former partner, at your old precinct. Tell me about that."

He shrugged. "It hurts."

"Excuse me, ma'am," said the waitress, barely able to balance the dishes she was juggling on both arms. She set the salads on the table in front of them and walked away. Orin sawed off the glowing end of his cigarette and parked it on the edge of the ashtray. The waitress had brought the wrong vegetables.

"Dumb," Juliet mumbled, then covered her mouth. "Oops."

"For shame, Doc. Show a little compassion for the wretched masses."

"Oh, dear, I know. I'm sorry." She laughed. "Okay." She made a show of recovering herself. "Back to business. Tell me," she said, "why do you think of yourself as a failure?"

"What would you call a thirty-eight-year-old alcoholic cop about to be divorced, who can't sleep right, hold down most meals, or get laid?"

"Is that what you are?"

"Yes."

"I think you need help."

"Terrific," he said, and pretended to reach for his wallet. "You want your money now?"

Juliet laughed again, tossing her head back, her wavy hair falling across her shoulders like a curtain. She liked him, his frankness anyway, and while she didn't think she'd enjoy meeting him in an alley at midnight, in a semiprofessional setting or in the office he was refreshing, attractive, in an earthy sort of way.

She said, "Listen. Seriously, to make the decisions that can change your life for the better, you're going to have to face reality, sober. Do you agree?"

"In principle."

"Okay. You feel 'sort of' powerless, somewhat guilty, and you agree about the importance of sobriety, 'in principle.' Listen, you're supposed to talk to me, sort of invite me into your world, and together we analyze what's working and what isn't, what feels good, what hurts, and together hopefully we'll learn why. Okay. No more trips around the bush. Let's talk about your emotional needs."

"I need to make love."

Juliet Cammer barely looked up from her plate. "Go on."

He cleared his throat. He said, "I hope you don't take this the wrong way. I realize this is not . . . usual. But I'm wondering about your emotional needs, too."

"I'm your therapist, Orin. We can't . . . I can't—"

"Yeah. I see."

"I'm flattered but—" She shook her head. "You're a man who wouldn't let an opportunity like this pass without giving it a try, and that's something actually attractive about you. However, there can't be any involvement if I'm to treat you. And that's my job, my professional duty. Just like yours would be to protect me from a criminal. It's what we committed ourselves to a long time ago, and we do it, no matter what. Which is something you need to stop evading and decide about—whether you are going to do your job or not do your job. My obligations don't stop at five o'clock, nor do yours." She pointed with her fork at the shoulder holster visible under his jacket. "Neither one of us is ever really off-duty."

"You're right," he said. "It's time to get on with business."

The maître 'd appeared with a phone that he plugged in at the table. "For you, Dr. Cammer."

She called someone "honey," said, "Me, too," and hung up, smiling. "Before we finish, I want to ask you to think of the worst thing that you have ever done in your life. Don't—"

"I deserted my chi—"

"Don't tell me now. Think about it during the week. Next session I want you to tell me why you did it and how it makes you feel today. Okay?"

George Clarke and Orin Boyd ran into each other on the steps of the precinct house. George stepped back to admire Orin's attire.

"Well, well—pink sunglasses, unshaven, designer jeans, black leather jacket, and probably striped underwear. How come you're all hipped-out. The bosses gonna start talkin' about you."

"I'm working with the vice dicks today. They called me at home."

"Oh, no," George said, making a face. They walked inside.

"Whatsamatter?"

"It's useless. It's just numbers, just a way to make the Man look good. You ain't gonna stop the hookers from selling, the johns from buying. Fuck it." George dismissed it all with a wave. "We kill eight any way we can around here. Just be careful. Some of the prossies have been setting up johns for stickups. The marks are easy, naked. Keep your pants on."

"Yeah," Orin said, "see you later."

George headed downstairs to the locker room; Orin went upstairs to the squad room and reported to Detective Shaw.

Shaw said, "You sure *don't* look like a cop. More like a low-life. Terrific. Look, you use your own car and just cruise the line between Belmont and Freeport. I'll be close by. If we get a live one, I'll say 'yes,' on the radio. If I say 'no,' keep rolling. Remember, we need a price and the offer to perform a sexual act. Ya gotta have both. Then throw the cuffs on her, or him. We got quite a few transvestites giving head, so watch your ass. They tape razor blades between their fingers."

Orin nodded. "Why some 'yes' and some 'no'?"

"Conservation. We sort of keep recycling them. We don't want to keep bagging the same snatch."

"When do we start?"

"When it gets dark. How about a couple of cold ones till then?"

Shaw killed a six-pack of ale in his car and didn't feel like working at all by sundown. He hated police work, he said; he liked women and weight lifting. He had three years to go on the job.

Orin had nursed two beers and was apprehensive as he finally climbed behind the wheel of his truck and rolled out in search of fluff. He kept checking the rearview mirror for Shaw's unmarked car.

They hit the Line and cruised. It was cold out but the street was full. On his third pass a thin, dark-skinned girl in a black micro skirt smiled knowingly at him. He circled the block again. The girl smiled again and put her foot on a fire hydrant. The radio said, "Yes."

He switched it off and hid it under the seat. "What's happenin', sister?"

"You and me. Mostly you."

"You partying?"

"Sure." She leaned into the truck on the passenger side.

"Coming?"

"Sure." She hopped in.

She was pleasant, had an attractive face and swollen hands. No jewelry. A scar ran across her neck like a worm.

"Go down the Line and make a left," she said. "My name is Shantel. What's yours?"

"Lloyd."

He followed her directions, acting like a rube. She told him to park next to a boarded-up turquoise cottage. He twisted sideways in his seat to face her. He said, "What are you going to do for me, honey?"

"What would you like?" she said, white teeth floating in coffee skin. Shantel was a pro and not about to name a game, or a price, to a stranger.

"How about some head?"

"Let's do some lines first."

"Sorry. Trying to quit. Listen, how much do you want for this?"

"Party with me, boy. I ain't gonna charge you. I wanna ball. I wanna get high and screw the pants off you. I don't believe the myth," she said, and laughed at her own joke.

Orin caught Shaw lighting a cigarette in the side mirror on her side. Sloppy, he thought. He wished he could call a timeout for a sideline consultation.

"You a nice-lookin' dude. Not like most of my flabby old white tricks. Let me party some. I can come with the right kinda guy."

She reached for him. He took her wrist and held it away.

"Listen, honey. I know you're working. I don't mind pay for play."

"Fuck the money, man. I'm not here on business. Can't I pop my own cookies for a change?" She put her other hand on him.

"I'm sorry about this," he said, and took her pocketbook.

"*Hey*, whatcha messin' with that for? Serious now."

He went through her pocketbook and found a cigarette pack filled with vials and joints and tossed them out the window.

"Hey!"

"I'm a cop."

"I ain't done nothin', not a goddamn thing. What did I do that you should bust me?"

"You really *didn't* do anything."

"You mean it?" she said, looking skeptical. "What is this, a joke?"

"No joke." He shook his head. "But there's a tough dude baby-sitting us. So you watch your ass tonight."

Smiling, she popped the door and slipped out. "Maybe another time, eh, homeboy," she said, and strutted away.

Orin switched on his radio again and drove on, slowly circling with Shaw in tow. He reported what had happened. Shaw scoffed: nobody down here gave nothing away. "She must have made you."

Around ten o'clock he thought he saw a familiar face and stopped. Lonnie Terrell, the slow, pretty kid he had met outside the Wilhelm Clinic, was easing some guy into a building. Orin reported that he was going off the air for ten on a break and put the transceiver back under the seat. He parked in a crosswalk, undid the nine millimeter strapped to his ankle, slipped it into his jacket pocket, and got out.

He went in the front door; the second door inside was jammed shut. The building looked decrepit, maybe abandoned. He knocked anyway. A skeletal junkie answered the door and Orin asked for Lonnie Terrell.

"Who's asking?" the cadaverous man wanted to know.

"Me, asshole."

"I'll go get her for you."

"Let me in, man."

"Sorry." The junkie closed the door.

"Me, too," he said, and kicked it open.

The junkie ran down the center hallway. Orin started after him but stopped when flickering images caught his eye, coming from a large room midway down the hall. He peeked in.

A smut movie was playing on the bare white wall across from the fireplace and five men in various stages of undress sat on couches watching and awaiting service, oblivious to the temperature. Lonnie was naked on the floor in front of one of them, going silently about her work, her toes curled into her feet against the cold. The guy sucked the glass dick of the crack pipe, using a lighter to flame the dream steam.

Orin walked casually into the room like he belonged. Hands on his knees, he leaned over into the guy's face. "Ey," he said softly, and flicked a fingernail against the glass works. The man's eyes were barely open.

Lonnie Terrell looked up, aghast.

"Who the fuck are you?" the man said. "I'm losin' the mood."

"Here," Orin said, and snapped his boot into the man's face. "Suck on that."

"Yo."

Orin spun in the direction of the voice, gun out, crouched.

"Ey, Mr. Po-lice." The Latino's handgun gleamed. "I see you got a nine. Nice. Very nice." He was smiling. "I got a sweet little Beretta. A pocket job, but it's got a kick, seein' how it's loaded with magnums. Cold, too. Ice-cold. Bought it off a brother."

"Lonnie, get dressed."

"I think we need to talk," said the Latino. "We are in trouble together. Maybe we can get out of trouble—together. You see, we maybe can't do business here anymore, after this, which fucks things up for us."

"What do you want, scumbag?"

The Latino stopped smiling. "Please, let's try to remain civil. We have a lot at stake here."

"Put your gun down and your hands on the wall."

"It ain't as easy as it looks, Mr. Po-lice. You're not playing by the rules. We got a business to protect. Employees. Payrolls."

Lonnie was dressed. Orin said, "Drop the gun or do it. Let's get it over with."

"Yeah," the Latino said, "waiting can be a bitch."

"My first shot will take your face out. Then I'm going to have you de-boned and sell you for a wetsuit. So let me hear the safety click or drop it. *Now.*"

The Latino dropped the gun.

"Against the wall, on your knees."

He complied. "You must be new."

"Hands on it."

Orin covered the five on the couch and the guy he'd made kneel facing the wall. They didn't move, except for the groaner with the missing teeth.

"You made a fuc'm mufsahe," the guy mumbled.

"Yeah," Orin said. "Why?"

"You made a fuc'm b' mufsahe."

"Hey. You want more root canal? Shut up."

"I think he's tryin' to tell you these premises are protected," said the Latino.

"Well, we enjoyed the show but we gotta run," Orin said.

Lonnie was panicky. Orin led her out, his gun trained on the room, then the hallway as they hurried out. On the street he shook from the adrenaline.

"How much do they pay you for that?" he said as he hurried her along, glancing back to see if anybody was in pursuit.

"Nothin'"

"Nothin'? What do you mean 'nothing'? Why would you do *that* for nothing?"

"They get me high."

"For God's sake!" He grabbed her shoulders and shook her. "Don't you know any better?"

She blubbered, her nose leaking like a child's. He walked her to the truck and put her in. She braced against the dashboard and began to hyperventilate.

"Stop," he said very calmly. "Right now."

Bobby Shaw appeared at the window on his side. "What gives?" he said, but sized it up for himself without being told. "If you want some advice," he said, "from a top high-school graduate, Officer Boyd, this is a tough precinct. We don't need any bleeding-heart bedwetters. First you let a full-fledged slut like Shantel walk. Then this. I don't fucking believe you."

"There's a porno crack house back there."

"Yeah. Ricky's," Shaw said. "That ain't exactly news."

"The guy in there said the place was protected."

"Yeah. By the Fourth Amendment. And whaddaya expect we can do about it, now that you kicked down their door without a warrant?" He shook his head and looked at his watch.

"You know," Orin said, "they got every kind of action you could want here, except one. No *bolito*, anywhere. Ever notice?"

"No. I'll speak to the State Gambling Authority and see if they're interested in bringing in some parlors. You're relieved, Prince. Get this pumpkin and your Cinderella bimbo outta here."

Gloria Mendosa answered the door in her pink satin robe. Her eyes were glazed and her cheeks were flushed; George knew immediately that she was drunk, but that was the risk when he popped in at two in the morning. He kissed her forehead; she wrapped her arms around his neck and smeared her rubbery lips all over his face.

George held her at arm's length and frowned. "Your breath is rude," he said. "You got a terrible case of 'zactly." He took a can of beer from her refrigerator and chugged it in self-defense.

Gloria laughed and walked unsteadily across the little living room— flipping the panty hose hanging from the extension cord away from her face—to the bottle of Champale she had been drinking. She bounced onto the couch and grinned at him playfully. "Margarita has my Anthony tonight, so I don't even mind that you are late."

"You know," he said, opening a second can of Bud. "We got to get you a bigger apartment."

"I don't want a bigger apartment. I want an engagement ring."

"Easy now," he said, stroking her wrist. "Everything comes to she who waits."

"Hey, George," she said, "I tell that story to my baby."

George wondered just how much money he needed to do it up right: to park Gloria on the boardwalk in Long Beach, feed a little luxury to Ella in dribs and drabs. He wouldn't retire when his twenty were up. He would work lots of overtime, raking in the money for their future. He could even find himself another local twist, one to fill his needs for companionship and creature comforts during the perilous hours on duty in the 13th. Promotions for everybody, he was thinking. Gloria moves up in style, some unknown chippie gets her big chance to break into the lineup, and Ella Clarke—ungrateful nag that she was—takes one more exalted step in the direction of sainthood. It was perfect, he thought. It was sexual as hell. The blood rushed south from his brain.

"I love you," he said to Gloria. "I just want to be sure about us. You know I've been hurt before."

"Now how is a little girl like me gonna hurt a strong man like you?" She stood up slowly and opened her robe, revealing to him her weaponry.

His jaw fell, as if she were the first woman he had ever seen naked. He chugged the rest of his beer without taking his eyes off her and threw the can in the direction of the trash basket. "I think I just remembered why I love you."

She hugged him around his head, grinding her bush into the stubble on his chin. He was pleased to note the lack of an offending odor, and kissed her.

"Oh, Georgie, what am I gonna do with you?"

"Everything, I hope." He stood up and placed his hands on her shoulders, towering over her while he switched the batting order. No words were necessary between them. She kissed his belly, then plucked open the buckle of his belt with her teeth, something she knew he loved. "It doesn't have to be a diamond," she said as she descended.

"I know," he said as he arose.

13

In the space of seven days Orin collared five felons, two of them armed. All but one were involved with Bubba Sims's operations.

After each arrest he returned to the street with an increased appetite. The time seemed to pass easier when he was doing actual work again, time that he had previously spent getting drunk or undrunk or just being bored. He even made a painful start at jogging to try to flush out the poisonous residues of years of hard drinking, and he felt something beginning to change, to turn again in him, almost like a wheel. Sobriety, however, was mysterious and frightening, and he knew deep down that back-sliding would be easy.

Those who cared for Orin were pleased, even admiring. Some of his superiors weren't, but then that was the main purpose of his one-man crime crusade. When his arrest record reached fifteen, Sergeant Ril summoned him to his office.

"Just what is it you're telling me?" Orin said after ten minutes of rambling intimations.

"Only that it isn't mandatory for you to make arrests that are better left for the Detective Division, due to their sensitivity."

"Whose sensitivity?"

"Look, Orin. There are forty-three thousand jail cells maintained by the State of New York, all occupied. And there are sixty-seven thousand drug busts a year. Figure it out for yourself."

"You're saying we shouldn't arrest people."

"I didn't say any such thing."

"Good. Because I wouldn't want any misunderstanding between us."

"Know this, Officer Boyd. You're a pain in the butt. It's unhealthy, unwise, and unseemly."

"Undoubtedly."

Ril turned away, the pleats of his shirt perfect. He fussed with his water carafe. "Get out," he said. "I have nothing further to discuss with you."

On his way out of the station house, Orin stopped upstairs to drop off the report of an arrest to the detectives. Against the wall on a bench, handcuffed between two black girls in the squad room, the retarded kid, Lonnie Terrell, was giving a version of her personal history to Detective Harry Foley, trail boss of the pussy posse at the 13th. Harry Foley was a tall and very handsome ladies' man who regularly rounded up new hookers as they appeared on the streets of Belmont. He felt it was his duty to lay down the law to them. He particularly hated free-lance whores and drug-crazed housewife amateurs.

Lonnie didn't see Orin standing in the doorway as she rattled off her life story while the girls on both sides of her slept curled up on the hard wooden bench. She spoke haltingly of a family in Flushing, her hopes for a future in cosmetology. She told Detective Foley of her confusion on the unfamiliar streets; she explained that she had merely been asking directions of the men she had hailed on Broadway. It was very upsetting to her that he thought something else.

Foley switched on a tape recorder and played back what Lonnie Terrell called "asking for directions." She listened to herself coyly offer to give an undercover cop a hand job for fifteen dollars.

"How many other times have you been lost on 'unfamiliar streets'?"

"Never. Please," she said. "I needed the money for bus fare home."

"Give me a break."

"I'm stupid," she said. "Handicapped."

"I don't know," Foley said, shaking his head at Orin and rolling his eyes. "It says here you've been lost in Freeport, and once in Hempstead, and once in Long Beach."

Lonnie Terrell started to cry.

Orin cleared his throat. Lonnie and Harry Foley turned to look at him, then Lonnie tried to press her face against her chest.

"Would you mind taking her cuffs off?" Orin asked Foley. "She's kind of a personal friend of mine."

"Yeah? Go ahead. I didn't know anybody knew her. I never saw her before tonight."

"Thanks." Orin pulled his cuff key from his gunbelt and disconnected Lonnie from her sisters in crime. She buried her face in her hands and began sobbing, leaning the top of her head on Orin's gut. "Okay, knock it off," he said. "The worst is over."

"He's gonna put me in jail tonight, Orin. I d-don't have a hundred dollars cash money for bail."

"So we call someone. What's the big deal?"

"She's ashamed to call her parents," said Foley. "I gave her all the options."

"That's crazy," said Orin. "Have you ever spent a night in jail?"

Lonnie sighed. "Yes."

Orin picked up Lonnie Terrell's PDCN Form #81 from the pile of papers on Foley's desk and grabbed a phone on the adjacent desktop.

Foley got out of his chair and tried to wake up bachelorette number two.

"They're probably not home," Lonnie said.

"Let's just give them a try," said Orin. "I'll do all the talking."

At the second ring a computer answered and broke the news to Orin that the number he had dialed had been changed, the new number was unpublished at the request of the subscriber. The computer thanked him for calling New York Telephone.

"Yes," he said to the computer. "My name is Officer Boyd, from the Nassau County Police. It seems your daughter Lonnie is involved in a rather humorous situation and needs you to come get her from the Thirteenth Precinct station house. Excuse me? I'm sorry . . . No, she didn't . . . Not at all . . . I'd be glad to loan Lonnie the money. Yes, sir, I completely understand . . . You're welcome. I hope that leg of yours heals okay."

Lonnie stared at Orin with her mouth open while he said good night and hung up the phone.

"How much is that bail?" Orin asked Foley, who was shaking the other hooker's shoulder.

Foley grinned at Orin, then at Lonnie, then at Orin. "For you? Make it twenty-five bucks."

"Thanks, Harry. I owe you one."

After Lonnie was fingerprinted and photographed, Orin bailed her out at the desk and walked her to the front door of the station house. "Where you going now?" he asked her.

"Home."

"Where's home? I mean, as long as we both know that Flushing is a fantasy. What about your father being some kind of cop? Was that bullshit, too?"

"I wouldn't lie about my father."

"So where do you live?"

"I got a place."

He nodded at her while he held open the door. She was an illiterate, poorly dressed girl, a failure even at hooking.

"You're all fucked up," he said. "I think you need some kind of help, like from Social Services maybe."

"Don't worry," she said. "You'll get your money back."

"I don't care about the money. I didn't want to see you go to jail, or get hurt on the streets."

Lonnie sniffled and wiped her nose with the sleeve of her windbreaker. "Why?" she said. "You got something you want me to do for you tonight?"

"What makes you say that?"

"The way the detective—"

Orin took hold of her upper arm and steered her outside to the stoop. The heavy door closed behind them, and Orin listened for a moment to the sounds of ghetto life: the boom of amplified drums, the screech of tires, laughter, shouting.

"Hey, Lonnie, I'd rather you were a bag lady than a whore. You understand?"

"I don't want to be either." Her eyes filled with tears. "What kind of help are you talking about?"

Orin brought Lonnie back inside and made the necessary phone calls to place her in a halfway house. An agent of the Social Services Department agreed to meet her in the morning.

"Come on," said Orin. "I'll buy you coffee."

Lonnie beamed. Together they walked to his truck.

Maybe the diner was a mistake. He could feel not only her desperation, but also the stares of other women in the diner—one of them a waitress whose heart he had wounded only yesterday when he just said no. Her name was Rita, and she was very interested in what he was doing. For a moment the chink and rattle of porcelain ceased.

To make matters worse, Lonnie pulled off her jacket, revealing a sheer blouse and breasts like footballs. Orin's face became a mask as he looked around the dining room; the uneasy patrons and overstuffed waitresses went back about their business, unusually subdued. Orin had a street cop's knack for that: a way of chilling what he turned his gaze upon. "Sit down," he said to Lonnie.

Rita, in her tight pistachio uniform, appeared at the table, pad in her hand, smirking. Orin ordered a cheeseburger and a chocolate shake for Lonnie. As he was feeding fifty cents into the Seeburg Consolette, Rita set the food in front of them without a word. Lonnie filled her mouth with four quick bites before swallowing once. Ketchup dribbled down her chin and between her fingers. Then, starvation averted, she told him a new version of the story of her life—that she lived in Queens, in a group home. In two more years she would be a qualified and duly licensed beautician.

Her mother and father were dead, killed in a car crash, but she said she had many friends. Just two months ago she had had her third abortion.

And Orin sometimes thought that he was alone in the world.

He invited her fishing with him that night, and after she finished her snack, he drove her out to the Swift's Creek Bridge. They sat under the parkway, in a pocket out of the wind, and she told him about life without mail. No letters, no money, no family. Watching *Family Ties* and wishing she could be one of the kids. She said she really didn't mind, and Orin nodded.

He dropped her at a subway station in Far Rockaway at midnight, and headed for home, or a reasonable facsimile thereof.

14

Orin parked under the elevated tracks at Main and Broadway. The Reverend Bubba Sims's main numbers writer—all 350 black pounds of Champagne Danny Bugs—was working the opposite corner like he was running for mayor, smiling and shaking hands with all the factory workers walking home. Orin could distinctly hear his rap when the traffic stopped on Main for the light.

"You got it, bro. Can't win if you don' play/Got to try your luck, every day./Hit the mark with Danny Boy/Flip on out and buy a brand-new toy."

Orin closed his eyes, feeling vaguely pissed off. A full-time crook ought to have the sense to walk a block away. These guys were blatant about their business. Orin considered taking up a position farther down the Strip, but of course each block had its barker. Besides, he needed to get in their faces some more. Champagne Danny glanced over at Orin. Orin's expression said: wise up, dummy. Danny just laughed, as if the cops were just there to protect his receipts, as if Champagne Danny was just another shopkeeper.

Orin considered waiting until later in the evening and making some overtime out of the grab, even though the money earned would be a thimble of water to the desert of his debt.

"Hell," he said to himself, and got out of the car. "Hey," he called, "Danny, come here."

Champagne Danny waved to him. "Busy now, Officer. I'll take care of you later." A pair of factory workers approached Danny. He shook his head. "When the heat goes away, then everyone can play."

Orin waited for a break in the Main Street traffic, then jogged across the street to Danny. "Hands on the wall, Fatso. You know the drill." Orin grabbed for Danny's coat, but the big man spun away with surprising quickness.

Danny started moonwalking backward. "Yo, cop. Get a grip, my man. You makin' a practical er-ror."

Orin continued to stalk the numbers writer. "Don't bust my stones, Danny. Let me see those wrists."

Danny stuffed his hands in his coat pockets and took another step backward. "Be cool, brother. Walk away."

Orin reached for Danny's arm again.

Danny swung a foot at Orin's crotch and missed.

"That's it," said Orin. "Let's get it on."

They faced off against each other, all semblance of civility discarded.

Someone nearby yelled, "Yo! The cop's fighting Danny," and from out of nowhere gathered raucous spectators, enclosing the combatants in a movable ring. From their third-floor rooms, pensioners leaned forward like gargoyles. A coffee truck parked on the opposite corner and honked its horn.

"Last chance," said Orin, "before your face lands on the sidewalk."

Danny wheeled and ran, to protect the action he kept hidden inside the extra pocket in his baggy trousers, to protect his absolutely spotless criminal record, and his reputation on the streets as a man of agility.

Orin caught him within five steps and shoved him roughly to the sidewalk. He stood over Danny while the crowd re-formed around them.

"Stay down," said Orin. "I don't want to hurt you."

"Why don't you go fuck yo'self."

Orin wished he had not left his nightstick and portable radio in the police car. They would have been valuable tools. Danny grunted and lunged at Orin's ankles. Orin sidestepped the attack and jumped on

Danny's back. He wrapped his hands around Champagne Danny's throat and tried to close off his windpipe, but Danny's neck was too thick and slippery. Orin rolled free and got on his feet, and the two of them squared off again.

"Somebody call the cops," Orin said to the crowd as he and Danny circled each other.

"Shit," said one of the onlookers. "Somebody call Bubba, too."

Both men were breathing heavily, Danny more so. Orin dropped into a crouch, searching for the opening for a takedown.

Danny said, panting, "Let's us jist drop . . . all this nonsense and . . . git back to bidness."

"Fine . . . You just walk over to the police car . . . and climb into the back . . . and everything . . . will be just fine."

"Yo, I means . . . fuggit about the whole affair."

"Forget about this." Orin exploded out of his crouch and drove his shoulder into Danny's mammoth belly, knocking the big man into the gutter between two parked cars and diving on top. They rolled wildly around in the confined space between bumpers until Orin whipped his black leather slapjack out and brought it down hard across the bridge of Danny's nose.

Blood bubbled up from a wicked gash, and his grip on Orin's other arm went slack. The cuffs were on in seconds.

After Orin caught his breath, he dragged the dazed and handcuffed man across the street to his police car while one of the spectators held up traffic. Orin wrapped Danny's head and face in enough gauze for a turban and drove his blind and bleeding prisoner away to the station house.

Sergeant Reagan was waiting for him just inside the door. The man did not look happy. "The inspector is very disappointed with you," said Reagan. "Did you have to open his fucking dome?"

"Why?" said Orin. "What difference does it make?"

"The fucking switchboard's lit up with brutality complaints, you moron. We're lucky the brothers ain't storming the fucking station house because of you."

"Yeah!" said Champagne Danny. He looked comical with his head wrapped in bandages, his hands behind his back. "I wants to make a complaint my ownself. We was having ourselves a fair fight until this officer here went high tech."

"Ah, Sarge, this baboon assaulted me. He had in his possession gambling records and seven hundred dollars in ones and fives. What did you want me to do? Give him a warning?"

Sergeant Reagan looked at Donnelly, who had appeared in the foyer. Donnelly narrowed his eyebrows and nodded.

"We wanted you to handle the situation professionally," said the sergeant. "Perhaps even exercise discretion."

"It was all a big mistake," said Champagne Danny. "One I'm willing to forget about, if someone would *please* unwrap my goddamn face. I was beautiful when I left the crib this morning. Now my face is all fucked up and my blinds is folded."

Reagan looked at Champagne Danny, then Donnelly, and then he shrugged with resignation. "Take him upstairs, Boyd. We'll put the fires out down here."

"Stop," said Orin. "You're making me cry. People forget, don't they? It's a jungle in here, too."

"Bobby Shaw can process the paperwork. Possession of gambling records and resisting arrest. He can walk for a hundred bucks."

"*Thank* you, Sergeant. Inspector. Come along, Chubby Butt."

A short while later Champagne Danny sat facing Bobby Shaw's desk, comfortably uncuffed, with a butterfly stitch on his nose. For the twenty-five minutes it took one of Bubba's other runners to arrive with a clean one hundred dollars, Detective Shaw typed an arrest card, a court information form, and lit Danny's cigarettes. Then Danny said good-bye to Orin and everybody else upstairs as if he had been a guest in their home. He thanked them for their courtesy; he apologized to Orin for the fight.

A plastic evidence bag filled with policy slips and cash was inventoried, tagged, and secured in the property locker. Orin signed the vouchers. Shaw signed over the tape.

After Shaw left, Orin returned to the shady side of town. He cruised the Strip until he found Abraham Wilson lounging on a milk crate with a bottle of red wine in an alley beneath the kitchen exhaust of the Player's Bar and Grill. Batman looked actually happy.

Orin called him over to the truck and told him about busting Champagne Danny and confiscating his gambling records; he explained that tomorrow Danny would have no way in hell of knowing who bet what, that anyone with the balls to run a bluff could collect on the daily number. Abraham Wilson just beamed.

Captain Blogg and Sergeant Ril, decked out in their best civilian suits, stood shivering by the front door of the station house, greeting the rank-and-file members as they arrived for the Kick-off Dinner. Dom Ril took attendance on a clipboard and handed each of the guests a peel-and-stick name tag. George Clarke, Orin Boyd, Dan Korengold, and Paul Kellog arrived late, direct from a warm-up session at Red's. They were under-dressed, in the manner of construction workers, loud, and unruly.

George Clarke took offense at having a name tag slapped on his chest: "Everybody here knows everybody else. What the hell we need name tags for?"

Sergeant Ril steered him aside. "Shut up, willya. Let him have his fucking fun."

"This is fun?"

"For Blogg this is eight days and twelve nights in Vegas."

"Good point," said George.

"He got it all from a textbook he read, something about helping us to accept who we are."

"I don't know how you do it, Sarge," said George.

"What's worse," said Orin, leaning into the conversation, "we don't know why you do it. Talk about hitching your wagon to one lame jackass."

Ril linked arms with them and led them inside. "I do it for slugs like you," he said, heading down the stairs to the muster room. "I do it because if I didn't, the lunatics would drag this precinct down the drain. You guys don't know the shit him and Donnelly come up with from minute to minute, every single day. It's scary."

"You're quite a guy," said Orin, messing up Ril's carefully styled hair.

"Quite a guy," said George, pulling Ril's red silk tie closed around his throat.

"*Come on*, you bastards!" he wailed, and struggled to free himself. "Don't fuck around."

Orin and George roughhoused Dominick Ril even as they dusted him off, loudly apologizing all the while.

"Jesus Christ," said Ril. He loosened his tie enough to allow air down his throat. "You fucking guys are off the wall."

"And don't you forget it," said George as Orin opened the door on the party. "We're a couple of wacky motherfuckers."

Ril ran back upstairs while George and Orin mingled with their fellow employees. Orin drank a can of Budweiser he had hidden in the pocket of his parka; George was sipping peppermint schnapps from a back-pocket flask. They stood next to the makeshift dais, plucking pieces of bologna and cheese from one of the six-foot heros and stuffing them into their mouths.

Orin watched a pale hand pour white powder into the blood red punch. Orin followed the hand to a shoulder, and up to an earring. Weird Arthur Leach grinned at him and winked. "Dexadrine," he said. "I figure, what the fuck."

Sergeant Ril opened the door and cried out, "Attention!"

A few of the guests raised their eyebrows. Someone noticed that the cable television was tuned to the skin channel and switched it off.

Archibald Blogg entered with his arm around Police Chaplain Monsignor Martin O'Rourke, an aging priest wearing a clerical collar and a wide grin.

"Gentlemen," said Blogg. "Please—take your seats. We'll be eating and drinking and making merry in a very short while."

While the cops jostled one another for chairs, Archibald Blogg took his place on the dais. Seated next to him, on either side, were most of the ranking officers of the precinct. Except James Donnelly.

"Thank you all for coming this evening," said Blogg. "We'll begin the program with a couple of words from the good monsignor." He sighed as he sat down, then took a deep breath, reacting visibly to the dentist's office smell emanating from the punch.

O'Rourke waved to the men and thanked them for having him. He said right up front that he had never had more fun, or felt a closer kinship, than the times he had spent among street cops.

"Gentlemen, I've known plenty of cops in my day. You've always been my heroes. But it wasn't until I started working with cops that I found out just how tough and lonely this job can be . . . how easy it is to get lost, to grow cold and hard, to give up. What I'm saying to you, boys, is that a stumble now and then is nothing to be ashamed of, and that I pray for each and every one of you, each and every night. I want you guys to know that if you've got a problem with anything, from syphilis to hemorrhoids, alcohol to zero motivation, I'm only a phone call away. And I don't break balls. Thank you, guys. God bless you."

The monsignor sat down to enthusiastic applause.

Captain Blogg moved from behind the dais to a table against the back wall where Sergeant Ril had assembled a stereo record player. Blogg took needle in hand and waited for silence before striking up the band.

"We Are the Champions," sang the rock band Queen while the men smoked and chatted among themselves. A dice game broke out in the corner. More than a few wondered what was going on. Weird Arthur lip-synched the lyrics.

When the song was over and Blogg was taking off the record, Orin punched George in the thigh. "That's it," he said. "That's my bullshit limit. I'm outta here like a brand-new suit."

"Let's hang for a while," said George. "I want me a dose of that punch."

"You want some of that punch? I'll get you some of that punch." Orin stood up. "Hey!" he yelled. "My partner wants some of that punch."

"Orin, please," said Captain Blogg. "Our best foot forward, now. We have company."

"Dreadfully sorry. It's just that me and some of the boys are parched."

"I'm sure you can wait a few more minutes," said Blogg. "We still have a slide show and then the presentation of awards. Please?"

"Fine." Orin sat down and lit a cigarette.

As Dominick Ril helped Blogg pack up the stereo, he went on record as having warned Blogg about George and Orin, and the trouble he foresaw when they walked in the door. Blogg told him that no one liked to hear the words, "I told you so." Especially superior officers.

"Right, sir." Ril turned the overhead lights out, leaving everyone in the dark. Then a square of white projector light appeared on the wall behind the dais. Silhouettes filled the square (a rabbit, a sea gull, someone's middle digit) then the black words **POLICE OFFICERS**, and, one by one, the official ID photographs of everyone in the precinct—those posed pictures the newspapers ran whenever somebody was shot. These were met by a stony silence, except for one falsetto voice that said, "I'd like to eat that six-foot hero."

The photographs of their superior officers paraded across the wall. The men showed their appreciation by making comments in disguised voices: "Scrote." "Wimp."

Archibald Blogg surmised that something had gone wrong. "That's enough, Dom," he said.

"Just two more, sir," Ril called from the back of the room as he slid the first of these into view. It was a slide of himself, sitting at his desk with his collar open, looking casual and generous, just one of the guys.

"Mini-geek!"

"Blow job!"

"I said that's enough, Sergeant!"

"Last one," said Ril, the underside of his face ghoulish in the projector light, the smile loony.

"Get the light, Officer Moses," said Blogg.

"Get the light your own damn self. We on my fucking time."

The men began to chant: "*Last one, last one, last one* . . ."

Blogg stood up and waved his hands through the shaft of light, to no avail; the picture poured through onto the wall, a picture of the captain himself, in full dress uniform, saluting an American flag.

"Geek!" yelled some of the men. "Geek."

"Stop that!" cried Blogg. "Stop that this very *instant!*"

A gunshot rang out.

The honored guests and their hosts dove out of their chairs onto the floor.

"*Sniper!*" Blogg screamed from his place of cover under the dais. "Nobody move."

Nobody moved.

Orin's face pressed against the cool linoleum floor, and he was reminded of nap time in elementary school. The air in the muster room filled with the smell of gunsmoke. Seconds passed uncomfortably. Somebody cut a fart that sounded like an eighteen-wheeler's air brakes. Cops giggled. Someone said, "Goose me one more time, Mikey, and I'll blow your fucking head off."

"Hold your fire!" Blogg screamed. "Everyone. This is a combat situation. You are all required to follow my commands."

The door flew open and the desk officer from upstairs turned on the lights. Bodies littered the floor like a bomb had gone off.

"What the fuck are you assholes doing?" Lieutenant Tripp shouted. "I got reporters upstairs and you guys are holding target practice down here?"

"Is anybody hit?" Blogg yelled from his place of concealment.

"That's a negative, Captain," said Dominick Ril, lifting the paper table cloth from in front of Blogg's face.

Monsignor O'Rourke sat up in his chair, wiping his brow with a napkin. "Mother of God," he said to no one in particular, "Does this happen often?"

Sergeant Ril yelled, "Oh, my Lord." He walked to the wall where Blogg's faint image could still be seen. A bullet had gouged a large chunk of plaster out of the ear.

Blogg's face grew pale; he put his hand to the side of his head as if to check for blood. Ril drew his gun from his customized shoulder holster and jumped up on the dais to announce that the muster room was now a crime scene. No one was to leave. Everyone would be required to give a statement. "And I want your guns, too, you fucking dipshits."

"Well," Orin said to Captain Blogg. "My morale is certainly sky-high. Thank you very much for the wonderful time." Orin elbowed George in the ribs. "What do you say we grab that punch and hit the highway?"

"Do it," said George. "I'm right behind you."

For it was George who held the smoking gun in his pocket, Orin knew. Orin stepped up to the dais and hoisted the punchbowl over his head and carried it out to the hallway like the Stanley Cup, right past Sergeant Ril, who was yelling for everyone to strip naked, and Archibald Blogg, who was saying that skin searches really weren't necessary.

The men followed him like some kind of victorious team. They watched in amazement as Orin stopped and raised the bowl to his lips. George got everybody chanting *"Boyd-brain, Boyd-brain,"* and then worked his way to the edge of the crowd and up the back staircase to the exit.

"Hey!" Weird Arthur said to Boyd. "That's dexi-punch, you moron. One little drink should be plenty. Trust me."

Orin smacked his lips and handed the bowl to Paul Kellog. "Tequila!" he cried. "Loose women, rum for my men. Tonight we ride."

The rest of the gang passed the punchbowl around and followed Orin up the stairs and out the door, an armed mob.

Captain Blogg and Sergeant Ril stood on the front porch in their wake, watching them pile into their private cars.

"We've lost them," said Blogg.

"We never had them," said Ril. "Nobody's ever had those guys."

Blogg put his arm around Ril's shoulders. "They're good men, you know."

Loud sports cars, Harleys, and pickup trucks ripped through the municipal parking lot, making further conversation impossible. Ril shrugged the captain's arm off and lit a cigarette. When the last of the rebel yells died away, he threw his cigarette down and eyed Archibald Blogg. "Captain, you say the dumbest things sometimes."

15

When Orin reported for duty, the locker-room gossip was that something was up. There had been yelling and screaming in the precinct commander's office. At roll call Inspector James Donnelly joined Lieutenant Fazio behind the desk, so the men gave their deportment more thought than usual.

Heads were gonna roll. Donnelly was given to quietly glowering at his men as they passed his office, not face-to-face confrontations with an entire tour. Most of the time he was either out of the building or locked in his office, with Dominick Ril coming and going like a waitress. Now as he stood before the assembled officers, Inspector Donnelly was staring at Orin's aorta. He told Lieutenant Fazio that he needed "just one fucking minute with the men." His face was flushed, his voice trembling.

"Listen up, guys. The inspector has something he—"

"I've had it with you, Boyd! You and anybody else here who thinks you're funny." He leaned out over the desk in a push-up position, his collar open, his tie tossed back over the broad, star-studded shoulder of his uniform. "You're a loser, Boyd. A fucking punk."

"What are you talking about, sir?"

"Where would you like me to start?" Donnelly replied. "Last night's little pep rally shooting?"

"Just how much of the awful truth do you know?"

Lieutenant Fazio said, "Knock it off, Orin."

Donnelly straightened. In a hoarse whisper he said, "I'll be waiting for you, Boyd," then he turned and walked back to his office, his regulation wing tips squeaking in the dead silence.

George glanced at Orin, who gave a non-committal shrug.

Orin returned to Broadway, where Champagne Danny was again working the blue-collar street trade, yesterday's bust just so much overhead. But when Danny saw Orin this time he stopped his sales rap and moved along down the block, finally ducking into a unisex barbershop that was guarded by a sleeping German shepherd.

Dog or no dog, Orin would have followed Danny, if only to gloat, but a radio assignment to a street fight on Sunrise Highway interrupted. He cursed loudly as he turned the police car around and roared off to the battle at Sunrise and Main.

He was disappointed to see it was over when he got there, already reduced to a couple of bleeding winos screaming curses at each other from the back seats of different police cars. Orin was told by Sergeant Leroy Bourbone that his services weren't needed.

"Who did who?" Orin asked. "They both look like they've been through a blender."

Bourbone flashed Orin the satisfied smile of a man holding privileged information. "Persons unknown did 'em both," he said. "We're still trying to figure out why. Something about some bullshit scam they tried to pull that didn't work. Thieves falling out, and whatnot. Frankly, I don't give a fuck."

A rookie cop, whom Orin had not yet met, saluted Sergeant Bourbone. He was very short and very wide in the beam. His uniform was crisp and new, his leather goods shiny.

"I think we should get them to a hospital, sir. They're both pretty badly cut up."

Bourbone said he had seen worse. "Relax, kid. They're okay."

"But—"

"I said relax. If I've learned anything in twenty years out here, it's that shit lives."

"What'd they say happened?" Orin asked the rookie.

"I really don't know. They were talking mostly gibberish."

Orin rolled his eyes and pegged Dugan for a dork. "What do you think they said, kid? Just repeat it, word for word."

Dugan shrugged. "Something about some dude named Batman drinking champagne and selling a guy tickets. Weird, right? Why do you think they talk that way?"

"To jerk off honky cops like you."

Orin returned to his police car. He called in, put himself back in service, and drove directly to the woods at the edge of the viaduct under the Meadowbrook Parkway. He parked the car on the grass and pushed through the wall of underbrush next to the overpass.

Batman was hiding out there, sleeping on a bed of pine needles and pizza boxes, using his Bible for a pillow. Orin bent over and shook him awake. "Yo," he said. "Rise and shine."

Abraham sat up slowly and rubbed his face. "Oh," he said. "It's you . . . I hope you didn't bring me no more good ideas."

"What happened?"

Abraham coughed and held his hand out. Orin filled it with a cigarette. The matches in Abe's pocket were soggy from sleeping in the woods; Orin lit the cigarette with his Zippo.

"Somehow Bubba got the action back for them. I don't know how. See, I knew Tommy Joe and Rocky had played with Danny yesterday, and I hadn't, so I said what you told me. They got their butts kicked by Champagne Danny and Sherman Clayborne when they tried to collect at the barbershop this morning. Now I hear everybody in town is looking for me."

Orin frowned, his mind climbing the chain of evidence to what had to be the broken link. "How many people know about this spot."

"Counting you, too damn many. I'm moving back to Brooklyn this afternoon, soon as Charlene's son shows up with a truck from his job."

"I feel terrible about this, Abe. I'm really embarrassed."

"That's okay."

"You want to stay at my place for a couple of days?"

Batman sniffed. "You're okay, Orin."

"Hey," said Orin. "I'm the one who got you into this."

Batman pulled a bottle from inside his shirt and took a slug on his pint of Night Train. "Mama always told me that you couldn't cheat an honest man."

"Yeah," Orin said, nodding. "My mother used to lie to me, too."

"Forget it," Abraham said, and painfully changed his position. "It's a damn crooked world. I been watchin' the same things go down since I was a kid. All of them motherfuckers gettin' rich. If they think you can hurt them, then they break you, like they done to me."

"You got a past, don't you, Abraham?"

"Much worse than that, Orin. Much worse than that. I'm just sorry Bubba Sims got to beat me one mo' time."

"I won't forget that," Orin said. "That's a promise."

"Wish I could." Batman winced as he changed position. "You best be careful, too. Some cops are hard people. They'll kill you soon as look at you . . . like they did Ossie."

"Who are you talking about?"

"Ossie King. He got hisself killed by the cops on the night of August 19, 1984."

"How do you know?" Orin pushed back the brim of his cap.

Batman was rubbing his arm. "We was playing dice in a vacant apartment behind the liquor store, smoking reefer and drinking Mad Dog. It was Ossie's regular game. Me, Tommy Hatcher, Leroy Atkins, Ossie. We was loud but we wasn't actually bothering nobody, I guess, until around ten o'clock. Then Ossie got all pissed off. The dice was draining out Ossie's money like it knowed he was due for bad luck. Trouble was, the game was in Bubba Sims's territory. That, and the noise I guess, brought cops. Ossie lipped off to them, sayin', 'Whatcha think we are, slaves?' The cops called another cop. Three of 'em. We turned off the light and shut up, but they kicked in the door on us and smacked Ossie a couple of times in the mouth with their sticks, then they threw Tommy on the wall and took his money. Leroy just upped and gave them his. Tommy and Leroy booked; the cops let 'em go. They put Ossie in handcuffs and leg irons and dragged him out by his feet. They never said what they were gonna do with him, just drove away, with Ossie all trussed up like a calf." Batman sighed. "You gotta cigarette I could hold?"

Orin tapped out another cigarette and lit it for Abraham Wilson. He didn't push, he didn't say anything.

"I waited about an hour for the cops to type him up, then I walked over the precinct to see about getting Ossie out. The man in charge of the desk told me they didn't have no one named Ossie King in the lockup. I asked if maybe they took him to the hospital. He checked the blotter and said no. So I went to Ossie's room on Centennial Avenue. The door was locked and covered with blood, like they'd tried to dump him there maybe and couldn't get in. I didn't see Ossie anymore that night or the next day. The blood on his door was all cleaned up. They found his body near a canal the day after that. He'd been beaten bad. I was so scared. That's when I went into the woods and built myself this little place where no one could find me. I spent a week here. Finally got up nerve to sniff around town. Went for some food and saw in the newspaper that the cops was in trouble for leaving an intoxicated man to die. The cops swore he had been tipsy but fine when they let him go, that they didn't know who beat on him, said he was fine when they drove away. Two or three months went by and just about everybody forgot about Ossie, almost even me. Then the reverend shows up, tells me to get in his car. He told me he'd protect me and see that nothing bad happened to me, that there was ways to handle the po-lice. The cops were in a jam but they had money, Bubba said, and sooner or later they'd get away with it anyway, and Ossie would still be dead. Wouldn't nothin' change that. This was a way to say they was sorry for what they done." Batman snickered. "I can still hear me asking how much. Bubba said ten thousand dollars, cash money, just to come in and say that I seen Ossie in the woods the day after the doctor said he'd died. Five thousand before, five more after. I could share the money with Ossie's family down in Charlotte if it would make the whole thing easier. God forgive me, I took the money. They gave me the first half and pretended like there was no more. I traded my own self respect for some chump change."

"Who were the cops, Batman?"

"Bobby Shaw, Ril and Jimmy Donnelly."

The lights were on in the kitchen window of the ranch-style home off Dogwood Avenue. Sergeant Daniels's unmarked Plymouth was parked in the driveway; the side door of the garage stood open and someone was hunched over a workbench. It was Daniels, wearing designer jeans and a pale blue sweater. He was painting a dollhouse.

"Sarge."

Daniels spun around, half scared to death, squinting to make out the figure in the shadows of the driveway.

"It's me, Orin Boyd."

"Step into the light."

Orin stepped into the doorway, holding his hands above his head like a prisoner of war. Daniels exhaled and told him to relax.

"Sorry," Orin said. "I couldn't talk to you at the shop."

"Yeah," Daniels said. "The guys are worse than women." He put aside the paintbrush and wiped a drip from his hand with a rag. "So how's it coming?"

"Well, I'm pissing a lot of people off."

"So I hear. What the situation in the One-Three?"

"It's been sold out. The Reverend Sims seems to be the mortgage holder."

The sergeant swept sawdust from a picnic bench and offered Orin a seat. "More than one rat?"

"Definitely. Shaw, Ril, Donnelly."

Daniels made a face. "Messy."

"What messy?"

"It means a lot of fall out, a lot of press. Commissioner Trimble is very conscious of media."

"What is he, running for office?"

"I'm just telling you," Daniels said, "the guy gets jumpy about newsprint."

"He's jumpy? I'm tweaking the snout of this thing and *he's* jumpy. Hey, this ain't about guys loading up at a store burglary scene, or copping a free blowdini. I'm talking protection of organized crime. Bubba Sims runs everything that moves in this precinct, and you know he's got to be supplied by even a bigger operation. As in mainline Mob. So tell the commissioner to chill out, or get me the hell out of here because it's gonna get worse before it gets better, and I gotta know there's somebody holding my ankles if I'm going to try sticking my head in this thing's mouth."

"I hear you," Daniels said. "By the way, you should know that Doctor Justice turned up."

"Yeah?"

"Yeah. Sheriff's office in Oneonta, New York, reported a body in the local reservoir."

"Suicide?" Orin said sarcastically.

"Yeah, really."

"At least they clean up after themselves," Orin said.

Part of his next seventy-two hours off Orin spent moving through the precinct like the shadow of a cloud. He watched crack dealers in BMWs, pot dealers on bicycles with beepers, numbers runners, loansharks, hookers with cellular phones—a small portion of the vast and profitable network of enterprise operated under the very nose of Precinct Commander James Donnelly.

Orin followed a white man home to Levittown, he followed a black man home to Roosevelt. Sherman Clayborne entered The Night Moves bar with a white girl on his arm at three A.M. Attractive female members of Bubba Sims's organization came and went from Bubba Sims's devotional hall like they were working a rugby tournament.

For the most part Orin kept to the alleys and rooftops, dodging cops and crooks alike, watching the energy, the action flowing across the checkerboard ghetto. Patterns began to emerge that made sense, patterns he committed to memory. He pissed behind dumpsters; his bowels never budged. He did not eat or sleep for fear he would miss something valuable.

Physically and emotionally exhausted, he sat on the top step of a rusty fire escape in an alley behind West Merrick Road as the sun set on the second day of his labors. His mind pored over details, possibilities, probabilities. He lit a cigarette, holding it cupped in the palm of his hand. The ocean breeze was chilly but restful. His eyes closed for a moment, his head bobbing forward, then snapping back. He knew he should sleep, that a plan would present itself to him if he slept.

He checked his watch. It was almost seven P.M. If he could force himself to stay awake, he could recheck the patterns he had come to observe. In a few hours maybe he could eat a meal and sleep for a short while in a soft bed on clean sheets. Or maybe not.

The sound of a sledgehammer thudding into brick jolted him upright. His skin was chilled, covered with a salty dew. Orin drew his nine millimeter from his belt and began a catlike descent from his perch.

The sledgehammering continued somewhere below him and off to his left. He heard a furtive voice grunting something in Spanish. He dropped from the ladder to the alley. The soles of his sneakers crunched shards of broken glass.

The grunting continued, to Orin's amazement. It was coming from the three-bay loading dock at the end of the unlit alley. Orin hugged the rear concrete wall of Tom's Discount Warehouse and worked his way closer. The grunting stopped. Orin froze.

For a moment silence so enveloped the alley that Orin wondered if he had been dreaming. Then a little man wiggled out of a dark hole in the white concrete wall, like a worm. Orin watched the solitary figure stand up on the platform, face the wall, and start tugging for all he was worth on what looked like the arm of an accomplice. Orin leapt onto the platform and put the barrel of his gun against the back of the little man's head. "Don't move a muscle, *amigo. Policia,* can you dig it?"

The man let go of the bass fiddle he had been trying to steal; the neck of the fiddle snapped to discordant attention like a hard-on. Orin looked along the neck of the fiddle into the hole, then down at the little man shivering by his side.

"You incompetent fucking asshole," he said. "You oughta be ashamed of yourself. You didn't make the hole big enough."

The startled burglar said nothing, just stared at Orin wide-eyed with wonder and regret. He looked to be about thirty years old, a Dominican probably, with long black hair that the fog had slicked to his skull. His pants were torn at both knees, his T-shirt was filthy.

"What the hell were you gonna do with a fiddle?"

"No *habla Inglés.*"

"Don't hand me that shit."

"*Por favor?*"

"I bang your wife on weekends."

The man's dark eyes never wavered.

"Okay, so you don't speak English. Now what the fuck am I gonna do with you?"

There was a call box half a block away. Orin could easily drag his burglar there by the ear and turn him over to one of the guys. That cop could lie that he had caught the thief red-handed. Who would ever believe the burglar's story that a superhero had appeared from the sky to capture him, and then disappeared again into the foggy ghetto night. But none of this was worth exposure.

The burglar clasped his hands in prayer. *"Señor, por favor . . ."*

Orin put his gun in his waistband and grabbed the man by his shoulders, standing him up and twisting him around to face him. Orin bent over and looked angrily into his eyes. "You no doey this again?"

"Sí . . . sí."

"And always make the hole big enough?"

"Sí."

"America, nice country?"

"Sí. Sí. Bery nice."

"Okay, *mi amigo*, no harm, no foul. You best *vamoose* the fuck on out of here before I change my mind-o."

The burglar knew right away what *vamoose* meant. He backed away from Orin to the edge of the platform, slowly, as if haste would spoil his good fortune. Then he dropped to the ground and ran helter-skelter to the nearest hole in the stockade fence.

Orin slid the neck of the fiddle back inside the building, and walked out of the alley, his hands in his pockets.

Orin had found James Donnelly's home address on an old precinct personnel roster, and drove up to Old Brookville after dark several nights running. A light rain dotted his windshield the third evening, making a paste of the dirt on the wiper blades. Once again he wore his covert activities ensemble: the five-shot Smith & Wesson revolver in an ankle holster, his blue jeans, black sneakers, a black sweatshirt, a black canvas jacket, and a black pullover ski cap. The village cop on 25A looked him over good while they were sitting at a light.

Orin got lost twice on unmarked woodland roads before he parked his truck one hundred yards north of Donnelly's driveway, next to a stand of evergreens. There, in the damp and the darkness, he counted to a thousand. He locked his truck and worked his way through the trees in the direction of the isolated house. Wet leaves smeared his cheeks, but softened his footfalls. The patter of raindrops covered his advance.

It was a large white colonial, backed into a leafy tuck in the woods. The front lawn was large enough to host a football game. Orin knew the price tag on a spread like this was well beyond the means of an honest civil servant. And if Donnelly had married money, it was unlikely he would have so brazenly risked it by catting around as he did.

At the edge of the forest Orin pulled a plastic garbage bag out of his jacket pocket and spread it out on the wet grass. He lay prone on his stomach and settled down to wait for Donnelly to show himself in one of the casement windows. He might as well be comfortable.

At eight-forty, Mrs. Mary Donnelly, who bore an unfortunate but uncanny resemblance to the late Babe Ruth, kissed her loving husband good-bye at the open front door, then squeezed into her silver Mazda RX 7 and drove away. At eight fifty-three, the inspector himself came outside in his monogrammed bathrobe and his boat shoes, smoking a cigar and carrying an umbrella. He had his dog on a leather leash, and though the large black Labrador growled and tugged in Orin's direction, Donnelly held on tight and made sure he did his business in the pachysandra near the garage.

The inspector did not dispose of the waste product according to the laws of the Village of Old Brookville. Orin held his position, enjoying the chance to watch his prey in its natural habitat. At nine-fifteen, a red-headed woman driving a black Mercedes parked in the driveway and walked quickly to the front door—which opened for her as if automatically.

Orin counted slowly to one hundred, then crawled across the lawn to the driveway to read her license plate: GIGI BNZ, New York. Then he crawled back to the woods and ran madly through the cool brambles and branches to his truck and the cellular phone he had rented.

He made the trip in under two minutes. Even a snatchhound like Donnelly would still be in the foreplay stage. The Police Department Communications Bureau operator took under one minute, giving him the ownership information on GIGI BNZ. The New York Telephone operator took only ten seconds to give him a home telephone number. "Thank you for using AT and T."

Orin felt giddy. "Hello," he said. "Mr. Raymond Glasser?"

"Doctor Raymond Glasser."

"Sorry for the mixup, sir. This is Captain Jonas from the Eleventh Precinct. I'm afraid I have some very bad news for you concerning your wife."

"Gigi? My God, what's happened to her?"

"She's been impaled, sir."

"*Impaled?*"

"For about ten minutes now, I suspect."

"What are you talking about?"

"Your wife, sir, is sitting on the lance of her lover, Jimmy Donnelly."

There was silence on the other end for several seconds, then the angry voice of a cuckold. "James Donnelly, the cop? From the country club?"

"They're at his house right now, humping like a couple of poodles."

"Thank you, Captain."

Click.

Orin figured it would take all of fifteen minutes for Dr. Glasser to make the trip from Roslyn to Old Brookville. That left Orin just enough time to report to the Long Island papers the homicide that had just occurred at the police inspector's home in Old Brookville.

After completing his call to the newspaper, Orin switched off the phone and raced back to his spot of concealment at the edge of the Donnellys' woods.

Less than three minutes later a second black Mercedes pulled up and parked behind the first. A tall man in a warm-up suit got out and jogged halfway to the front door, stopped, stood on his toes by the front picture window, then banged the copper doorknocker.

Orin saw two heads appear briefly in an upstairs window, then James Donnelly was downstairs, opening the front door, saying, "Ray, please. This isn't at all what it looks like."

Donnelly had changed from his robe to red golf slacks and an orange tennis shirt that clashed. He was barefoot. His hair was standing up in the back like Ronald Reagan's.

"Where is she, you bastard? I want to see Gigi this fucking minute!"

"She's in the bathroom, Ray. Calm down. She stopped by to see my Mary, but unfortunately just missed her. I built her one little drink, and now you're here, looking terribly upset. What the hell is going on, Ray? I hope you two don't plan on dragging your friends into your marital troubles."

Dr. Raymond Glasser landed an uppercut on Donnelly's jaw before the inspector could react, sending him down for the count, his back propped up against the doorjamb. Glasser admired his work for a moment, then stepped over the comatose body of the inspector and entered the big white house.

Orin heard screams through the open door, then saw the doctor dragging a half-dressed Gigi from the house by her frizzy red hair. Every three steps they stopped, as if waltzing, and the doctor smacked her on the back of her head. Twice she fell on the grass, the last time refusing to rise again. Before the doctor could get her to his car, the lights of another set of headlights froze them on the lawn.

Assuming the Mineola press corps was landing in force, Orin couldn't help gloating, congratulating himself on the exquisite timing of the operation. But things worked out even better than that. Mrs. Donnelly had changed her mind about stopping at the library and returned from her church meeting an hour before she was expected. She parked her silver Mazda RX 7 behind RAY BNZ and GIGI BNZ.

And then the mini-van mini-cams arrived.

Orin watched television at Red's, surrounded by his hard-drinking brother officers and several women of ill-repute. He ignored them one and all, staring sullenly into his martini glass, chain-smoking Marlboros, in full pursuit of an angry bender, the kind where someone else would pay.

Sometime after two A.M. Orin handed Newt a twenty-dollar bill, snatched a bottle of gin from the bar, and left Red's without saying good-bye to his mates.

He drove back to the station house and used his copy of the precinct master key to take a patrol car from the parking lot without permission. He switched on the dashboard radio and listened to radio assignments for family fights and burglar alarms. God, how he hated this place, he thought, and after less than a year at that. He hated the hopelessness, he hated the hardness. And worse, tonight he hated the helpless victims. He wanted to get even with them, too.

He cruised the run-down sections of the precinct, loaded with street dealers, announcing over the roof-rack public address system an impending Iranian attack: "Move all your food, liquor, and valuables into your basements. Clasp your hands firmly behind your heads. Place your head between your knees. Red alert. Red alert. The mullahs are coming. Red alert."

It was surprising how many actually took his advice and huddled together in their basements. However, thirty-five angry complainants took the trouble to dial headquarters, which resulted in an entire squad of Internal Affairs detectives from Mineola swooping down on the precinct and totally disrupting the night's drug dealing and scattering the street walkers.

Orin drove the borrowed patrol car full bore when he saw the unmarked Chevy on his tail, taking advantage of his local knowledge and taking chances no prudent man would. Hard left, hard right. A couple of one-way streets done backward at high speeds, and he lost the shooflies long enough to ditch the police car behind the station house. He locked the doors, then duckwalked unseen between parked cars to his truck. His thighs burned and his chest was heaving as he lay across the seat.

Red and white lights flashed on the torn cloth ceiling of the truck. He closed his eyes and concentrated on the blood pumping through his temples, the fruity smell of his breath. He heard voices close by, radio squelch, and footsteps. Someone said something about calling out the dogs.

A minute passed, then another.

The searchers were slowly moving away from him. He propped himself up on one elbow and looked over the dashboard. He could see a marked patrol car idling at the curb at one end of the block, and another one at the other end. Very tricky, he thought. What a waste of time. Because if there is anything a cop can do, it is make himself comfortable in an automobile. Orin took another swig of gin and settled back on the seat. Two hours later, when he awoke chilly and stiff, the perimeter had been dismantled, other calls for service draining off the searchers.

Orin popped a couple of antacid tablets into his mouth and called it a night.

16

Orin got up early to appear at a preliminary hearing in Family Court. The papers had been served on him at the station house, in Lieutenant Fazio's office. "It's cheaper to keep her," Fazio told him after the process server left. "Believe me, I know."

He met Judy by chance on the steps of the large white courthouse. Her cheeks were rosy in the cold, her eyes bright. He held the heavy door for her while asking after Dawn. She did not reply, only looked at him stonily, and then moved away to join a handsome young preppie on the other side of the lobby.

The young associate took her by the hand and sat her on a bench under a portrait of the current county executive. Judy pointed at Orin; the rookie lawyer gave him the once-over and nodded grimly.

Orin sat down on the other side of the lobby next to a fat black woman surrounded by teenage daughters and infant grandchildren. He introduced himself and then pointed out his wife. "That's the bitch," he said. "Her and one of her sweethearts. Ain't even got the decency to wait till the judge says it's over."

"You must be kidding," the woman said. "Why your poor heart must be breaking."

One of the grandchildren took this opportunity to escape from her clutches and run for the door. "Taiisha," she said to a daughter in a sweatsuit and gold chains. "Get Jamal back on this bench 'fore I whup your butt. Lord have mercy," she said, turning back to Orin, "but this younger generation is dumb. You gots to tell 'em every damn thing about everything, and you gots to say it over and over."

While Taiisha was rousing herself from the bench, a uniformed court officer walked briskly into the middle of the lobby. "Boyd versus Boyd," he said. "You're on in 208."

Orin said good-bye to the overburdened matriarch and followed Judy and her lawyer to a hearing room on the second floor. Family Court Justice Bertram Cowles, a plucked-looking man in a business suit, and a redheaded stenographer in a tight black dress were waiting for them. "Boyd versus Boyd?" asked Cowles.

"That's correct," said Judy's lawyer. "My name is Jonathan Mullaney, attorney for the plaintiff."

Judge Cowles seemed unimpressed. "Preliminary hearing for divorce and division of common property?"

"Yes, sir."

"And I see you are also seeking an order of protection at this time," Cowles said, reading from the annotated calendar.

"We'll reserve that right at this time," said Mullaney.

"Protection from me?" Orin said.

Judy turned to him quickly. "Your drinking," she said.

"I see," said Orin. "We're here to play hardball."

"Orin, I—"

Mullaney cautioned Judy to remain silent. "Your Honor, the defendant in this case has a long history of substance abuse, both illegal drugs and alcohol, dating back to his late teens and early twenties. He has been disciplined by his employers for drinking on the job. He also carries a gun twenty-four hours a day. When you hear in sworn testimony from his wife some of the irresponsible and dangerous acts he has committed, you will, I feel confident, see the propriety of such an order."

Judy started to cry. She pulled a tissue from her bag and dabbed her sky-blue eyes.

"Please try to relax, Mrs. Boyd," said the judge. "This is really no big deal."

Judy put her glasses back on and looked at the judge in horror. "It is to me," she said.

Her lawyer hushed her again.

"Mr. Boyd," said the judge. "Look at me. Listen to me. Is what Mr. Mullaney telling me true?"

"I don't know," said Orin. "It sounds like he was there, to hear him tell it. I wonder where he could have got his information."

Cowles had another question: "Do you drink alcoholic beverages, Mr. Boyd?"

"Yes, I do."

"Do you drink to excess?"

"That's all according to who's giving the breathalyzer."

"What you consider to be excess?"

"Sometimes."

"Do you take drugs, Mr. Boyd?"

"No, I do not."

Judge Cowles nodded. "Mrs. Boyd, please tell me something of your marriage to Mr. Boyd, and try not to make it sound like *Queen for a Day.*"

Judy froze, unsure of where to begin. Hearing Orin interrogated on her behalf, watching him answer embarrassing questions truthfully, flooded her with regret.

"Mrs. Boyd? . . . Hel-lo?"

"I'm sorry."

"Did your husband ever push, punch, kick, slap, choke, or otherwise physically abuse you?"

"No," she said. "Not physically."

"Did he run around with other women?"

"No, not that I know of."

"Gamble away his paycheck?"

"No . . . he was always very generous."

Cowles turned his attention to Orin, carefully looked him up and down. "So, what's the problem?"

"Mental cruelty," said Jonathan Mullaney. "No, make that mental torture. Games, rules, harassment, emotional abandonment, the willful and deliberate obstruction of her career."

Orin's face grew pale. "Hey," he said, "asswipe! Just because I don't beat my wife don't mean you're gonna make it to your car tonight."

"Your Honor!" cried Mullaney.

Cowles banged his gavel. "Sit down and shut up, will you, Counselor. And you, Mr. Boyd, you watch your mouth as well. You do yourself no favor to prove their case against you. In fact I strongly suggest you bring legal representation to the next stage of these proceedings. Every time you open your mouth you do yourself damage."

"Yes, your Honor. I'm sorry."

"In the meantime," Cowles said, sliding on a pair of bifocals, "the Court grants plaintiff's request of half the defendant's salary, to be temporarily divided between alimony and child support. My law clerk will work out the details with you."

The judge stood up and stretched, Mullaney sat down, the bored stenographer headed for the coffeepot.

Orin shook his head. "That's it?" he said. "I don't get to say anything about her?" He had come prepared to cite Judy's crimes of omission; he was ready to drag that faggot boss into court by the balls. Why did it seem that the case had already been decided?

"Forgive me, Mr. Boyd," said Cowles. "You have something more to say?"

"Doesn't everybody at a time like this."

"Sometimes, sometimes not. Go right ahead, though. I'm all ears."

Orin's glare stopped the stenographer in her tracks. "I want this on the record."

The stenographer returned to her chair and sat down. The judge stopped gathering up his papers. "Now please, Mr. Boyd. We're very busy here, you know."

Orin turned and looked at Judy. She was pulling on a black leather glove. He squinted.

"For the record," he said, "I'm sorry as hell about all of this."

The call came in through the CB switchboard to "shag that bum from behind the luncheonette." Orin put aside the latest issue of *The Sporting News* and pulled out of the coop behind the empty unemployment office. He figured one of the wet-head skels, who drank all day on Main Street, must have curled up in the cold weeds for a nap, and Maria wanted to close the back gate and lock up. Something like that. A little taxi service probably. A little neighborhood beautification.

Orin's guess was mostly right. Maria wanted to close early and she said she couldn't get the man lying back there to move. She opened her back alley door and pointed to a derelict. "Maybe he's sick," she said. "He smells so bad I wouldn't go near him."

"I see," said Orin. "He stinks, does he? You wouldn't go near him. You sold him Colt .45s from eight o'clock this morning, and now that he's shitfaced with ca-ca in his pants, you call me to scrape him up. Does that sound fair to you?"

"No," she said, pulling on her overcoat, tossing keys into her purse. "But who said anything is fair."

"No big deal, Maria. You call, we haul."

"Thank you, Officer Orin." She closed the door behind Orin and slid the dead bolts into place.

Orin found Abraham Wilson face up against the fence with his eyes open in the knee-high weeds, dead-of-winter frozen, the pupils Airwick green. An exit wound bloomed like a rose in the middle of his chest. The fingers of his left hand gripped the bottom of the chain-link fence. Orin knelt next to the body and checked for a pulse. Abraham Wilson was cold and hard, like wood.

Orin made the sign of the cross, then pulled the walkie-talkie from his belt and notified headquarters. He heard himself request a doctor and a detective be sent to his location, also the crime scene search unit, the medical examiner, the wagon and basket. Then, dazed with guilt and regret, he walked around the building to his patrol car and took a yellow disposable blanket and perimeter tape from the trunk. After he roped off the crime scene, Orin covered the swollen body with the blanket, tucking the corners under the shoulders and feet. He and Abraham would be together now until all the clinical experts were finished collecting data; they might as well be comfortable.

A black Plymouth sedan stopped at the curb near the open chain-link gate. Detective Bobby Shaw got out and took a cursory look at the body. He told Orin to call for a doctor. Orin told Shaw that after fifteen years on the job he knew what to do when he found a dead body. Bobby Shaw had garlic on his breath, and shine on his cheeks from too much wine with lunch. Shaw borrowed Orin's clipboard and copied Orin's notes while Orin trembled.

"Did you notify his relatives?" Shaw asked.

"I don't know if he had any. He lived outside, in the woods by the Meadowbrook Parkway."

"Terrific," Shaw said sarcastically. "Any friends?"

"Some of the other winos, I guess. And a woman who tried to look out for him . . . Charlene King. From that big rooming house on Washburn, near Main." And me, he thought, as much as anyone. I'm a wino, too.

"That house full of hard-ons at the corner?"

"That's the one."

"That's fucking beautiful, Boyd. I really wanted to spend my afternoon taking statements from degenerates in a whorehouse that smells like gorilla shit."

Orin turned his head and spit. "I ain't the fucking landlord, Bobby."

Shaw did not smile as he said, "Be nice to me, Boyd. I'm mostly one of the good guys, remember?"

"Sure, Bobby. One of the good guys."

Just then the crime scene search unit arrived in their clean white van, and two cops in blue jumpsuits hopped out. They checked in with Shaw, wrote down his instructions, then began to scurry about the empty lot. They searched the long-dead grass around the body for blood, hair, fibers, semen, saliva, urine, feces; also spent shells and cigarette butts, anything at all produced by man. They collected and catalogued these puzzle pieces with great care. Orin watched in reverent silence as they uncovered the body and took photographs from a dozen different angles.

Bobby Shaw taped paper bags over the lifeless hands and feet to preserve any microscopic evidence, a look of distaste on his tanned and handsome face.

"That's enough of this shit," he said, standing up, dusting off his trousers. "Let's call it a wrap."

"A couple more," one of the cops said to Shaw. "Black Dan is catching today, and I only want to do this once."

Detective Sergeant Daniels arrived a moment later and took immediate command of the scene. He said hello quickly to Orin and the others, looked at the body, then asked Bobby Shaw, "Whaddayagot?"

Shaw gave Alonzo Daniels the basic facts as he knew them and explained that he had ordered a complete search of the entire lot. "I don't think he was killed here, Sarge. From the lack of blood and all. I think somebody tossed him here."

Daniels gave Shaw a list of nine more things to do, and then pulled Orin off to the side. "How's it going," he said as they walked out of earshot.

"I'm doing okay."

"You look like something's bothering you."

"This job is bothering me."

"I mean something personal," said Daniels.

"This is personal." He shook his head. "You wouldn't believe me if I told you."

Daniels slapped Orin on the shoulder and returned to his examination of the evidence. The medical examiner arrived. Ten minutes after that the assistant district attorney on-call found his way to the scene of the crime. Everybody did all that they could for the deceased. Then upper management left the empty lot, the yellow tape was pulled down, and the crime scene secured. Everything was as it was before the body was discovered.

Orin helped load Abraham into the green rubber body bag and slid him into the basket. He asked the Reaper to stop by the house of Charlene King. He hoped Shaw would be there, wrinkling his nose; and he thought Charlene might want to see the body. "Five minutes?" he said.

The Reaper shrugged. "Whatever. I'm here until midnight."

"Thanks."

Bobby Shaw's unmarked car was not parked in front of the ramshackle rooming house. Orin imagined another drink had been in order for Bobby, maybe down by the water. A wino's case could wait.

Orin climbed onto the wooden stoop and knocked on the door. "Charlene?" he called out, sticking his head inside. "Charlene King?"

Charlene waltzed into the front room with a cooking spoon in her hand. She recognized Orin and smiled at him. "Hey, sugar cop. What it is."

"It's Abraham, Charlene . . . I'm afraid I got bad news."

"Did *he* get hisself locked up again today? 'Cause if he did you can tell him I ain't bailing him out this time. He can stay inside and eat their food if he thinks it's so good. And tell him take a goddamn shower, too."

"He's dead, hon. Abraham got himself murdered."

The cooking spoon dropped to the carpet, splattering tomato sauce on her slippers. She tightened her bathrobe over her breasts. "Murdered? Is that a fact."

"We found him in the lot behind Maria's Corner Counter. Somebody shot him in the back."

She nodded slowly, her face impassive, as if she had always expected news like this and had already dealt with her grief.

"I need his personal papers for the detectives, if you've got them. His birth certificate and Social Security card—things like that."

"They in my car," she said, "in the glove department." She slipped on a pair of rubber boots. He followed her outside to the driveway, where she retrieved Abraham's wallet from her Buick Electra and gave it to him solemnly. Inside the brown vinyl wallet Orin found faded parole papers from the State of New York, newspaper clippings on the death of a man in the Belmont woods, and a birth certificate from Oxford, North Carolina.

"This is it?"

"He didn't have no license or bank books. I did all of his bookkeeping, what little of it there was. He showered here. Ate a meal now and again. You know we was lovers once, but he fell too low for me."

"And the rest of the time he lived outside?"

"Yeah. In that hideout of his."

"Why?"

Charlene's eyes filled with tears. "I guess 'cause he couldn't stand hisself."

"You want to see him before we go?"

"He in that van?"

"Yes, he is."

Orin and Charlene walked to the end of the concrete driveway. Orin opened the back door of the morgue wagon and helped her climb inside. Her hand was large and strong, but trembling. Orin unzipped the body bag down to Abraham's throat, exposing in the dim light only the face. She bent over and stroked his cheek with the back of her hand.

"I loved you like a brother, Abraham, long after I loved you like a man." She kissed his lips and his forehead, her face dripping tears onto his. "Good-bye, my baby. Be at peace."

▪ ▪ ▪

Orin slipped his key in the lock of his own door, then remembered he had left in his usual dazed rush that morning, and had not locked his door. "I'm losing it," he said softly.

He shoved it open and felt along the concrete wall for the light switch. A man's fist struck him in the solar plexus and he dropped to his knees, stiff, gasping for air.

"Get up, motherfucker, 'fore I puts you out fo' good."

Orin squinted through the haze, but saw nothing to attack. Drowning, he bobbed and weaved on his knees like a drunk until the arms of a human forklift picked him up and held him against the door.

"You know why I'm here, doncha boy?"

Orin recognized Sherman Clayborne's baritone but didn't have the air in his lungs to respond. Sherman smacked the bottom of Orin's jaw with the top of his rock-hard forearm. "Let's try that again," he said. "Does you know why I'm here?"

"Yeah," Orin said. "I know why you're here." He had his arms around Sherman's ample waist, his head resting on his shoulder. They might have been dancing, from the dreamy look in Orin's eyes.

"But now you know that was a mistake you made, that you ain't never gonna make again. Ain't that right, white boy? You gonna watch out for your ownself from here on in."

Orin was hanging on in the clinch, slowly regaining full consciousness. He needed time. "Yeah," he said. "You've heard the last . . . from me."

"Don't jive me, homeboy. Don't make me visit you again."

"I promise . . . I'll never forget that."

Sherman Clayborne gave Orin a viselike bear hug to remind him, just in case.

Orin gave Sherman a viselike ball hug and school was suddenly over. Sherman's throat opened wide and he screamed bloody murder. He shoved Orin away and grabbed his own crotch. Orin lunged straight into Sherman's kneecap, driving his shoulder into the bone, then locking his hands behind the ankle.

He tried to lift Sherman backward, but Sherman was no flipped-over Volkswagen. There wasn't a car in the world that could throw a double-fisted rabbit punch.

Orin crashed to the floor chest-first. Sherman grabbed him by the hair and hoisted him up, and ran him head-first into the dresser.

Orin dropped to both knees, then toppled slowly onto his side, his head ringing and his field of vision drastically narrowed. Sherman stood over him, wounded but triumphant. He rolled Orin over with the tip of his pointy gray shoe.

From flat on his back Orin leg-whipped Sherman Clayborne to the floor, then both men staggered to their feet. Orin glanced around the dark room for weapons and grabbed a pitching wedge from his golf bag in the corner.

Sherman wiped the sweat off his brow. He seemed to have a smile on his face, a white blur in the darkness.

Orin held the golf club by the head and whipped the shaft back and forth like a sword. Blood was dripping into his mouth, making his stomach feel sick. He could hear heavy breathing in the distance, but his vision was again blurred, his sense of outrage much reduced. As he wobbled on his feet, concussed, his mind played back a highlight film from his high-school years: himself, being carried from a gridiron on a stretcher, to the polite applause of an away-game crowd.

An inappropriate smile spread across his face.

Sherman Clayborne must have sensed the vacant gaze in Orin's eyes— that his unexpectedly formidable opponent was almost out on his feet and that he was suddenly free to go. For he took the opportunity to back out of the Hole and disappear.

When Orin woke up it was morning. He took four Tylenols and put an ice bag on the knot on his head. He brushed his teeth, ate a bowl of dry Corn Chex, and fell back onto his bed. His body and face were killing him: the bruises on his cheekbone, the tender cut on the bridge of his nose, his gut. He was dreaming of various forms of violent revenge when George Clarke knocked at his door, a six of Bud and pair of hero sandwiches under his arm.

"I brung you a CARE package," he said. "Hey! What happened to your face?"

"I fell down getting out of my truck."

"Smooth move." George pulled an aluminum snack tray off the stand and set up lunch in front of the benchpress. "I'm glad you were here. I couldn't take the old lady another second. She's been looking at me funny again, going through my wallet and shit."

George handed him a chicken cutlet hero. Then he sat on the bench, resting his foot on a barbell, squeezing his can of beer as he drank it. He tore bites from his meatball sandwich and spoke with gobs of red food in his mouth: "So what do you think? What the fuck are you up to today?"

Orin held a cold can of beer against his forehead. "I didn't really fall out of my truck. Sherman Clayborne stopped by last night to rearrange my face."

"Fo'get abou' it."

"You forget about it. In fact, you'd better stay away from me from now on. You gotta know I'm gonna dump napalm in his holy water."

"Yeah?" said George, grinning. "What do you have in mind?"

"It won't be a pretty sight."

George pulled another beer from the plastic rings. He stretched out on the bench, staring at Orin with that look men have when they're considering divorce. "You gonna blow someone away?"

"I couldn't afford the ammo to do the job right. No, I'm thinking of something a little smarter, starting with a collar. No way that fuck strolls into my face."

George shook his head of salon curls. "Did you call the cops last night? Did you make a report? Did you go to a hospital? Substantiate your injuries."

Orin stared at George in disbelief.

"Don't look at me like I'm some kind of pussy. Any good desk officer will laugh your ass out in the street, you try to charge the dude with Burglary First and Assault."

"His ass is mine."

"You're fucking crazy. They're just gonna retaliate."

"Hey, George, ain't nobody paying me to look away."

"This ain't the Bronx, you know. You'll never get away with it. You know goddamn well the job won't back you up. Not with your record."

"My record's not *that* bad."

"I'm telling you, this is out of your league. These ain't no teenage punks from the Strip. And you don't have no fallback position, either. What about your kid wants food with her meals?" George looked around the apartment, taking note of the soiled clothes on the floor, the barren walls, the ground-level daylight. "Believe it or not," he said, "it can get worse than this."

"I'll be retired before they ever know how good I got them. We're talking time-release revenge here."

"Yeah, right," said George. "Dream on. You'll be sitting right here with your thumb up your ass, waiting for Internal Affairs to pick you up, just like everybody else they nab, then you'll hide your face from the cameras when they walk you into court. And that's if you're lucky. That's if someone doesn't gun you down in the freaking street."

Orin dismissed that scenario with a wave of his hand. "Oh, yeah? Gerry Reilly? He told me guys from my old outfit are making five grand a month in Honduras, showing training films and fucking the ass off teenage señoritas. So believe me, if the job sends me Dixie, we're talking bang, zoom, then *astala* bye-bye."

"I knew I shouldn't have got you that *Soldier of Fortune* subscription for Christmas."

"Maybe alone is better."

"I'd love to help you, guy, but—"

"I don't need your help, old buddy. The pleasure of this exercise will be entirely mine."

Orin drove the old red truck into the crowded parking lot of the Church of the Midnight Light. The upper row of side windows were open and Orin could hear the Reverend Sims exhorting his parishioners as he stepped from the cab. Bubba Sims was promising happiness and good fortune for those who chose to support his mission.

The double front doors were open. Orin walked right in. He was the only white man in the place. The black people standing at the rear of the church smiled at him and made room. The reverend stood six-feet-six, looked about fifty-five, and dressed like a dandy: sharkskin gray suit, white shirt, lavender tie, and many rings. The tone of the preacher changed from exultory to angry. He screamed into the microphone that an infidel had entered the House of the Lord. Orin looked at his immediate neighbors and shrugged.

"I meant anyone who comes to mock us. We are protected from such intrusions by a little piece of paper your kind habitually ignores, the Constitution of the United States of America. I want to know what you are doing in my church."

"Hey," said Orin. "You came to my house."

Bubba stepped away from the pulpit and the microphone. "You're deluded."

Following Sherman Clayborne's lead, some of the younger men in the congregation stood up and left the pews, forming two columns along the outside walls, slowly advancing on Orin at the rear of the church.

"Watch yourselves, men," Bubba said. "He's got a gun."

"Actually, I just wanted to see what you were telling these good people," said Orin. "I wanted to see for myself if they knew where you got all your money."

Bubba's hand dropped behind the lectern. A small red light on an amplifier next to him blinked off. A fat woman in the front of the congregation rose to her feet.

"We give it to him, Mr. Po-lice-man," she said proudly. "The reverend lives good and decent 'cause we a prosperous people."

"Amen," said everybody else. "Praise the Lord."

Orin pointed up at the pulpit. "We have a date, Reverend."

The deacons closed on Orin, yet his demeanor remained calm. A squat black man in his fifties moved to Orin's side. "You a brave man, Officer," he said out of the side of his mouth. "And you had a chance to say your piece. Now I suggest you book whilst you still can."

"Well," said Orin. "I'll take you up on that."

17

They sat at the end of the bar in Red's. The place was empty at that hour of the morning. Newt had barely opened for business when they arrived.

"Actually," George Clarke said, "I think you were freaking nuts to crash the Sunrise Highway sermonette. And goddamn lucky you're not being brought up on charges."

"Me? The lying fuck jumped me in my home, however humble it might be." Orin ate the ice from his ginger ale.

"You're making yourself crazy here, Orin. Who cares if Bubba Sims runs a little numbers thing here, a little pussy there, who cares if he dusts the streets with drugs. If it wasn't him, it would be somebody else, maybe a really bad son of a bitch who hated cops."

"Yeah. And Bubba's just a sweet guy who shoots bums in the back."

George shrugged. "You don't know that. You couldn't prove it."

"Don't think it was luck I didn't get jammed up," Orin said. "I heard Donnelly had the legal bureau burning the midnight oil, looking for a hook to hang me from. What they found, to their deep regret, was that I got the same constitutional rights that he does."

"You're dreaming," said George. "Ten cops put together don't have the rights that Bubba has. Or the firepower."

"Only in America." Orin hoisted a beer. It was a little after eleven in the morning.

"Donnelly probably wanted to have you tortured," said George. "He's such an asshole sometimes. I hate this fucking job."

"Calm down, buddy. It's not like you to bring the job home. What's the matter? Feeling a little stress?"

"You better believe. I'm sick to death of breaking my ass for this freaking place."

"Now, now. Let's not kid ourselves," Orin said.

"Eight hours a day I wear that freaking target, I'm doing my freaking job."

Orin raised his finger to object. "Take the average tour. We begin our intensive motor patrol with free coffee in the diner, we read a free newspaper, we stop by the firehouse and make personal phone calls. An accident report, a quick trip to the medical center. Then dinner and dessert on the arm. After that—"

"What exactly are you saying?"

Orin blew a smoke ring; George followed its progress the length of the bar. "I'm saying the surest way I know to fuck up is to start believing your own act. Kenny Demarco always told me that. If you're working, you're working. If you're screwing the pooch, bring it dog biscuits."

"You're fucked up," said George. "I gotta get another partner."

"I just need to get some more collars. Hey, Newt," Orin called into the kitchen. "Can a couple of heroes get a goddamn beer?"

Newt stepped into the doorway, wooden spoon in hand. He was wearing an oversize apron covered with blotches of chili. "Get 'em yourself. I'm knocking out my side work so I can close this dump on time tomorrow morning."

Orin strolled behind the bar to pour their beers. "You want one?" he called to Newt.

Newt answered in the negative. He said he didn't care for watered Rheingold, didn't matter who was buying.

George slurped his beer and stared at the picture on the wall of the fat white softball players and their shiny new fire truck. He plucked a pack of beer nuts from the rack and spilled them on the bar. "Did you hear what Donnelly did yesterday?" George said.

"Nope," said Orin. "But every day it's something new."

"Donnelly was shithoused yesterday afternoon when I saw him. He had this foxy Spanish broad sitting on his desk, complaining about her old man kicking her butt. Then he comes running out and grabs me and two other guys and sends us out to pick the bastard up while he and the little lady start sipping cocktails in his office. It was awesome, man."

"Get out of town," Orin said. "Did you put in for the overtime?"

"Now what do you think? That asshole paid me two hundred bucks to ride over to the Night Moves Bar with Davy Slater and Conner O'Connell and smack the shit out of Julio Ramirez, which I woulda been glad to do for nothing."

Orin shook his head. "Can you imagine if we did something like that?"

"I have done something like that," George said. "And lived to talk about it."

"Yeah." Orin nodded. "I guess I have too."

"You ever feel guilty?" George asked. "About the shit we do?"

"What are you, nuts?" Orin didn't want to think about guilt, on or off the job. He didn't want to think about home. He wanted to think about starting his life over where nobody knew him, just him and his daughter, with money to burn.

"I don't know," said George. "Maybe I am depressed."

"You?" said Orin. "The man who has it all?"

George sighed. His wife, Ella, had come to him two weeks ago, to ask about the possibility of separate vacations—in this, their first year of wedlock. She thought they needed time apart to get their heads straight. He said to her he didn't know what she was talking about. Everything was great. "Can you believe it?" he said. "She said there were things about the relationship that bothered her. She said talking with her mother would help. I wanted to kick her fucking teeth down her throat."

"What'd you tell her?"

"I didn't tell her nothin'. I'm thinking about it. Every day I tell her I haven't made up my mind yet."

Orin touched George's forearm, a gesture of sympathy for a troubled friend. "This is no time to be an asshole. Tell her it's okay, encourage her even."

"When did you turn into Phil Donohue?"

"I didn't. I'm saying let her go see her mother and you and me can hit the open road."

"How you gonna pull that off?"

"I don't know. Easily, I suppose. I'll charge it. How do you usually do it? I don't know if I've told you this lately, but you're looking at a guy who needs to get away."

"I believe you," said George. "The word isn't good on you out there. You got an ongoing problem."

"Anybody giving odds?"

"You don't wanna know."

"Thank you, George, for confirming my suspicions. I'm indebted to you for even taking the risk of sitting with me."

George glanced around, a look Orin knew meant he was suddenly worried.

"They wouldn't dare do anything in Red's," George said, not sounding completely confident.

For the next hour, George bitched about his wife screwing up his plans. Orin slumped on his barstool, chewing Tums and burping, thinking of novel ways to tell George to shut up.

"I'm sorry, Cap," said Dominick Ril. "The old man is tied up for the rest of the day. Maybe if you sent him a memo."

"Tell him it's in regard to this." Blogg handed Ril a copy of the teletype order. "Maybe he'll be able to squeeze me in."

Sergeant Ril read the order, his lower jaw dropping as bells of panic rang in his head. "Well, well, well," he said, patting Captain Blogg on the back. "If that don't beat all. I tell you what, boss, I'll see what I can do. You wait right here."

James Donnelly was sitting in his chair, his feet resting on the steam radiator behind his desk, a telephone stuck to the side of his florid face. He spun around and raised his bushy eyebrows at Ril, put his finger to his lips. "Okay, baby," Donnelly said into the phone. "I'll have to get back to you," he crooned, and hung up.

"Which one was that?"

"Sally Ann."

One of his main skirts, Sergeant Ril realized. Donnelly would go through the roof if he knew half the men had been there first.

"Archie Blogg's outside."

"What, is the flag ripped again? Don't tell me we've got roaches."

"I wish that was all it was. Actually, he's got orders in his greasy little hand that say he's gonna be the next commanding officer around here. I guess your transfer came through quicker than you thought."

"Last night, to the Intelligence Division, thank God," said Donnelly.

"You, working terrorists?"

Donnelly put his hands behind his head and smiled. "You suck enough ass in this job, it can pay in ways you'd never believe. From now on I spend my days reading magazines and talking trash to hot clerk-typists. No more bullshit, no more pressure, no more crazy fucking niggers. Just two-hour lunches and golf with the deputy commissioner."

"Sounds nice," Ril said, a little surprised at the tremor in his voice. "What about me?"

"I got you covered, Dom. I've always had you covered. You know we're still a team." James Donnelly launched into a recital of all the things he would be able to do for Sergeant Ril from his new and prestigious position.

"We've come a long way together," he said.

"What should I do about the Geek? He's waiting."

"Will he go away if we ignore him?" James Donnelly hated male visitors to his office more than phone calls from his bookie.

"Do you think that's wise?"

"No," said Donnelly. "Not really." He got out of his chair and picked up the pink plastic bat from the garbage pail. He faced the door and took a few practice swings, then cracked one out of the park, slow-motion, coming out of his shoes like Mantle. "Send in the goddamned Geek," he said. "But stick around. I want you in his lap from the get-go."

Ril ushered Archibald Blogg into the office and sat him in the chair opposite Donnelly. Then he walked behind Donnelly's desk and stood at his commander's side.

"May we speak privately?" said Blogg.

"We are," said Donnelly.

"I see."

"Dominick Ril is your right-hand man, Archie. You want something done around here, he's the guy you see."

"Why thank you, James. That's exactly what I'm looking for."

James Donnelly was about to wish him well, and would have, had not Detective Sergeant Daniels barged into his office at that moment, rage all over his face.

"I didn't hear you knock, Sergeant," Donnelly said.

"That's right, Inspector. You didn't."

Donnelly was taken aback at the anger smoldering in the sergeant's eyes. "Excuse, me, Sergeant. I'm in the middle of something here."

"I wouldn't be the least bit surprised."

"You'd better watch your tone of voice," Donnelly said.

"Fine. I'll just try my tone of voice out on the district attorney then."

Donnelly raised his eyebrows, then smiled wearily, nodding his head in resignation. "Hold on a second. Let's not have any of that crap. Archie— okay if I get back to you?"

Blogg was already headed for the door. "No problem," he called over his shoulder. "Whenever's convenient." Dominick Ril followed him out.

"Have a seat," said Donnelly as the door closed.

"Thank you."

Donnelly's face was flushed, there was a quiver to his speckled hands. "What's all this noise about the district attorney? What the hell have the boys done now?"

"Nothing. Your detectives do nothing, they know nothing. I mean, looking the other way. I mean, driving around with blinders on."

"Look, I'll admit we've got less than the elite of the force down here, but—"

"Don't insult my intelligence, Inspector. I can tell when we've gone Dixie. And I can tell when someone shits in my face. I just lost one of my old narc cases in a suppression hearing because one of your detectives admitted that he forgot to read the defendant his Miranda rights. Can you believe it? Security guards at a flea market know better than that."

Donnelly shook his head in unsurprised sorrow. "Mea culpa, mea culpa. This is a piss-poor precinct because I'm a piss-poor administrator. The commissioner knows it, *Newsday* knows it, even my fucking wife knows it. So I did the only honorable thing. I opted out. Starting March first, I'll be buried in Intelligence, finishing up my thirty-year career a disgrace."

"At seventy-five thousand dollars a year."

"About that, yeah. What of it?"

"Nothing," said Daniels. "I just hope there's a soft seat around for me when my time comes."

"Things are changing in the job," said Donnelly. "You never know. You've done pretty good for yourself as it is."

"I've worked for it. Longer and harder than most. And I don't like being made to look like a fool. I climbed onto that witness stand today totally prepared. Of course the defendant was read his rights, I say, knowing full well that even if he wasn't, there ain't no detective in the world dumb enough to admit it."

"But—"

"Except for Detective Bobby Shaw, from where else but the Thirteenth Precinct, sitting up there after me, saying, 'Ooops. Yeah, I did forget.'"

Donnelly grimaced. Such an error really was beyond belief.

"I was one guy away from a major wholesaler with that case. My perp was scared shitless of going to jail and ready to wear a wire. Then Shaw talks to him and it's like night and day. He don't want to talk, he don't know nothing from nothing. Am I crazy? he wants to know. He was very cocky for a guy going down the tubes—like he knew he was gonna beat the rap."

Donnelly laced his hands together behind his head and put his foot up on the desk. "You know I don't get bogged down in individual cases."

"Maybe you should, Inspector."

Donnelly didn't answer right away. He opened his desk drawer, removed a roll of Tums, and popped one in his mouth. Then he lit a cigarette. "I really wasn't cut out for a desk job," he said to Daniels, "keeping up with the paperwork and the local politics. I was always strictly a uniform patrol guy. Service with a smile and skeedaddle."

Sergeant Daniels picked up his briefcase and rose to his feet, his lack of satisfaction apparent. "Shaw tanked the case, Jimmy."

Donnelly remained in his chair, wondering if this was the last wad of crap to land on his desk, or if Daniels planned on going over his head.

"Sergeant Daniels," he said. "Thank you for bringing this matter to my attention. I assure you that I'll fuck up Shaw's life at the earliest possible opportunity."

■   ■   ■

With his truck parked outside the luncheonette, Orin opened a tunafish sandwich and ate half of his bachelor's dinner. While he was checking the mirror to see that he had wiped his mustache clean of mayonnaise, he noticed the black unmarked Plymouth pull up behind him. Detective Shaw got out and made his approach as if he had just cornered a gang of armed felons.

"You following me?" Orin asked him when he got to the window.

"Matter of fact," he said.

"Go away, Bobby. I don't want to play this scene."

"No scene," said Shaw. "Just a little advice. Can I sit?"

"As long as you don't get fresh."

Shaw walked around the side of the truck and slid into the front seat next to Orin. Both men rolled up their windows. Shaw played with his diamond pinkie ring while he talked about fishing and drinking and the chasing of skirts, the good life a veteran cop ought to have. Then, almost out of nowhere, came the offer to end the bankruptcy of alimony. "You're going nowhere," he said. "Don't you think it's time to cut yourself a slice of the pie."

Orin didn't mind paying child support; he thought it was one of the nicest things he did. His signature on the front of the check was a kind of penance, Judy's on the back a form of grace.

"Not that crooked preacher's pie," he said. "No fucking way."

Shaw nodded, as if he had expected this objection. "If I can't appeal to your wallet, maybe I can get through to your brain. You're stepping on toes, Orin, and for nothing, as far as I can see. It's not worth it, you know. Nobody cares. Not even you, really."

"Whose toes, Bobby?"

"What difference does it make? All this static is totally unnecessary. Why don't you wise up and get on the damn bus."

Orin laughed softly. "I got too much keeping me up nights as it is."

Shaw laced his big fingers together and cracked his knuckles. His gaze was fixed and distant, the look of a frightened man. Orin also stared out the window, like he and Shaw were at a drive-in movie. He wondered what it felt like to be Shaw. He stared at him, but Shaw's face offered little in the way of clues. He was a functionary in this, a messenger boy.

Shaw nodded to himself. "I figured that's what you'd say. They made me try you anyway."

"Come on, Bobby, who is 'they'? Who is so worried about what a slob like me could be doing?"

Shaw grabbed the door handle and started to get out of the truck. "Pray that you never find out."

Orin smiled cruelly, accepting the challenge with relish. "Friends in high places, eh, Bobby?"

"More than you've got."

"You're gonna need them."

Shaw exhaled contemptuously, as if to belittle his plight. "Don't worry about me, Boyd. Worry about yourself."

He got out of the car and slammed the passenger door.

Sherman Clayborne maintained a crash pad in a HUD apartment designated for a family of four. It was on the second floor of the housing project on Lincoln Terrace North. It was a place for him to be alone, to entertain the friends that he could not bring home. To his mind, the jet-black walls and jet-black rug, the chrome and glass tables and shelves, the big-screen TV, and the lines of cocaine the size of cigarettes equalled success. And nobody fucked with his car, either.

Present at the dining-room table were the Reverend Walter Sims, Police Inspector James Donnelly, Detective Robert Shaw, and Sherman himself. The meeting was called to order by the reverend. He summed up their agenda: "Orin fucking Boyd."

James Donnelly was unsurprised when Bubba laid it on him hard, jabbing a bejeweled finger in his face.

"Yo, man, that brazen motherfucker, he's the only son of a bitch dumb enough to take us on. And he one of yours."

"What the fuck do you want?" Donnelly said.

"Results, James, jus' like every other businessman. The motherfucker strolled into my finances, my church, next thing he'll be fucking my women . . ."

"I tried, Bubba."

"Look, James, I'm not attacking you personally, but maybe Intelligence ain't the right gig for you. Maybe you need to get closer to your roots, back on the street."

"Listen to me, you black fucking bullshit artist, don't even think about telling me what I gotta do."

Sherman Clayborne bristled in his chair, then looked to the reverend for a signal. Detective Bobby Shaw slid his right hand closer to the holster on his belt.

Bubba smiled and held his hand up. He seemed to enjoy watching Donnelly lose his cool. "There ain't no need to get racial, Inspector. I'm not saying you ain't intelligent. I'm just saying you standing in a Mineola rainstorm with your umbrella out, and I'm here in Belmont getting soaked to the bone. Your boy Archie Blogg is good for a lunch on the water now and then, but he ain't gonna be any kind of help with Boyd."

"What about Dominick Ril?"

"He's like dealing with a woman, James. You know that."

Donnelly said nothing. All he really wanted to do, he thought, was to get out of this housing project before any cockroaches made a home in the cuffs of his trousers. He was terrified to be where he was, and who he was with on a Friday afternoon in broad daylight.

"I'm not saying you useless, only that you less valuable than before."

"You do have a way with words, Bubba."

"Try these out, then, Mr. Inspector. You and Bobby Shaw here gotta do more for me or the gravy train is over."

"Personally, Bubba, I don't fucking care. I got what I came for, and more."

"Me, either," said Shaw. "I want out."

"Yeah?" said Bubba. "Well I want Officer Boyd."

In the courtyard under Sherman's living-room window, small groups of all ages were gathered around radios, listening to rap and soul and reggae. Donnelly had the sinking feeling a sacrifice was being prepared. "What about after?"

"What *about* after?"

"Then we never met each other, Reverend. You don't know me and I don't know you, forever and ever, amen."

"What if I want Orin Boyd dead?"

"That's between you and your Maker," Donnelly said.

"He's ashes, then," said Bubba Sims.

James Donnelly had heard enough. "It's ancient history," he said. "All of it. We did what we had to do, and that's it."

"A beautiful sentiment," Bubba said. "Maybe I'll use it in the pulpit Sunday."

Bubba Sims sat back in his chair and smiled at Donnelly, then Bobby Shaw, then Sherman.

Donnelly's bushy white eyebrows formed a steeple. "That's it?"

"Hell, yeah." Bubba stood up. "Gentlemen," he said. "It's been a pleasure."

James Donnelly and Bobby Shaw left the apartment and walked side by side from the door of the housing project, across the crowded courtyard, where they were momentarily surrounded by dancing Negroes and criminally loud radios enveloped in a marijuana fog. Like ducks, the black boys at the curb were calling, "Crack, crack," at every passing car. Then, insolently casual, they discoed away from the unmarked police car.

"What is it with these people?" asked Donnelly when they were safely locked inside the automobile. "Every time they see a cop, it's American Bandstand? I feel like I'm supposed to give them a grade."

The crowd parted for the police car. A transvestite hooker flashed them store-bought tit.

"They're animals," Shaw said. "One step up the evolutionary ladder from wiping themselves with rocks."

Donnelly said, "Tomorrow you come up to my place and I'll give you cash. Then, pal o' mine, we're gonna go our separate ways. I don't want to see you, this town, or any more fucking niggers ever again."

Bobby Shaw laughed out loud. He opened the window and let the wind blow the exhilaration of canceled debts into his lungs. It was finished, for better or for worse. He was nearly free.

18

The change of command at the Lucky 13th took place on an unusually balmy winter afternoon. Inspector Archibald Blogg was installed in a brief ceremony in Donnelly's office. The outgoing inspector gave the incoming commander the keys to the nicest car and a list of the best waterfront restaurants.

"Great. Wonderful. Thank you for all your help." Blogg was openly anxious for Donnelly to depart.

"There's nothing else you'd like to ask me?" Donnelly said. "Somehow I'd imagined there would be things you'd want to know. In fact I figured you to break my balls on everything from overtime expenses to paperclips."

"No, James. You're free to go." Blogg pressed the buzzer on his phone.

"You're not interested in personnel matters pending, or the status of ongoing investigations? Wouldn't you like to know which community groups you can tell to fuck off and which ones require kid gloves?"

Blogg said, "No. Everyone starts with a clean slate."

"Fine." Donnelly nodded. "Then I'm only too happy to get the fuck out of your hair. Have a ball, Archie."

Blogg spent an hour alone after Donnelly left. At four P.M. he came out of his office and stood up behind the desk to address the change of tours. One captain, two lieutenants, three sergeants, and thirty-six police officers were ordered to stand at attention by Sergeant Dominick Ril.

"Men of the 13th Precinct," the new inspector began. "For too long now this precinct has been the Sodom and Gomorrah of Nassau County. We have the highest crime rate and the lowest arrest statistics; we're second in percentage of sick time used, the leaders in excessive force complaints. Not a single woman officer has ever asked to work here, not one. Blacks and Hispanics don't want to work here. In fact, we're the only precinct in the entire county that is not allowed to give tours to the local schoolchildren."

George Clarke raised his hand and Blogg acknowledged him: "Yes, Officer Clarke."

"Most of them kids are gonna get a private showing one day anyhow, sir. Why duplicate the effort?"

While everyone was laughing and slapping one another five, Inspector Blogg looked to Lieutenant Fazio for help; he found none. Sergeant "No Relation" Reagan finally told George to knock it off.

"I know what goes on around here," Inspector Blogg said. "Don't think that I haven't been watching."

The front door opened and the room fell silent while a pair of detectives escorted an elderly female robbery victim to the upstairs offices. Then Blogg resumed his inaugural address: "You men have been reading pornographic smut in the police cars, and sleeping away your midnights behind the factories. Anything but your frigging jobs, for which you are being more than amply compensated."

No one was moved enough to make a rebuttal.

"All of this willful dereliction of duty will cease. No more drinking on duty, no more personal phone calls, and the next man to fart into his microphone will be summarily fired. You have no idea how embarrassing I find it to carry a live walkie-talkie in this town."

Sly smiles spread across faces. An oooh went up from the back.

"I know how much you yearn to change," Blogg said, his voice growing husky with emotion. "I know that deep down inside, your professional lives disgust you."

"Amen," said Paul Kellog.

"Say that again for me, Officer Kellog."

"I said, 'Amen.'"

"Everybody!" Blogg said.

"*Amen.*"

"Beautiful," said Blogg. "Just one more thing. There will be no more abusing our positions of public trust, and by that I mean acts of fornication with the Negroes and Puerto Ricans. Are we clear on this point?"

"Fine," most of the men said. "Right." "Crystal clear."

"Absolutely not," said George, under his breath. "Not now, not ever."

"Excellent," Blogg said. "Now. Let's look in another direction for a moment. The art of police work, as practiced in the old One-Three. Does anyone have any comments? Is there anything we can do to improve our performance?"

No one had any comments. No one had any new ideas.

"I expected as much," Blogg said. "Or as little. Good day to you all, men. I'll be praying for you."

Blogg retreated into his office. Dominick Ril held open the door and followed him in.

"Jesus Christ, boss. What the hell was that?"

Blogg massaged the tip of his bony nose and searched the face of his subordinate. "Nothing."

"You were announcing something," Ril said.

Blogg shrugged.

"Inspector, please. You gotta listen to me. I can run this dump so you won't hear the motor. Stay in your office and cut out paper dolls—please. Drink, screw around, go to the movies, go to the beach, play golf with the detectives. Just don't talk to no reporters, and try not to fuck with the men."

"I don't answer to you, Dominick. I don't answer to James Donnelly anymore. My job is to lead these men, Sergeant. For your information, I'm planning an aggressive management: taking risks and encouraging initiative. There are sleepers in this precinct actually capable of law enforcement. My method will draw them out."

Ril sat down in the chair across from Blogg's big desk and propped his head on his hand. "There's a couple of sleepers here all right."

"Those are good men out there, Dom. They are fathers and brothers and sons, decent men. Policemen who took an oath." Blogg walked around the desk and stared out his office window at the junkies smoking dope. "If we can't believe in them, this place is lost."

"Those decent men think you're a douche-bag."

"I refuse to believe that."

"They've already—"

"Want to know the truth, Dominick? I don't give a damn what the frigging men think. I'm still gonna do this my way. The bullshit, my good man, is over."

"Guess again, sir." Ril stood up and opened the office door enough for Blogg to see the last few day-tour cops signing off-duty, every one of them grinning like an idiot. "Those are the happiest working cops in America right now, and do you know why?"

"Why?"

"Because their new boss don't know his ass from a hole in the ground."

Blogg frowned.

"Honest to God. I'm showing you the future, unless you wise the fuck up and let me run things. Knowledge is power, Inspector. I got it. You don't."

"And if in spite of all this evidence, I insist upon doing things my way?"

"You will drown in a river of red tape, rules, and horse shit, sir. No one will be able to save you." Dominick Ril hovered on one foot by the door. "Will there be anything else before I go, Inspector?"

"Yes," said Blogg. "I would like a couple of aspirins and a container of chocolate milk."

The two prowl cars sat sixty-nined window to window in the litter-strewn lot behind the movie theater, Jerry Santos sipping his third cup of coffee, and Orin slurping pork lo mein and a shrimp roll. His briefcase, on the seat beside him, was covered with packets of duck sauce. It wasn't his meal period but he was eating now because he had things to do on his actual lunch break. Like see his divorce attorney.

"*Headquarters to thirteen, twenty-one,*" the radio barked.

Orin acknowledged the call. "Thirteen, twenty-one."

"Aided case, cardiac arrest, reported at five-four Halston Street. Respond forthwith."

"Thirteen, twenty-one. Okay."

He looked over at Jerry. "It never fucking fails. I swear they got cameras hidden in these cars."

"Or monosodium glutamate detectors. Relax. I'll head over there and hold the fort."

"Thanks, man. I'm right behind you."

Jerry Santos flipped on his roof lights and siren and dropped it into gear. Bouncing over the uneven ground, he raced out of the lot while Orin folded down the covers on the cardboard food containers and chucked his garbage out the window.

It took Santos four minutes to reach the address, a single-family dwelling in serious disrepair. He slid to a stop, killed the siren, popped the dashboard trunk-lock and hopped out of the car. He gathered up the first aid kit and the oxygen tank, and the Hope Bag so he wouldn't have to swap spit with some dying derelict who needed resuscitation. He jogged across the dead brown lawn, lugging the equipment and panting just a little.

The screen door opened as he came up the steps and a black boy held it open with one hand, a shotgun in the other.

"What the fuck?" Jerry said, but he knew, like any cop would. The first blast hit him full in the neck and face.

Orin heard the retort as he turned onto Halston Street, saw Jerry on his back, Jack Gaines just arriving as the black kid leaped from the porch and ran for the side of the house. The car jumped the curb as Orin drove after the kid, across the lawn, through hedges, banging down garbage cans and scattering lawn furniture, the kid right in front of him, screeching to a halt with the kid pinned against the garage.

He was young, maybe seventeen, with a gold chain around his neck and a Georgetown sweatshirt. His hair was in a peak, like Gumby, razor cuts down the sides of his head. He was trying to pump the shotgun slide, to chamber another shell.

Orin thrust his pistol out the window left-handed and fired, missing with many, hitting with a few. The boy spun sideways and crumpled.

Orin got out of the car and made sure the kid was dead, then ran back through the flattened hedge, around the house to the front where Jerry lay, blue eyes open, his life leaking into the dead brown lawn. Sirens wailed.

Neighborhood people were cautiously approaching, some with hands to their cheeks, dismayed. Orin re-loaded.

19

It was a nice funeral. The line of blue stretched six deep along Merrick Road for over a mile. Some had come from as far away as California and New Mexico. There were thousands of them, lean ones with chests filled with medals, soft ones who looked like they most enjoyed giving motorists directions to the county fair, each with a black band across his shield, each having at one time or another imagined himself in that heavy black coffin under the flag. They stood at attention, bursting with a threatening, violent pride, locked together for a moment by a bond of blood and honor.

After the mass on the steps of the Catholic church, Orin and Moses removed the flag from the lid and folded it with military precision, it being a ceremonial duty not unfamiliar to either. Bowing slightly, Orin presented the flag to Christine Santos.

She almost hadn't come, feeling lost and left out of the spectacle of a policeman's death, but Orin had convinced her that it was a moment much more hers than any goddamned police department's, no matter what any of them blathered about the brotherhood. What bothered her, though, was how little say she had had in the arrangements; she had not even been consulted. She had thought to bury him in a favorite suit, but of course they laid him out in full uniform. Such was the tradition, the way it was always done, and always would be.

Moses leaned forward to kiss her cheek. "We loved him, too," he said.

She nodded and backed into the cluster of immediate family and close friends, holding the flag to her heart. Orin stepped to her side and put his arm around her waist.

Just behind her, alongside her eldest daughter, stood Jack Gaines. He almost looked sadder than he had a right to be, as if it were his fault, or as if it was he who had suffered the greatest loss. Maggie stood with Consuela a few people back. Looking for Paul, Jack had found Maggie instead. He had been the one to tell her. She had sat down quickly at Paul's kitchen table for a moment and then had run to the bathroom, sick to her stomach. She returned to the kitchen ashen, her hair wet, hands shaking, like his.

The motorcycle contingent, a combined honor guard from New York City, Suffolk, and Nassau seventy-five strong, lined up in front of the hearse. Behind the flower-covered open tumbril a squad of mounted police sat at attention on horses braided and blinkered, working hard on the reins to keep their frightened mounts in line. The silver hot engines of the motorcycles roared, then—with a wave of the leader's hand—fell silent.

The beat of drums, muffled and haunting, was heard. The kilted Emerald Society Pipe Band formed a circle on the steps of the church and stood resplendent in bright green and scarlet tartans. The sun, firing glints of light off metallic snare drums, stabbed at the eyes of the crowd. The muffled beat ceased. The whole of Merrick Road was still.

A lone piper stepped from the circle and moved smartly to the top step. He stood to attention, the chill wind ruffling his feathered cap. He filled the Scotch plaid bag with hard-earned air and played "Baldur the Brave, Keeper of the Rainbow Bridge."

A whining thread of sound from his pipes led into "Amazing Grace." At the second stanza, the entire band joined in, sending up a strident howling. Drumsticks twirled, cymbals crashed. Christine Santos buried her face in Orin's chest, then recovered herself. The music stopped.

The motorcycles exploded. An uncle replaced Orin, who joined the other pallbearers. The coffin was laid gently in the hearse. The procession moved away, like a long blue scarf unwinding along the avenue.

Headquarters was making Jack Gaines nervous. At the door to Daniels's office, he checked his uniform, knocked and was summoned in.

"How are you doing, kid?" Daniels said. "Sit down."

"Fine, sir." Jack sat. "So what's this about?"

"I just wanted a preview of your Grand Jury testimony tomorrow, is all. And, again, I'm terribly sorry about Santos. I know you were close."

"Yes, sir. Thanks. He was going to stand in as father-of-the-bride at my wedding this summer." Jack felt tears building along the lower edge of his lids. He tipped his head back, and away slightly, to contain them. He found a spot over Daniels's shoulder and focused on it: a photograph of a small black boy, well dressed, beaming. Daniels tossed a pencil onto the desk.

Daniels said, "You were the third officer on the scene, is that correct?"

"Yes, sir."

Daniels didn't say anything, giving the young man time to compose himself.

Jack said, "I never saw anybody die before. That day I saw two. One of them was just about the kindest person I've ever known."

"The kid was dead before he ever hit the ground."

"I'm sure Boyd didn't intend to outright kill him."

"You're sure, I'm not."

"He was firing left-handed."

"So he says."

"He's a first-rate officer, Sergeant."

"I've got to admit, at one time, yes. Boyd was a tremendous cop early on, maybe his first five or six years. He changed."

"The job changes you."

"Whatever. But as a rookie he never would have done what he did. That seventeen-year old would still be alive."

"And Jerry would still be dead."

"That's what a cop gets paid for—taking that kind of risk. The shotgun was jammed. Orin Boyd put two out of six shots in him. Why did Boyd feel the need to execute an essentially disarmed kid?"

"The kid was holding the weapon. He had just killed a cop, what, ten seconds earlier?" Jack shrugged. "How do you expect me to know what he was thinking or the kid was thinking. I don't even know what I was thinking. It was so fast . . ."

Daniels propped a foot on an open drawer and tilted back his chair. "You plan on doing twenty here?"

"I suppose," Jack said.

"Do you know that I could make them the worst years of your life. Get your transferred around. Get you on all the shit details when you got there. Footposts and like that—the whole Buoy 9 routine. You know what I'm telling you?"

"Sure I do. I half expected it, to tell you the truth."

"Do you care?"

"Yeah, I care. I've seen what's been done to Boyd. I know you've got plenty enough power around here to fuck me up for good."

"So."

"So several things. Do you really think you could make all those years worse than being branded a rat by every cop on the job? Two: how can I give him up when every damn day for the rest of my life I'm going to regret not having emptied my whole gun into that fucking kid sooner than he did so that maybe Jerry Santos wouldn't be holding down a permanent fucking footpost out at Fairleigh Memorial Park. Orin's a hero, Sergeant, if you haven't heard."

"Hero, huh?" said Daniels. "Well,"—he rubbed his eyes—"I guess you're gonna do what you gotta do. It's a shame, you know. The other cops going deaf and dumb doesn't surprise me, but I thought, somehow, with your background, you might have seen it differently." He nudged the drawer shut that his foot had been on and sat up. "Don't worry about me screwing you. You called my bluff. I wouldn't waste my time." Gaines got up. "Oh, while you're having your daily regrets, you'd better pray that someone else doesn't cross Boyd in his remaining time with us. I'll see you around."

Officer Gaines left. Detective Sergeant Daniels tossed the thick, dog-eared work record of Orin Boyd back into his out basket. Less than a minute later Orin Boyd was announced.

"Are you serious about jumping on my shit about this shooting?"

"No. I thought I'd best make it look good though." He pointed to a thick file on his desk. "The shooter's. Seventeen and his file must be three inches thick already." He sat down and pointed to the other chair. "The kid was a member of Bubba Sims's junior league. I presume you realize the target wasn't Santos."

"Yeah," Boyd said.

"They must be upset with you."

"No more than the brass in the Thirteenth. So what's the story with the commissioner?"

Daniels made a face. "He is, as the shrinks would say, conflicted. He wants results, now. He wants to know. And he doesn't wanna know. 'Good idea, poor execution,' is his new line on this investigation. With Donnelly gone, I get the impression the commissioner wishes it would all go away, quietly."

"Then what am I doing here, with my ass hanging out the window?"

"Police work is what you're doing here. It needs doing. The Thirteenth has gotta be cleaned up. You got to get something on these people."

"How about a murder?"

Daniels straightened. "You're serious."

"Yeah. Maybe you remember it. A vagrant named Ossie King. Ril, Shaw and Donnelly iced him—beat him to death. August 19, 1984."

"Jesus. What have you got for evidence."

Orin sighed. "A dead bum's testimony is about it."

"Yeah," Daniels said, "that will hold up. Great. I can just see the DA salivating over that one. Are you sure there's nothing, nobody else?"

"Nothing."

Daniels rubbed his face; there were too many long nights in this job. "Maybe the commissioner is right."

"He wants to tank this?"

"Not exactly, but he's leaning that way. We haven't come up with anything and it's been quite a while."

"And it's not going to make him any friends in high places, or in the Department."

"Yeah." Daniels sounded resigned.

"Well, tell him it's too late. They've gone too far, and I'm in too deep."

Daniels put on his game face. "If we say it's over, it's over. You understand, Boyd? You're not some fuckin' cowboy. You're a police officer doing a job."

"Yes, sir," Boyd said, "I'll try to remember that the next time I talk to Jerry's wife. Be seein' you."

20

Police Commissioner David Trimble pushed the folder away, removed his bifocals, and rubbed his eyes. This Blogg fellow had to be a titless wonder, he thought, a supervisor of clerks. The man's title had been Administrative Officer, and his duties included the issuance of equipment, the maintenance of vehicles, and the raising and lowering of the flag. The only up side was that Commissioner Trimble was confident the man was honest. Internal Affairs had given him their highest rating for integrity. Still, Trimble had been reluctant to entrust his most violent, racially divided precinct to a clod whose closest brush with an emergency decision was a broken traffic light.

The commissioner rubbed his cheeks and examined his manicured nails. The 13th Precinct had desperately needed a new commanding officer by March, yet after screening the men eligible for the job, he felt like he was searching for a martyr. From the forty candidates, he had received exactly one letter requesting the post—Blogg's. The other captains had chosen to bide their time and wait for less volatile commands to come open. Three thousand cops under his command and *one* had come forward.

James Donnelly had been an unqualified disaster for at least the last ten years. His macho management style—once the norm among the Irish brass who dominated the department after World War II—failed to impress the younger cops. But Blogg . . .

Trimble sat back in his high-backed swivel chair, filled his pipe, and studied the latest report from Daniels. The phone buzzed: his secretary announcing Detective Daniels on line 4. He thanked her and picked up.

"Sergeant."

"Yes, sir. Good morning."

"Not exactly correct," said the commissioner.

"What is it?"

"Some complications in that confidential matter we've had under review."

"Bad news?"

"Bad news."

Orin quietly took his place in the muster room among the men. Someone had written BOYD-BRAIN on the blackboard using the side of the chalk. Word was out. A couple of guys patted him on the back. Paul Kellog returned the raincoat he had borrowed, Kole returned the leather jacket. Moses caught him up on station-house gossip, including the news that Archibald Blogg was now reluctant to speak out loud. "He thinks the place be bugged, so he's into sign language. Ril does the interpretation, seeing as how he's almost as fucked up as Blogg."

Orin said, "I'm glad to see nothing changes."

"Only thing changes around here is the number of days I got left to retirement."

Archibald Blogg and Sergeant Ril entered the muster room like a comedy team and sat down at the head of the table. A star-shaped smattering of spackle filled the bullet hole in the wall above their heads. Ril read a list of significant items to the men, then a sheet of paper that Blogg shoved in front of his face. "Oh, yeah," he said. "The boss wants each of you to take a yardstick out on patrol from now on. We're gonna start measuring the hedges at intersections this week and citing owners who allow growth of more than thirty-six inches."

There was more than the usual grumbling from the men, which was odd, considering how few hedges were left in Belmont.

Dominick Ril slammed his hand on the table. "Just do it, for Christ's sake. Why do you guys always have to bitch?"

" 'Cause you don't," said Jack Gaines.

"Now, now." Archie Blogg stood up behind the lectern with a stack of file cards in his hands. The floor was muddy, the air smelled of leather, wool, and cigarettes. Blogg cleared his throat and called for their attention. "Gentlemen, a moment of your time, *por favor.*" His tone of voice was cheerful, self-satisfied. "I have an announcement of the utmost importance."

Insolent expressions of disbelief appeared on every face because the last time he came to them with one of these con jobs, they were forced to contribute five dollars apiece for the removal from the locker-room walls of graffiti, the content of which, he informed them, bore the unmistakable mark of poorly motivated police officers.

"It is my great pleasure to report to you that our Live and Let Live Initiative for dealing with the various ethnic groups in this precinct has been an unqualified success. Assaults are down since the beginning of the year, robberies are down, we've even gone thirty-six days with only two homicides. I'm proud to say, we've improved every statistic so far this very remarkable year, except for chain snatchings and automobile accidents. May I say to you men, well done."

The uniformed policemen breathed a collective sigh of relief and loosened their death grips on their wallets.

As the men dispersed, Orin was cornered by a gloating Sergeant Reagan and ordered to report upstairs immediately to the commanding officer of the precinct. None of the guys behind the desk or at the switchboard looked at him as Reagan accompanied him to Inspector Blogg's office door. Orin stopped in the hallway and tried to pry from him advance notice of his problem, but all No Relation would say was that this time he had really fucked up.

Orin nodded gravely, then knocked on Donnelly's—now Blogg's—door.

"Come in."

Archibald Blogg offered Orin a seat, but Orin said that he preferred to stand.

"Fine," said Blogg, who also remained standing. "See if I give a damn."

"What seems to be the problem, sir?"

Blogg looked him up and down, as if he were the lowest slime on earth. "How could you?" he said.

"How could I what?"

"I'm so disappointed."

"About what?"

"It's not good, Orin. It's not good at all."

"Sounds like?" Orin said, tugging on his earlobe.

"You've been charged with repeatedly porking a retarded girl, a girl mentally incompetent to give her consent."

Orin laughed out loud. "Is that all?"

"Is that *all?* Surely you jest. We're talking statutory rape here, Boyd, for diddling some mental retardate."

"I refuse to believe that Judy failed the test!"

"Judy?" said Blogg. "The unfortunate named in this complaint is a Lonnie something. Who the hell is Judy? Just how many nuts have you cracked?"

"May I face my accuser?"

"Of course not. As this is not a criminal matter yet, your civil rights are extremely limited."

"That sounds fair."

"How do you answer the anticipated charges?" said Blogg.

"What charges?"

"You know, that you're frigging this Lonnie . . . Terrell," he said, finding her name in papers on his desk.

"It's bullshit," Orin said. "Very dangerous bullshit."

Blogg sat down wearily in his chair and assumed the posture of a father correcting the behavior of a wayward child. "You're going to have to do better than that," he said. "I understand she gave a statement."

"Archie, the girl can't even read."

"Give me some kind of explanation. Say anything, for God's sake. I have to send in these disciplinary forms . . . I'm supposed to conduct a preliminary investigation. For the Trial Board, I'm afraid."

"Do what ya gotta do," Orin said.

Archibald Blogg buried his head in his arms. "This is terrible," he said.

"Jeez, Arch, try not to take it so hard."

"But we were so close."

"Ah, yes," Orin said. "That we were."

"Really?"

"I mean, we didn't slash our wrists and mix the blood, but we were cool. We got along."

Blogg smiled warmly, as if appreciating an old friend anew. "I don't believe a word of it, you know. I told them you were Catholic."

"Answer a question, buddy of mine. Is my accuser a cop from this precinct or somewhere else?"

"Ah-ah-ah. Don't presume on our friendship. All I can say is that certain members of the force have come forward with certain information. That, and I must warn you not to have any contact whatsoever with Miss Looney Tunes. I don't think the Department would have any trouble at all charging you with tampering."

"Am I suspended?"

"Not yet. The investigation is continuing. You have just been advised of active and pending charges, per your contractual rights."

"Well, you know what then, sir? Fuck you and the horse you rode in on. You may consider my refusal to explain away these charges a personal declaration of war. Don't forget to tell your douche-bag friends."

Orin squared his shoulders and turned for the door, showing Archibald Blogg his Parris Island posture, the steel in his weary spine.

He called Judy at her office. He told her that he needed to see her right away.

She said, "I was just about to call you."

"Oh, yeah?"

"Yes. I just got to work."

"You?" he said. "Late to work? Has anyone alerted Wall Street?"

"I'm late because a very large man was waiting outside the house this morning when I went to put Dawn on the bus. He called out to me, asking for you. I told Dawn to run back into the house."

"That was good," said Orin. "Then what?"

"I told him that you didn't live there anymore, that you never came by, but he insisted on leaving a package for you. A shoe box."

"You didn't open it."

"Would you stop talking to me like I'm a child."

"You are a child," he said, "in situations like this. You panic, Judy. You burst into tears if someone spills beer on your carpet. Now what did this man look like?"

"He was big, much bigger than you."

"Height, weight, age, race, any facial hair . . . scars, marks, deformities, tattoos. What was he wearing, Jude? Describe his manner of speech. Did he appear intoxicated? How did he get there? How did he leave? Little things, Judy. Simple little things."

"He was black. He had a car. It was red."

"A black man in a red car. Great. What kind?"

"I don't know. Full size."

"And the license plate number was . . ."

"I didn't get it."

"You *see* what I'm saying? Dawn should have sent *you* inside. Then I'd have some way of finding this son of a bitch and stopping his clock!"

Judy turned icy. "I didn't *have* to take down his license, Orin. He left a business card. His name is Sherman Clayborne. He said his business was imports, exports—and funerals."

Orin's knees went weak. "Meet me at the house."

"My lawyer doesn't think that would be wise."

"You called your *lawyer* about this—before you called me?"

"Who was I supposed to turn to?"

So maybe I'm not through rolling with the punches, he thought, stunned at how quickly the distance between them had grown. How alone he had left his wife and his child. Judy, in a moment of terror, had run into the kitchen and called that punk legal eagle before she had called him.

"I'm sorry," he said. "I . . ."

"I'll meet you there in forty-five minutes."

As Orin pulled into the driveway, Judy stepped from the front door wearing a turquoise business suit and black high heels. She had a yellow flower pinned to her lapel, and though she wore makeup, her face was pale.

"Where's the box, Judy?"

She made a petulant face at him. "Around back. By the shed. And hello to you, too."

"Stay right here," he said. "On second thought, go get me a martini."

"I don't keep liquor in the house anymore."

"You're kidding. That faggot boss of yours stopped drinking?"

"Don't make me say something that will hurt your feelings, Orin. You wanted to help me, so help me."

"Where's Dawn?"

"At school."

"Beautiful," he said. "Good. I'm sorry I got on your case. Now stay put." He walked around the house to the shed, where he found the green shoe box on the ground near the white wooden door. He looked back over his shoulder and saw that she had followed him as far as the fence, where she was standing next to a bush, her arms folded beneath her breasts, coat open, staring at him in wonderment.

Fuck it, he thought, she's earned the right to watch.

He got down on both knees and sniffed the box, then picked it up in his fingertips and weighed it, everything an experienced officer does not do when confronted with a bomb. The package had not the heft of a bomb, or any heft at all, though it could be plastique, he supposed. Holding his breath, he lifted the lid.

There was a piece of cardboard with a strip of masking tape attached. Crudely written on the tape was his daughter's first name. He recognized it as the one she had so proudly printed and attached to her cubby hole at preschool. He replaced the cover on the box, stood up, and tucked it under his arm.

Judy walked toward him like a zombie. "What is it?" she said. "What's going on?"

"Could we go inside for a minute. I won't stay long."

"Don't I know it," she said.

A spasm of pain creased his face, and he suppressed the urge to retaliate in kind. She was right, he thought. He was a midnight mover, a ghost, and not at all the kind of man with whom a woman ought to build a future. He looked over her pretty head to the roof that needed patching, the trim crying out for a second coat of paint. He did not have even the consolation of leaving her well off.

She led him into the quiet little house, and they sat facing each other across the kitchen table. She offered him a cup of coffee, which he refused. "How about a sandwich or something? You look like you're losing weight."

"No thanks."

"So what is it, Orin? What the hell have you got yourself into this time?"

"A bit of a jam."

" 'A bit of a jam,' " she repeated.

He opened his checkbook and started writing. "Here's four months of payments in advance . . . actually all I've got. That ought to hold you till I get my act straightened out."

She picked up the check and examined it. "Trouble at work?"

"You think I socialize with that undertaker?"

"No."

"Listen to me carefully: Take your vacation now, beginning tonight. You're gonna have to pull Dawn from school for a while. Bermuda, Florida, hell I don't care if you go to Newark, as long as you pay for your tickets in cash."

"You are even more than normally out of your mind. I can't do that, Orin. I have to finish a presentation by next Wednesday. Our lives can't simply stop because you've got professional difficulties. What's the matter?" she said. "Why are you staring at me like that?"

"Because I'm mad enough to smack your goddamn face!"

The color drained from Judy's cheeks; she put her hand to her lips and held her breath.

Orin's voice was shaky: "There is nothing that you will ever do for that asshole boss of yours that is more important than what I'm telling you to do for me. Your life is in danger. Dawn's life is in danger. I've got a tiger by the tail and I can't let go."

"It's that bad?" she said. "Really? I mean you've told me lies more farfetched than this to get a night out with the boys."

"You're not hearing me, Judy. Listening is more than waiting for your turn to talk."

"But—"

"It's bad."

"Enough," she said, suddenly holding up her hand. "Spare me the sordid details. I'll pack some of our things. We can go to my sister's house."

"Thank you. For my part, I promise to bring this situation to a swift and certain conclusion. I know how much you need your strokes at work."

"Just don't get yourself killed," she said.

"Mikey Garrett has my will in his office, just in case. I left all of it to you and Dawn, all of my worldly goods that aren't already yours."

"Is there anything else?" she asked, looking at the check, her watch, the cuticle on her index finger. She was rattled.

"What more could we possibly say at this stage of the game?" he said.

"I don't know. Maybe millions of things, maybe we haven't even scratched the surface yet."

"Maybe someday we won't hate each other. And maybe Dawn will be okay."

Her eyes were sparkling with tears. "Why the hell did everything have to change? Why couldn't we have changed together?"

He shrugged and slumped lower in his chair, remembering. "I don't know," he said. "But we made Dawn. That's worth it all."

"First you got old, then I got old. You thought I was a jerk, I knew you were a jerk . . ."

"Then it was over."

She bit her lower lip and complained, "It all seems so suddenly final. Like without even noticing it, we missed our last chance."

That was true, he thought. He had also always assumed they could pull the marriage out of the loss column with a stirring fourth-quarter come-back. Now the game was over.

"God," he said, "I feel like . . ." Orin stood up and walked behind her chair, bent from the waist and kissed the top of her head. "Give Dawn one of these for me every single day," he said.

"I will," she said. "She'll need them."

Dawn came home from school on the bus while Judy was still packing. Orin took her outside. They cleared the unmelted snow from the walk and built a small snowman, which they then took turns pelting with snowballs he made, until it was time to go in.

Judy Boyd sat at the kitchen table drinking coffee.

"I don't wanna go," Dawn said as he held the door for her to walk into the house. "I wanna stay here with Daddy."

"Hurry up," Judy said to her. "Get your doll and let's go."

Orin followed them out to the car. Judy was quiet as she strapped Dawn into the front seat. Lines creased Judy's pale forehead.

"Look," he said. "I—"

"Just don't say anything, okay?" She started the engine and rolled up her window.

"Hey," he said, to get her attention but their car was turning into the road. "I love you, kid."

Standing at the end of the blacktop driveway, looking at his small brick house and then the other houses on the block, Orin was struck by their pathetic similarity; cape after cape, one square lot after the other. Orin's had no garage, but it did have the patio that in summer was surrounded by cotton-candy rosebushes. A selling point, should they be forced to sell the place.

He went inside and poured himself a cup of coffee and a bowl of Captain Crunch. Putting the milk back, he noticed an original crayon masterpiece affixed to the freezer door with strawberry magnets: an open-faced house with a mommy and a daddy and a baby and a cat. He turned away and sat down at the breakfast table.

Peace and quiet and Judy's paper. Who had it better than he? Scanning the regional section, his eye caught a photograph of Bubba Sims in a business suit. He was accepting the grateful appreciation of a local state assemblyman for his work with disadvantaged youngsters.

How does he get away with it? Orin wondered. He looked at his watch. On the radio the soothing voice of the Reverend Sims was melodically welcoming any and all interested sinners to join the great march to heaven. Salvation, he cried, was near at hand, if only man would see the Midnight Light.

Orin threw his hand in the air. "I see it, Reverend. I feels it. And you will, too."

He pulled on his jacket and left quickly, the kitchen door locking itself behind him. He did not have a key anymore.

21

Inspector Blogg's preliminary report on the allegations made against Police Officer Orin Boyd arrived at headquarters on Monday. The Trial Board immediately set aside all other business and considered the matter that same afternoon. There was the damaging written statement, with the childlike signature at the bottom, and the deposition of the investigating detective, Detective Robert Shaw. There was the report from the intake psychiatrist at the hospital stating only that Lonnie Terrell had many times been sexually abused in her life. The evaluation did not mention Orin Boyd. The Trial Board considered Orin's hostile reaction during his interview with Inspector Blogg. They considered Orin's previous record.

The following morning a pair of detectives from the Internal Affairs Division responded to the 13th Precinct station house and called Orin in from the street. Downstairs in the muster room they advised him of his constitutional rights to silence and counsel, then delivered formal notification to him of his suspension without pay. His two .38-caliber revolvers, his shield, and his ID card were confiscated, bagged, and tagged for the Property Bureau, pending the outcome of the investigation.

During this ritual stripping, Orin said nothing to either detective. Then Detective Sergeant Arthur Hanley, the older of the two dicks, tried to good-guy a statement of admission out of Orin: to get the truth down on paper, he said, to clear the stench from the air. He must have thought Orin was intimidated. He must have thought Orin — like almost everyone else these bullies flopped — was thinking of his unpaid bills and family responsibilities, his disintegrating reputation in the community.

What Arthur Hanley didn't know was that the moment they had taken his guns and his tin, Orin felt not the lack of strength they might have hoped for, but the rush of exhilarating freedom.

Orin draped his heavy arm over Hanley's shoulders and whispered softly into his ear, "Get fucked, Handjob. I didn't do it."

"Good. Then you'll get off."

"I don't want to get off. I want to get even."

Detective Hanley seemed to droop under the weight of Orin's arm.

"Did you hear me?" Orin said. " 'Cause I'd like it to get back. That's what you girls do best, isn't it, carry tales?"

"Come on, Boyd. Let me go!"

Hanley's partner, a chubby young cop named Rankowsky, took one small step closer and asked Sergeant Hanley if he was having a problem.

"Yeech," Hanley squawked.

Orin tightened the clinch around Hanley's neck. "You tell your no-balls boss that I've done everything on this job but rob a bank and fuck a faggot, and you punks still don't have a clue."

"Oh, we'll tell him," said Rankowsky. "You can bet your ass we'll tell 'em."

Orin released his chokehold on Hanley and shoved him into his partner. "Come on," he said to them, his hands at his sides, palms up, taunting them like a kid in a schoolyard. "Just me and the two of you. What could be fairer? I'll bet after sucking hind tit all day, you guys could use a little workout."

Hanley and Rankowsky closed ranks, telling each other how they wished they were free to kick Boyd's butt.

Orin laughed. "The only thing 'tween you and me is air and opportunity. Let's get it on."

Hanley and Rankowsky backed out of the muster room. Orin followed them slowly like a dog they couldn't take their eyes off. Hanley and Rankowsky ran up the metal staircase, screaming for their lives, right into the arms of Archibald Blogg, who was lounging by his doorway, eating an ice-cream cone.

Detective Rankowsky explained to Inspector Blogg what had happened, while Hanley rubbed his throat from time to time and quacked like a duck.

Orin was approaching. Other cops behind the desk and civilians on the bench stopped talking.

"Inspector Blogg," Orin said loudly, stopping in front of the desk. "These two character assassins just told me they have pictures of you and Sergeant Ril taking little boys into a closet. They said you're members of some man-boy love organization."

Blogg's eyes flew open wide. "You stop that kind of filthy talk."

"They showed me the leather masks, the spiked belts, those tiny, tiny briefs."

"Orin, you get into my office at once."

"Alone? With you? Bullshit, my duce. I see the way you're licking that cone."

Blogg's face turned white. He turned to Lieutenant Fazio who had the unfortunate luck to be the desk officer at this particular moment in precinct history. "Wipe that stupid smile off your face, Lieutenant. I'm ordering you to have this man placed in a straitjacket."

Fazio looked over the top of his eyeglasses at Blogg. "Water it, sir. Maybe it will grow."

Blogg's jaw fell open, his face blanched. "You're suspended, too!"

Fazio stood up and threw down his pen. "I am? Really? That's great, sir. Now *you* get a fucking ambulance for the pregnant lady on Pearsall Avenue, and you find out where that fucking doctor—who's supposed to make that pronouncement on Ray Street—went. And when you're done with that, go upstairs and find out if the guys are torturing the prisoners again, or if all that screaming is someone jerking us off. Then, Inspector, figure out how you're gonna cover the school crossings this afternoon while you also decide what you want from the deli for lunch."

Archibald Blogg looked away and raised his hand. "I get the point, Lieutenant. Forget I said a word."

"Inspector," said Rankowsky. "If you'd like our help subduing this man—"

"*Hey!*" newly reinstated Lieutenant Fazio screamed from behind the desk. "What kind of rank are you guys carrying?"

Arthur Hanley said that he was a sergeant.

"Well that ain't gonna be fucking good enough," said Lieutenant Fazio. "*Capice?* Now I'm ordering you out of my station house. Or I'll have Officer Boyd physically remove you." He glanced at Officer Boyd. "You'd do that for me, wouldn't you, Orin? Even though you're temporarily off the clock."

"I mean, hey, Vinny, for *you?*"

"We're going," said Hanley. "What the fuck do we care."

"And don't come back," Orin said.

"I hope I never have to see this nuthouse again."

A uniformed crowd gathered downstairs in the locker room to provide moral support for Orin Boyd and to roundly curse Inspector Archibald Blogg, Police Commissioner Trimble, the system in general, and the two shoofly motherfuckers who were at that moment racing for headquarters with Orin's guns and shield.

Orin thanked George and the boys for being there, then told them there was nothing nobody could do. He was gone, he was ashes, he was *astala* bye-bye. Thanks, but no thanks. He was standing in front of his locker, taking off his uniform, when Moses offered him money.

"Thanks, bro. But I'm doing okay. I got things I can sell," he said, lifting his cold nine millimeter pistol from the top shelf of his locker into his gym bag. "When I'm done with them, that is."

They were the only customers in the Stallion Bar.

"What did they say you did?" George asked.

"You don't want to know." Orin bent closer.

"Did you do it?"

"No."

George started to scratch his chest. "Did I *not* do it with you?"

"Not even close, George."

George winced as he shifted his weight on the barstool. "Where's it coming from?"

"The reverend."

George lowered his voice. "What about inside the job?"

Orin shrugged.

"Ril." George said.

"Ril?" Orin looked skeptical. "Me and him have never crossed swords."

"He hates your guts from the kick-off party. He thinks you were the one threw the round."

"That was you, George. Remember? I'm the one who sacrificed his chromosomes and drank the punch that saved your career."

"I know that, and you know that . . ."

"Beautiful, George. Another name for my list."

"Don't put nothing past Dom. I'm serious. When Donnelly was here, the little cocksucker was ruthless." George looked up into Orin's pale eyes. "What are you gonna do?"

"Boogie."

Juliet Cammer had just plugged in the Mr. Coffee when Orin flew through the open office door. She looked him up and down and frowned. His hair was disheveled, he needed a shave, there was tar on his blue jeans and words on his sweatshirt said: On the 8th day God created Jerry Garcia.

"Did you hear?" he said breathlessly. "I got suspended from the job."

"They called a little while ago."

Orin had to laugh. "You know, it's truly amazing the things they're good at."

Juliet Cammer was in no mood for jokes. "Orin, you can't stop coming right now. This is a critical time. I'd like to carry you for free for the time being, if that's okay. You can pay me back later when everything works out."

"I'm overwhelmed by your offer, but you know I can't accept it."

"Why not?"

" 'Cause that's the kind of guy I am."

"You're a fool."

"I'll take that under advisement. What I would like, however, is for you to appear in my behalf at the departmental trial, as my one and only character witness. I need you to sit up there like a big girl and tell them I wouldn't boff a retarded kid. Can you do it? The insubordination charge from Blogg and the harassment from Hanley I can deal with by myself."

Juliet's auburn hair fell forward, concealing all but the tip of her nose. "I wish I could," she said. "But I can't."

"Why not?"

"I haven't been working with you long enough to make that kind of judgment under oath. The department psychiatrist would destroy me on rebuttal."

"So some guy who doesn't know me at all will testify about my depraved sexual appetites, and everyone will take it as gospel. While you, who I've been spilling my guts to, won't say diddly squat in my behalf."

"Spilling your guts?" she said incredulously.

"Who else do I tell my problems?"

"You never even mentioned a Lonnie Terrell, Orin. I had no idea who they were talking about."

Orin shook his head in sorrow. "I'll catch you around the campus, Dr. Cammer. Thanks for all your help."

"Would you call me next week. Let me know how things are going?"

"No," he said. "I don't think so."

"Daniels," Daniels said into the phone before he was even half awake.

"It's me."

"Yeah, I recognized the voice. Wait a second." Daniels switched on the light, tossed the receiver under his pillow, switched off the light, and padded out of his bedroom quietly so as not to wake his wife.

He went into his den across the hall and closed the door. The night sky was bright, the room silvery. He picked up the phone and slumped into his lounger.

"I'm here," he said.

"I'm there," said Orin, "way out there. And I want to check the scoreboard."

"Right," Daniels said. "You've been suspended. They've got the girl out of the county somewhere. The Trial Board has passed on the charges to the DA—statutory rape, incompetent incapable of consent. That's a tough charge for a cop, Orin."

"You know it's bullshit—smoke to cover themselves."

"It's doing a good job of fogging things up."

"So what's the score."

"You're off the case."

"Trimble?"

"Yeah. He says you should get a good lawyer, but we're not to recommend anyone. Maintain maximum distance."

"And the Thirteenth?"

"He thinks it's turning around by itself. Blogg's an idiot, but controllable and too stupid to be corrupt, which I guess was the idea behind putting the asshole in charge."

"And Abraham Wilson and Jerry Santos are in their warm beds."

There was an uncomfortable silence. Finally Daniels said, "If you keep a low profile, I think the interest in you will cool. There's no season ticket on you that I've picked up on."

"I'm so relieved. My wife will be, too. We can rest assured now that our kid won't be threatened—again."

"You sound pissed."

"How can you say that?"

"What are you going to do?"

"I'm not telling."

"What else is new."

"But do give the commissioner my regards and thanks for his concern. I am touched. He should have a Happy Easter."

"Orin—"

The line went dead.

George Clarke was waiting for him in the parking lot behind Alimony Acres, slumped half asleep behind the wheel of his T-Bird. He jerked upright when he heard Orin's knock on his window. He asked Orin where he had been. He had called and called, then finally come over to see if Orin had ended it all. But there was no sign of anyone.

"I've been here and there," Orin said. "Running errands. I can't stay in the Hole anymore. But, hey, thanks for thinking I'd kill myself."

"Don't mention it."

"How's your cold?"

George beat on his chest like a monkey. "Nobody gets a piece of this rock."

Orin grinned. "I need some information, George. About Shaw and Bubba, and Ril."

"It's all eyewash, man. Let it be."

"No way."

"They're scum. What more can I tell you?"

"A whole lot more, I hope. Like about beating a man named Ossie King to death a couple of years ago."

"Never happened. Ril and Shaw beat the case in the grand jury. They couldn't even hang a negligent homicide beef on them."

"What about Donnelly?"

"What about him? He didn't have nothing to do with that." George paused. "Did he?"

"How'd they beat the case?"

"I guess they lied good. How does anybody beat a case? They had a secret witness come forward, said he'd been with the dead guy after Ril and Bobby, and everything was hunky-dory."

"I wish I'd known this shit earlier."

"Hey," said George, "all you gotta do is ask."

Then George announced that he had done a lot of thinking since Jerry got shot, that he was forty-five years old and didn't have nothing going for himself but a little extra pussy on the side. His future, unless he won the lottery, looked predictable and drab. God forbid he should have to retire to Florida with all the other dirtbag cops. Twenty years from now, okay. But not now, in the prime of his life.

Maybe it was time to take a shot at the freaking moon, he said. "Time to roll those laughing bones." With enough money he could go out west, maybe Vegas. "I think I hear Mr. Opportunity knocking on our doors."

"Our doors?"

"That's right."

"You think I'm about to do something illegal."

"And lucrative," George said, grinning.

"We've been together too long."

"You're gonna scheme something and split. You got the look."

"What makes you think it'll double the money if you help?"

"Because . . . shit, I don't know. Two heads are better than one?"

"Don't expect me to talk you in to it," said Orin. "A really good friend doesn't encourage a buddy to throw away his pension."

"Who said we're gonna get caught?"

"Who said we're gonna get away with it?"

George was getting dreamy-eyed, drifting away from the subject of risk. "Money that you find you don't mind spending. We could have us a freaking blast."

"One shot ain't gonna make you rich. Five, ten, twelve, thousand, George."

"There's got to be more than that."

"Maybe, maybe not."

George refused to be dissuaded. "You got a plan?"

"I got the big picture down."

"What do you have in mind?"

"Don't jerk me off, George. First, are you in or are you out?"

George exhaled deeply. "Fuck it. I'm in."

"And you're gonna keep your big fat mouth shut?"

"Hey!" said George, wounded.

"Don't kid yourself, son. I'm a manic depressive and you're a shameless gossip. That's a terrible combination for success."

"I swear to God that I won't say a word to anyone. You and me, we're going it alone."

Orin cast George a cold, appraising look, weighing the pros and cons of such dubious assistance. He looked down the dismal street.

"Come on, man. What are we doing?" said George.

"I'll give you that on a need-to-know basis."

"You don't trust me?"

"Of course I don't trust you. You might be wearing a wire right now for all I know."

"That's bullshit."

"Think about it, George. If you were me, would you trust you?"

George thought about it for less than a second. "Of course I would. I'm your partner, for God's sake. We got to trust each other or we're freaking doomed. Man, I know I got a big mouth. But this time's gonna be different. This time I tell no one nothing, not a peep, not diddly squat, *nada*. And then you and me, we laugh all the way to the bank."

"Maybe," said Orin.

22

Orin was on the floor of the van as he assembled his arsenal, supplies he had gathered over twenty-four hours: a portable radio, flashlights, flares, Smith & Wesson handcuffs, the cold nine millimeter and three full clips, one hand grenade, one smoke grenade, hi-gloss white enamel spray paint, condoms, masks, surgical gloves, rope, his United States passport, and a picture of Dawn in her lavender swimsuit, taken on Parent's Day at summer camp last year—she on starting blocks at the end of the pool, girls on either side of her perched like birds with their wings spread. Behind them a counselor points a starter's pistol in the air. Dawn stands erect, grimacing, her fingers in her ears. His child, he thought, more than Judy's.

It was time.

George Clarke was waiting for Orin in the parking lot of the Sunrise Mall, a monstrous blaze of concrete and glass. It was one-thirty in the afternoon, and George sat low behind the wheel of his T-Bird. He was also dressed in earth tones.

"I told my wife we had a stakeout," he said. "You really think we'll be done in forty-eight hours?"

"Don't annoy me, okay? I got five thousand things running around in my head and you want me to validate your parking sticker."

"Hey, fuck you, okay. At least I still got a wife I have to answer to. You know what I'm saying? If you're gonna be this way about things, go do what you gotta do by yourself."

"Fine," said Orin. "Me and Gloria can turn the trick without you. Go home and mow the lawn. I'll give you a grand right now to forget you ever met me."

"But—"

Orin curled his upper lip. "Beat it."

"Look," said George. "It's just that I'd feel better about laying my pension on the line if I knew what you had up your sleeve . . . if you'd just tell me you're—how shall we put it—filled with confidence."

Orin said, "Aren't I always?"

George frowned. "I'm gonna regret this. I know it."

Orin had George follow him west on Sunrise Highway to the 13th Precinct. They got off at Main Street, and several blocks later parked both vehicles in front of the Stallion Bar. George got out of his T-Bird and walked up to Orin's truck. "I still can't believe you talked to Glo behind my back."

Orin rolled his eyeballs at George. "Give her your keys," he said. "Tell her again what I told you. Quickly. Don't even think about dipping the wick."

Gloria was waiting for George at the door, her brown eyes beaming. She wore a gray-and-white striped tank top, gray sweatpants, and red rubber sandals. Her hair was wet from a shower, combed straight back from her face. George gave her the keys to his car, again told her Orin's instructions, then asked her to repeat them one more time.

"What do you think I'm stupid? Orin told me, too—twice. I watch Bubba's house and take down all the license plates. If he goes anywhere, I follow him. What's the big fucking deal?"

"Just don't fuck up the car, okay. Stay to the right and go slow. Try to remember everything I showed you down at the beach. And throw all your cigarette butts out the window."

"Do you love me?" she asked.

"You'd better believe it." He kissed her cheek and patted her rump. She giggled and squirmed on his thigh. "I gotta go now. Orin's waiting downstairs."

"You gonna make us a lot of money?"

"I sure as hell hope so."

"Be careful," she said.

"You, too."

Orin Boyd checked his watch as George stepped onto the sidewalk in front of the bar. Five minutes. Not bad. "Get in," he said.

George yanked open the passenger door and climbed into the truck. "Step two?" he said, rubbing his hands together.

"Step eight," said Orin. "Step two was getting out of bed."

They drove to the Main Street entrance to the parkway, then along the grassy shoulder to a jagged break in the woods, where Orin jerked the wheel hard right and pressed the accelerator to the floorboard.

George screamed, "What the fuck?" as the truck hurtled toward the forest wall. He braced his arms on the dashboard, pumped his foot on an imaginary brake.

Through the windshield it looked as if they had driven off a bridge: the blurred splash of pine needles beat on the glass like rain, then the truck slid to a halt in the middle of a perfect clearing. Dust from their plunge through the barrier of branches hung in the air like the golden glow on old photographs.

"Well I'll be damned," said George. In the back of the grove, old milk cartons had been arranged around a steamer trunk, a hammock fashioned from dead branches, and pizza boxes above the pit-like sunken living room. "You have been a busy scout."

"You could say that."

George's spirits soared, buoyed by the knowledge that preparations had indeed been made, that Orin wasn't going off totally half-cocked.

"And screw those helicopter cops, too," Orin said, pointing to the foliage overhead. "This place is fucking invisible."

"You rigged this up by yourself?" asked George.

"It was left to me. Want to see the garage?"

George scratched his head and looked around. "Sure."

Orin hopped down from the pickup truck and slammed the door. He walked to a stand of pine trees at the northern edge of the clearing and yanked on a rope. The trees fell forward, revealing to George a recently borrowed, freshly painted white step-van.

"Hey!" said George.

There was a company name—VAN-GO NUTS . . . WE DELIVER GOOD-NESS—amateurishly stenciled on the vehicle. Off to the side was a camper cap to mount atop the back of Orin's pickup so as to make it a legal passenger vehicle on the parkways.

Orin slapped George on the back and pointed. "The license plates belong on Ril's Firebird. The number on the driver's door is Archie Blogg's home phone. And, of course, the van belongs to the Church of the Midnight Light. I stole it last night, God forgive me."

George was aghast. "You've lost your freaking mind."

"Do you really think so? I mean, I have gotten into this project, I know. But I need it to work, George. My family's involved. And I'm only gonna get one chance."

"I know," said George. "It's just that . . . this shit is spooky. It's like you're deliberately leaving them clues."

"That's exactly what I'm doing, good buddy. I'm signing my masterpiece."

"Looks more to me like a suicide note."

Orin threw his hands in the air in exasperation. "God, you're depressing. I told you that the day we met and not a fucking thing has changed."

"That's not true," said George. "Plenty has changed. You used to have a job, a wife, a house, and a kid."

"I haven't forgotten my failures. I'm talking about what I gotta do."

"You still want to go through with this?" George said. "It's not too late to turn back, man. That's the beauty of it! We haven't broken any laws yet, right?" He grinned like a showman.

"You haven't broken any laws yet. I, however, stole that truck and those plates, crimes for which you must now arrest me or face criminal charges yourself."

"I forgot about that. It's already too late to back out."

"That's probably what a jury would conclude."

George paced one more lap around the hideout, kicking at the dirt and cursing under his breath.

"George, my man. If they wind up thinking I did it, ain't no one gonna be looking at you."

"I never thought of that."

Orin held his hand out to George, to shake on their bargain.

George's palm was sweaty to the touch.

They crossed the Rubicon at 2:45 P.M. crashing out of the woods in the Van-Go-Nuts like they were riding in a tank. The police radio waves in the 13th were relatively calm. They heard 1308 catch a gun run at Mosley Park, and four cars dispatched to various family fights at the Lincoln projects. The other five two-man patrol cars were cruising the streets or were parked in front of the station house when the stolen van rolled by.

Champagne Danny was first, as it was Orin's preference to tackle the hard parts right away, those moments of maximum exposure.

The delivery truck rolled to a stop at the corner of North Main Street and Lillian Avenue. Orin hopped from the passenger side, wearing a Porky Pig mask over his face. He hit Danny upside the head with his blackjack, then threw a sleeper hold around that fat black neck and held on for dear life. For a moment, stretched over Danny's back, he felt as if he were moving heavy furniture down stairs, and losing control, but a second clip with his blackjack settled the match.

The overhead door on the back of the purloined van rolled up. George Clarke hit the pavement like a paratrooper and helped Orin abduct the goon before anyone on the street realized anything untoward had happened.

A client in the beauty parlor across the street noticed a delivery truck had parked in front of Champagne Danny. When it drove away Danny was gone—sort of. It was strange.

When Champagne Danny regained consciousness, he found himself handcuffed to a pie rack on the bouncing metal floor of the van. Cinnamon crumbs and granules of sugar vibrated before his bloodshot eyes. A white man in a John Travolta mask was watching him, pointing a thirty-eight revolver at his chest. "Oh, wow," said Danny. "Bubba gonna shit."

"Shsssh," said the man in the mask, holding the barrel of his gun to John Travolta's lips. "I don't want to kill you."

Orin turned south on Rochester Street, and then east on Merrick to the car wash at Albany Avenue. It was three o'clock in the afternoon, the end of watch. The night shift moved in with dry rags. The black boys who had dried cars all day peeled off their yellow rubber suits.

Orin slid down in the driver's seat of the idling van and watched Darnell Reeder (who sometimes walked with a limp and sometimes didn't) climb on his ten-speed bike and push off in the direction of the Langston Hughes Housing Projects.

Orin was betting Darnell had, hidden on him somewhere, the day's take from the fleet of foreign cars that made island-wide deliveries from Belmont before returning home for their evening wash and wax.

Orin whipped a U-turn across Albany Avenue, cutting off a county bus, whose driver could be seen flipping him the bird from inside his motorized aquarium. Orin caught up with Darnell Reeder in the middle of the crowded block, then rode even with him until they came to a stretch of empty lots with no parked cars. Orin cut the wheel slightly to the right.

"Yo, motherfu—" he heard Darnell Reeder scream.

Orin faded right another foot, causing the boy to hit the curb and fly headfirst over the handlebars of his bike. He landed in a graceless sprawl on the sidewalk. Stunned, bleeding from the nose and forehead, he was quickly handcuffed by Porky Pig and thrown into the back of the van. Reeder looked momentarily relieved to see Champagne Danny until John Travolta kicked him in the balls.

George closed the overhead door and locked it from the inside. Then he systematically stripped the clothes from Reeder's frail, quivering body and tore them into pieces. He pulled a screwdriver from his back pocket and pried the heels off Darnell's shoes. A flattened wad of twenties and fifties fell from each. George gathered them up and passed them through the sliding interior window to Orin, behind the wheel. The gears ground loudly, the truck lurched forward.

Is this beautiful or what, Orin was thinking. It's like we're practically invisible. There was nothing on the precinct radio but accidents and aided cases. Crime could continue unmolested. He wondered if Bubba Sims knew something was going down yet, if word of strange occurrences had reached high places. He wondered how long the truck would be cool, how long a man wearing a Porky Pig mask could drive a bogus donut van around a suburban ghetto before he drew unwelcome attention. Probably for days, he decided, because everybody else was busy doing their own fucked-up gig, hoping they wouldn't be caught either.

A couple more numbers drops, he decided, then vanish and regroup for the grand finale. And then, he thought wistfully, it would be time to fly the friendly skies.

He grinned ruefully and sang out loud: "Don't cry for me, Mineola . . ."

By six-thirty in the evening the van was full of chastened, frightened prisoners, even the Spanish *bolito* numbers man newly signed on to diversify operations. They headed into hiding. Five street-level dealers and numbers writers, and their action, had been confiscated during the afternoon, costing the Church of the Midnight Light forty-eight thousand dollars and change.

The eight-to-four cops had gone home, the third platoon still settling in. A new signal monitor had taken over the desk at the One-Three, a new cop nicknamed Tongue-Twist.

Orin heard him assign 1305 and 1306 to an *"awarm at the wicker stowe, a wobbewy in pwogwess."* Moments later he dispatched an *"ambuwance to 505 Sunwise Highway."*

"Blogg," George said, as if that explained everything.

The Reverend Bubba had to be going out of his mind, Orin figured. Word of the Van-Go Nuts bandits had to be spreading through the precinct. Wholesale daylight abductions—unimaginable, and conducted with the man's own van, too.

He parked between two dry-docked cabin cruisers in the massive boat yard west of Cow Meadow Park. Van-Go Nuts, Incorporated, was about to go out of business.

While George remained inside with the manacled prisoners—who were now arguing vehemently among themselves—Orin got out of the van and turned the hose on the sidepanels. A little soap and a hard bristled broom and the water-based white paint came off as easily as advertised.

Van-Go-Nuts became again Meals-On-Wheels.

Orin pulled Dominick Ril's license plates off the van and threw them into the murky waters of the canal. He imagined the little asshole standing on line at the Motor Vehicle Bureau during one of his precious lunch hours: better yet, he imagined Blogg doing it for him.

■　　■　　■

A cool ocean fog had rolled up from the beach and hung heavily in the trees above the hideout, the salty mist enlarging the sounds of parkway traffic: the stretched-out sounds of angry horns and internal combustion engines.

Tongue-Twist sent three cars to a street fight involving knives and sticks. On Bayview Avenue an illegal alien was giving birth to a citizen. A man on Russell Place was in *"wespiwtowy distwess. Thirteen-oh-seven, we-spond wiff caution."* In the steeple of the Lutheran Church on Nassau Street, a black woman and her infant had been found, quick-frozen like vegetables. Detectives were responding.

The several prisoners had long since given up hope of rescue and had fallen silent. George and Orin smoked cigarettes in the earthen hole that served as the living room, keeping watch over the locked-up van. It was 7:20 P.M. and the sky was solid black and starry.

"Peaceful, ain't it?" George said. "Sitting in the woods always makes me feel like a little boy with his first *Playboy.*"

Orin jerked his thumb in the direction of the red-and-white van. He was in no mood to hear confessions. "Take another look at our POWs," he said. "I don't want them croaking out on us because of an exhaust leak, or something."

"They're asleep, I told you. They don't care. Didn't that always amaze you . . . how they could curl up on the detention bench and sleep while we ruined their lives."

"No," said Orin. "Check 'em, anyway."

The next phase of the scheme was one Orin would handle alone. In Phase 3, though, he would need his partner again. When George returned from bedcheck, Orin laid it out for him. George listened carefully, then said again that he didn't want to wear his uniform at any time during the caper; he thought if caught in it he might face additional charges. "I told you that when you said to bring it along."

"Come on, George, you've been impersonating an officer for twenty years. What the hell is one more night? Even if they catch us, you can't be shot as a spy."

Charlene King did not look at all surprised to see Orin standing on the back stoop of the rooming house she owned. "Come in," she said. "I was wondering when you was coming by? I lef' a message for you two days ago, at the precinct."

Orin stepped into the kitchen and said hello to six black adults in soiled underwear at the kitchen table. They all smiled and said hello, and wasn't it a lovely evening.

"I don't work there anymore," he said.

"You a bigshot detective now?"

"No, ma'am."

"Well, whatever, I'm glad you here."

Charlene turned her sultry gaze upon the semidressed wino horde at her large kitchen table. Without so much as a word, they scooped up their cups and glasses and limped from the kitchen as one.

Charlene sat down and waved for Orin to do the same. She took a moment to gather her thoughts, then said, "You want some coffee?"

"Yeah, sure. Light and sweet."

She turned on the copper kettle and took down a jar of ground beans.

Orin put his head down on the table. The fatigue was winning. His neck and shoulders were tense, his breath bad, and his eyes were burning and raw.

"You want me to fix you a sandwich or something?"

"Thanks, Charlene. I haven't eaten or slept in a while."

"I'm hip," she said, grinning. "Sure sounds like you been busy."

"I got a whole lot more to do," he said. "A phone call to make, if that's okay."

"Do it up," she said. "You on a roll."

While Charlene got busy at the refrigerator, Orin dialed the home telephone number of Inspector James Donnelly. It was time to put the squeeze on, to make the bastard sweat.

"Donnelly residence." An older woman, maybe even the Babe.

"Mary?"

"Mrs. Donnelly doesn't live here anymore. I am Marta Rodriguez, the housekeeper. Mr. Donnelly was called away on business. Unexpectedly. But he should be back later this evening.

"Gee," said Orin. "Things haven't been going too good for the inspector, have they?"

"No," she said. "I'm afraid not."

"They're about to get worse," said Orin. "I suggest you get paid in cash tonight."

"I always do," she sniffed. "May I tell him who called?"

"My name is Ossie King, ma'am. Would you please tell the inspector I'll be in touch?"

"I'd be glad to."

Click.

"Oh, my Lord," said Charlene. "Is you a devil or what? I should have Auntie Lucinda at the church teach you something 'bout roots and spells. That man you just called is gonna worry some tonight. He gonna have torment and grief until I don't know when."

"Fair is fair," said Orin. He reached into his pocket and pulled out eight hundred dollars and laid it on the table in front of Charlene. "For the phone call, for shelter, for feeding me."

Charlene barely looked at the money. She allowed as how Orin had been good to Abraham and her, and what he was offering wasn't necessary. Real nice, she said, but unnecessary.

He said, "It's only money, and I want you to have it."

"Well fine, then, Officer Orin. I'll use it for a down payment on a proper headstone. It just ain't right, Abraham still don't have a roof over his head."

"That's perfect," said Orin.

She smiled and patted his hand. "You want to take a nap?" she said. "My room's quiet and clean, and won't no one disturb you till you say so. Grab your things and follow me."

Charlene gathered up the money in a brown paper bag and led Orin through the crowd in the living room watching reruns. Her derriere wiggled seductively under her robe on the way up the stairs to the third-floor landing of the rooming house. There was only one door at the top of the stairs. Charlene pulled out her key ring and opened the two double-cylinder dead-bolt locks. "Don't you worry 'bout none of them niggers coming up here. They know if they do they dead."

Her bedroom was enormous, running fully the length of the house. The floors were of highly polished black wood, the walls a blend of white shag carpeting and mirrors. The bed in the middle of the long room was round and covered with white fur. Music was playing somewhere, a little ditty by Barry White. She opened her personal refrigerator and offered Orin a bottle of Colt .45.

"No thanks."

"Mind if I do?" she said.

"Not at all." Orin dropped his bag at the side of the furry bed and sat down.

Charlene King sat at her dressing table, a lavish contraption of mirrors and track lights. The chair was made of elephant's tusks. Charlene sat on it with the air of an African princess.

"What time you want me to wake you up?" she asked.

Orin looked at his watch. "About an hour, if that's okay."

"Whatever you say, Officer Orin. Consider yourself a paying guest." She closed the fake-leopard shades for him and turned the overhead high-hats to dim. "Good night," she said at the door. "I'll check on you in a while, if you want."

"Sure," he said.

Orin removed his dirty clothes and rolled them into a ball in the bottom of his duffel bag. Then he stretched out on the gray satin sheets and wrapped himself in her furry white comforter. His leg muscles quivered, a chill ran up his spine and out his arms.

He had so much to do, so much to think about. His wife, his child, James Donnelly, Bubba Sims. Faces paraded before him. Orin was facedown in Charlene's pillow when the tumblers clicked on the double locked door. He wrapped his hand around the nine under the pillow.

The door closed, the locks tumbled again. Then Charlene was sitting at his side, placing a hot moist towel across his shoulder blades.

"Relax," she said. "You way too tense. I could hear the bed springs vibrating from all the way downstairs."

"Thanks," he said. "That feels good."

Charlene ran her hand along the curve of his lower back, down as far as the comforter would allow. "Would you like a massage? I've got some Indian oils from Manhattan."

"I'd love one."

"Here," she said. "Lift."

As Orin lifted his hips from the bed, Charlene pulled the comforter down to his knees. Without a word she began stroking his back and thighs with oil, sliding her long lean fingers lightly to and fro. When she felt there was sufficient lubrication, she began to knead his hamstrings strenuously, bring him great pleasure as she bounced his leaden body on the bed. She spread oil across his buttocks and anus, letting her fingertips drag across the base of his balls. Orin adjusted his hips to make room for his erection.

"Feel good?" she asked.

"Oh, yeah."

Naturally Judy came to mind, as she had been wont to do over the last few days, the last few years. Orin wondered what her yuppie lawyer would do with color photographs of this little escapade. He wondered what she would think. Then he decided that he didn't care.

"You want to roll over?" asked Charlene.

He thought about this while she gently cupped his balls in the palm of her hand. If he flipped onto his back the fantasy was over. It would be Charlene King, all hot and horny, not the Nubian Goddess of the Nile. Batman's woman, come to think of it. Probably pretty stiff competition in the hardware department. But, if he was headed for Honduras, he would have to get used to dark-skinned women again, so why not get started.

"You don't have to," she said, withdrawing her erotic attention from the space between his legs, then starting in with energy and good spirits on his shoulders and his neck. "I just thought that maybe downstairs, when we was laughing . . ."

Orin flipped over onto his back and closed his eyes.

Her breasts fell softly on his face. Her robe was gone, the camisole worn so haphazardly as to be useless. He could feel her breath on his face, smell the just-brushed scent of Crest. His dick was so hard it was killing him. Charlene kissed his forehead, his nose, his chest, and then his belly, wiggling like a reptile in a southerly direction. She took his lily white woody into her silky black hand and smiled at it knowingly. "Hello," she said. "It's nice to see you." And then she unscrewed the head and crossed the wires.

23

Traffic on the parkway was light; the occasional glare from the head-lights of southbound cars splintered on the Lincoln Log divider, great legs of cubic light strolling into nowhere. He would remember this scene, he knew, years later. He would remember this quivering sensation, this trembling on the edge of resolution, as one of those rare moments when a man is free to begin again or die.

He switched on his radio and punched up WBAB, which could be counted on for splendid rock and roll, hopefully pre-1975.

Orin made Brookville in twenty minutes, and traveled the now familiar path through Donnelly's dark woods without mishap. He squatted by the edge of the treeline in the moonlight.

He was not surprised to see Dominick Ril's shiny black Firebird—with a temporary plate taped to the back window—parked in the gravel driveway, nor Bobby Shaw's unmarked Plymouth in the two-car garage next to Donnelly's company car. A gathering of eagles, thought Orin, feeling with his hand the warmth of Ril's air-scoop hood. Or rats on a sinking ship.

Orin knelt by the side of the car and absorbed and filed the lay of the land. Then he circled the house on his hands and knees, darting from shadow to bush to tree, dodging moonlight on the lawn, until he found just the right spot under the two large open casement windows of the den. There he struggled to quiet the sound of his breathing as he made himself comfortable on the pungent earth. He wanted a drink, bad. He wanted a drink with Kenny, bad. Just once more the golden glow of cocktail time, the mirth, the brotherhood. He wanted to tell the world to pound salt. And have Kenny standing there, backing him up. But he didn't. Wouldn't.

He could hear voices from deep inside the house, as if they were on stage.

Ril's: "Getting rid of him is like getting a bubble out of wallpaper."

Donnelly's: "Bastard!"

Shaw said, "What kind of evidence about Ossie King could he have? He wasn't here back then."

"Maybe nothing, Bobby," Ril said. "Maybe he's blowing smoke up our butts. Probably he just heard the scuttlebutt. I don't see why everybody's flipping out."

Donnelly said, "The motherfucker deliberately ruined my marriage, for Christ's sake. Now he's leaving me messages from dead men? I'm gonna kill him. I'm gonna blow his fucking brains out with a bazooka."

Orin stared at the mossy bricks of the patio.

Ril said, "You know, boss, from the day he set foot inside the One-Three he was bad news."

"Don't kid yourself. He's a candyass when you get right down to it."

Shaw disagreed: "Dom's right, boss. All these sellers disappearing off the street must be his doing, too.

"So what do you want me to do? Roll over and play dead? Let this asshole ruin my life? Bullshit."

Ril cleared his throat. "This guy is nuts. First thing Monday morning I'm putting in my papers. Archie Blogg can learn to wipe his own nose."

Shaw sighed. "I'll drive you up to Albany myself. We can do it together, make a day of it."

"Wait a minute!" Donnelly barked. "You guys really think it's that bad?"

Shaw snickered. "Are you willing to gamble that it ain't."

"Hey, now, Bobby. Let's nobody panic here, okay. We just stick to our story and this horse shit will dry up again and blow away."

Ril tried to sound like he was buying it. "Yeah. Nobody do nothing stupid now. Let's not turn this into a foot race over to the district attorney."

"You know what?" Shaw said. "If he had anything resembling probable cause, the three of us would be sitting in cages. So right now all he's got is a sneaky suspicion."

"What he's got is the truth," said Ril.

"Big fucking deal," Shaw said. "I say we wake up fuckhead Bubba and his boys. Maybe we should help waste the prick and be done with this once and for all."

"I like it," Donnelly said.

Ril said, "You guys are out of your minds. I never heard a word you just said."

"Trust me," Shaw said. "All we got to do is stand together. I'll go get Bubba myself."

"I'm leaving," Ril said. "Tell the rev I said to have a nice life."

The players moved to a room at the front of the house, from where Orin could no longer hear them clearly. The front door opened and closed. He heard footsteps on gravel. Then two fast cars drove away at speed. Donnelly returned to the den.

"Give me the number for Aer Lingus reservations, please." There was the familiar and delicious sound of ice landing in an empty glass. "Hi. My name is James Donnelly. I'd like to make a reservation on your morning flight to Shannon Airport tomorrow . . . that's right. I'm traveling alone . . . correct . . . one way . . . I see . . . I can give a credit card number now to hold the seat but I plan on paying cash . . . Beautiful."

Donnelly hung up and then methodically walked around the house, locking up. He stopped at the windows, under which Orin hid, and his shadow fell across the lawn as he rolled them closed.

In spite of the pleasant weather outside his open bedroom window—the cool breeze moaning in the branches overhead, the stars bright and twinkling—James Donnelly was sweating in his bed. When he rolled onto his side the sheet moved with him, so he threw the sheet off and then felt terribly exposed. Goose bumps rose on his flesh. He considered another Rob Roy.

A branch snapped in the woods, then another.

A motorcycle was downshifting somewhere far off, its gears whining in protest at speed and grade.

"Bastard," he said softly. If there was someone sneaking around in the woods, it was too noisy to tell. He slid his right hand into the bedside table drawer and wrapped it around the grips of his revolver. He eased from the bed to the open window with the view of the backyard.

The moon ducked behind high clouds, and his scan of the shadows from the patio to the pool told him nothing. Maybe kids, he thought, scratching his balls through his boxer shorts. Maybe the possum that had been dumping the goddamn garbage. It was 1:30 by the digital clock on the bedside table. Then 1:31. Another branch snapped in the woods.

Donnelly put on his heavy green velour robe and slippers and tucked the gun into the pocket of the robe. He was thinking about all the money he had saved over the years and hidden in the woods, his contingency cushion against disaster. Mary couldn't find it, accountants could not count it, and judges could not freeze it. It could only be lost, he knew, to a bigger thief than himself. He thought of life in Boca Raton. Oh, well. Not with Ossie King floating up out of the past.

He tread softly down the center hall stairway and through the dark and quiet house to the back door. He drew the curtains aside and squinted through the glass, then turned the dead bolt and slid back the door. With his gun in his hand he stepped from the house to the patio. The wind sighed in the treetops.

Donnelly walked purposefully across the yard, holding his robe closed at his chest, relying on familiarity to guide him past obstacles. An acorn stabbed the ball of his foot through his slipper. He stopped next to a white wrought-iron bench and looked around self-consciously. His heart was pounding as he tramped through the underbrush in the darkness, ignoring the thorns that pricked his bare shins, the stray branches whipping his face. He stopped in front of a dying oak, put his revolver in his pocket, and dug his hands into the hollow of the tree the way a child digs into a toy chest. The waterproof toolbox was right where it had always been, under the pile of damp leaves. He shook it with both hands, then tucked it under his arm like he was a half-back and walked quickly back to his house.

Once the door was locked behind him, Donnelly carried the toolbox upstairs to his room and set it down at the foot of his bed. He returned to the window for a moment to listen to his yard, and it occurred to him that he might have been clutching a box of shredded newsprint to his chest; the money might have been stolen hours ago by that bigger thief he so feared. He opened the toolbox and dumped the contents on his bed sheet: two hundred and forty-one thousand dollars of United States currency. Fifties. Hundreds. Thousand-dollar bills. His lawyers could sell the house and cars, cutting it fifty-fifty with Mary; with his stocks he would still have almost a million to retire on. It had taken years to accumulate all this, years of accommodating others, practicing the fine art of selective enforcement. Fuck 'em, he thought. Fuck 'em all. Donnelly sat on the edge of the bed, smiling, his hands buried in the cash. "Thank you," he said. "Thank you."

There was a flash of light. "Why, James! You little crook, you."

His head snapped around. Orin Boyd stood in the doorway of his bedroom, with one hand on the light switch, the other pointing a pistol.

"Boyd!"

"In the flesh, sir. And the money, sir—damn good spot. I know *I* would never have found it."

Donnelly's face turned as white as the hair on his head. He was trembling when Orin snatched the revolver from the pocket of his robe, actually gasping for breath as Orin led him to a chair.

"Easy, boss," said Orin. "It's only money. And what the fuck. You stole it to begin with, so it ain't like it's really yours."

Donnelly's respiratory distress continued. Orin considered calling for medics. But at last some color returned to the man's face and he managed to catch his breath.

"Get out of my house," he croaked at Orin.

"I will. I want to make sure first that you're alive when the homicide dicks arrive to lock you up."

"What are you talking about?"

"I'm referring to Ossie King, a no-account black man you and Shaw and Dom beat to death, though from what I heard, I'll bet it was mostly you."

"Good luck, asshole," said Donnelly. "I wasn't there."

"Wrong."

"Not even a negligent homicide, Boyd. And that was years ago, when the evidence was fresh. What makes you think what you've heard would mean a fucking thing in court?"

"Remember a guy named Abraham Wilson? Batman, to his friends?"

"A useless neighborhood wino for the last twenty years."

"He's dead, you know," Orin said.

"I wasn't aware of that."

"Sure you weren't. Did you know that he was a lot smarter than everybody gave him credit for?"

"What are you talking about?"

"He could read, he could write, he had a memory, he had fears and dreams and regrets—just like you, James. Just like me."

"You're beating your meat, Boyd. You haven't got a thing."

"I got a dying declaration, is what I got, sir. From his lips to my ears, just before he died. I even taped it, just in case."

"Come on. Get the fuck out of my house. I don't care what no nigger wino says happened way back when; a grand jury won't care what he says. You can wipe your ass with that tape for all the good it's gonna do you."

"Wrong again, boss. I'll be wiping my ass with your hundred-dollar bills."

Orin ordered the inspector to remove his robe and underwear. He walked him downstairs at gunpoint and handcuffed him, nude, to the radiator in the front foyer, out of reach of a telephone but close enough to beg for help from the first person to come to his door.

"You're history, Boyd. Your ass is mine," Donnelly said from his hands and knees.

Orin laughed out loud. "But now your ass belongs to the Big Bamboo at Attica State Prison. God, I get weak in the knees just thinking about it. The passion, the savagery."

James Donnelly curled into a sitting position on the rug. Orin tucked the money into his pockets and sleeves and dropped the empty box on the floor.

For Marta Rodriguez, Donnelly's cash-only maid, and her sense of modesty, Orin hoped Sergeant Daniels got to the front door first.

Bubba's red Caddy, with its whip antenna and flashy chrome wheels, stood out in the wealthy wooded hills of Glen Cove like a downtown hooker at a tea party. Those with old money in passing Ferraris cringed; most figured Bubba as a suitor to a maid. Bubba just cruised, oblivious.

But even though Bubba was easy to follow, Gloria was nervous behind the wheel of the unfamiliar T-Bird. Winding roads through the woods were a far cry from circling the empty parking lot at Jones Beach with her panties off. She didn't know how close she could come to Bubba without spooking him.

The smell of the land reminded her of a day with her son at Bear Mountain. She lit a cigarette and felt her heart pounding. George was not worth this kind of fear, she told herself. Maybe no man was.

She flipped on her headlights and followed Bubba Sims deeper into the darkening woods. She told herself to try to remember landmarks: the stone gate of a large estate, the twinkling lights from a chandelier high on a hill.

At a stop sign she turned on the radio, flipping the dial over to a Spanish station, which she had trouble finding and then fine-tuning.

It was hard to look at the road and radio at the same time, but Gloria thought a familiar voice would help her relax. She took a deep and satisfying drag on her cigarette, then checked her golden hair in the rearview mirror. When she focused again on the road, Bubba was gone. Just like that. The two red dots she had followed for better than ten miles had vanished.

He must be ahead of her, just around that bend. She could catch him if she hurried. Losing touch with him would make her seem more innocent.

Gloria Mendosa burned rubber as she took off in hot pursuit. Gray smoke filled the evening air behind her. She rode the car hard over bumps and around blind corners, frantically scanning the side of the road when she flew past a driveway or the entrance to a private road. The homes of kings, she thought with envy, here and there the palace of a god.

At last she saw something up ahead of her, climbing a hill on her right. She sped past an octagonal red road sign that was nearly overgrown by a fir tree and did not see the Glen Cove police car inching out in front of her from the hedge until it was too late.

Orin drove his pickup the three short blocks to the Albany Avenue boat-launching ramp. George followed in the Meals-on-Wheels van. Neither wore a mask. George parked the van in a corner of the empty, littered lot, next to a brick-face factory wall. He shut off the headlights and cut the engine but left the keys in the ignition. Locking both doors, he hopped down from the cab. He banged hard on the side of the van, asked if anyone was in there, listened with glee to their calls for help, then ran across the lot to Orin's pickup.

"Relax," said Orin. "There ain't no one around to see us."

Orin was right. The only human movement visible at all was on the water, near the mouth of the canal, kids illicitly drinking beer in a dinghy. The radio calls were all of the usual variety. George asked Orin what was going to happen next.

"I don't know."

"What do you mean, you don't know?"

"I mean we could stop now." Orin blew on his hands. "We could walk away clean with a few bucks apiece."

George sighed. "I was thinking about that myself. Things have been just a little too easy, you know? How much exactly do we got so far?"

"Not enough to change our lives—maybe twenty-five grand each."

"Do you think we made any mistakes?"

"I'm sure of it," said Orin. "Not that I think we're gonna get caught by the cops."

"Really?"

"Hey, we wore gloves, we wore masks, we switched vehicles, and we robbed criminals. Who's gonna say the bread was theirs?"

"So what do you want to do then?" asked George, with the impatience of one not used to making irrevocable decisions.

"I want to shoot the moon."

"Well, fuck it, then. Roll 'em."

"Which means it's time to climb into your uniform, George, without another word. I'll get the flares from the back of the truck."

When Orin returned to the cab, George was lacing up his combat boots.

"Awright," he said, "you lookin' bad, George."

"I love it," said George. "You do in three days what our squad of defectives hasn't done in three years . . . And doesn't Bubba got some set of balls, running a delivery business through the middle of the precinct." He covered his shield number with a black mourning band. As George strapped on his revolver, he frowned at Orin. "Has it crossed your mind that the County of Nassau might be able to produce a complainant for this?"

"Yes, it has."

"Just asking. Don't get pissed. What makes you think these mopes will drop their money to a guy they don't know?"

"Hey, does Charlie Krenshaw work every single day of the year? Someone's got to collect on the man's day off. The signal is flashing the high beams on and off."

"And how are we going to get our hands on the bus?"

"That's where you come in."

Gloria Mendosa sat handcuffed in the back of a Nassau County ambulance. A chubby blond paramedic wrapped gauze around her head. She was, as she understood it, being arrested for unauthorized use of a motor vehicle and driving without a license. Any other charges would depend on the severity of the injuries to the policeman driving the patrol car she had wrecked.

Glen Cove Police Officer Howard Ragusa told her that a computer check of the registration showed that the crumpled T-Bird being hauled away on a flatbed towtruck belonged to George Clarke, of Bellmore, New York.

"Georgie Clarke," she screamed. "He's a cop; you could check it out."

"Yeah, right," said Officer Ragusa. "I know plenty of cops who loan their cars to Puerto Ricans who can't drive."

Charlie Krenshaw saw the cop, holding the flashlight and the flare, step from the woods on East Merrick Road just seconds after he passed his last opportunity to turn his Nassau County bus north, back to his scheduled route. He blinked his eyes and shook his head; he told himself he needed to get more sleep. Then he downshifted the empty bus and followed the officer's hand signals to pull to the side of the road.

The cop turned his back on the bus and began to lay out a line of flares between it and an old red pickup truck that was parked by the side of the road. Krenshaw watched, mesmerized by what he thought was great stupidity. The flares belonged behind the bus, if anywhere, not behind a piece of shit pickup truck. He flipped on his emergency flashers and mumbled, "Jesus H. Christ!"

When the last of the five flares had been lit, the dopey cop held it in his hand and stood twenty yards away, waving it weakly at cars as they passed.

Charlie thought it awfully rude of the guy not to approach the bus and apprise him of the situation, whatever the trouble might be. He leaned out the window and called to the officer. The officer waved back at him.

Krenshaw yelled, "What's the holdup?"

The cop held his hand to his ear, as if to indicate deafness.

"Fine. Great. Just like a politician. I got it, you fat fucking asshole. You want me to come to you."

Krenshaw set the emergency brake, then grabbed the door handle and flung it open. He stepped down to the street alongside the rumbling bus. Suddenly someone had him bent over in a headlock that felt like he was drowning.

"Evening, Charlie," Orin said to him softly. "I'm afraid the jig is up."

Doubled over, Charlie Krenshaw didn't know what to say, nor would he have been able to say it if he did. His shock at being attacked from the darkness increased exponentially when he realized that his attacker was wearing only sneakers and a pair of polka-dot boxer shorts.

"And I know that you know that I know what I'm talking about. Right, Charlie? Drool if that's correct."

Charlie Krenshaw gagged. He was holding onto Orin's bare thighs, perilously close to a coma. He dropped to his hands and knees, then he was face down on the pavement with a sneaker on the back of his neck. His hands were cuffed behind his back. A plastic garbage bag was pulled roughly over his head and shoulders, enveloping him in total, terrifying darkness.

He knew then that he was going to die—horribly. A knee pressed against the small of his back. He begged: "No, God, please don't kill me."

"Now relax a second, Charlie, and listen to me. I'm not going to kill your dumb ass, so please don't shit your pants . . . I have to wear them later."

"But—"

"I'm serious, Charlie. I can do without the hysterics."

"Okay, okay."

"I'm your guardian angel, Charlie. And I'm sick and tired of you fucking up. The only reason I don't kill you is because you're a stupid fucking guppy swimming in a pool full of sharks. That and because you've got a little boy at home who needs you, don't you, Charlie? Don't talk, okay? The Lord wants you to wiggle if you understand what I'm saying."

"You've been to my house?"

"Did you hear me?"

Charlie Krenshaw, face down on the road, wiggled like a snake.

"Good. You're fired. From here on you only work for the bus company. You're never going to do this other bad thing for Sherman Clayborne ever again. Understand?"

Charlie wiggled.

"Attaboy. I think we understand each other. It's better than standing trial, don't you think?"

Charlie wiggled some more.

"Okay, now I'm gonna take the cuffs off. You'll need your hands free to take off your clothes."

Charlie stopped wiggling and started to scream. "Oh, God, no! Please."

Orin slapped the bowling ball head in the bag until Charlie stopped begging and started to weep.

"You done yet?" Orin said. "You stupid son of a bitch, I told you, I want your clothes so I can wear them. I need to borrow the fucking bus."

Charlie retched, as if he were going to vomit.

"Hey, do you want to get home alive tonight or not?"

The bus driver started gatoring like a freshman at a high-school sock hop. Orin helped Charlie to his feet and led him into the woods, the bag still over his head. He removed the handcuffs and stepped back while Charlie rubbed his wrists.

"Drop 'em and cough, little buddy. To the skin."

Charlie stripped without further protest, handing Orin first his pants, his shirt and jacket, then, reluctantly, his underpants. Orin put on the blue shirt and gray uniform jacket and pants. He threw Charlie's briefs up into a tree.

"Good luck," he said, "in whatever you choose to do next."

"But—"

"But nothing, Charles. It's over. It never happened. Say thank you tonight when you do your prayers."

Orin stepped quickly from the woods and climbed onto the bus. The flares had been extinguished and collected. He put on Charlie's forty-mission cap, released the hand brake, and flashed his hazard lights at George Clarke, who was at that moment stepping from the woods fifty yards ahead, pulling up his fly. He was all in black again, the ultimate thug.

George gave Orin the finger, then jumped behind the wheel of the pickup. Orin jammed the gearshift into low and pulled onto the roadway in the right-hand lane. In his rearview mirror, he could see Charlie Krenshaw prance gingerly to the side of the road, wearing the garbage bag like a diaper to cover his nakedness.

At the Buffalo Avenue projects, and then at each succeeding stop, Orin flashed his brights twice before pulling over to the curb. Each time he performed this simple task, a black kid or two got on the bus without paying. Each threw an envelope into Charlie Krenshaw's open lunch box. Each got off at the next stop down the line. None of them looked at Orin closely. None of them noticed the pickup truck following the bus, holding steady on the wing.

Orin kept his eyes on the busy road, remembering with a childlike sense of wonder when he passed the collection basket at eleven o'clock mass. He remembered the temptation to bolt from the church. At each bus stop he felt a sense of brotherly love for those thrusting money upon him and forgave them their trespasses. The receipts piled up.

George trailed bus number 241 along route 27B, watching the crack dealers get on at one stop and off at the next, where another dealer got on. Seven different dealers all together, playing leapfrog across the precinct. Every one of the slimeballs threw a bundle into the box.

"Fucking money!" George hooted.

At the last stop within the precinct, a dark and desolate corner of northwestern Belmont, Orin let the bus stall out, then feigned an inability to restart it. He slammed his palm on the steering wheel theatrically, and pretended to radio the dispatcher for help.

He did not face his few passengers, nor offer explanations. While they grumbled softly about the miseries of public transportation, Orin opened the door and got off the bus with the lunch box in his hand. While they argued about how long it would take to fix the bus, Orin opened the engine housing and lay down on the road to look inside.

His passengers were swapping favorite road stories when ten minutes later someone noticed that the driver was missing.

24

Officer Howard Ragusa had a hard time deciding what charges to file against Gloria. He cuffed her to his desk and opened a copy of the New York State Penal Law. He had already written out her summonses at Glen Cove Hospital while her scalp was stitched. There was really nothing he could do here about criminal charges until he heard from the doctors or placed a call to the owner of the Thunderbird, this Officer Georgie Clarke she kept yelling about.

He asked Gloria for Clarke's home number.

"I don't have it with me."

"You don't know it by heart?"

"No. I usually call him at work."

Officer Ragusa went to the trouble of looking the number up, then he placed the call.

Ella Clarke answered on the third ring. "Hel-lo?"

"This is Officer Ragusa, Glen Cove Police Department. To whom am I speaking."

Ella cried out in grief. "Oh, no. Not my George. Is he all right? What happened? Is he dead. I thought you people sent a car."

"What I'm calling about is a car, ma'am."

Gloria's eyes flew open wide and she sat up straight in her chair, clanging the cuff on her wrist against the desk. "Some fucking bitch answered Georgie's phone?"

"Who is that?" Ella Clarke asked Officer Ragusa.

"Who is this?" Officer Ragusa asked Ella.

"My name is Ella Clarke. My husband is Police Officer George Clarke."

"Oh, boy."

"Is that his cleaning woman?" Gloria asked Ragusa. "He said he has someone come in to straighten up."

"Who is that in the background?" Ella Clarke said.

"Just a car thief, Mrs. Clarke. Don't pay her any mind. Listen to me, I'm not calling about your husband. I wouldn't know him if I fell over him. I'm calling about what's left of a T-Bird, and a woman here who claims your husband loaned her the car."

"Husband?" said Gloria.

"That's impossible," said Ella. "My husband is on a stakeout. He's got the car with him."

"And where might this stakeout be?"

"How does she know about the stakeout?" Gloria said, tugging Ragusa's sleeve with her free hand.

"I can't give you the details," said Ella. "How do I know you're really a cop? Actually, how do I know you're not helping my husband goof on me? How do I know this isn't a joke at my expense?"

"Forget it, lady. I'm sorry I called." Ragusa took the phone from his ear and leaned over his desk to hang it up.

Gloria grabbed his arm. "Don't hang up! Find out how she knows about the stakeout."

"Hello? Hello?" squealed Mrs. Clarke.

Officer Ragusa handed Gloria the phone. "Here," he said. "You two must have a lot of catching up to do."

George Clarke had never sat in a bar with forty-nine thousand bucks in his pocket. He had never enjoyed the expense-account thrill of spending someone else's money. He was so filled with the afterglow and satisfaction of wealth, he considered buying a round of drinks for the house.

Unfortunately, there were only two other patrons at the Players Bar and Grill, and they were already drunk and swapping spit in a booth in the back. George didn't think they'd properly appreciate the freebee, so he refrained from waving his arm like a cowboy and shouting, "The drinks are on me." Instead he smiled at the Dominican barmaid and ordered himself another tequila sunrise.

He wished Orin had stuck around to celebrate. He didn't think a bar was a dangerous place to be at a time like this. After they had split the money, and dumped the masks and the gloves and the flares and Charlie Krenshaw's uniform, it was over. What was the big deal?

Orin said to pick up the T-Bird from Gloria and go home. Find out what Bubba did, and who he did it with, while Rome was burning, then go home and lock the doors. Go to work every day. Don't tell nothing to nobody. Don't talk on the phone. Don't spend any money. Don't fucking brag.

George thought Orin had a lot of nerve, talking to him like that after all they had been through together. Just because his plan worked okay was no reason for him to act superior. And why did they steal all this money if they weren't gonna spend it? What was the freaking point?

He looked at his watch. It was almost Saturday morning coming down. Where, he wondered, was that sleazy bimbo with his car. He had to get home. Ella had long ago bought his last lousy excuse. He chugged half of his cocktail and burped; he remembered that he had not eaten dinner, that Orin had neglected to schedule a pit stop. Damn, he thought, looking at his watch again, if Gloria didn't get there soon he was going to have to call a cab.

The barmaid was mixing him another drink when he saw Gloria's dark face pressed against the window over the neon Michelob sign. George told the barmaid to cancel his order, and left a five-dollar tip on the bar. He met Gloria at the front door and took her by the arm into the alley. "Where the fuck have you been?" he said, looking around. "Where the fuck is my car?"

"I had an accident, George. The cop said your car was totaled."

"No," he said. "You're kidding. My beautiful, just-waxed car . . . You did say totaled, right? You wouldn't be jerking me off?"

"To-taled."

"Oh, Jesus."

"Forget about your car."

"What do you mean forget about my car? As long as you're all right, can't I worry about my car? What the hell is going on with you? How did you get here?"

"What makes you think I'm okay? Did you ask, you son of a bitch? Do you even care?" Gloria bent forward and spread the hair on the top of her head. "I got ten damn stitches in my head, and for what?"

"For money, my darlin'. For love."

"Bullshit."

"You look beautiful to me, babe," he said, taking her hand in his. "How about a little mouth-to-mouth?"

She turned to walk to the door; George yanked her back to attention. Gloria pulled free, then curled her lip and sneered at him. "Don't mess with me, you son of a bitch. You don't know who you've been fucking with."

George stopped dead in his tracks, paralyzed by an unreasonable fear.

"What?" he said. "Gloria, what happened, baby? Why are you so uptight?" He pulled wads of money from his pockets and flashed it in her face. "It's all over, baby. We did it."

Gloria shrugged and turned her back. He followed her to the back door of the building, then the five long blocks over to her apartment and into it. He threw the money on the kitchen table the way he imagined cavemen once threw meat onto the fire. Gloria poured herself a glass of red wine and lit a cigarette, refusing to acknowledge the presence of the hard cash.

George could not understand this. Piles of money caused him to hallucinate: visions of shiny cars and gold jewelry, the ocean from the deck of a condominium, women—beautiful, docile, happy women with frosted hair, wearing strapless gowns, serving him big pink drinks packed with ice.

He told Gloria of their daring as he and Orin swept through the night untouched, modern subterranean heroes on the side of good and profit. He described the appropriation of the bus, the dumb-sheep idiocy of dealers handing over money. "To us," he said. "A couple of swashbuckling motherfuckers."

"Big fucking deal," she said.

"Say what?"

"Jou heard me."

None of it mattered, he could see. Gloria Mendosa lacked the sophistication to imagine what money represented. Talk about pearls before swine, he thought, about telling shit from Shinola. If this low-duck bitch wasn't moved, then fuck her. There were millions of broads he could buffalo. "You got no class, Gloria. That's your freaking problem."

"Says you."

George began to gather up the money. "Where's my car, Gloria? I got places to go and people to see."

"The detectives have it."

"And why do detectives have my car?"

"They're holding it for evidence . . . in case the cops I hit die."

"This isn't funny anymore, Gloria. What the fuck are you talking about?"

"Sit down a minute, Georgie. Don't be in such a rush to go home to an empty house. I'm gonna tell you everything about everything. And I am going to tell you the truth, something which you have never done for me."

George's throat went dry and his palms were sweating. There was an icy fury in Gloria's voice, the kind when more than idle threats are involved, a fury certain of action. George had the feeling he was fucked as he sat down slowly on the arm of her secondhand couch. Gloria casually knocked off the rest of her wine.

"Well?"

"I followed Reverend Sims, just like you said, but then I lost him for a while, and then I hit a cop car. You with me so far? Then they took us all away in an ambulance, and then they took my pretty ass to jail. They said I stole your car, Georgie. They had me under arrest, you son of a bitch. They said there was no way a man like you would give his car to a spic like me."

"Why those racist—"

"Then they called your house," she said suddenly.

George felt short of breath. "Yes?"

"Your wife told the cop the same damn thing."

"My what?"

"The woman—Mrs. Ella Clarke. She said her husband wouldn't loan his car to a spic. She said her husband hated spics."

George slapped himself on the knee. "Ella Clarke told the cop she was my wife? I don't believe it. I really do not believe it. Man, is that chick flipping out, or what?"

"What are you saying, Georgie? Don't lie to me anymore."

George took Gloria by the shoulders. "Ella Clarke is my crazy little sister. I swear to God, Glo. Sometimes she thinks she's my wife, sometimes she thinks she's my mother. Just last week she told the next-door neighbor that I was holding her *prisoner*. She's an overdose casualty. Too much LSD in the sixties. We humor her."

"That's not what she told me."

"You spoke to her, too?"

"For about ten minutes, you lying motherfucker. And then I spoke to some detectives, and then they spoke to some other detectives. Then those guys called the fucking commissioner of police, that guy Trimble you're always calling a scumbag, and then he even came to see me . . . and then they all drove me down here to meet you."

George smiled stupidly, stealing a glance around the room. "You're kidding, right?"

"They're waiting outside to talk to you."

George laughed nervously and grabbed his chest. "Knock it off, will you Glo. You're scaring the crap out of me, not that I don't deserve it."

"Really," she said, lifting the bottom of her tank top to show him the tiny transmitter taped to her stomach. "They're recording us now." Gloria curtseyed, then opened the door. "Commissioner Trimble?" she called into the hallway. "George will tell you now that he did lend me his car. And then I want an apology from each and every one of your men."

"Which you shall have, Mrs. Mendosa. Which you shall have." Commissioner Trimble stepped into the seedy apartment with Detective Sergeant Alonzo Daniels and Inspector Archibald Blogg, followed by two detectives from Internal Affairs. One of the shooflies closed the door behind them. Gloria offered to make them coffee.

George took a look at the second-story window, one more look at Gloria, then he exhaled deeply and smiled. "How's it going, Commissioner? Inspector? What brings you to this neck of the woods. Sarge? Long time no see."

"I don't have time to play games with you, Officer Clarke," said Commissioner Trimble. "You can cooperate and become an active participant in this investigation—which still might involve administrative charges being brought against you—or you can go to jail for five hundred years. The choice is yours. You have a minute to make up your tiny mind."

George looked to Archibald Blogg for a glimmer of understanding, some gesture or advice, but Blogg was only along for the ride on this. Blogg was clucking his tongue and ogling Gloria as if George were already dead and gone. Sergeant Daniels was looking out Gloria's window near the couch, enjoying the same view of the precinct that George had loved so long. The two boys from IAD George didn't want to know.

"What exactly do you mean, 'cooperate'?" he said.

"Exactly where you got the money? How you got the money? Who helped you? The basics, Clarke. Don't make me any madder than I already am. The only way to cope with this fiasco is to play it all the way through to the end. If you can prove you were acting as a police officer, disrupting the bad guys and confiscating the money, you might even save your pension."

"I want a lawyer," said George.

"A lawyer can't help you."

"That's bullshit."

"Sink or swim."

George stared at his palms and tapped his foot. He had to urinate, but didn't dare ask to be excused. He tried to think. What had they done? Nothing, really. Temporary stuff. Crimes he had committed almost daily for twenty years. Except that he knew the district attorney could take the same set of events and make it sound like assault, robbery, kidnapping, and several counts of unauthorized use. His tongue locked in his throat. His eyes begged for mercy.

"Cuff him," Trimble said to the pair from Internal Affairs. "He goes down."

"Later for that noise," said George. "I'll talk."

"I thought so," said Archibald Blogg.

"Where's Orin?" asked Daniels, turning back from the window.

"Orin?"

Commissioner Trimble exhaled loudly. "If you waste one more valuable second of my time, I'm going to feed you to the fucking wolves."

"He's home, I guess. Orin said he was going home."

Daniels said, "You're full of shit, Clarke."

George could only shrug and stare at the floor, contemplating various measures of revenge against Gloria, the least of which would be the ass-kicking of her life.

"So whatever you two clowns were up to is over?" Trimble asked. "There are no more crimes being committed as we speak?"

"Yeah," said George. "It's over."

"Is this all the money?"

"It's half." George looked at Gloria. "Our half."

"Fine," said Trimble. "Let's go pick up Boyd."

The detectives from IAD helped Daniels pack the money into evidence bags while Commissioner Trimble thanked Gloria for her assistance and the use of her lovely apartment. He told her he was sorry one of his men had played her for a fool. He hoped the laceration to her scalp would heal properly.

Gloria blushed happily at all this masculine attention, George couldn't help but notice.

George Clarke paced approximately two and a half miles around the headquarters bullpen on the night of his biggest mistake, until his flat feet hurt and his eyes went blurry in the overhead fluorescent light. He drank four cups of strong black coffee and pissed six times.

He also left three different messages for his wife on the answering machine at his house.

It drove him crazy, answering the commissioner's questions while his wife was not answering the phone. Before he called home the first time he pulled his shield case from his back pocket and removed his wedding ring from the safety pin and put it on.

He said, "Ella, honey. Please pick up. It's me. I know you're there. Honey, don't do anything rash, okay? Wait for me. I'll be home from work around seven in the morning. I love you, baby."

At 5:10 in the morning, George Clarke told his own answering machine that it owed him at least the opportunity to explain, that Gloria Mendosa had just happened, and now that the truth was out in the open he could see what a fool he had been. He ran out of time on the tape before he could add that it never would have happened if he'd been getting enough attention at home.

At 5:30 A.M. George left another message: "I'm on my way home, Ella, and if you're not there I'm gonna kick your ass."

Sergeant Daniels told him to relax. She would probably forgive him in a decade or two. He called George a taxicab and then walked him to the front door of headquarters. Daniels said they would call him at home when they needed him again. The day tour would finish processing the arrests of last night's "victims." George was to check in immediately if he heard from Orin Boyd. Any fuckups now, any failure to follow through, and George was going down the tubes without grease. "Get some sleep," said Daniels.

"Yeah, I will," George said. "Thank you, I guess."

"Don't kid yourself, George. We didn't do it 'cause of you."

George walked down the front steps, across the wide sidewalk, and, with a sad, sober look on his face, ducked into the waiting yellow cab.

He had only a ten-dollar bill that he had borrowed from the sergeant. Everything else, even his own cash, had been confiscated. ("This is no time to get cheap on us, Georgie boy," the commissioner had said.)

The cab rolled south on Franklin Avenue, Garden City's golden artery, past Bloomingdale's, Saks, and Lord and Taylor's, Sweeney's and Leo's, foreign territory to both the Arab cabbie and his passenger. The only time George spent in Garden City was with his divorce lawyer, and that was only now and then. George stared glumly out the window and imagined what a time he could have had here with forty-nine thousand bucks.

When the cab reached Hempstead, George lost all interest in his surroundings. He spent the rest of his ride in deep thought, examining various excuses for Ella, testing lies for plausibility. He would have tried them out on the driver, but Abdul Hammsid's English was limited to the streets of Nassau County, the points of the compass, the denominations of American currency, and various sexual acts.

"Turn here," said George, when they had reached his cross street on Newbridge Avenue. "Three doors down . . . the green one . . . that's great work, Abdul. Here." George thrust the ten dollars over the seat to the driver.

"Twelve dollars," said the driver. "Plus tip."

"For a five-minute camel ride? I'll give you the tip of my dick."

"Fuck you! Twelve dollars. Plus tip."

The mood George was in, he considered blowing the persistent little bastard back to Mecca. Then he considered going into his house, locking the doors, closing the blinds, and ignoring the entire situation. "What am I, nuts?" he said out loud. He imagined the wizened driver loading up his cab with dynamite, praising Allah, then burning rubber down the street, hard right up the driveway and slam into the house. "Wait right here, my man. I got the money inside."

Ella's Sunbird was not in the garage, nor did she answer his calls for assistance from the foyer. Her coats were gone from the closet, likewise the money in the cookie jar. George felt panic in his chest as he ran up the stairs to his bedroom. It was true, he was thinking. The bitch had booked.

Ella's things were absent everywhere, as if a team of F.B.I. specialists had scientifically removed all traces of her presence. He was finally and suddenly alone.

Stunned, he returned to his living room and stood stock still for a moment, then ran through each room of the empty house, searching. There used to be money everywhere, in envelopes for the paper girl, in piles on the top of his dresser, between the cushions of the couch, with the pretzels and cheese curls.

Nothing. He was penniless and all alone. Then George thought of one last possibility. He ran back upstairs and opened his cedar closet; it was a dead-solid lock there was money in every pocket of every suit that he owned, along with matchbook covers with phone numbers.

Unfortunately, that same thought had also occurred to his wife. She who had taken a jagged-edge sewing scissor to each, rather than rummage around. "That fucking Orin," George said to himself. All of this was his fault.

The terrorist cabdriver outside hit his horn sharply several times, jarring George back to fiscal reality. He walked out of his house and across the lawn to the curb.

"Two more dollars," said the driver. "Plus tip."

"No two more dollars," said George as he wiggled out of his wedding ring. "Take this instead and get out of here."

"Fucking A, okay," said Abdul. "Got to go."

George felt very sorry for himself as the cab rolled away from the house with his ring. Sorry for himself, yet tragically proud. He wished there were cameras present to record the moment, or neighbors, watching from their windows in tears. He was not really as bad a man as everyone might think, not way down deep inside.

Orin knocked softly on Gloria Mendosa's apartment door.

"Georgie?"

"Orin."

Gloria opened the door. She had a glass of wine in her hand and her mascara was smeared beneath her eyes. He saw her flattened hair, the neon discoloration of betadine.

"For a minute I thought it was George," she said.

"Wasn't he here when you got home?"

"They took him away."

"Who exactly took him away?"

"The cops . . . Commissioner Trimble."

Orin stepped inside and locked the door. He sat down at Gloria's kitchen table. "We didn't fool them for long, did we?"

Gloria sipped her wine and sniffled. "Yes you did. You would have. It was all my fault."

"No," he said. "I'm the jerk who thought it up."

"I told them about you," she said, "because you knew he was married, and you didn't say. You knew all the time." Gloria began weeping in earnest, begging forgiveness.

"It's okay," Orin said. "It's okay. But I think it might be the time for us to get out of here for a while."

25

The upstate telephone information operator gave Orin the number he needed: 914-555-COPE. He hoped the good father was not out on the links or downtown bowling for milk shakes.

"Camp Cope, may I help you?"

"Monsignor O'Rourke?"

"Speaking."

"Bless me, Father, for I have sinned. It's been twenty years since my last confession."

"Hey, Orin. I just talked to Alonzo about you. How's it going down there?"

"Lousy, sir. And you were the only one I could think of to call."

"You haven't been drinking have you?"

"No, sir. It's nothing like that. I think you'd better turn off your tape recorder, though."

A moment passed silently, then O'Rourke came back on the line. "Well?"

"You know I got suspended, right?"

"Yes. I know."

Orin looked at the waitress behind the counter of the roadside diner. He pointed to his empty coffee cup, and she got up to get him more.

"What did the boys at headquarters have to say?"

"The whole world is looking for you after last night. They want you to give yourself up. They said it's not too late to cut a deal."

"The answer is no, Father."

"Listen to me, Orin. Your partner George Clarke is cooperating with Internal Affairs and the district attorney's office. They're talking about calling the whole thing a legitimate sting operation, albeit one with some procedural errors. Inspector Blogg is already trying to grab the credit."

"I refuse to play the pivot man in their circle jerk."

"Daniel's pretty pissed off at you. He told me you and he were working together on this. He said something about trust among comrades, and patience. He also said he was glad that you and your family were safe and together, but that Shaw was out there somewhere, too."

Orin smiled, picturing Internal Affairs detectives guarding his empty ex-house for him. He thanked God that George did not know where they were.

"He said he'd look into any matter for you, immediately."

"That's beautiful," said Orin. "I couldn't have asked for a better retirement present."

"Daniels thinks you're close by, maybe still on the Island. He said not to spend any of that money if you want this thing to look kosher."

"What money?"

"The money you confiscated as evidence from those dealers you—ah— arrested."

"What dealers?"

"Orin."

"I'm leaving the job, Father. In fact I'm on my way out of town."

"Are you sure you don't want to come in?"

"Positive, Father. I've gotta take care of some business."

"Are you armed?" asked O'Rourke.

"Yes, Father. I am."

"Good."

▪   ▪   ▪

George knocked back his fifth shot of scotch and chased it with an ice-cold beer. His legs felt rubbery, his cheeks flushed. His world had collapsed, his women had flown. And his career, well, that was still up in the air. He pulled on his coat and walked outside into the clear, cold dawn. Didn't bother to lock the front door. The NatWest cash machine was only two blocks away. What was left behind to steal?

Alone inside the lobby of the bank, he made a face at the security camera and slid his card into the proper slot. He punched up a request for withdrawal of five hundred dollars. The machine declined. Reenter. Which George did.

The machine said, Insufficient funds.

George said, "Get the fuck outta here." He requested a look at his balance. The machine showed him goose eggs and spit back his card.

George shoved the card back into the slot with the palm of his hand. "You don't like it? You can *eat* it! What do I care?"

Orin couldn't rest. It was not that the bed of soft branches was uncomfortable, nor that the woodland noises disturbed him. Stretched out on his back, he had tried for an hour now to kid himself that the local bush war was over and that he had won. He had personally spanked James Donnelly and Bubba Sims, and everyone on the street and in the station house would know it. The money didn't matter. Right and wrong didn't matter. It was simply a question of honor. He had been wronged, challenged; he had played the game well. Sayonara, suckers.

All a comforting fiction. He knew he had not really won anything. Not when things were tallied at the end. Walter Bubba Sims would remain in power, getting fatter and richer and probably more cruel. He'd eat other cops, the way he had eaten Orin, or he'd buy them, the way he bought Donnelly, Shaw, and Ril. Bubba's friends inside the job would multiply. Shit cops would force good cops to kiss his fucking ass. He'd be feeding his face at the PBA picnic.

Orin Boyd, on the other hand, would be looking for gun work in Honduras and points south, forever on the dodge, without family or friends. He imagined Dawn telling his grandchildren about her father who ran away when she was five. And Judy, alone.

Orin sat up and lit a cigarette. He realized that he was crying and wondered when he had begun, and why the thought of Judy living alone was sadder than the thought of her living happily with another man.

What was it in him, he wondered, that would let him abandon his family and live like Abraham? What would Batman have done in a fix like this?

That was easy. He'd have trucked on over to Charlene's and let her take him in for a while, that's what. God knows she'd have never called the cops on him. She had food, heat for the body and soul. Batman would have gone to Charlene or got drunk in the middle of Main Street.

Orin did not feel like getting drunk anymore. Still, it seemed too much to ask, to choose his life again as he had chosen it the first time around, step by bloody step. He was much too tired to pick up any pieces.

Let it be, he thought. Leave it alone. The flight to Mexico City was hours away. Which meant he had the rest of the day to hide and sleep, or risk exposure to settle his affairs. Either way, he thought, it's over.

He struggled to his feet and urinated against a small tree. Then he tiptoed out of the clearing and washed his face and hands in a stream along the viaduct. He spent the next thirty minutes installing the camper cap and spray-painting his pickup with glossy white enamel. He restored the original—expired—plates.

Almost street-legal, he thought, tossing the wrench into his tool box. Judy could drive it anywhere, however poorly she might handle the stickshift and clutch, or, more likely, she could sell it for junk.

And wouldn't she freak when she saw how much cash could be rolled inside two Campbell soup cans. Seventy-five, twenty-five: Her cut and his: tomato rice and chicken noodle, side by side on the ground with the rest of his groceries. At last he was the good provider.

He was changing his shirt when he heard the noise behind him. His gun was in the back of his pants. His gun hand was trapped inside his right sleeve because he had not unbuttoned the button first. Someone had him dead to rights. Too tired, he thought.

"Freeze," said Shaw, stepping from the side of a tree, his revolver pointing at Orin. Ten yards away Sherman Clayborne appeared, holding his favorite pistol.

Orin raised his hands above his head, his work shirt hanging from his wrist.

"You fucked up, buddy," said Shaw, keeping his distance. "Me and Sherman here found the old man chained up nude. Donnelly died of some kind of breathing problem, but not before telling us what happened."

"What happened?" asked Orin.

"You know, about the money."

"You're a bad guy, Bobby. Your parents ought to be ashamed of you."

"Where is it, fuckhead? Unless you want to be tortured first, *before* I blow your brains out."

Orin couldn't help but look at the groceries, then down at his feet.

"Look in the bag," Shaw said to Sherman.

Sherman snorted like a bull. "Man, he's jerking you off. Cain't you see that. Look any other damn place beside the bag, if you want to find it."

"Humor me."

Sherman looked inside the grocery bag. "What the fuck did I tell you."

"Tear the truck apart, then. He's got to have it here. Don't you, Orin, you slimy fuck."

Orin looked up at the sky. "Of course I have it here. Where else would I have it?"

Sherman pulled the nine from Orin's belt and raised his own gun into Orin's face. "How about I shoot off an ear to start?"

"Start any place you want," said Shaw. "I can't do nothing with the guy."

"Whoa," said Orin. "Maybe we can do business."

"This ain't business," Shaw said softly. "This is pleasure."

"And if I give up the bread?"

"I promise I'll make it quick."

Orin motioned with his head. "Rolled up in those three soup cans."

Shaw stepped sideways to the groceries and picked up the chicken noodle. When he turned it over he saw that the bottom had been removed and a large quantity of money rolled up inside it. "Cute," he said. "I'll bet you think you're fucking slick."

"Let me see," Sherman said, picking up the can of tomato rice that had been similarly stuffed. "Hot damn, that's a nice chunk of change."

Shaw's hand jerked up the chowder can, expecting weight and finding none. He heard a funny ping and saw that the can was empty, then the hand grenade, without the spoon, on the ground. No pin.

Sherman said, "What the fuck?" Shaw stood transfixed.

Orin knew two of six significant seconds had elapsed and launched himself headfirst into the sleeping pit. He landed on a pile of leaves, then pressed in against the side of the earthen wall. A ghost inside his head said, "Sin loy."

Sherman Clayborne said, "Oh, shit."

After the sound and smoke blew away, Orin stood up and dusted himself off. He quickly packed up the truck, taking care where he stepped when he recovered one soup can. The bankroll from the other floated in the air all around him. With the motor running, he poured gasoline over the living-room furniture, the pit, hammock, latrine, the bodies. He lit a match and flicked it onto the bed.

The flames spread quickly, filling the base camp with heat.

George Clarke was wide awake and roaring drunk, thinking of Ella and Gloria, and how they had fucked him over—and how bad he wanted to get even. He worked himself into such a rage that he called the cab company and asked for Abdul by name, then asked him to return, which Abdul was more than happy to do.

George met him out front and negotiated a deal. His ten-speed bike for a ride to Gloria's apartment and back. Abdul nodded and said, "Plus tip."

As they drove away from the house a twenty-one-year-old rookie, plucked from his academy class by Internal Affairs, keyed his mike and said softly, "Eagle Two is on the move. For some reason, they got a bicycle stuffed in the trunk."

His commanding officer answered, *"Ten-four, kid. We have him."*

At Gloria's, George banged on the door for a couple of minutes and then felt compelled to kick it down. He stepped through the wrecked wood into an empty apartment. She was out of there. George plunged his hands into the overflowing box of refuse she had left in the middle of the bedroom floor, searching for clues to her whereabouts, some indication of the next ghetto she planned to inhabit.

He found the copy of Gloria's travel itinerary about halfway into the garbage pail. It was in Spanish, from the travel agency down the block. She was booked on Flight 102A to San Juan: one adult, one child, one way.

George checked his phony Rolex. There was time to catch her, time to ask her to marry him. God, how he loved her, how he longed to see her again.

He stepped over the broken door and ran down the stairs to the street. "Abdul," he said. "Abdul, my man."

For his Sony VCR and a copy of the *Star Wars* video, Abdul agreed to drive George to the airport.

"Pan Am," said George. "Chop, chop."

Their subsequent route back to the Southern State Parkway was tracked and reported by Detective Conboy Baker, who was then ordered to disengage. The choppers were up and ready to take over.

He signed over the New York registration of the pickup truck to Judy that morning in the Medford kitchen of his soon-to-be former sister-in-law. Judy Boyd sat at the gray Formica table, rubbing sleep from her eyes, wearing running shorts and one of his old police T-shirts. "Give me a second. My head is still in a fog. I detest not sleeping in my own bed."

Feeble sunlight was leaking into the room. The smell of coffee brewing.

"So now what?" she said.

"Now you drive me to Kennedy and then we say good-bye. Drive the truck home and get it registered." He looked from the V-shaped furrow over her brow to the soup can full of money on the counter by the sink.

Judy cleared her throat. "My, God," she said. "All that money."

"Not a bad tip for a ride to the airport. Marrying me worked out better than winning *Family Feud*."

Judy rose from the table and walked barefoot to the door, keeping her face hidden as she lit a cigarette. Orin studied her back.

"What do I tell your daughter?"

"I don't know. The truth, I guess, when she's old enough to handle it."

"You son of a bitch. She'd better be old enough to handle it right now. Her daddy's running out on her at five. She'd better be one tough kid."

"She's still got you."

"What's left of me."

"Tell her I loved her."

Judy shook her head. "No way. You tell Dawn good-bye someplace between here and Kennedy Airport. You tell her to her face what your plans are."

"Fine," he said. "Maybe you're right."

"I want this to stick in your craw," she said to his back as he went into the guest bedroom.

How long had it been, Orin wondered, since he woke his daughter from sleep and smelled the sweat on her forehead, or studied the curve of her neck? Would she remember him, he wondered, or would he years from now return to find the house repainted by another daddy, and a balance to their lives he could not provide; or would he find them alone, never fully recovered?

"Sweetheart. It's Daddy."

Dawn seemed glad to see him; there was not nearly the trouble dressing her that he recalled. He kept a steady chatter going with her, frightened of the desolation they might see together in silence, frightened by the temperature of his heart—that he could do this to his baby.

When her shoes were tied and she was ready, he picked her up and carried her downstairs to the kitchen. Judy had a blue hooded jacket on, and she was packing the money in her Tupperware. "I'm truly stunned," she said. "I've never seen so much money in my life."

"Hide it good when you get back. Maybe at your mother's house. And try to remember how long it's got to last you."

"How long?"

"You'll be okay," he said, as if he hadn't heard her.

"I asked you, 'How long?'"

He could only squeeze his little girl and stare at Judy. She returned his stare, her backbone stiff. Dawn, sensing the solemnity, began to whine. Judy dipped her eyes and turned away.

She locked the house behind them and they squeezed into the cab of the truck, a snapshot of a family on an outing. The neighborhood was bustling as they drove off the block, onto Route 112, and then the westbound Long Island Expressway.

Judy tried another tack: "You're sure this isn't some bogus . . . You could tell me the truth, you know. Just tell me that we'll see you again. Tell Dawn that her daddy will see her next Christmas."

"Someday, when she—"

"You're full of shit, Orin. Face it."

Judy looked out the side window and bit her knuckle. Dawn began to cry.

■　　■　　■

The truck bounced down the exit ramp at the 150th Street entrance to John F. Kennedy International Airport. Traffic inside the airport proper was heavy going past the cargo sheds and Quonset huts, where tractors without trailers were lined up at loading docks like burros. Must be getaway day for lots of folks, Orin thought as he searched the directory signs for Pan American. A brand-new shuffle of the deck.

Orin drove past American, United, the International Chapel, the entrance to the Long-Term Parking lot; he stopped to allow a sailor in the crosswalk safe passage. A halo of diesel exhaust surrounded the airport, filling Orin's nostrils with the scent of adventure and risk.

"I want to thank you," he said to Judy as he parked the truck in the loading zone in front of the Pan Am terminal. "For raising my child, for taking care of business in spite of everything that's happened. Once upon a time you were my very best friend. I won't ever forget that . . . no matter where I wind up."

"Don't give me that 'best friend' crap," said Judy. "You wouldn't do this to Kenny."

He bit his lower lip. She was right. He leaned over Dawn to kiss Judy's cheek. Dawn buried her face in his lap. He could feel her tears through his jeans, her little warm palms.

"Good-bye, guys. I love you."

The departures board overhead showed the San Diego flight to be on time; he had thirty-five minutes to pay for his ticket, clear security, and get on board that westbound bird. For better or for worse, he thought, my life begins anew.

The pretty brunette at the ticket counter tapped the magic codes into her terminal, conscious of the line behind him. "Will that be cash or a major credit card?"

A commotion caused him to turn his head. George Clarke was holding his badge in front of him, hurrying through the terminal, followed closely by an Arab with a limp.

"Sir?"

Orin turned his back to George and smiled at the counter girl. He slouched his shoulders and spoke into the collar of his parka. "I'm sorry. How much is it?"

"Four hundred twenty-five, seventy-five."

"Jeez, is it that much?" He had only two hundred dollars in his pocket. The rest of his money was stuffed inside his sneakers. "I don't have that much right now. I'll hit a cash machine and be right back."

"Of course. And thank you for trying to fly Pan Am." She smiled.

"Miss?" Orin heard George Clarke call rudely to the reservations clerk two stations away.

She raised her eyes. "Yes, Officer?"

"When does the next plane for Puerto Rico leave?"

The ticketing agent did not need to consult her computer for the answer: "Boarding now, sir. Gate twenty-one."

"Thanks."

Orin watched George and his manservant trot off in the direction of gate 21. He wondered if he should stop George from making an ass of himself, as he was sure to do if he caught up with Gloria. He'd be kissing her ass and slapping her face, calling her a whore and begging her to stay. The stewardesses would be screaming at him. The kid would cry and kick him in the shins. The airport cops, if they had the brains they were born with, would yank old George's gun and shield and toss him in the lockup. All around, an ugly scene, not that the dopey bastard didn't deserve it.

The doors flew open again and a white male with a radio in his hand sprinted by the counter, then a black, then Inspector Archibald Blogg, and Sergeant Alonzo Daniels, and Monsignor O'Rourke, all of them walking rapidly in the direction of gate 21.

Orin took that moment to cup his hands and duck his head to light a cigarette. When he was sure the entire entourage had passed, he started after them, slowly, unable to resist disaster.

He knew he should flee in the other direction. It struck him as amusing and uplifting that he should find himself in pursuit of those who were pursuing him.

He picked up his pace, humming a Roy Orbison ditty, and closed the gap to a scant ten feet by the time the procession reached the metal detectors. "Seal off the area," he told the startled security guard. "No one in or out."

"Yes, sir!"

The waiting area at gate 21 was almost empty, the last of the passengers inching into the accordion walkway. Gloria Mendosa and her son were among them, she dragging K-Mart shopping bags and clutching their boarding passes to her breast. The sound of running men approaching made her turn her head.

"Freeze!" George screamed at her, causing the remaining travelers to immediately dive behind the molded seats.

"No, *you freeze!*" screamed the white man with the radio who suddenly had an automatic pistol in his hand.

George became an ice sculpture, holding a position on one foot. Abdul turned into a quivering mass on the floor. They were quickly surrounded by police officers who patted them down and slapped on cuffs.

Orin lingered at gate 20, pretending to fuss with a pay phone. He could hear the Arab begging for mercy, explaining that he had done nothing wrong, vowing to burn George's house to the ground if he did not receive a certain VCR.

Daniels grabbed George by the shoulders and shook him. "Where the fuck is Orin Boyd?"

"How should I know?"

"Then what the hell are you doing here, Clarke? We told you to stay home by the phone."

George turned around to see that Gloria Mendosa was gone, the ground crew scrambling like ants to get their million-dollar investment out of harm's way.

"I came to say good-bye to a friend," said George. "I was late. End of story."

"Fine," said Daniels. "The deal is off. You're under arrest."

"But I—"

"Save it, George," said Archibald Blogg. "Nobody cares. We plan a perfectly good operation and your hyperactive penis stabs us in the back."

This was more than Abdul could bear. He began to cry loudly, and would not be comforted until Daniels determined he was not involved in any criminal activity. Once the cuffs were off, Abdul began a recitation of plagues and bad fortune that would visit George and his descendants until a year before the end of time. George offered Abdul his watch if he would pick him up at arraignment in Mineola. Abdul told George his watch was "big bullshit piece of junk. I divorce you, I divorce you, I divorce you." Orin thought that a remarkably fast adjustment to George, for a guy who had only just met him.

Daniels said, "Remind me to never give a guy a break again."

"Not even just once more?" Orin said as he stepped into view with his hands in the air.

"Well, I'll be damned," said Daniels. "Ain't you a sight for sore eyes. Are you sober?"

"Haven't had a drop."

"Beautiful." He smiled and shook his head. "Take the cuffs off Clarke and let's get out of here. We can work this out back at the barn."

"Really," said Archibald Blogg. "Think how this must look to foreign visitors."

They surrounded Orin like Secret Service men for the trip through the terminal. Abdul carried his duffel bag. When they stepped outside into the morning sunshine, Orin felt like he had just returned from a long and difficult journey.

Daniels opened the back door of the unmarked Plymouth for Orin. Blogg joined him in the back seat and put his arm around Orin's shoulders. "Don't worry too much," he said. "Basically, ya done good."

"Real good," said Daniels, sliding behind the wheel, as George and Monsignor O'Rourke got in the front.

Orin shrugged. "But not by design."

Blogg disagreed: "I wouldn't say that. In fact—you'd better not say that."

Orin smiled.

Blogg said, "I got a call this morning from the district attorney. Dominick Ril surrendered himself last night around four. He sang quite a tune. When the detectives went to arrest James Donnelly at his home, they found him dead. Handcuffed. Possibly heart failure, possibly suffocated."

"You don't say."

"Two more bodies turned up in the woods. Burned beyond immediate recognition."

"Probably smoking in bed," said the monsignor. George looked pale.

"Bubba's thinning out his choir," Orin said.

Blogg said, "The reverend flew the coop. The guys found his office cleaned out. His wife says he went fishing in the Caribbean."

"They killed Abraham Wilson, too."

"We know," Daniels said. "Ril is giving us everything."

"Then it's over?" Orin said. "I can go back to being a crossing guard?"

"After we all do a great deal of paperwork," Daniels said.

"And I'm back on the payroll?"

"As soon as you turn over the bucks you confiscated during your raid."

Orin looked at Daniels in the rearview mirror. "This is your deal?"

"This is called cutting my losses."

"You wouldn't shit me now, would you?"

"No, son, I would not."

"How's Monday morning, when the banks open up?"

"First thing Monday morning. Not that I think you put the money in a bank."

"Deal."

Orin noticed that traffic was backed up on the entrance to the Belt Parkway, and considered it odd for the time of day and their direction of travel. He felt sleep coming over him and rested his head against the window, his eyes closed. Archie Blogg pulled the burning cigarette from between his fingers and stubbed it out. It was only when Daniels rode up on the grassy shoulder to skirt the tie-up, caused by the stalled white camper pickup, that Orin opened his eyes again.

"Well, I'll be damned," he said. He grabbed Daniels by the shoulder. "Do me a favor?"

"Sure . . . whatever you need."

"Sarge, stop the car."

"Huh?"

"You heard me. Let me out."

Blogg's eyebrows arched and his smile disappeared. "Uh, Orin, I'm not sure we ought to just let you sashay—"

"I'm not going nowhere. That's my wife and kid in that truck."

Daniels slammed on the brakes. "Orin," he said. "On your knees if you have to."

Blogg looked him in the eye. "You'll meet us at headquarters this afternoon?"

"Boy Scout's honor."

"Go," said Blogg. "All the best of luck."

Orin nodded and opened his car door. "You'll all appreciate this in the long run. I make fewer mistakes when they're around."

Orin slammed the door, stepped away from the unmarked car and resolutely stuck his thumb in the air, and in that one giddy moment of freedom he struck a deal with his ghosts: He invited them to stay.

His girls were along in a moment. Motorists stuck in the smoking truck's wake could be seen cheering wildly behind their windshields as Judy pulled to the side of the road.

JOHN WESTERMANN was born in 1952. He attended Trinity College in Connecticut, participating in several sports, and joined the police force of a Long Island, New York, community. He served as an officer for 15 years and was several times cited for bravery and excellence. He is the father of two and lives with his wife, Lisa, on Long Island. His previous novel, *High Crimes*, was published in the U.S., England, France, and several other countries.